THE POISONOUS TEN

TYLER COMPTON

Tyler Compton
Los Angeles, CA 90046
www.tylercomptonbooks.com

Publisher's Note: This is a work of fiction. Names, characters, places, and incidents are a product of the author's imagination. Locales and public names are sometimes used for atmospheric purposes. Any resemblance to actual people, living or dead, or to businesses, companies, events, institutions, or locales is completely coincidental.

Book Layout ©2013 BookDesignTemplates.com

Ordering Information:
Quantity sales. Special discounts are available on quantity purchases by corporations, associations, and others. For details, contact the "Special Sales Department" at the address above.

ISBN 978-0-9893845-2-0 (paperback)
ISBN 978-0-9893845-1-3 (ebook)

For my parents

PROLOGUE

The dial tone from the phone used to place the 911 call echoed throughout the multi-million-dollar home up above the Sunset Strip. The person who had placed the anonymous call either had vacated the premises or was in a condition that now prevented him or her from hanging up the phone. The original distress call had come in at 8:23 on that otherwise uneventful Wednesday morning, the last Wednesday in the month of August.

When the dispatcher first answered the call there was no reply, and as she checked the computer to see where the call originated, an alert immediately came up of a tripped silent alarm in the same residence. The dispatcher called the private security firm that handled the gated community and sent out a call for a 211S—robbery with a silent alarm. When the private security company failed to respond within a timely manner, the LAPD were then contacted.

A real estate sign was posted in the front yard of the 22,000-square-foot lot that sat within the private, gated community nestled off Mulholland Drive, looking down over the city. The information brought up on the home had it currently listed as unoccupied. The driveway in front of the house lay devoid of any vehicles, a requirement of the homeowner's association. The front door showed no signs of anyone having broken in, other than being ajar a few inches.

The rear patio doors looked out at the canyon below, making the view alone worth the asking price. The valley view was serene, giving off a false sense of paradisiacal hope; the sounds of lawnmowers running in the distance. The city showed no signs of the usual intoxicating smog building up, but it was still early, with the temperature already rising above eighty. The smog would come soon enough.

The small, undeveloped yard below appeared incongruous with the expansive mansion behind it. But then again, people didn't move into houses like these—in these locations—for the yards. The multiple-story houses lined the hills as if dropped there like sprinkles on a cake. For these houses, it was all about the view.

At the rear of the house was a room, completely white, from the carpet below to all four walls and the ceiling above. Four floor-to-ceiling windows on two of the walls opened up the room to allow for the maximum amount of sunlight, though the room still felt stuffy, the air inside polluted somehow. There was a faint, musty smell in the room, somewhat nutty and sweet.

The room was barren, save for a woman who sat in a single, white chair, her back to the door while she stared out the windows at the valley below. The only other color in the room was a circle of what appeared to be dark-purple paint on the carpet around the woman, as if keeping her in some sort of otherwise invisible force field. The woman wore a white, polyester cocktail dress with matching heels. Her hair was curly and blonde, put up in a twist; casual, yet elegant, as if she had done herself up to go out on a date. Her eyes were open and glossed over, as if covered in milky eye drops, never to blink again.

Her cheeks were rouged, now slightly off-putting as the color clashed with her decaying skin, while the bright, luscious color of her lipstick-covered lips stood out like those on a porcelain doll. Her skin had an off-color, yellowish-blue tint to it, that would have appeared to be cold to the touch had anyone been watching her, despite the fact that she was quite warm. Her head tilted off to the side, slightly leaning back, stretching the skin of the front of her neck, the veins in it staining her off-color skin like branches of a leaf-less tree against a cold autumn sky. A few drops of the same purple paint that circled the woman were on both sides of the otherwise pristine, form-fitting dress.

The final touch to this otherwise macabre display of affection had the corpse with both her hands in her lap, each clasped around a bouquet of various purple-hued flowers, as if eternally waiting for her true love to show up and give her a kiss that would bring her back to life.

A kiss that for Allison Tisdale that was both too late and never to come.

PART ONE

1

Detective David Parks of the LAPD's Robbery-Homicide Division stood in the darkness of his bathroom, not yet ready to turn on the light. Not yet ready to face the day. Or his own reflection.

And if *he* wasn't ready, what would that say about anyone else?

He had been on his third cup of coffee and putting together a five-thousand-piece Ravensburger puzzle of the Tower of Babel in his living room when he received a call from the watch commander letting him know that his presence was needed up on Mulholland at the scene of a homicide. Parks had stared at the frustrating puzzle before him and made a mental bet at which would be easier to solve. He took down the information and promised to be at the crime scene within thirty minutes. Then he looked back at the puzzle taunting him—one side away from having the entire outer edge finished—and realized it would be closer to forty.

Parks reached for the light switch, his hand hovering over it for a few seconds—*come on, it's just a light switch, not the end of the world*—before he finally flipped the switch. He caught his reflection in the mirror above the sink and ran a hand over his head, which had been shaved at the hospital three weeks prior so the doctors could stitch up the numerous cuts he had received. While his stitches were still prevalent, his bruises had all but disappeared.

He had spent the last two months tracking down an unknown culprit who left apples and candy filled with razor blades in several of the local elementary schools, each one of which had found its way into a child's hands or mouth. Over a dozen children had to be hospitalized, most requiring stitching and/or cosmetic surgery of some sort to repair the physical damage that had been done. One child had even swallowed a razor blade, and was saved after four hours of surgery.

Both teachers and parents became frenzied to a state of panic, to say nothing of the children, who were dumbfounded by the whole situation. Teachers were questioned. Faculty members. Janitorial staff. No one had any idea who was attacking the children or how the perpetrator got onto the school grounds. Leads had been growing thin when Parks finally identified the assailant as Peter Kozlov, a former substitute teacher who had lost his own son six months earlier and, subsequently, his job.

Deciding that taking the life of his wife was more important than fleeing, Kozlov tried to run her over, ultimately missing and taking the life of Parks's partner, Detective Aaron Levinson, in the process. In Parks's attempt to apprehend Kozlov, he found himself on the wrong end of a razor blade, his arms, hands, and face receiving the brunt of their carnage.

After the events, which were praised by the LA Unified School District and numerous children's parents, as well as the LAPD, who awarded him the Medal of Valor, Parks was ultimately given a department-paid "recovery period." Though with the department questioning and reviewing Levinson's less than ethical actions during the Kozlov case, Parks—by association as the man's partner—felt it was more a forced time-out while he too was reviewed.

He should have been there for him. For his partner. If only he had been then perhaps none of this would have happened. Levinson wouldn't be dead. He wouldn't have been suspended. Didn't matter what they called it, he knew what it really was. This time off allowed the department to review every detail of his entire career with a fine-tooth comb. He knew that much. They just needed him out of the way so they could go over his caseload. See if his actions were just as questionable as his partner's was. See if they needed to find a more permanent home for him besides out solving murders. Even worse than any of that, they were checking his past to see if he too had made any mistakes that would now result in the release of killers, rapists, and other deviants harmful to society. They were worried, and he understood why. He was one of the best they had in the department. One of the most decorated. A spotless record. An impressive record. Then Levinson had been caught—manufacturing false evidence, no less—and suddenly Parks's actions were put into question. Forget all the good he had done. He was simply fruit of the tainted tree. After all, how could he be partners with someone for five years and not know just how devious they had been?

Parks turned on the water and filled his cupped hands before splashing his face. He needed to get over this. He had been asked back. Would they really have done that if they still questioned him? His dedication? His loyalty? His ethics?

It had now been three weeks of watching game shows, working out at the gym, running seven miles a day, and figuring out his thousand-plus-piece puzzles; and he was close to going over the edge. He was a working man. He needed the job. For him, there was little else. No wife. No kids. No friends, to speak of. He had spent the last fifteen years dedicated to the job.

He noticed his hands shaking, from the adrenaline that surged through his body and realized he felt like a student on their first day of school.

Pull yourself together, Parks thought to himself. *You have nothing to prove. You have done this a hundred times before.*

Was it adrenaline? Or was it his pills? They had put him on a new prescription and his body was still working it through his system. He'd often found himself suffering through insomnia, heat flashes, and blurry vision, all of which were due to the new meds. This could be another side effect.

He turned off the faucet, glanced at the two orange prescription bottles on the counter, and nodded approvingly. Three weeks earlier, he had had four times as many bottles. As both bottles were currently empty, he would have to stop by the department shrink's office later that day if he expected a refill. He had never cared for pills and didn't see any purpose in getting more. If he was good enough to come back to work then he was good enough to put his physical limitations behind him as well.

Parks pocketed his cell phone along with his wallet and identification and headed to the bedroom, where he picked out a distinguished-looking tie that he wasn't even sure matched the rest of his outfit. He noticed a coffee stain on the front of his shirt and considered just throwing on a jacket, hoping no one would notice. He contemplated this for almost half a minute but knew it was unlikely no one would and quickly changed his shirt and tie. He then grabbed his department-issue standard weapon, the coldness of the weapon feeling good against his hands. It was the first time in three weeks he had touched his gun. He hadn't even made it out to the gun range for some practice on his down time. That wasn't like him. He was focused, always in tune, always prepared—or getting prepared—for whatever came next. He had been lazy the last few weeks, a condition he was more than willing to blame on his meds. He mentally scolded himself and left the condo, walking down the wooden stairs, around to the side of the building where his dark-grey Acura TL sat waiting for him.

As he was about to start the car his cell began to ring, he figured the watch commander was wondering what was taking him so long.

"I'm already on my way," Parks said, by way of a greeting. But there was no reply, only silence coming through the other end. "Hello? Hello?" Suddenly he could hear a child's laughter and then the line went dead. Parks stared at his phone, trying to comprehend what had just occurred, when he figured he had been the object of someone's practical joke or unintentional butt dial.

He started the car, checked the address he was going to again, and pulled out, driving north along Beverly Glen toward Sunset Boulevard.

After a few miles, he turned right, heading east toward Hollywood. Fifteen minutes later, he pulled off Sunset onto Crescent Heights, which turned into Laurel Canyon as it snaked its way up the hill, leading high above the city. He turned onto Mulholland Drive, driving along the cliffs that overlooked the city below, before arriving at the security gate that protected the more respectable gated community within from the rest of the cesspool-infested world. He flashed his badge at the security guard, who noted it in his logbook. As he did this, Parks noted everything, from the age and phys-

ical attributes of the guard to the semi-protective gate and the open-
ness of the area. He wasn't sure how far away the crime scene actually was, but while the illusion of protection was in full force, the
reality of it was a different matter. The guard flipped the switch for
the gate to open and waved him on without any further trouble or
comment. Parks recalled the first time he had been called to the Par-
amount Studios lot, where he had been given a map of the grounds.
If he got out of here only half as lost and confused as at the movie
studio, he figured he'd still need a stiff drink to calm his nerves. Just
one of the many benefits of working in Hollywood, though after
being on the force for over a decade he was now pretty skilled at
maneuvering throughout the various studio lots within his jurisdic-
tion.

A few winding turns later, he finally found the four-
bedroom/five-bath modernized, mid-century home atop the hill.
The house was three stories, though it only appeared to be two, with
the third, lower floor off the side of the hill down below street level.

The house was blocked off by four black-and-whites in the middle of the street on either side of the property. Several neighbors
stood gawking and taking photos on digital cameras and cell phones.
Parks sighed. These days he didn't even have to worry about the
paparazzi any more. They would simply approach the neighbors and
offer a finder's fee for the photos. In this day and age where anyone
had access to a recording device and the Internet, everyone was a
freelance photographer for the right price. Nothing was sacred or
safe from the public's scrutiny.

He hesitated for a second, his hands gripping the steering wheel,
his knuckles blanching. He took a deep breath and tried to clear his
mind. Flashes of Peter Kozlov coming at him with a razorblade filled

his thoughts. It was over with. He had survived and with Kozlov incarcerated. Hopefully for life. He had nothing to fear. He had been attacked and injured numerous other times. PTSD had never affected his abilities before. He simply didn't work like that. This was just like any other time.

Parks exhaled, grabbed his notebook and exited his car. He looked up to see two news choppers close by, most likely reporting on the murder down below. He slammed his car door shut and started for the house when several reporters rushed him.

Son of a—Parks caught himself and put on a fake smile.

The first reporter he ran into was Charles Wyler, the lead crime reporter for a quickly rising, independently financed local station. It was common knowledge that Wyler often blackmailed and harassed his subjects, reporting false information if it "benefited the public," all for the "good of the people." Where other reporters may have held back out of fear or respect, Wyler had no issue with pushing the law to his benefit, which is why other reporters were often at his heels, like jackals waiting to pick at the scraps.

"Detective Parks," Wyler began as he shoved a microphone in Parks's face, staying with him step for step. Parks kept his eyes on the house and zoned in on his target without taking the bait. "I see they've let you back on the force."

"I was never off it. Just on vacation."

"Sure you were. But what's another corrupt cop on the LAPD?"

Parks hesitated for a second but kept walking toward the crime scene. He wasn't going to let Wyler get to him. Not on his first day back. But Wyler was relentless. There was always another angle.

"What can you tell us about the murder here?"

Parks smirked at Wyler as if to say, I just got here myself. What do you think I know?

"Detective—"

"No comment at this time," Parks said calmly as he faced the crowd of reporters. His heart jumped a beat and his whole body froze for a second as he thought he had seen Kozlov standing in the crowd of onlookers. Then a reporter moved, the sun glared in his line of sight and the image was gone.

Don't do this. Not today. Pull yourself together. He's locked up where he belongs. He's not coming after you, and what's more important, the children are safe.

He cleared his throat. "I'm sure Media Relations will have something for you all shortly."

He lifted the yellow caution tape and walked past two officers who held up their hands to stop the reporters.

"Detective!"

Parks made his way between two of the black-and-whites to find Jake Fairmont, who at thirty-four was the youngest member of his team. Fairmont held two cups of coffee while he leaned up against a stone hedge that outlined the driveway leading to the crime scene beyond.

"Heya, boss," Fairmont called out as he handed off one of the cups then ran a hand through his curly, sun-bleached hair. He turned around and stole another glance at the house behind the Prada sunglasses that were usually on his face or up on his head to hold his hair out of the way. He wore fitted Armani jeans and an equally expensive button-up shirt, tailored to his lean, muscular body, contrasting nicely with his deep surfer's tan. He had on a navy blue jacket that Parks figured wouldn't last long with the heat that was forecasted for the day. Thermometers were inching over ninety and it wasn't even ten yet. The smog had already begun attacking Los Angeles, giving the city a broken-down automobile-and-gasoline smell that made it even more difficult to breathe.

"Morning, Jake. Good to see you. So what do we have?" Parks asked, assessing the situation, eyeing everything and everyone at once. Everything outside the house was neatly trimmed and in its proper place. The grass was evenly green, the flowers in full bloom, the house recently painted. All windows cleaned, brass knobs polished. A side gate leading to the back yard was slightly ajar—something to check—and the flower garden under the front windows had been disturbed in some way, as if someone had been stepping in the area, spying in through the window.

Another thing to check out.

Everything else looked perfect. Pristine. And fake. As if the place was a movie set.

"Not sure. I took overalls of the area and the house from outside, including onlookers," Fairmont answered as he gestured at the house and the crowd building in the street, referring to the photos he had taken. Fairmont was stiff, uncomfortable, not sure how to behave himself. Parks had been worried about this but knew there was nothing to do but let it take its time and pass. Fairmont had been working for the LAPD's Crime Scene Analysts division as their primary crime scene photographer and recorder for five years before becoming a detective and joining Parks's team the year before. He had originally dreamed of owning his own gallery and selling his photographs to rich patrons who wished to decorate their luxury office buildings with his exceptional black and whites, but had since moved on from that dream in these hard economic times and found a more profitable use for his degree in photography. Parks knew that

Fairmont also used his photography skills to take headshots of actors and actresses looking to get a foot in the showbiz door. Luckily, in this city, he had a never-ending supply. Even though Fairmont would never admit it, he made more money snapping photos of kids who would never make it as background extras on the CW, let alone feature films, than he did taking pics of homicide victims.

"But they haven't even let us in to see the body yet."

"What do you mean? We got an active crime scene here. I was called. We're in charge. What's wrong?"

"Not sure," Fairmont answered. He reached into his pocket, took out a packet of Nicorette gum, and popped a piece into his mouth. "We were ordered to stay out until the CDC clears the place. They're in there now." Fairmont nodded over to a white van with the words CENTER FOR DISEASE CONTROL on the side. "You ever try this shit?"

It took Parks a second to realize Fairmont was asking him about the gum before he shook his head. He had never smoked other than the few cigarettes he'd tried back in high school. Unlike several other vices he indulged in, smoking hadn't stuck with him.

"Works for shit if you ask me," Fairmont continued. "But who knows. Only my first week on it. Swear this stuff's more expensive than cigarettes."

"CDC?" Parks said, interrupting Fairmont's train of thought. "This is a homicide. What are they doing here? Other than contaminating my crime scene."

"Rumor has it the two responding officers who found the body collapsed at the scene and barely made it out alive." Parks turned at the words and saw his assistant supervisor and new lead detective, Rachel Moore, approaching. He welcomed the woman who would most likely have information for him. He could tell everyone was anxious to be on a case and working like they had before the Peter Kozlov fiasco. He could see it on their faces. They wanted to prove their loyalty—not just to the force, but also to him.

"What's that?" Parks had only partially heard Moore's explanation.

"No one's sure why, so they're being checked. They say there's a possibility of contagion and we're not to go in until the area's been cleared."

Rachel Moore was dressed for business and always ready for it. Wearing a slick, gun metal-grey pantsuit that nicely complemented her figure, she appeared a full decade younger than her forty-eight years. Her Gucci sunglasses hid her almond-colored eyes, each graced with a light touch of eye shadow that was almost unnecessary with her facial structure and skin tone. With her jet-black hair tied back away from her face, she had her equipment case at her side, ready to barge into the house upon Parks's command.

"Who says?" Parks looked from Moore to Fairmont and back again, squinting as he studied their reactions, wishing he'd remembered sunglasses like both of his co-workers. Even if his were the cheap ten-dollar drug store brand and not name ones like his employees often purchased.

"It's okay, sir," Fairmont said, catching Parks's eye line. "Maybe it's for the best you don't have them. You know . . . out in public."

"What? My sunglasses? What's wrong with my sunglasses?"

"Nothing, sir. I'm sure whatever pair you bought at the gas station on the way here would totally elevate your cool status by a whole half a point."

"Rachel?"

"Yes, sir?" she replied still staring at the house.

"It sounds like Jake is harassing me on our first day back on the job. Is that what it sounds like to you?"

"I wouldn't think that would be the wisest move for him to make on our first day back, sir," Moore said, holding back a smile and eyeing Jake with a slight shake of her head.

"I can have him transferred, you know. Is he aware of that? I hold that power over him. I hear Watts needs a new photographer."

"I'll have the paperwork drawn up and ready for your signature as soon as we get back to the office," Moore said.

"You know, I'm surprised they haven't created an app for that yet."

"What's that, sir?" Fairmont asked.

"Transferring unruly help. Just press a button on my phone and—bam. New location. New photographer." Parks smiled. They were getting their groove back.

"Wait, you got an iPhone? Really? That seems like an awful lot of power for someone like you to have control of. Sure it isn't just a cutout of an iPhone. From like an ad?"

"Someone like me? What's *that* supposed to mean?" Parks turned to Moore who shrugged.

"You hired him," Moore mumbled.

"What? I did no such—"

"Where's C.C.?" Fairmont asked out of nowhere. "She still on her way?"

Parks sucked in a deep breath then slowly let it out through his nose. "Miss Cain is no longer a member of our team."

"She what?" Fairmont asked looking from Parks to Moore. It was obvious from the look on Rachel Moore's face that she had anticipated this, and Parks couldn't say he was much surprised by the fact either. Chyna Cain—commonly referred to as C.C. by her peers on the force—had been part of the fallout from the Kozlov/Levinson debacle.

"Wait," Fairmont said, still not buying this. "She doubts you? She thinks you're just like Levinson? She doesn't really doubt you, does she?"

"We're all adults here," Parks said. "You're free to make up your own minds and decide what to do with your lives. I can't tell you what to say or think."

"What did she say at the inquiry?"

"Was I there for yours?" Parks asked, looking to Fairmont. He hadn't been. They had all been one-on-one interviews as they always were. They each knew that.

"But she left because she thinks you're just like Levinson, didn't she?"

"I don't know why she left and it doesn't matter. She's gone and it's not my job to get her back. It's my job to solve his murder. So how about it?"

Fairmont looked too Moore, obviously wanting to discuss this further but knowing it wasn't worth the fight. That was just life. Maybe C.C. did think Parks was just as guilty. Maybe she simply didn't want to be part of a scandal. Maybe she couldn't handle the looks and whispers. All were possible, and none of them mattered. They still had a job to do.

Moore gazed toward the two patrol officers who guarded the walkway to the house. Fairmont snapped his gum as Parks left him and Moore and approached the two guards.

"Sorry, sir," said the guard on the right. "No one's allowed in until the scene's been cleared."

"Cleared by whom?" Parks asked. "I'm the lead detective in charge here."

"Just following orders, sir."

"Whose orders?" Parks asked impatiently.

"Mine," said a female voice from behind the guards.

"And who are you?" Parks asked as he looked past the two men at a woman approaching him. She should have been on a runway or in the movies, and he figured that's what had originally brought her to Los Angeles like so many others who ended up here. As she got closer he saw how her height might have hindered her career aspirations, barely standing at five feet five. Her hair, a brilliant blaze of orange and amber, was tied back and out of her way so that she could work unobstructed.

"I'm Doctor Jacqueline Isley," the woman replied, making her way to Parks. The woman removed a facemask to reveal a small, pointed nose, covered with a light, almost unnoticeable smattering of freckles, and a thin-lipped mouth with a strong jaw that added to her commanding appearance. Her face was all business-like, controlling and attentive, almost as if she should have been a nun, ready to disburse disapproval. She snapped off one of her latex gloves and offered a hand, all business-like and professional, to shake. "But you can call me Jackie."

2

"Doctor?" Parks asked.

"Yes. But like I said, you can call me Jackie. I'm a forensic toxicologist with the county coroner's lab. Poisons are my specialty. So you're the detective in charge?" Her words were rapid, precise, and to the point. She had a job to do and didn't want to waste any time getting to it.

"I should be," Parks said as he sized the woman up. She wore a white biological hazard suit, which she now unzipped and worked her way out of to reveal a light green blouse and matching skirt that revealed just enough legs—shapely and strong—alluring yet still professional. He could tell she was athletic, a runner or swimmer, though knowing women nowadays she most likely did kickboxing or yoga. Parks got the slightest scent of jasmine, not overpowering, just potent enough to hide her natural scent without being distracting. "But to be honest with you, I'm not sure what's going on around here."

"It's all right," Jackie said, addressing the two guards. "The area's been cleared. Assume regular protocol. Detective . . . ?"

"Parks," Parks answered. "Dave Parks."

"Detective Parks is in charge here," Jackie confirmed, nodding just once to let them know that she gave them permission to follow him.

"And why was I ever not in charge of a case I was called in on?" Parks asked as Jackie turned and led him down the cement walkway toward the front door of the house. Parks motioned to his team and started after the woman who he felt was still running things, despite what she said. So far he wished he had stayed home with the puzzle.

"This morning a 911 call was placed from this address," Jackie explained. "Two officers answered the call to find the house abandoned."

Parks stepped into the home with its sixteen-foot ceilings and admired the exposed wood beams that held it up. Below him were glazed over, walnut-colored floors that appeared darker than their natural color. Each window had white gossamer drapes that floated into the rooms as a slight summer breeze blew through the house.

"Abandoned?"

"Yes. Except for this room," Jackie said, leading him into the room with the single chair containing the dead woman within the painted, purple circle.

"Then what happened?" Parks asked, standing in the doorway, not entering the room.

"One of the two officers approached the victim."

"All the windows were open like this when they got here?"

"Unfortunately not. My people had to open them," Jackie said with regret on her face. "Sorry about your crime scene, but we had to be sure. We laid plastic down for the pathway we took to the body and windows. I hope that helps. One of the officers collapsed in the doorway and blacked out. By the time his partner made it from the victim, over there, back here, he also collapsed. Luckily he was able to give off an officer-in-distress alert before he did. Otherwise, these two men would be just like our victim there." She was curt, professional, and uncaring, simply laying out the facts for him to evaluate.

"And how is our victim?"

"Dead," Jackie replied matter-of-factly.

"I can see that."

"From all the way over there? You sure? She won't bite, you know?"

"Well, I'm not wearing my doctor-prescribed glasses but I'm pretty sure the woman in that chair isn't going to be moving again. If she is, she's gonna have one hell of a crick in her neck. Maybe you should have called a chiropractor instead of us."

"We did. But he doesn't do house calls," Jackie said. "Plus, you're cheaper."

"I—" Parks paused a moment. He hadn't been expecting her to match him beat-for-beat. She had been professional so far, almost cold. Maybe this was an olive branch for having his leadership challenged. "I bet. So how did the vic die?"

"Poisoned."

"Some bio-chemical—"

"Cyanide. Good, old-fashioned cyanide." Jackie threw on a smile but quickly replaced it with a look of sadness. She was giddy about what she did. Not about the fact that there was a dead body to investigate, but the hows and whys of it. She liked her job and it showed. Parks made a mental note that though his puzzle might have been easier, this was becoming more fascinating.

"Cyanide, huh? You have some kind of expensive breathalyzer

that you can hook up to the victim and out pops your poison of choice?"

Jackie smiled and Parks could see he her cold exterior chipping away.

"The team who responded to the officers' distress call realized there might be poison in the room and quickly dragged the two men out and called the CDC, who dispatched a vehicle and gave me a ring. An Officer Hernandez lost consciousness before I arrived, but one of the responding officers said he mentioned something about almonds."

"Almonds?" Parks sniffed the room and got nothing then looked back at the windows and realized that if he had been able to smell the scent that he'd most likely be seconds away from hitting the floor.

"Don't look so displeased. The almond scent isn't a tell-tale sign of cyanide. A genetic trait allows very few to be able to smell a faint, bitter, almond scent. We're lucky Officer Hernandez was one of those few, or else we might not have been able to determine the poison in time to save them."

"So they'll be okay?"

"They've each been given an injection of sodium thiosulfate to counteract the cyanide's effects. We'll keep a close watch on them for the next couple of hours, but I'm hopeful."

Parks looked around silently for a moment, studying the crime scene before him.

"And you think this is our actual murder scene?"

"I do."

"Why?"

"The cyanide gas. It was concentrated mostly in this room,"

Jackie explained. "See, I believe the victim was posed in this chair post-mortem. There appear to be light ligature marks on the wrists and ankles—"

"So she was tied to the chair?"

"It appears so. I'd say she was tied to the chair when the gas was released. She died and the killer reentered and cut her loose then drew this circle around her on the ground and left."

"Why come back to draw a circle? Why not just do it before and be done? Why risk the poison affecting him as well?"

"I don't know. I don't get into the minds of killers. You think I'm wrong?"

"No. Not necessarily. I'm just talking the scene out. That's what I do. The ligature marks. What held her to the chair? Where are the bindings? And why is she still holding onto the flowers?" Parks surveyed the room again, purposefully avoiding eye contact with Isley. She was attentive. The evidence said she was right. But why? He looked back to the body then turned to Fairmont.

"Start taking mid-range shots and close-ups of the vic. We need to process this room."

Fairmont took a step into the room and stopped.

"It's safe," Parks said with a roll of his eyes.

"You sure?" Fairmont asked, eyeing the room. "You know the state doesn't exactly provide the most beneficial medical coverage. I'm not sure what their policy on toxi—"

"Just do your job, okay?" Parks looked to Jackie for help of some kind.

Fairmont turned to Jackie, who pursed her evenly proportioned lips while trying to hold back a smile, and nodded in agreement that it was safe.

"Anything you say, boss," Fairmont said as he entered the room and began to take pictures of the body.

"How's this coming along?" asked a voice from behind Parks, causing him to turn and come face-to-face with the Assistant Chief, Jane Hardwick. His superior stood before him, all six feet of her, in a cross-stitched blazer and matching pants, her styled, caramel-colored hair cut perfectly to outline the rest of her slim face. Parks had worked for Jane Hardwick during the nine years she had been with the LAPD and found her to be an extremely strict yet honest and fair superior, something he figured she learned from the first twenty years of her policing career in Chicago.

"Chief," Parks acknowledged. "Good morning."

"Parks," Hardwick said, looking past him to Jackie. "And you're Doctor Isley of the county coroner's office, I presume?"

"I am," Jackie nodded.

"Good." Hardwick smiled back sharply. "I talked to your superior this morning. Based on what few facts I've been given, you're on loan to us until this case is wrapped up. You two will be working together. I assume there won't be any territorial, childish behavior I should have to worry about?" Both Parks and Jackie remained quiet. "Good. Now, Doctor Isley, Detective Parks here is one of my best men."

"Yes, ma'am," Jackie replied.

"And you," Hardwick said, turning to Parks. "I think Doctor Isley's expertise in this subject area will be of great use to you. I know you can accept help when it's being offered in the interest of the case and the department. She's here to help. This is a particularly grue-some killing with what I've been told is a particularly nasty sub-stance. I want this perpetrator behind bars as quickly as possible, or

I'm going to have all your asses."

"Yes, ma'am," Parks replied.

"How long you been working in your position?" Hardwick asked Jackie.

"Almost six years now," Jackie answered with firmness.

"And what's your assessment of the crime scene?"

"Truth be told, poisoning isn't all that common a way to kill someone. Hasn't been for decades. It's complicated. Intricate. Requires knowledge and patience."

"Premeditation," Parks commented, politely taking control of the conversation.

"Yes," Jackie agreed rather quickly. "Almost always. You get full of rage, you stab someone to death or shoot them. You don't go find some poison and a syringe and inject someone to watch them suffer."

"Unless that's what you want," Parks countered. "To make someone suffer."

"Correct," Jackie continued, speeding up her words. "And that suggests planning, patience. Poisonings are a more intimate way of killing. Here we have a more personal connection between the killer and victim."

"You think this is personal?" Hardwick asked.

Jackie wavered from foot to foot and glanced at Parks for help, theories not being her strongest suit. She liked dealing with facts, as she had admitted to him earlier.

"On several levels—yes," Parks jumped in. "This body wasn't hidden. It's out in the open, for all to see. This shows pride. On the killer's part. He's not ashamed of what he did. He's proud of his work and wanted it to be found. That speaks of a bravado and confidence in a job well done."

"But you've no proof this will turn into a serial," Hardwick said. "And before we have proof one way or the other that this *is* the work of a potential serial, I suggest we nab the bastard as quickly as possible."

"Yes, boss," Parks agreed.

"Then I'll leave your team to it," Hardwick replied with a nod of her head. "Oh, there is one other thing," she said, gesturing to a young man who had been standing behind her, unnoticed until now. "Tippin."

The newcomer was a kid, no more than nineteen or twenty, with big Bambi-eyes and chocolate-colored hair cut close to the head in a sort of faux-hawk style. He was of average height, with a thin posture, like a walking skeleton. He had a blue, white, and black plaid, button-up shirt over a matching blue crew-neck with black pants that were so tight Parks wasn't sure how the kid was able to breathe. A pair of blue low-top Converse finished off the wardrobe.

"Everyone. Moore. Fairmont. Pay attention," Hardwick called out, looking last at Jackie to make sure she too paid attention. "Everyone, this is Milo Tippin. He's going to be joining your team in light of its recent . . . thinning. He's been sent over from the CSA department. He has a background in computer science, so anything you need computer-wise, I suggest you ask him. He's spent the summer bringing our backlog of case files online to make them more"—Hardwick looked to Tippin for help but found the word she was looking for before he could offer any—"available for cross-referencing. Anyway, he's aware of crime scene procedures but has yet to process an actual crime scene, so help him along. Remember where you all were when you started."

Nobody said anything, everyone simply staring at Hardwick and Tippin.

"I can buy that he's completed all of the exams and whatnot. But how old is he?" Parks asked then turned to Tippin himself. "How old are you?"

"I'll be twenty-three next May," Tippin answered.

"He looks sixteen," Parks said to Hardwick. His biggest concern was that no one would take the kid seriously when he tried to interview a suspect or question a witness. He'd never had that problem before and wasn't sure how to deal with it. "Has he even put in his time as a patrol officer?"

"I graduated fast and early," Tippin replied. "Look, I've applied for patrol duty. Several times. I keep being denied and shoved in the back of an office or the basement surrounded by files and paperwork. Why should I be punished for being smart and young? I want to do this. I'll gladly go put in my four years on patrol duty if you can get someone to accept me there."

Parks stared at the kid, taking in what he had said and why he said it.

"So then, how is it he's ending up with us?" Parks looked to Hardwick.

"I received an anonymous email with his personnel file," Hardwick said. Parks immediately turned to the kid, knowing he had most likely hacked her email account himself. "Let's just say I was slightly impressed. Just because he's not street-wise doesn't mean he's not helpful. You have experience between everyone else on your team. He needs a start, and against my better judgment—which has never been wrong—I decided to be the one to give it to him. He looks too young? Then blame his family's genetics, not him. We're lucky whenever we can get new people on the force to help us out, especially in the detectives and CSI units. The process to get in here is long and tedious, and we aren't exactly batting them off."

"Yes, I know. I'm sorr—"

"I personally go over the files of every applicant that gets into this department. I know every person here, and I'd like to think I damn well know what I'm doing when it comes to assigning people to where I choose. That includes Tippin here. He'll work well with your team. I don't give a flying squat if you like this or not. The kid's legit. You need him. Whether you want him or not. Detective Levinson's gone. Detective Cain, as you all know by now, as well. So no more coddling you all like babies. We have to move on. For the good of the team and the job. Make it work. Now I have to go outside and organize that zoo of reporters. Someone sure doesn't know how the hell to keep their damn trap shut." Hardwick turned and marched out the door.

Tippin was even more on edge, rocking from foot to foot, and Parks began to feel sorry for the kid. There was no sense in taking out his frustrations about the morning on him.

"Look, kid, it's been one hell of a morning, and you're not at fault for any of it." Parks looked to Jackie and felt the same way. She was just doing her job as well. He had been thrown a lot on his first case in three weeks. He had been complaining of boredom at home. Well, the universe was complying. "No one's to blame. It's just me getting the best of myself. And we have a dead body we need to process."

"Um . . . not to be rude, but who are you?" Tippin was embarrassed by having to ask this question.

"Sorry," Parks chuckled, looking out the doorway where Hardwick had just disappeared. "I'm Dave Parks. Lead detective. It's my job to try and keep this rag-tag group of people in check."

"Though more often than not he's the one who needs to be kept in check," Fairmont joked, gathering a chuckle from Moore and a smile from Parks.

Parks needed to keep this light. His first impressions to both Jackie and Tippin weren't exactly his most shining moments.

"This is Rachel Moore," Parks said as continued. "She's my assistant supervisor. She's been with the LAPD for almost twenty years now. And working on and off with this me for close to . . . what? Six? Seven years now?"

"In one way or another," Moore agreed. "I started out a detective, then transferred over to the CSA division when they were short people. My main area of expertise is in trace. I find the hairs, fibers, fingerprints, and other little things that most people look right over and don't notice."

"She's got hawk eyes. Don't even try to get away with anything around her," Fairmont joked. "She's also our resident mama bear."

"And that's Jake Fairmont," Parks said, keeping the introductions moving. They still had a body to examine.

"Photography's my gig," Fairmont said with the wave of his camera. "I'm the one who'll record everything in this room for our reports. You need to look back and refer to anything that was here today, I'm the one you see."

"Good. Our team's sort of been out of commission for the past few weeks," Parks admitted. "We've lost two members of our team due to our last case, which is where you two come in. Tippin, why don't you follow Detective Moore as she begins on the hunt for fingerprints? We're a family here. We all work together. I prefer it that way. Everyone has their specialties, but we help each other out when needed. If someone asks for help, I have a strict policy that anyone that can help does so. If you have a problem with that, then I suggest you ask to be transferred to one of the other teams."

Tippin nodded enthusiastically.

"Okay. And finally that brings us to our newest temporary member," Parks said, turning to Jackie. "From time to time we get cases that have certain special qualities about them. Such as this victim behind us, a victim who appears to have been poisoned. So we've got ourselves a poison specialist to help out with the case."

Parks stood silently while everyone stared at Jackie.

"Oh, right." Jackie smiled as she realized what they were waiting for. "I'm Doctor Jacqueline Isley. I've been a forensic toxicologist with the Los Angeles County Coroner's office for the past four years now, though I spend half my time with the CDC as well. Been working there for six years. Our victim was poisoned by cyanide, but the room is safe for us to be in. So that's it. I suggest we start in on the body."

"All right then," Parks said. "Fairmont, you finish with the body so we can get Doc—I mean Jackie—working it. It's time we find out what exactly happened here."

3

"Hello, boys," Medical Examiner Amy Tanaka called out as she walked into the room with a glow about her that made her coworkers wonder if she was pregnant or had just had morning sex instead of having just arrived from another crime scene. At her side she carried her examiner's kit, which looked as if it weighed more than the small woman and often made observers wonder how she stood upright while holding it. "And women. I apologize. How are you, Rachel?"

Moore smiled silently, focused on her task on hand. She was halfway through the room while Tippin looked intently over her shoulder to see how she worked the laser system that read for latent prints on the wall, scanning anything abnormal into the computer system.

Tanaka walked up to the dead woman and set her kit on the ground then stared at the body. It was a full minute before she noticed Jackie next to Parks.

"Hey, girl," Tanaka beamed. "Why, if it isn't my two favoritist people in the world. So what do we have here?"

"A tardy slip with your name on it," Parks quipped.

"Sorry, teacher, but the principal gave me a pass. I knew she was coming here"—Tanaka gestured toward Jackie—"so I knew I'd have some time before they let me in to see the body."

Tanaka worked her way closer to the body of the dead woman in the chair and looked down at her. The woman's eyes remained open, forever staring off through the windows at the valley below, while the skin around the eyes had a dark-purplish hue to them, as if she were wearing a lot of mascara. There was a sad look to the woman that affected the inspectors as they stared silently for a moment, giving the victim her last respects.

"Does she look familiar to anyone else, or is that just me?" Tanaka asked, breaking the silence as she began inspecting the body.

"Can't say that she does," Parks admitted.

"Me neither," Jackie said with the shake of her head.

"Probably just me," Tanaka said as she went back to inspecting the body. "There are slight abrasions on the wrists and ankles, proving she was held against her will. I'm not sure by what yet. No residue was left behind so I'd rule out duct tape, plus it appears thinner in circumference. More like small rope or wire. Somewhat hard to see, so whatever it was, it was probably something soft to the touch. It didn't cut through the skin when pressure was applied. So that probably rules out wire."

Tanaka began shifting through the purple flowers in the victim's hands and looked curiously at a gummy substance that came off the flowers, sticking to her gloved-hand.

"What do you have there?" Parks asked.

"I'm not sure," Tanaka said as she brought her fingers to her nose and moved her head back in confusion. "But it smells like . . . honey." She motioned for Jackie to get something out of her kit. "I'll take a sample and have it tested."

"Honey?" Jackie asked, handing over a sample container. "Why?"

"Not sure," Tanaka admitted. "But it appears to be all over the bouquet of flowers in our vic's hands. You get pics already?"

"Roger Dodger," Fairmont called from behind Tanaka.

"Thank you, hon," Tanaka said. "Then I'm going to get this entire bouquet tested. Just to make sure. Maybe there's something else in here."

"Could that be how the poison was administered?" Parks asked as he scribbled into his notepad.

"No. The poison was in a gaseous form," Jackie replied, not looking away from the body. Parks wasn't sure how often she wound up at crime scenes or if she was used to seeing dead bodies, but she appeared in control of herself considering the situation.

Tanaka finished wrapping up the flowers then handed them to Jackie, who set them next to her kit to take with them later. She then went back to focusing on the body, moving her attention from the woman's hands to her face.

"She was poisoned? That was determined?" Tanaka asked, looking to Jackie.

"Cyanide gas," Jackie explained. "The windows were closed throughout the entire house. And the door to this room was closed."

"Are you sure, girl?" Tanaka asked. "I mean if you were locked in a room filling with gas, wouldn't you be found dead at the door, claw marks on it, hoping to get out? Or why not throw the chair through the window and get fresh air in the room?"

"Because she was restrained," Parks said, motioning to the ligature marks. "She was found in this chair, holding the flowers, behind an unlocked door because she was posed this way. Postmortem."

"True. But none of those are the reasons why I know the killer stayed here until after the victim expired," Jackie said.

"And why's that?"

Jackie pointed to the purple circle that surrounded the woman in the chair.

"He could have painted that before she died," Parks repeated from earlier that morning.

"Nope," Jackie disagreed. "That's not what you think it is."

"You mean purple paint? Then what is it? Grape juice? Prune juice?"

"The victim's blood."

Parks looked down to the circle around the body with confusion and let out a deep sigh.

"*Urusai*," Tanaka said in a whisper.

"You'll have to have your team test it to be sure, but I already know it is," Jackie said. "Look. See the two marks on the side of her dress? That's not paint. That's where the killer cut her and drained her blood. Then he took her blood and painted the circle around her. The darkened discoloring of the blood is from the poison in her body. Cyanide can sometimes do that. That's how I know the killer stayed here after she died. He had to have been here after she was poisoned in order for her blood to change like that."

"I can't say I've ever seen that before," Parks said. "But should be easy enough to test." Parks looked to Tanaka, who would get samples.

"I didn't find identification on the body anywhere," Fairmont said. "We'll have to take her prints and check IAFIS. Hope we hit something there."

"Thanks," Parks said. "Any thoughts on the clothes she's wearing?"

"No idea." Jackie shrugged. "Not within my budget, so not really my area of expertise."

"They're expensive," Tanaka said, placing goggles over her eyes, before beginning to inspect the victim's mouth and eyes. "The dress is worth close to a thousand. The shoes are Jimmy Choo's. That's seven hundred, easy. And the necklace is a Stephen Webster studded collar worth probably around a grand and a half."

"You're telling me she has on around three thousand dollars' worth of clothes?" Parks couldn't believe it, and had the information come from anyone but Tanaka, he wouldn't have.

"Hey," Tanaka huffed, "just because I can't afford it doesn't mean I can't look. And try on. And admire. And dream about." Amy looked up at Jackie and winked. "I believe in following the Boy Scout motto. Maybe one day I'll find me a man who can afford them. You never know."

"Uh-huh," Parks replied. "Been perusing the pages of sugardaddy dot com again, I see."

"Well, since I didn't see your face anywhere on there, it must have been. Speaking of older, well-to-do, who's the twink?"

"The what?" Parks looked around the room wondering what she meant, before he saw her looking at Tippin.

"You mean the kid?"

"I said twink, didn't I?"

"What the hell's a twink? And you were talking about sugar daddies. I was looking—oh, never mind. That's Milo. Newest member of the team. Milo Tippin, this is Amy Tanaka, our resident smart-ass and chief medical examiner."

"Pleased to meet you." Tanaka smiled up at Tippin.

"Since I don't see your assistant, if you need any help don't hesitate to put him to work," Parks said, looking back at his notebook and the few notes he had so far. "We're still finding him his niche."

"Oh goodie," Tanaka said. "Young buck like him should have eyes like a hawk. Why don't you come over here and give me a hand. Unless you're still using him, Rachel?"

"Put him to work," Moore said, waving Tippin on.

Tippin started for Amy's side when she stopped him. "Grab some gloves and one of those containers in my kit and get the tweezers as well. You're going to help me get samples and collect what's under the vic's fingernails. Got it?"

"Got it." Tippin replied.

"Oh, lookie at him. He obeys. I like him already."

"Just like Amy to get into the groove of things by ordering a man around," Parks mumbled.

"I thought you might have wanted a break," Tanaka replied as she got back into the dead woman's face and continued her examination. "But then again, if you're feeling left out I can always—"

"Hardly. Where is Robert anyways?"

"Sent him back to the lab with samples from the double shooting in Koreatown. Figured I could handle this one on my own since your team was here."

"Oh my," Tippin called out, interrupting Tanaka and startling everyone in the room.

"What is it?" Parks asked.

"I know who she is."

Parks and the rest of the team moved in closer for a better look.

"Told you she looked familiar." Tanaka said with a smile. "Twink's on my team. Already called him."

"Who?" Parks asked.

"Him," Tanaka said, pointing to Tippin.

"No. Not—who is *she?*"

"Allison Tisdale," Tippin answered.

"And who's that? Some movie star?" Parks asked, hoping he was wrong. The last thing they needed on their first day back was to get a celebrity. In this town they were treated like royalty, making investigating a case that much harder to maneuver through.

"Really?" Tippin asked. "None of you?" He turned from one person to the next, all of them shaking their heads.

"Who is she?" Parks asked again.

Milo motioned for Parks to follow, and he led his boss out of the room and through the hallway to the front door. Along the way Parks noticed that both Rachel and Jackie had also followed. Milo continued out the front door and headed toward the end of the driveway.

"Where are you taking us?" Parks asked as he glanced over toward the news vans that were multiplying by the minute like vultures surrounding a recently expired piece of carrion. He wondered how they had even gotten in past the security guard and figured the man was most likely making up for his lackluster salary today. That made him wonder who else might have also gotten in past the gate, and he made a mental note to check it out.

Milo turned toward the lawn and pointed. "See?"

Parks turned and shielded his eyes with his hand as he stared back into the sky-blue eyes of Allison Tisdale, her face plastered across the realtor's FOR SALE sign planted in the front lawn of that very house.

4

"I want to know everything there is to know about Allison Tisdale by the end of the day," Parks ordered. "I want her background. Family. Work. We obviously know who her employer is, and judging by the kinds of places she sold"—he waived his arms at the luxury of the house surrounding them—"she must have done fairly well for herself. We need info on coworkers, her history with the company, where her office is . . . everything. Fairmont, I want you and Tippin to dig into her life. Find out what you can."

"Wait, so who is she?" Tanaka asked, examining the body's scalp.

"She's the realtor for this residence," Parks answered, removing his jacket.

"So that's how the killer got access to the house," Fairmont surmised.

"I would think so," Parks agreed as he found a nearby officer standing guard outside the room and tried to hand off his coat. The officer simply stared at Parks and refused to move. Parks stared back when the officer finally took the coat. Parks had a feeling he might never see the article of clothing again. "We find keys or anything on the body?"

"No keys. No wallet. No purse or any other forms of identification," Moore answered. "She's wearing the dress, the shoes, and the necklace. That's it. Nothing else."

"But I did find these," Tanaka said, holding up two small, plastic baggies, each one with a different pill in them. "Little yellow one is Percodan, and the white one is codeine."

"Where were they?"

"She's got two pockets on that dress. One on each side below where the purple marks are, almost as if they were leading to them."

"Rachel," Parks said. "Let's find out if she was prescribed those medications. It's odd that there would be one pill in each pocket."

"I'll run a tox on her blood to see if either is in her system," Tanaka said as she put the pills away and went back to the body.

"I want to know when she was last seen and by whom. I want to know her every move up until she disappeared. And I want to know how long she's been missing, if she's been missing, and why no one reported it. Unless someone has."

"On it," Fairmont said.

"I want to know where she lived. If she lived with anyone." Parks knew most of his team was aware of what he wanted, but he wanted Tippin to know what was going on and what was coming next.

"She worked out of an office on Wilshire in Beverly Hills," Tippin called out.

Parks turned, somewhat surprised, to see his newest team member standing with an iPad that he had been using since he came back into the room.

"You got an address?" Parks asked, rolling back his sleeves.

"Yes," Tippin answered. "And I pulled her DMV records too. Got her home address. She has a house in Beverly Hills not far from her office. And she's . . . she's married."

Tippin looked up, suddenly concerned. They would have to do a next-of-kin notification.

"Go on," Parks nudged.

He wouldn't have Tippin anywhere near a NOK notification on his first day. He hated them himself, an unfortunate part of the job, but a requirement none the less. And one that he preferred to take on himself as much as possible, sparing the members of his team the reactions that came with such an announcement. You never knew how someone would take the news concerning the loss of a loved one. Some cried. Some went into hysterics, going public with their turmoil, while others hid it for moments that are more private. Some masked the pain. Some tried and failed. Some didn't know how to behave, as if years of watching scripted reactions on Law & Order had stilted their ability to react appropriately. Some were angry. Others relieved. Some even joyful. But no matter their relationship with the deceased, everyone felt something.

"Been married for about five years," Tippin said as he went back to his computer and began punching at the screen. "Husband's name is Douglas Tisdale. He's a professor at PSU. Nothing stands out on his record. Few parking tickets, but that's all. No complaints or reports filed against him. They make a decent living. Mostly from what she brings in."

"Okay, good," Parks said. "Rachel? Anything?"

"So far? Nothing," Moore said. "No trace evidence. No prints. Fibers. Hairs. Nothing."

An officer stuck his head in the doorway to the room, looking as if he had something important to relay without wanting to catch whatever deadly contagion had been unleashed within the space.

"What is it, officer?" Parks asked.

"Did the door-to-door with all the neighbors. So far nobody's seen anything of worth. Want us to give it a second try?"

"That's okay. Wrap it up. We'll come back to them if something comes up. Thanks." The officer then disappeared quicker than he had shown up. Parks signaled Tanaka and Jackie. "Is it okay if I leave you two ladies to keep at the body?"

"Oh, no. What will we ever do without a big, strong man here to help us? Oh, maybe there's a jar of pickles in the kitchen you can open for us or a car that needs its oil—We'll be fine," Tanaka said without looking up from the corpse in front of her. "We'll be at least another half hour here. Then I'll have the body moved. Luckily for you, with a poisonous agent introduced to the body—and therefore possibly to the rest of the city—it gets a high priority. City will push aside all other autopsies for this one. I'll personally handle it myself. You should have a report on your desk by the end of the day. And that's rushing it."

"Pickles? Really? You better not be getting pregnant on me, Tanaka. Fairmont? You and Tippin go and check out Tisdale's office. See what her co-workers have to say about her."

"Will do, boss." Fairmont saluted.

"Rachel, get Allison's home address from Tippin and we'll go notify the husband. Tippin? You wouldn't happen to be able to see if the husband has classes today or if he might be at home?"

Tippin played around on his computer for a few more seconds.

"Fall quarter doesn't begin until September sixteenth and classes don't start up until the nineteenth. He might be at the school planning for the fall quarter, but there's nothing scheduled."

"Okay. We'll go check for him at home. If he's not there . . ."
Parks looked to Fairmont and Tippin. "Just keep your phones on. I'll
contact you if I need anything else. You work ten times faster than
anything I could get from our own people back at the station."

Fairmont winked at Tippin, who smiled back, having made a
good impression.

"Oh, and speaking of which, pull phone records for them as well.
Home. Cells. Everything."

"Will do." Tippin mock saluted.

"Any other questions?" Parks asked to no reply. "All right then,
people. Let's get going."

5

arks pulled up in front of the Tisdale's house on Crescent Drive just below Sunset and put the car in park. He glanced down the street, away from his intended target, willing himself the strength to knock on the front door and change a man's life forever. He wished he had had his pills that morning. If ever there was a part of the job that he hated, this was it.

"You're grinding your teeth," Rachel said from the passenger seat.

"Sorry," Parks said, stopping the tic.

"Sooner we do this the sooner it's over."

Rachel Moore had spent the drive in silence, re-reading her notes, to let Parks mentally prepare for the task.

"I know," Parks replied. He sounded calm but could feel his heart beating. The movies and TV shows rarely got this part right. The suffering that was about to be inflicted on the living. Death always left an echoing mark throughout the lives of those who remained.

"Just ignore all the bullshit and focus on the job you know how to do."

"Huh?" Parks turned to Moore.

"I see the way they've been looking at you. The other officers. And I see you noticing them. Letting it get to you. Don't. They do not hate you. They don't know what to feel. Half of them think Levinson did the right thing. It led to you being able to stop Kozlov. They know it was wrong, but Kozlov was the greater of two evils. They want to congratulate you and pat you on the back. But they know it was wrong. Therefore, they're conflicted. Plus you're one of the most moral people on the force. How much did you know? Did you let it happen? If so, was that your call to make? Are you so moral you can stand in judgment over others about things like that? And if so what's to stop you from doing it to anyone else you deem fit to judge?"

"You know we never talked about what all really happened."

"And we don't need to," Moore said. "We've worked together for almost ten years. In one way or another. And I was also a part of that team, in case you forgot. And I know you Dave Parks. I know what you go through. How you think. Why do you think I'm still standing here beside you? Despite all the whispers and gossip, which will die out, I'm still here and I'll continue to be so. Overall, you're a good man. A good detective. People know it. Your pros will outweigh this one con. Besides, I don't care what others think. We don't need to have a talk because I know what I need to know. The rest doesn't matter. So how about we go in and notify Mr. Tisdale about his wife."

"Okay. Let's do this."

Both detectives got out of the car and made their way up the walkway through the neatly manicured front lawn, matching perfectly with the neighbors' on both sides. The lawn was short and evenly green with flowers lining the walkway that lead up to the double-story box-shaped house, which had a picturesque and homey feel. The fresh paint job gave the appearance of having been applied within the last year, with a matching trim that helped keep the house in symmetry with the rest of the street.

Parks knocked twice and rang the doorbell. The door opened to a man in his mid-forties who would have blended in with the usual Hollywood crowd, no one giving him a second glance as his good looks were a dime a dozen in this town. He wore a faded-blue, button-up shirt that had the top two buttons undone to reveal a recently acquired pinkish tan. His face was reddened, showing signs of being in the sun, and highlighting the few crow's feet around his eyes.

"Are you Douglas Tisdale?"

"I . . . who are you?" the man asked in reply.

"I'm sorry," Parks apologized, retrieving his identification from his jacket pocket. "I'm Detective Dave Parks and this is Detective Rachel Moore. Are you Douglas Tisdale?"

"Yes, I am," Mr. Tisdale answered, turning pale. "What's wrong? What happened? Is Allison okay?"

"Is Allison Tisdale your wife?"

"She is. What's wrong? Oh my God. What happened? What—"

"May we come in?" Parks asked as he glanced around behind him. "It might be better if we take this inside."

"What's happened to my wife?"

"I'm sorry to have to tell you this, but your wife was found dead this morning. Please, Mr. Tisdale. May we take this inside?"

Mr. Tisdale began to shake and stepped aside to allow the detectives entrance into his house. He closed the door behind them and made his way into the neighboring living room where he pointed to a couch and collapsed in a nearby sofa-chair. He tried to catch his breath in between the tears and dry heaving that controlled his body.

Parks glanced around and took in the surroundings of the room. It was quaint, with nothing too expensive, while giving an air of sophistication. There were pictures of the couple throughout the room and hallways. Pictures of vacations to beaches and other tropical places showed the couple had a happy relationship. At least on the surface. There was a beauty to the Allison Tisdale in the pictures that hadn't been evident from the pasty corpse that had been poked and prodded by his team that morning. But there were no children. No pets. No family members, at least in any of the pictures. Just the couple.

"We're sorry to have to do this right now, Mr. Tisdale, but we need to ask you a few questions," Parks said as he waited for the man to compose himself. The husband glanced around the room, avoiding eye contact with the detectives as if this made the news they had delivered not true somehow, as if he could outrun it in some way and thereby make it not so.

"I'm sorry," Mr. Tisdale finally said. There was a somewhat gravely, calming sound to the man's voice, which probably helped keep the attention of his students when he lectured. "Yes. Of course. How . . . how can I help?"

"As you know—"

"Did she suffer?"

Parks stared at the grieving man. "I'm sorry, but we don't have all the details just yet."

Mr. Tisdale nodded to show he understood.

"We found your wife's body up in a house on Mulholland." Dave paused, hoping the man would pick up and add whatever knowledge he had. Most people did that, anything to avoid the silence. Especially in a time like this when all that was probably going through his head was his wife's death. It was manipulative but effective for rooting out the hidden truths.

"How did she die?" Mr. Tisdale asked as if he hadn't heard what Parks had said.

"I'm sorry, but we're not at liberty to discuss the details of the investigation at this time," Parks answered, hoping he didn't sound as cold as he felt. He tried to keep his voice calm, soothing, yet forceful enough to invoke reassurance that everything was being done that could be. "It's still an ongoing investigation—"

"Because I'm a suspect," Mr. Tisdale said, more as a statement than a question.

Parks neither confirmed nor denied the statement, sitting patiently until Tisdale finally continued. It wasn't like in the movies where the detectives were racing against a clock and a movie or TV show's run time. Parks could wait all day if it helped make the person interviewing more at ease. He had patience. It was one thing he was good at. Frustratingly so, according to his former partner.

"She was showing a house up on Mulholland all weekend. She's a realtor. She had an open house that started Friday. So that's probably where you found her."

"When was the last time you saw your wife?"

"Um, this, um, morning. This morning. She left early. About six-thirty. Quarter to seven. I was still in bed." He paused as if recalling a thought. "She kissed me good-bye. I offered to come with her and help, but she told me to catch up on my sleep and keep organizing for the upcoming semester. I'm a professor."

"What do you teach?" Parks asked, sounding interested. He already knew the answer but hoped the question would divert the man's focus from his wife's death onto something else. Distractions often worked. As long as they weren't too obvious. Then all one did was focus on the matter at hand.

"Biochemistry and molecular biology," Mr. Tisdale answered. "I took the last two years off from teaching classes to focus on research. I start up with courses again this semester. I've been working on my semester syllabus, which is why Allison told me to stay home. I've been having some difficulty with it."

"What kind of research?" Parks asked, appearing indifferent though he felt the opposite. From what Tippin had found, they were well aware of what kind of studies he conducted, which was what had piqued their interest in him even more than usual.

"Cancer," Mr. Tisdale said. "Allison's sister passed away from breast cancer about two years ago, and my father had pancreatic cancer. So it's . . ."

Mr. Tisdale broke off and stared into space.

"So you were here all morning?"

"Yes, I was," Mr. Tisdale continued. "I was alone. Just me and the TV while I worked in my office." Mr. Tisdale gestured across the hallway to a neighboring room with the door ajar. "No one can vouch for me. I'm sorry. But I swear to you I didn't kill my wife."

"How would you describe your marriage?"

Mr. Tisdale paused, not as if trying to think of what to say but rather as if being caught up in past memories. Parks stared at the man's reaction but didn't feel he was hiding something, only that he was shocked by the question and knew he was about to forfeit personal information that he might otherwise not want out.

"It was good." Mr. Tisdale smiled and wiped his face, his tears and nose running together. "But I'm sure everyone says that. We travel. Love to travel. We're good. We enjoy each other's company. Hang with friends. Don't fight. I mean nothing physical. We've had little tiffs here and there. But who doesn't?"

"Sex?"

"Excuse me?" Mr. Tisdale shot out, taken aback.

"You two still sleep together? Same bed? Separate beds? With other people? Open marriage? Into anything . . . different? I know I'm getting personal here, but we need to explore all avenues. If there might be a third party involved, then—"

"No," Mr. Tisdale interrupted. He had begun fidgeting, and his eyes were no longer leaking. They had clearly touched a sore subject with the man. "No, nothing like that. It's just the two of us. We still sleep—*slept*—in the same bed. Only us. No one else. Nothing out of the ordinary. Just plain, good, old-fashioned sex. And yes, we still . . . did it."

"No affairs?"

"I love my wife," Mr. Tisdale reassured him. "I have never."

Parks stared at the man, taking in the chosen wording.

"Do you know of anyone who might have wanted to harm your wife?" Moore asked, taking over the interrogation. Parks had done his job and was now viewed as the bad cop. Tisdale wouldn't trust him anymore. Time for her to step in. "Any enemies? Recent events that might need to be brought to our attention? Anything that might help us."

"Nothing that I'm aware of," Mr. Tisdale said. "She worked. But I don't know of anything or anyone causing any problems there. You'd have to talk to her people at the office."

"We will, Mr. Tisdale."

"I know there are people who are pissed to be out of their homes. I mean, the economy's hurting people right now. Houses get foreclosed on, and Allison picked them up. Turned them around and sold them. Or there were people who hired her to sell their houses and might have thought she sold them too cheap. For less than what they were worth. But I don't know of any specific instances. Nothing that bothered her enough to tell me about it. Other than that, we mostly keep to ourselves. We do wine tasting. We started taking a few cooking classes at the Grove. Just to try and get out more. During the summer at least. I'm too busy during the school year. But nothing to take note of. No threats. No fights. Nothing bad with the neighbors. Most of the neighbors are . . ."

"Yes, Mr. Tisdale?"

"We've had no problems with them. No one I could think would do this. We had no problems with anyone. Sorry. I'm sorry I can't be of any more help. So you have no idea who did this to my wife?"

"Would you like me to get you some water?" Moore said, leaning forward in her seat, glancing from Parks to Mr. Tisdale.

Mr. Tisdale nodded and remained seated as Moore got up and made her way out of the room. This was a tactic that Parks used to perform with Detective Levinson. It was the first time he had done it with Moore, but she was on top of it. True, she was getting the distraught Mr. Tisdale a glass of water to help him cope, but she was also taking a quick look around the house to see if anything jumped out at her that would tell her something was wrong with the otherwise picturesque image of the Tisdales's lives.

Other than the dead wife.

"Oh, the kitchen is—"

"I'm sure she can find it," Parks interrupted, trying to keep Mr.

Tisdale's focus. "Does Allison have any family in the area? Friends?"

"No family here," Mr. Tisdale answered. "She's from Florida. Her father's deceased, but her mother and one of two sisters still live there. I can get you names and numbers if you want."

"That would be great," Parks said. "Any friends?"

"Yeah, a few. A Candace something. And a Melissa and Natalie. I'm not sure about last names. I know them, but I can't think—"

"It's okay."

"You can check her iPhone. Everything's in that. Schedule. Appointments. People's information. The names will all be in there."

"Mr. Tisdale, we didn't find an iPhone or purse or wallet or any identification of any kind on your wife's person," Parks explained. "Could she have left them here?"

"Not possible. She had her phone attached to her twenty-four seven. And leave without her purse or wallet? No. She had all her cards in there. She would have left with them."

"Okay, so—"

"Then how did you know it was Allison?" Mr. Tisdale asked. Parks could tell that for a second the man had hopes that maybe the police had identified the wrong woman and that his wife was and could possibly still be alive.

"One of my men identified her from her realtor sign in the front yard," Parks said. He let the explanation hang in the silence for a moment, and when he was sure it had been accepted, he continued. "How did your wife get to Mulholland from here?"

"She drove," Mr. Tisdale said. "You found her car, right? Maybe that's where her personal stuff is. She drives a silver BMW convertible."

"We'll get an APB out on the vehicle and try and locate it," Parks said, trying to reassure the man, who was getting worked up.

"We've got BMW Assist," Mr. Tisdale continued. "Call them and they can activate the GPS tracker on the car. They'll tell you where it is."

Moore made her way back into the front room and handed Mr. Tisdale a glass with a brownish liquid in it.

"Thought you might like something a little stronger," Moore said, smiling.

Tisdale simply held the glass, staring at it as if it was a foreign object he had no idea what to do with.

"We'll do that, Mr. Tisdale," Parks continued. "Thanks."

Parks caught Moore's eyes as she slightly shook her head from side to side.

"Anything else you can tell us?"

"I don't think so. Like I said, nothing special or out of the ordinary with us. I have no idea why someone would do this to her."

6

At seven o'clock that evening, Parks and his team assembled around a table in the downtown LA conference room of the Detective Bureau of the Office of Special Operations to go over their progress on case so far. The Special Operations building was only a few years old, the result of the city finally agreeing to spend some money on the department, hoping to give the LAPD a major facelift in the eyes of the public. It was also built in hopes of ridding the communication barriers between divisions and eliminating some of the overlap that occurred when it came to certain duties. This late in the day there wasn't a lot going on in the office as the other detectives had mostly finished their shifts and were already headed home.

Parks sat at the head of the table; to his left sat Rachel Moore and Jake Fairmont, while opposite them on his right was Jackie Isley and Milo Tippin. Assistant Chief Hardwick entered the room and stood near the doorway to observe.

Various wrappers from vending machine junk food and half empty cups of coffee were spread atop the table as the team tried their hardest to stay awake and focused. Everyone was stressed out and tired from a day of reading, studying, squinting, and focusing on every minute detail of Allison Tisdale's life. The day had been humid and the sun had drained the team of energy, making everyone sticky and smelly. Files were spread out in front of the group, along with notepads of scribbled notes and Milo's MacBook. Up on the murder board was a picture of Allison Tisdale near the middle and various notes written on both sides of her picture.

Parks threw away an empty chocolate bar wrapper and picked up a fresh mug of coffee, finishing half of it before he addressed the team.

"So what do we have?" he asked, breaking the silence. "Let's start with the crime scene."

"No forced entry from what we can tell. But we didn't find a key to the place anywhere on the victim's person or on the grounds. All windows, doors, and locks were intact and working," Fairmont said, reaching into his pocket for another piece of Nicorette.

"What about the house alarm?" Parks asked.

"From the time the alarm went off to when the responding officers first arrived was less than ten minutes," Moore responded.

"Ten minutes?"

"Yes. The neighborhood is gated and has its own security," Moore continued. "It's a private company that does security for several gated communities. The officers on duty were in a neighboring community responding to a B and E or else they would have been there. But since they were delayed, the LAPD was dispatched to the address."

"Even though they have their own security?" Parks asked, somewhat confused.

"When they can't be reached immediately LAPD gets called.

Quickly. Rich people."

"Any way to tell if the B and E was related?" Parks asked. "Like as a distraction."

"No reason to think that's the case." Fairmont shrugged as he leaned forward in his chair and scribbled some notes on his pad. "But we can look into it."

"So the killer didn't trip the alarm until after he had left. No time to set the alarm and do the murder," Parks said, more to himself. "Any prints?"

"We checked the alarm pad. There were no prints on it. We checked with the security company, and they confirmed that the alarm went off when the PANIC button was pressed on the keypad. So it was done intentionally. In addition, the reason we didn't find a phone in the house was the key-pad has a direct line in it to call 911. We think the killer placed the 911 call then disabled the line so no calls could be made or received from the key pad."

"Any other prints?"

"No," Moore continued. "Nothing. No prints were found in the room, near the front entrance, or at any of the doors or windows. We've collected a few fibers and hairs from the kill room, and they're being tested, but so far nothing."

"Speaking of which, what about the flowers?"

Fairmont sat up. "We checked Allison Tisdale's credit cards and there's no evidence that she bought and brought the flowers herself, so unless she paid with cash, we're under the assumption that the killer brought them with him."

"Though we did find one connection," Rachel Moore said. "Apparently her husband used to buy them for her a few years ago. Weekly, according to her co-workers. But that only lasted a few months then stopped."

"The husband?" Parks said. "Anything significant about these flowers in particular?"

"Not really. They consist of a dozen lavender roses with purple statice and Israeli ruscus. It's commonly called a Passion for Purple Rose Bouquet and can be obtained from most every flower shop, in person or online. Costs about fifty dollars. We've checked and found that within the LA area there were about two dozen of them ordered within the past week. We checked every online order and in-store purchase paid with a credit card and found none of them to be missing, so they've all been ruled out. That only leaves the paid-in-cash purchases, of which there are eight. So far it's been a dead end. Shoddy bookkeeping. And cash doesn't leave much of a trail."

"Keep checking. They had to mean something to the killer if he brought them himself. We're sure Allison Tisdale didn't pay cash for them herself?"

"Why would she?" Moore asked. "If she bought them for the open house then wouldn't she want a record of them? Write-offs and all that?"

"Agreed, but make sure. Show her picture at the local flower shops. What about the honey?"

"Nothing special there either," Rachel Moore continued. "Regular store-bought, every-day household honey. Nothing added to it. We're running tests to see if we can track where it came from or where it was sold, but I've a feeling it's so ordinary that we won't get any help from that angle."

"Any guesses as to why it was there in the first place?"

Moore motioned at Tippin from across the table for him to continue.

"Um, uh . . . There's nothing really all that special about honey, but . . ."

"Go on," Parks encouraged.

"There are a few things. It's a symbol of sweetness. We use it here in America as a term of endearment. Hey, honey. Hon. Et cetera. Um, in ancient Egypt and some Middle Eastern cultures, it was used as a way to embalm the dead." Tippin looked up and shrugged. Parks was impressed. The kid was doing a good job so far. Tippin looked back down to his computer screen and continued. "Min, the fertility god of Egypt, was offered honey."

"Make a note to ask Tanaka about that," Parks said to Moore. "Please, God, don't tell me she's pregnant. Anything else?"

"The Mayans regard the bee as sacred."

"Noted. Next?"

"It's a symbol for the new year in Jewish traditions."

"Noted."

"The Christians have several mentions of it. 'Land of milk and honey.' Stuff like that."

"Okay," Parks said, looking at his empty mug, which he didn't recall finishing. "I think we have all we're going to get out of this topic. Rachel, make sure we run all the tests and get me the results when they come in."

"Will do." Rachel agreed.

"And, Tippin, good job. Get your findings and add them to the murder book. Not sure there's anything of note there, but you never know. What about the pills found on the body?"

"Tanaka was right," Rachel began. "One tablet of Percodan and one of codeine. From what we could determine, Allison Tisdale wasn't taking either. Neither she nor her husband has ever been prescribed either pill by any of their doctors, and Tanaka said she didn't find any trace amounts in the victim's bloodstream."

"So it could be assumed they were left there by the killer. On purpose."

"It's a good assumption. But why?"

"That is one of the many million-dollar questions about this case. Make a note of it. What about the house itself?"

"It's worth seven point three million," said Tippin, once again taking the reins in the conversation as he began to type away on his computer, clearing the screen of the honey information and bringing up a new file. "It's been on the market for five months, though the previous owners haven't lived in it for six. They're currently down in San Diego, something to do with the owner's job. They haven't been back since they turned the house over to Allison Tisdale to sell. She had it overhauled and fixed up—painted, fumigated, cleaned, et cetera—back when she first inherited it, but otherwise there have been no worker-type people anywhere around the house for three months."

"What about gardeners?" Parks asked. "That yard was maintained. You can't tell me Allison Tisdale was out there every week mowing the lawn in her pearls and high heels."

"No," Fairmont interjected. "There's a yard service that takes care of most of the houses within the gated community. We're going to go interview the workers and the company tomorrow. We don't think it will turn up much—they only get to that yard every Friday—but they're always in the area so maybe they saw someone or something suspicious."

"Good," Parks commented. "Stay on it. What did you guys learn about her job?"

"Nothing out of the ordinary," Fairmont said, digging through his notes. "Works for herself. Used to work for Coldwell Banker but broke off and started her own real estate group about three years ago. She has two other agents who work under her. They do fairly well considering the current real estate climate. Mostly up-scale homes and mansions. Beverly Hills, Bel Air, and Hollywood Hills areas. Everyone is paid; and on time. No outstanding debts, creditors, or anything of the like. Had to take out a small business loan to get started, but it's been paid back in full."

Fairmont looked to Tippin, who continued with what he had dug up online.

"There are no outstanding personal debts that the Tisdales owe, either her or him," Tippin explained. "They have the house, pay the mortgage on time. Both have good credit. The most expensive thing they have is her car, but that's a lease and she has another thirty months on it. That seems a little pricey for the rest of their lifestyle, but it might make a difference to the clientele she's trying to bring in so that's probably the reason for the car."

"Did we find the car?"

"We contacted BMW and had them activate the GPS tracker, and so far, nothing. They're assuming it was disabled," Fairmont said. "We have a BOLO for the vehicle and Highway Patrol's been notified."

"All right. Anything else?"

"Other than that, no children, no pets, no outstanding debts, nothing. No major financial changes or withdrawals within the last six months."

"Interesting," Parks said. "So nothing in their financials sticks out?"

"We only made it back as far as six months," Rachel answered. "But we'll stay with it tomorrow if you want us to keep digging."

"Yeah, do that. Go back a year, maybe two."

"What about the husband?" Hardwick interjected from the back of the room.

"The husband's got no solid alibi. Then again, we haven't been able to find a motive for him either."

"He's a man and he's married to a woman. I've learned sometimes that's enough."

"That and he lied," Parks said.

"Oh?" Hardwick said as she looked to Moore, who shrugged, not knowing what Parks meant. "What about?"

"He got short when I brought up their sex life."

"So. Most people do. That's private."

"True. But I think he was holding something back. He got flustered when I mentioned an affair."

"So he was stepping out on his wife."

"I don't think so," Parks disagreed.

"You think she was?"

"I believe so. It was the way he handled the questions. He said he loves his wife. He never cheated. But . . . something happened. I don't think it was him, though. His reactions—"

"Well, then maybe it was him that killed her," Hardwick suggested. "She was sleeping around and he lost it."

"No," Parks disagreed. "This so-called, alleged affair, if there was one, happened a while ago. It was as if they had reconciled and he had forgiven her. Almost forgot about it until I brought it up. It wasn't how he wanted to remember his dead wife."

"But if she did it once," Hardwick said not dropping the subject.

"Old habits and all that."

"True. Whatever the case, right now he's our prime suspect. Our best shot. But his grief struck me as genuine when we broke the news of his wife. I'm not saying we're writing him off—like I said, he's our best bet—but I don't think it's him. Pull his history, financials, co-workers, family, the works. Who knows, maybe we'll get lucky. Maybe it is him. Rachel and I will handle the Mr. Tisdale angle. The rest of you go at this murder as if it isn't him. If it's not him then there has to be a reason our killer picked Allison Tisdale as his victim. Some reason he knew her. A client maybe? The man who sells her her coffee. Her car lease agent. Someone. Somehow, he knew her. He was able to abduct her from her regular daily life and kill her without anyone knowing she was gone for two hours. How was that possible? He had to know her schedule."

"According to her secretary, Allison Tisdale wasn't scheduled to come in to the office today until the afternoon," Fairmont offered. "She told the office she was going straight up to the house on Mulholland for the viewing."

"That coincides with what the husband told us," Parks said.

Parks's team stared at him as he got lost in his own thoughts. He looked up and saw Hardwick staring back, and he shook out of it.

"What else do we have? Jackie? You and Amy find anything out about the body?"

"The tests confirm that our victim was poisoned by cyanide," Jackie began. "This could have affected our killer just as much as the intended victim. It not only takes a lot of patience but, well, balls to pull this off. It's dangerous."

"What kind of a time period are we talking about here?" Parks asked. "I mean, considering when she left home to the time when we found the body was around two hours. Maybe less? Is that possible?"

"Yes." Jackie said. "Inhaling a toxic dose of cyanide—and in a gaseous form—can cause immediate unconsciousness. Convulsions even. Death can follow within fifteen minutes. Swallowing takes longer, which is probably why our killer chose the gas form."

"How did our killer get his hands on this cyanide gas?"

"Not sure. But it's a poisonous toxin, so it should be traceable. I'll check on it."

"What about the purple blood?"

"It's a side effect of the poison," Jackie explained. "It's often called 'chemical asphyxia.' What cyanide does is prevent the body's red blood cells from absorbing oxygen, which we all know is what turns blood the reddish color we generally see."

"And what about the circle put around the body?" Hardwick interrupted. "What does that mean?"

"Nothing as far as I'm aware of."

"We feel it's a sort of calling card from the killer," Parks admitted, not sure. "Either that, or they just wanted to make a spectacle. Perhaps they're theatrical."

"Speaking of calling cards," Amy Tanaka blurted out as she burst into the conference room. "I think our killer left one. And it's not the bloody circle."

"What is it?" Parks asked.

Tanaka took the photos she had in her hands and passed them around the table. They were of some part of the victim's body with a small symbol carved into the skin.

"What's this?" Parks asked.

"That was carved into the victim's body near the vaginal area. Postmortem."

"A cross?"

"God dammit," Hardwick huffed. "Does that mean this a religious killing then?"

"It could be," Tanaka replied, nodding. "But I don't think it's a cross. It's too symmetrical. All four ends are equal."

"A plus sign?" Fairmont asked.

"Could be." Tanaka shrugged.

"But you don't think so?" Parks asked. He wanted answers. And another damn cup of coffee. "So what *do* you think?"

"I don't know," Tanaka admitted. "I just know what I thought of when I first saw it. But I think that's more of a cultural thing. It probably is a plus sign. Or something else."

"What did you see?" Parks asked again.

"Jū," Tanaka finally answered.

"Jew?" Fairmont asked. "You mean, like, this is an unfinished swastika?"

"No," Tanaka said with a roll of her eyes. "Not a Jew. Jū." The examiner pronounced the word with more emphasis, and most around the table heard the Japanese in the word.

"You mean like ten?" Parks asked.

"Oh," Tanaka paused, the look on her face showing her surprise that Parks knew the Japanese number for ten. "Yes, exactly. Jū. The Japanese character for ten."

"So what are you saying?" Parks asked, his eyes glassing over.

"Not saying anything," Tanaka admitted. "Just that I think it's the symbol for the Japanese character for ten. I don't know what it means. That's your job. I just bring you what I find. And it could just be a plus sign. Who knows?"

"But it means something," Moore added. "It has to. The killer wouldn't just put that on the body for no reason. It means something."

"Most likely," Parks agreed. "Okay. We have some research to do. We need to run a check to see if there have been any similar murders with matching symbols carved into the bodies or left at the crime scene. Check with VICAP. Then we still have to find out how and why Allison Tisdale was chosen. I think that's just as important as why our killer's doing what he's doing. He chose her. For a reason. We need to know why. And how he came across her path. Does he know her intimately? Professionally? We need to tear Allison Tisdale's life apart piece by piece and then put it all back together again. This could be about anyone in Allison's life. So we're going to have to dig deep with this."

"We're on it," Moore said, motioning to Fairmont.

"Oh, Amy. The victim . . . was she pregnant?" Parks asked. Tanaka made a face, so Parks offered an explanation. "We're crossing off potential reasons behind the honey."

"Not sure what honey has to do with pregnancy, but for the record, Allison Tisdale was not pregnant."

"Good. Perfect. Milo, we're also going to have to do some research on the number ten and poisons," Parks continued. "What I think we should do is find out all we can about the number ten. What's its significance to anything? Locally? Historically? Universally? Anything and everything. But that's not a priority."

"Got it," Tippin said.

"Jackie, you're on the cyanide. See if there is anything significant that's been stolen in the last six months. At least. Anything reported missing. Universities. Chemical plants. Not just cyanide. Everything poisonous. I'm not talking Tylenol and simple household items. Our guy is theatrical. He's going for big and showy. The exotic. See if anything sticks out. I understand this is a needle in a big-ass haystack, but it's at least a start."

"I'll make some calls. See what I can find out," Jackie offered. "I know certain people in the right circles when it comes to poisons."

"All right then," Parks said, standing back up to end the meeting. "Everyone do what you can. Go home, get some rest, and be back early tomorrow. We have a full day ahead of us."

Parks noticed Hardwick motion for him to follow her out of the room. He followed her to her office where she asked him to close the door behind himself.

"Is something wrong?" Parks began. "With the assignments I just—"

"No, no," Hardwick said, brushing Parks's comment off and motioning for him to sit in one of the chairs opposite her desk. "You know what you're doing. You know how to lead an investigation. You don't need me eyeing your every move."

"Though the higher-ups would probably prefer that you did, considering recent events—"

"Believe it or not, but the higher-ups, as you so put them, are actually looking out for you."

"As well as their own asses," Parks said, making sure they both knew where they stood.

"True," Hardwick said, giving him the courtesy of the truth. "But that's not what I need to speak to you about right now. You've been reinstated. IA has found no evidence of any wrongdoing, on your behalf, on the Peter Kozlov case, or any of your previous cases. If they had, believe me, you wouldn't be here right now. You'd be talking to your union rep and enjoying the life of a retiree or guarding a cotton candy stand in Calabasas."

"So what's this about?"

"Peter Kozlov."

"What about him?"

"Well, he's shit. You know that. I know that. Most everyone who can read a paper or watch the late night news knows that."

"He's more than that. He attacked children. That makes him—"

"I am aware, and I agree. But that doesn't make his rights, as a US citizen no less, any less than yours or mine."

"Don't tell me. He's got a lawyer."

"He's got a lawyer." Hardwick replied. "Adam Wolfe."

"Son of a bitch," Parks cursed. Adam Wolfe was a well-known, and much cursed name around the LAPD when it came to high profile defense cases. "And he's claiming what?"

"That he was framed," Hardwick answered.

"Son of a—*and?*" Parks repeated. Hardwick stared, remaining silent. "And what? You're saying he could walk? Seriously? He fed razor blades to children. He attacked his wife. Killed my partner. And he could walk? Seriously?"

"Levinson planted evidence," Hardwick said calmly. "It's pretty well known by now."

"But *I* didn't."

"No. So what we need right now is to separate your investigation into Kozlov from Levinson's. All files. Notes. Everything. I've already got a team going over everything. The only way we're going to nab Kozlov is by painting you as a saint, which luckily for me, you damn near are. And—"

"And painting Levinson as the devil," Parks finished.

"It's going to be ugly," Hardwick said, confirming his thoughts. "But if we want to get him for this then there's no other way. Otherwise—"

"He could be a free man," Parks spat. "Seriously?"

"You need to make yourself available."

"For?"

"Adam Wolfe for starters. Anything he needs. Files. Documents. You. If he has questions, you better answer them and have the evidence to back them up. This thing is being rushed to court within the next few weeks and Wolfe is already aiming to have the entire case thrown out."

"I'm surprised he hasn't convinced Kozlov to be deported back to Russia," Parks said.

"Oh, he won't do that," Hardwick said reaching into her side drawer and pulling out a file. "We came across this last week while you were on vacation."

Parks made a face, challenging her word choice.

"What's that?" Parks asked, accepting the file.

"Let's just say you caught on and identified Kozlov a hell of a lot faster than they did over in Russia," Hardwick said.

Parks picked up the file, flipped it open and immediately shut it. Inside were dozens of pictures, each person obviously the target of Kozlov's wrath.

"How many?"

"Thirteen dead. Nine adults. Four children," Hardwick said, her expression stone cold. "At least another fifteen harmed. Three of those children."

"This asshole goes after children," Parks said, running his hands over his face. There was nothing more to say. He picked back up the file and flipped through it again.

"I'm aware of that," Hardwick said. "It appears he started after adults but then realized it was easier to . . . trick children."

"I'm surprised someone from the Russian mob didn't cut his dick off and feed it to him."

"They never identified Kozlov as the attacker over there. The attacks simply stopped. And he never touched a child."

"No, he never molested a child; he just fed them razor blades and watched them suffer."

"Now you get how serious this is? This man killed thirteen people and attacked another two-dozen, including children. This man cannot be let free."

"Whatever you need." Parks said.

"The case files are being gone over by a team," Hardwick said. "That you don't need to worry about. Probably better if you don't touch it until they're done, but once they are, it would be recommended that you go over every detail so you know it like the back of your hand. And any meetings you do have with Wolfe you better make sure you have our legal representation there as well. I don't need any bullshit accusations being flung about. Not any more than already are being slung."

"Consider it done."

"And Parks," Hardwick said, breathing deeply. "There better not be any fuckups by you or your team. Adam Wolfe is just looking for that one step out of line that will set his client free."

"Great," Parks smiled. "All I needed on my first case back."

"What's that?"

"More pressure."

7

"Detective Parks? Detective Parks."

Parks turned around to see Jackie Isley following him out the front doors of the station.

"Doctor," he said. "What can I do for you?"

"For starters, it's Jackie. Remember?"

"Jackie." Parks smiled. "And when I'm off the clock, it's Dave. What can I do for you?"

"Well, Dave, I was wondering what your plans were."

"I just broke down what everyone needs to focus on. I believe—"

"No. No," Jackie cut him off, smiling. "Not about the case. I mean right now. Would you like to get a drink? I was just . . . well, I'd like to talk. Pick your brain. If you have the time, that is? I promise to be more sociable."

Parks noticed several officers passing by, no one paying them any attention. The sun was still up over the horizon but looked ready to disappear within the next half hour, hopefully to relieve them of the heat that had bore down on the city all day. Despite living his whole life in Southern California, he never thought he would get used to the heat. And each passing year it just got worse.

"I'd like to apologize," Jackie said when Parks didn't respond.

"What for?"

"My behavior earlier today. I realize I might not be the warmest person when it comes to first impressions. I guess that just comes from my line of work. Most people assume that because I deal with toxic chemicals and contaminants all day long, I myself might also be infectious. I notice the looks I get. It's the general behavior I get from other men and women in the department, and I guess that over time I've put up a shield against it. Stay professional. Get in, do my job, and get out. The truth of it is that I do work with toxic contaminants all day long and it is a serious business. Lives are at stake and can continue to be so if I do my job incorrectly. But you and your team seem different. I just—"

"Sure." Parks smiled, stopping her babble. He wasn't really in the mood to socialize, thanks to the news Hardwick had just given him. But then again, he could use a drink. "A drink sounds good."

*   *   *

Thirty minutes later Dave Parks and Jackie Isley sat at a table in the corner of the front patio of a dimly lit Mexican cantina on Sunset. The music was louder than Parks would have preferred for conversation, so he chose the gated patio area, allowing for a little bit of privacy.

Behind the bar rested a wall covered with various tequilas, each one used to make a different flavored margarita. Two wide-screen televisions were plastered up in the corners above the bar, currently displaying the Dodgers, who were ahead by five points, continuing their winning streak.

"So how'd you find this place?" Jackie asked as she took her seat.

"Passed by it one night on the way home," Parks said. "Cheap drinks. Good food. On Tuesdays the tacos are a buck each. On our salary, every penny helps."

"Oh, I get you there," Jackie said, taking his thought and running with it. "Imagine being a single mother on what we make. Gotta love those high-paying city jobs."

Jackie took a sip of her margarita and brushed a strand of her reddish-brown hair out of her face. Parks noticed for the first time that day she had untangled her hair from up above her head, allowing the twists and turns of her naturally curly hair to fall down around her face. He also caught the vibrant colors that helped complement her natural beauty, especially after a day of working and not applying a fresh layer of makeup.

"So you have a kid?" Parks asked, not noticing a ring on her finger. He wasn't sure why he was conflicted to hear the news but felt he should pursue the subject since she had brought it up.

"Well, I guess I shouldn't really call him a kid anymore." Jackie shrugged. "He's twenty. Just starting his second year at PSU this fall."

"Twenty?" Parks asked.

"Yeah," she replied and blushed, fiddling with her napkin. "I had him when I was young. I was kind of a lost teenager—well, not really. I mean, I was focused. But I guess when I rebelled I did it in the strongest way possible and, well . . . live and learn." She took another swallow of her peach-flavored drink and continued to play with the rim of the glass as she spoke. "Not that I regret having Ricky—that's my son. Not that I regret having him for one second. He's the light of my life. I can't imagine him not being a part of my life."

"And the father?"

"Who knows? Not around, that's all I know. He didn't want anything to do with Ricky. Wanted me to get rid of him before I had him. He wasn't the fatherly type. Just the type you get rebellious against the parents with. Anyway, he didn't want to be around, and I didn't want him. I've rarely ever seen or heard from him since. But that's okay. I had my mother to help me out, and everything has worked out so far. At least that's what I tell myself. Honestly, every now and again, I wonder if I didn't screw up my son by raising him on my own. Not that I feel I did a bad job. Just that I wish I had had a father figure around for him growing up."

"And how's school going for Ricky?"

"We don't have to talk about him if you don't want," Jackie said, blushing again.

Parks took a sip of his drink. "No, please. It's fine."

"School's good for him, I think," Jackie continued. "Sorry. Not used to being on a date and having a guy actually interested in my child. Oh, I'm sorry. Not that this is . . . Sorry. Not that this is a date. I didn't mean that. Just that I'm not used to other people asking about my kid." Parks smiled, understanding what she meant. "But school's good for him. As best as I know anyway. He tries to pretend to not want me to butt in all the time, but he still loves me and tells me what he can. He's majoring in physical therapy. Or maybe it's called sports medicine. I'm not sure. He's always been one of those health-nut types. Always played sports in school. But then in high school, well, he had a rough time. Personal stuff. But when he played football, he dislocated his knee and tore several ligaments. And that was the end of his playing days. I told him it would be best to try and move on, but he loves the game and decided that studying something to do with sports would be the way to still be around it."

"So he's strong willed and independent. Wonder where he gets that from?" Parks smirked and took a swallow of his drink. "That sucks about the injury. I can relate."

"Can you now?"

"Yeah. Injured myself my senior year. Playing baseball. It was just as well for me. It's not like I was ever going to go pro with it."

"What position?"

"Shortstop. Sometimes outfield. I had the arm for it. It was high school. They moved us around."

"Shortstop. Like Kyle Oni," Jackie said referring to the Dodgers' current superstar. Anyone who followed the Dodgers knew who Kyle Oni was, with his picture plastered all over town. Front pages of newspapers, magazine covers and on billboards for the team. Everyone in town worshipped the superstar.

"Oh, I was nothing like Oni."

"No unassisted triple plays in your short-lived career?"

"Hardly." Parks chuckled. "So, you follow the game?"

"Ricky's the true fan. Spring through fall there's always a game on the TV or radio somewhere in the house. We usually try to catch a game or two just the two of us if we can fit it in. You know, that may be what I love most about my son. No matter what's been thrown at him in life—no father, injuries, whatever—he still fights on and doesn't let it get him down. He's a fighter, my son. I'll give him that."

"I'm sure the apple didn't fall far from the tree."

"So anyway, what about you? Any children?"

"Uh, no," Parks said.

"A perpetual bachelor for life?" Jackie smiled at him, and he stared at her, soaking in the light that beamed off her personality.

"Actually, I was married once," Parks admitted, taking another swallow of his drink at the mention of his ex-wife.

"Oh?"

"But it didn't last."

"What happened?" Jackie immediately blushed. "Sorry. I shouldn't have—"

"No. No problem. Who knows? Life. Nothing. Everything." Parks shrugged as his right leg began to shake, his body filling with nervous energy as he recalled his previous life. "We were high-school sweethearts. Then we got married and that only lasted five months."

"The marriage killed your relationship?"

Parks shrugged. "Life killed our relationship. We both helped though. Anyway, about five years later she remarried. To a cop, no less. And a few years after that they moved to Santa Barbara."

"I'm sorry," Jackie blurted.

"Don't be," Parks said. "I'm just not used to having personal conversations with another person, let alone a . . . It's just . . . Well, it's like with your son. These aren't topics that get brought up often. I don't do this a lot—if ever. I spend most of my time alone. At home or wherever. On the rare chance I'm out it's usually with other people from the department."

"You seem dedicated to the job."

"You could say that. It's what I have right now. No family to speak of. My mother's—no idea where she is. She hasn't been around most of my life. Since I was a kid. My father . . . took his life when I was four. I was mostly raised by my aunt and uncle. They live in Newport Beach, so I only see them a few times a year, mostly around the holidays. No siblings. No wife anymore. But I still have my job. I like it. I'm a bit of a loner. But I like it. Being on my own. In my head. Thinking a problem through. I'd be scared for anyone else who tries to settle down in there. In my head, I mean. Who knows, maybe I am a perpetual bachelor for life. There are worse things."

"Did the job interfere with any of those things? Like your marriage?"

"I was a good husband." Parks took a sip of his drink and rethought his last reply. "She had . . . has emotional, um, problems. Well . . . let's just say she just wasn't up to married life. At least not with me. Truth is I didn't start on the force until after the divorce. I sort of became lost when we separated. That's when I stumbled upon the LAPD. It's possible I wouldn't be here right now if she hadn't left me. So who knows?"

"We kind of just dove right into the personal stuff, didn't we? I really did mean to talk about the case. Why didn't we just stick to favorite bands or places to eat?" Jackie laughed, breaking the tension.

"Bet your favorite band is Poison."

Both immediately burst out laughing.

"Sorry about that. Oh, I don't know," Parks admitted. "You asked and it just felt right to answer. Who knows why we do half the things we do."

"So, how long have you been a detective?"

"I've been a cop in one way or another for about . . . what, oh, fifteen years now."

"Fifteen years?"

"Yep," Parks said, recalling the exact dates of things. "Became a patrol cop at twenty. Did that for four years. Followed by three years with the GND."

"GND?"

"Gangs and Narcotics Division. Then took my detectives exam and transferred over to Robbery-Homicide. Been working with them for about eight years now with the last three strictly through IAS. That's the Investigative Analysis Section. That's why I have the team I have. Usually detectives work in two or three-man teams. CSI comes in and does their analysis of the crime scene then hand over their findings to the detectives, who put it all together and try to solve it. Since I work in accordance with the IAS, I keep closer contact with the other analysts that I wouldn't usually work with after their initial investigation into the crime. Keeps us closer. But keeps us busier, as we're usually given more cases to solve." Parks stopped talking and took a sip of his drink as he collected his thoughts. "Who knows. There have been rumors running through the chain of command about changing things around in the department. Possibly get rid of the IAS teams. Just keeping the CSIs in their own group and the detectives in another. In a year or two I might not even be working out of this division any more. Or with these people. It changes all the time. I try to make the best out of what I've got. Try and do what I can with what I have while I have it. The rest doesn't matter."

Jackie mulled over Parks's comments. "So what's with the Frankenstein look?"

"The wha—oh." Parks smiled and reached up to his face, rubbing several of the stitches. "It's not as bad as it looks. The last case we worked. We tracked down Peter Kozlov—he was that teacher—"

"Oh God, I heard about that," Jackie gasped. "You guys worked on that?"

"That was us. Anyway, after we figured out who it was, Levinson and I—uh, Aaron Levinson—he used to be part of the team. Well, we went to arrest Kozlov and he put up a bit of a fight. Went after his wife. Accused her of turning him into us. Levinson tried to save her and was run over. Crushed him. He died quickly, all things consider-ing. Due to Levinson's death, him being my partner, and whatnot, I was placed on immediate mandatory leave."

"Then how'd you arrest him?"

"Yeah, sometimes I hear what I want to hear. Sometimes I hear it but I still have this . . . drive that fills me. Like adrenaline pumping through you. Only way to fix it is to finish the problem. I knew where Kozlov was. I wasn't going on leave until he was off the streets. So, unofficially, and without the backup of my partner or the law, I went to apprehend Kozlov. He came after me with a razor blade. And that's how I got these." Parks held up his hands and showed Jackie the cuts on his palms before pulling back his shirt-sleeves and revealing the scars on his forearms. "So you see, my face isn't all that bad. They had to shave my head to stitch up all the cuts on top. That was three weeks ago. The hair is growing back. The cuts are sealing up. I'm still alive, and Kozlov is in jail, awaiting trial, where he'll never hurt another kid as long as he lives. Small price to pay, if you ask me."

"I seem to recall a slightly different story in the news?"

"Yes, well, we can't have vigilante officers of the law running around LA cleaning up the streets, now can we? The public has a very slanted view of the LAPD. Rampart. Rodney King. OJ. And Kozlov's apprehension actually helped skew that view in the posi-tive. Unfortunately, now evidence is coming to light that shows Lev-inson might not have followed every step in accordance with the law. So the public is becoming concerned with Kozlov's possible release and the rest of the department is looking down on Levinson. But since he's not alive to be looked down upon—"

"And since you are both alive and were his partner . . ."

"Exactly."

"That explains the looks around the station today."

"I was cleared of any wrongdoing, which is why I'm back on duty. So I got my team back. Well most of it. So I agreed to some time off, to attend some department therapy sessions, and they'd help take care of the rest. It also helped that I was able to talk Levinson's widow out of hitting the city with an unlawful death lawsuit." Parks paused, not sure if he should continue. "Of course I've just been informed that Kozlov's lawyers are filing an injunction to have him released based on false and planted evidence."

"He could walk," Jackie said, not believing him.

Parks stayed quiet, not able to bring himself to answer that question.

"And you'd do it all again. The same?"

"With the exception of Levinson, I'd do it all the same, yes. I mean, I wish I had been there for him. To help him through whatever it was he was going through that made him feel he needed to do what he did. Maybe I'll never know. Either way, I'm alive, no matter the scars. Physical ones aren't nearly as traumatic as the emotional ones. I have tattoos that were more painful than what Kozlov did to me. At least he's off the streets and won't be able to hurt anyone anymore. That makes it worth it. He's not the first and he won't be the last. Someone new always comes along. As you saw proof of this morning."

Jackie sat back, thinking. Before she could respond, Parks added, "Which isn't actually something you see all that often, considering your position, now is it?"

"Yeah, like I said earlier, people rarely actually poison one another as a form of murder. We usually have one, maybe two, cases like that per year. Most of my investigating involves chemical imbalances during traumatic events."

Parks's brow gave away his confusion.

"Like, for example, say a college student goes on a rampage and slices up his family with a priceless Japanese sword his father had in his study and in the process of being stopped is shot by the police. Yes, this really happened," she said to Parks's questioning look. "Anyways, my job is to test the blood of the student to see if perhaps he wasn't on something. PCP or the like. For legal purposes, in case during the course of the trial he wishes to challenge his sanity or whatnot. Also, as uncomfortable as it may be, I have to test the officers on duty for alcohol and drugs in their blood to make sure their actions during the apprehension were sound and justified. It's an ugly snowball that just keeps rolling. If you get my drift?"

"I get it. I had no idea—"

"Most people don't. It's not personal. It's just a job. But sometimes I'm only seen as a step away from IA. That's why my social skills, or lack thereof, are what they are. Again, I apologize."

"You have nothing to apologize for." Parks smiled and signaled the bartender for another round of drinks.

"So, tattoos, huh?" Jackie said as she quickly did a once-over of him.

"Nothing that can be seen while on the clock," Parks said, chuckling.

"Uh-huh," Jackie said, smiling. "Regretting that drunken night in college when you wanted to impress a girl by getting a cartoon character tattooed, aren't you?"

"That's it."

"Or is it a flower? A heart with mommy's name in it? Or was the tattooist drunk as well and misspelled the declaration you wanted pronounced for the rest of your life on your body?"

"Guess you'll just always have to wonder."

Both sat quiet and took in the noise of the rushing freeway nearby.

"You got this look in your eyes when Amy brought up the symbol carved on the body," Jackie said, changing the subject. "You don't think Allison Tisdale's an isolated event. You think there will be more?"

"We don't know what that symbol stands for. Could be the number ten. Could be something else. Doesn't matter either way. Fifteen years on the force has taught me to trust my gut when it tells me something. And it's telling me something's up with Allison Tisdale. I'm not sure what. But something's off. I just hope I'm wrong."

"For the record, even though I don't have your experience working homicides, I agree with you."

"Thanks. I just hope we'll figure it out before anyone else loses their life."

"Do you think we'll be that lucky?"

Parks took another swallow of his drink and watched the passing cars without commenting one way or the other.

PART TWO

8

Assistant Chief Hardwick was having a quick late afternoon meeting with Detectives Parks and Wilkes, notifying Wilkes of a possible 459—burglary—and 187—homicide—that he was now in charge of. A short-tempered man who had worked his way up through the ranks, Detective Mark Wilkes felt himself to be more deserving of his position and special privileges than most others. He usually went along with the flow of the department and whatever decisions Hardwick made concerning him and his partners. Most of his career it had just been him and Cal Ramirez, though a year ago they had been assigned Detective Lewis Hayward, a twenty-year vet from the east coast. Wilkes was in his late thirties, with pronounced, becoming features, and the air of someone who used to attract attention based on his looks despite years of partying and reckless living that had yet to fully catch up with him. He had a tanned and lined face, particularly around the eyes, while the stubble along his neck was starting to grey. It wasn't hard to see why women would find him attractive. That was until he opened his mouth, usually to say something offensive.

"Are you serious? I thought you took us out of rotation?" Wilkes asked as he stood on the opposite side of her desk. He tried his best to be intimidating, with his hands on his hips and a look on his face that would have scared Medusa. At barely five nine, Hardwick stood a good three inches over him, and even if he had a good fifty pounds of muscle on her, she was still his boss and didn't care how he stood or barked his replies. Parks knew she had seen tougher and rougher men (and women) in her career as a law enforcement agent and wasn't about to let some snot-nosed, trust-fund brat tell her how to run her department.

"You know my team has to be ready to testify in the Cosway killings," Wilkes continued.

"I'm aware of that," Hardwick said. "And I've been informed by the DA that you and your team members will not be called for at least another week. That gives you plenty of time to process the crime scene and give your analysis of what happened. If for some reason one of your team members or yourself needs to be pulled early to appear in court, I will have the case reassigned." Hardwick looked to Parks who acknowledged that he would be the assuming detective. "Until then, it's yours."

Wilkes cracked his knuckles and ground his crooked teeth, not sure which step he should take. He was a fit man, having paid extreme focus on his health with daily exercise routines and with the food that he put into his body. He believed his body was a temple, felt no reason to treat it as anything less, though apparently that rule didn't apply to booze and cigarettes, which he went through at an impressive rate. This was also why he felt himself deserving of as many women as he could get, part of the reason he juggled both a wife and mistress—a supposedly little known fact that most of the department was well aware of. Including Hardwick and Parks.

Regardless, the information had never been used against him. And with his sister married to the mayor, it just might never be.

"Fucking hell," Hardwick continued when Wilkes just went on staring at her. "Look, Nelson's already handling a full caseload, and she just took on the Koreatown double shooting. And I'd give it to Parks, but it's his team's first week back from their mandatory hiatus"—Wilkes huffed at this comment—"and they're already working the Tisdale poisoning and that has a high priority from the mayor himself. Until we have further details, I want him and his team focused on that. Not to mention the Kozlov bullshit, which I know you're well aware of. Would you like Kozlov to walk?" Wilkes remained quiet. "Like I said, if you need to be pulled, then I'll reassign it. Parks will take over. Until then, it's yours."

"Yeah, right," Wilkes huffed.

"Look . . . Parks, what are you up to right now?" Hardwick asked.

"Nothing life altering. Just going over notes again."

"You have a free hour or two?"

Parks eyed Hardwick, knowing where she was going with this but knew he should keep the peace. His team had a lot of leeway their first week back.

"Sure thing."

"Good. Then I want you to shadow Wilkes on this homicide. Just stand back and observe the scene. That way if I do have to reassign the case then you're at least a little familiar with it. Okay?"

"Yes, ma'am," Parks said.

"That sounds agreeable to you, Wilkes?"

"Do I have a choice?" Wilkes asked, turning to leave.

"Wilkes," Hardwick said, looking down at the paperwork on her desk.

Wilkes stopped at the door.

"Don't worry about those two bastards. They'll get their day in court and what's coming to them. I won't let you miss that or mess it up for anything in the world. Now go on."

Wilkes left the office and Parks hung around.

"Are you sleeping okay? You look like shit."

"Just a late night," Parks said, shaking his head. "I'll catch up tonight. I promise." Truth was, ever since the Kozlov case his sleep had become less and less frequent with each passing night. Most nights he stayed up too late working the case and when he finally did hit the sack, his dreams were mostly images of Peter Kozlov and razor blades. But he knew better than to ever admit that.

"So how'd your deposition with Wolfe go?"

"Legal said it went positive for us. Wolfe's still going to find a way to try and spin it. But they said as far as we're concerned, there's nothing more we can do about it. You hear anything?"

"Judge Vogel is going to hear pleas by the end of this week," Hardwick said sitting at her desk.

"Vogel? That good or bad?" Parks wasn't familiar with the man enough to know how he would vote on the dismissal.

"He's a grandparent so he's sure as hell not going to want Kozlov out free on the streets," Hardwick began. "But he's also considering running for office so he's going to follow the law. He'll throw out all evidence that Levinson touched or had anything to do with. We're going to have to prove we had enough without Levinson's help."

"I lead the team on this investigation," Parks began. "And he was my number two guy. He had a hand in everything."

"I know."

"They're going to throw out the entire case."

"Most likely." Parks looked up, concern on his face, and Hardwick shrugged. "There's nothing we can do about your case. It's tainted. It's all garbage. I can't have Wilkes looking into it because he's got the Cosway case being looked into by IA as well. So I've got Nelson's team going over the entire case to see if she can find anything new."

"But if she's basing her new findings off my old case notes then her findings would be corrupt as well. That won't work either."

"There's not a lot we can do. I know he was one of your closest friends but right now Levinson has left us royally fucked. It's a gamble. There's nothing new we can do. Just hope to God that the fact that this man attacked children will outweigh the illegal means through which we captured him."

"Either that, or hope that if he goes free a pissed off parent will take justice into their own hands."

"He better not get free," Hardwick said. "For all our sakes. You think we have image issues right now? Hell . . . you better hope to God that man doesn't go free. Or else then we're all in deep shit."

"What about the wife?" Parks asked, the thought just coming to him.

"What about her?"

"He attacked her. Plus, you can't tell me she didn't or doesn't know things that could be used against him. I could talk to her?"

"You, will have nothing to do with anything having to do with the Kozlov case from here on out. But it's a solid idea. I'll make sure she's approached."

Parks breathed deeply but knew she was right. If they wanted Kozlov locked up for life then there was nothing he could do about it. He had to play by the rules of the game. And right now he was very close to going over the edge.

"All right. Just let me know if there is anything else I can help you with."

"You know I will. Now go help Wilkes."

*   *   *

"So the cause of death is . . .?" Wilkes stood over Amy Tanaka as she did her best to examine the dead body called in by the building super at a little after six that evening. Identified as thirty-four-year-old Ian Harris, the deceased was an up-and-coming photographer who had recently been receiving accolades for his eccentric and somewhat extravagant setups that were planned down to the most-minute detail. His most-noted piece of work thus far in his short-lived career was a photo spread he did for Vanity Fair with the cast of Twilight, recreating the famous dinner scene from The Thin Man, even though most fans of Team Edward vs. Team Jacob probably had no idea who or what The Thin Man was. The photograph was even detailed and dated to look as if taken during the 1930s. Each actor was dressed in authentically recreated costumes with numerous trinkets and clues spread about the picture to give hints related to who the actors were in real life, who their famous Twilight characters were, and who the killer at the crowded dinner table was. That was if the observer was willing to put the time and patience into scrutinizing the photo to find the answer. Rumor had it that Harris had recently been hired to reassemble the Harry Potter cast, though nothing had been officially announced and usually never was until the photo was revealed.

"No comment," Tanaka replied as she lifted the orange reflective glasses from her face having finished observing the body for biologicals.

"You're not a damn celebrity," Wilkes shot back.

"Hold your horses," Tanaka snapped while jotting down several notes.

Wilkes wasn't her favorite person to work with, but she had never let that stop her from doing her job. She was, as always and no matter what, a true professional. That also happened to be Wilkes's problem. He was a professional pain in the ass as far as most were concerned. Not that he didn't have his pluses. He closed cases. And quite often. It was his ability to close cases that he felt forgave his rough exterior was accepted. Wilkes was the "bad cop" to every other officer's "good cop." Most on the force agreed he was a good detective. He just wasn't the most agreeable person to be around.

"My horses don't need to be held," Wilkes replied. "They need answers."

Tanaka glared over at Parks, standing silently in the corner, and prayed for his participation in—or possibly commandeering of—this case.

Sitting before them in a sofa chair, slouched over a kitchen table, was Ian Harris's body. Across the top of the table, underneath the victim's head and several rolls of film, were the numbers 313 written in women's red lipstick. The tube of lipstick left on the corner furthest from the victim's head and had already been photographed, bagged, and tagged. Tanaka tried maneuvering around the body as a pool of blood had formed on the table around the man's face and on the floor below him where it had dripped off and collected. When they lifted the victim's head back from the table, they saw his face was contorted and covered with blood that appeared to have leaked out through the man's eyes. With most of his body bloated and his hands, arms, and face discolored, it was difficult to get a positive visual identification even with the super letting them know who lived in the loft. Tanaka maneuvered the corpse's hand and held several fingers up to her scanner, the prints fed into IAFIS. Five minutes later, while she examined the eyes for lacerations, there was a confirmation on the corpse's identity.

"Can't you just say the man bled to death and let my men get to the body?"

"I could say that," Tanaka replied without looking up at the detective. "But that doesn't necessarily make it true. Now, do you want the truth or just whatever half-assed theory I can throw at you to shut you up and get me the hell out of here? It's your report, Detective."

"So you're saying he didn't die from bleeding to death from his eyes?"

"I'll have to get him to the lab to do a full autopsy to know for sure," Tanaka answered. She could sense Wilkes's internal groan so continued. "Did he die from blood loss? It's possible. There is a lot of blood here. Was it enough to kill him? Only if he didn't quickly receive the proper medical attention. But you're looking for what caused the blood loss as his reason of death. What that cause is, I don't yet know."

"But what could cause that?"

"Officially?"

"Just whatever you can tell me off the top of your head. I know you need to wait for your damn autopsy to be official. Your guess will do me fine just now."

"Off the top of my head? Trauma. Infection of some sort. Thrombocytopenia. That's decreased blood platelets. Leukemia has been known to cause bleeding from the eyes. Hereditary disorders.

Liver disease. Hemophilia or an anticoagulant of some sort. And there's also hyphema which is bleeding between the cornea and iris. Or a face fracture."

"Does his face look fractured to you?"

"No it does not, Detective," Tanaka answered, studying the body. "But this is one of the most violent crime scenes I've seen in a while."

"That's it?"

"That's it. You want a reason, then pick one of those. I won't know for sure until—"

"You complete your autopsy," Wilkes finished for her as he waved her off. "Son of a bitch. All right. So when will that be?"

"The autopsy?" Tanaka knew she was about to disappoint the man. "Sorry, but I have a backlog a mile long. On top of that, it's Monday evening and today's Labor Day. Half the department is working overtime already, and it isn't exactly a slow time with it being a holiday. Probably won't get to it until Wednesday. Maybe Thursday."

Wilkes breathed deeply to announce his disappointment. But this wasn't his first homicide, and it wouldn't be the last time she would tell him to wait. He usually had someone he could call somewhere and get strings pulled and people pushed around. Unfortunately, there wasn't much to be done about a line of dead bodies.

"All right," Wilkes said, giving in. He wasn't done with this yet, but as far as she needed to be concerned, he was. "One last thing. I need to know how to pursue this investigation. Was our guy here possibly the victim of homicide?"

Tanaka stared at Wilkes, feeling sorry for the man. "Look . . . officially, I can't tell you anything just yet. Off the record, the door and windows were locked, so how did someone get out of here? Then again, it appears there was some sort of violent spasm by the victim before he died. Was that from contact with another person? I have no idea. There are no obvious markings or lacerations on the body anywhere to show signs of violent trauma. So who's to say? For everything that says this is a homicide there's something that says it isn't. Have I ever seen anything like this before to suggest one way or the other, homicide versus accident? No, I haven't. But my gut, based on other crime scenes, would say this is."

"Thank you." Wilkes smiled sarcastically. "That will do just beautifully for me for now. Contact me as soon as you know anything definitive."

"Will do, Detective."

"You get all that down, Boy Scout?" Wilkes asked Parks as he walked by the man and out of the room.

Parks shrugged at Tanaka who rolled her eyes and went back to her body.

Thirty minutes later she finished her inspection of the body and backed off to make room for the members of Wilkes's team. Detective Cal Ramirez was a family man with a pockmarked face and beady eyes who always had a dirty joke ready. The third man in Wilkes's team was Detective Lewis Hayward, who had only been with the department for almost two years, though, at forty-five, was far from its youngest member.

Hayward relayed that he had been going door-to-door to interview Ian Harris's neighbors, checking for signs of anything out of the ordinary, from suspicious people lurking around the building to vehicles that didn't belong, which along that area of Beverly and Western wasn't all that uncommon. An hour later he had come to the conclusion that while Ian Harris may have been a dick from time to time, most of his neighbors knew little about him.

No one appeared to be holding any grudges.

No one appeared to wish him any ill will.

Overall, most people didn't know him.

"All right," Wilkes said, addressing his two men in the front room of Ian Harris's loft. The forensic people had finished with the scene, having lifted numerous fingerprints and other hairs and fibers, all labeled and ready for the lab to analyze. There were several half-empty glasses of booze and a brown-paper-wrapped package that was empty of whatever it had previously contained. Hopefully they would get lucky with the fingerprints that were all over the box.

Unfortunately, he had to wait for the autopsy results before he could give any definitive direction to the case, but until then they would hit all of the usual channels. Family. Friends. Neighbors. Business associates. The works.

"Tomorrow, I want you two to hit up the vic's work space. Hayward, you're better with computers than Ramirez or me. I know he was a freelance photographer, but get a hold of his agent and manager if he has one. See if he has any shows in any galleries. Assignments he may have been working on. See if he's pissed anyone off lately or if he's behind on anything. There're a few photos around the place that make it look like he might have been hanging with the paparazzi lately, and we know how loved they are. Then, if you can, go over his financials and see if there's anything outstanding there. I want to know if he was in any sort of trouble. I'll be notifying the family and coming up with a timeline leading up to his death. Okay. Any questions?"

No one had any.

"Then get your asses moving, people. We have a dead body that's getting colder by the minute." His team members disbursed and he turned to Parks. "You have any questions? No? Good. Not like you're going to ever touch this case anyways. I don't care what she says. We both know I'm getting screwed here. Thanks."

9

"Son of a bitch." Parks threw the binder across the table, and it flew up and slammed against the wall before hitting the ground, most of the papers inside coming free from the three rings that held everything together.

"Sorry," he mumbled to no one in particular as he picked up his cup of coffee, only to find it empty. He crushed the cup and went to throw it but resisted the urge and dropped it into a trash can instead. He could feel the stress building inside, and the endless supply of caffeine wasn't helping.

The rest of his team was in the conference room going over various aspects of the Tisdale crime scene from five days earlier. So far they had found nothing of any significance and weren't any closer to identifying who had murdered Allison Tisdale. There had been no further poisonings or messages delivered to the police or anything of the sort. Parks felt the case coming to a halt. Five days after the fact with nothing to show for it wasn't a promising start. Apparently he had been wrong about the possibility of a serial poisoner.

Jackie Isley had to go back to the coroner's office to continue with her day-to-day activities considering the lack of forward motion on the case. She had informed them that if they needed any further assistance from her, she was only a phone call away and happy to oblige.

They had brought Mr. Tisdale in for further questioning, all of which he passed without signaling any red flags other than the fact that he had no solid alibi. He hadn't proven himself enough to be wiped completely off their suspect list, but at the same time, Parks knew it was pointless to continue pursuing him when they had other avenues to follow up on. Either way, Doug Tisdale's photo stayed up on the murder board under their list of suspects. If the department could afford to spare a few lower-level officers, maybe he'd have some men keep an eye on the man just to be sure.

Not to mention the threat of Peter Kozlov's possible release weighing heavily on Parks's mind, making his focus and concentration difficult to keep under control. A child killer could be back out on the streets within a few weeks.

"Sorry," Parks repeated with a little more force this time.

"It's okay," Moore reassured him as she helped pick up the binder. "We understand."

"It's just . . . this guy is good. He's thought of everything. Paper trails. Fingerprints. Evidence. He's left nothing out of place. It's like he's a phantom. A ghost. And there's been no other murders. It's almost like Allison Tisdale was an isolated event. If we don't discover something soon, I'm not sure what's going to happen to this case. It's turning cold and fast."

"You need some coffee?" Moore asked softly, her mothering instincts kicking in. She did that effortlessly, a trait Parks found interesting considering the woman had never actually had any children of her own. At least as far as he knew. "Go on. Take a break."

"Hardwick's putting us back into rotation today. Let everyone know."

"We know. It's not like it wasn't expected. We were lucky to have as much free time on this case as we did. The truth is there are homicides every day, and this case cannot take up all our time anymore. It's okay. We're ready to work. This case isn't finished; it's just on hold pending new information. What's going on with Kozlov?"

"No idea," Parks said. "That's what I really hate. The waiting. I've got parents of the children calling here day and night. Hell, they're even showing up in the parking lot. Accosting me. Asking me how I can let that man who attacked their children go free?"

"They see you as the knight who vanquished the dragon," Moore said.

"Yeah, well now that dragon might go free and it's this knight's fault," Parks said, shaking his head. "My, how they turn on us so quickly."

"They don't blame you. But you stopped the monster once. They just want you to do it again."

"Yeah, well it's looking like I'd have to kill the monster in order to achieve that."

Moore stared at Parks, knowing he would never do any such thing. That by simply saying the words, putting them out in the universe, was dangerous enough. Parks turned from Moore, not able to handle her glare, glancing over at Fairmont and Tippin. Fairmont was digging through several binders of charts, forms and other various papers that Tippin had printed off for him, while Tippin himself typed away at his laptop.

"You two got anything new?" Parks called out.

"Nothing so far," Fairmont said, leaning back, stretching in his chair, raising his hands high above his head before bringing them down and covering his face. "Nothing in their financials to make anyone suspect."

"And the affair?"

"What affair?" Fairmont shot back, talking through his hands. "Sure she had one? There's no evidence she ever did anything outside her marriage. No receipts. No secret getaways. No hidden love notes. Text messages. Whisperings behind her back. Nothing."

"What about coworkers?"

"None of them are suspect," Fairmont answered.

"Really?" Parks asked, looking to Tippin.

"Of the five men she worked with, two are gay, one is over sixty, and the other two have been there less than a year. Which doesn't exactly feel like enough time to have had an affair, have the husband find out about it, and all be worked out and forgiven by now . . ." Tippin trailed off. "They're all in the clear."

Parks stayed quiet, thinking, staring off into space.

"Parks?" Moore asked a minute later. "You on to something?"

"It's just while we were searching through the Tisdales' financial records, I realized something. They loved each other. I believe that. But Mr. Tisdale wasn't exactly spending the big bucks on his wife. Other than holidays, birthdays, and anniversaries he rarely ever spent anything on her."

"Okay . . . ?"

"So remember how you said the flowers that we found Allison holding were the same ones she received a few years back for a few months from her husband. What if they weren't from her husband? What if they were from whoever she was having an affair with?"

The group remained silent for a moment and processed what

they had been told.

"Can you guys trace the flower orders?"

"It was two years ago," Fairmont replied, unenthusiastically.

"Yes. But I figure a bouquet of flowers every week for three months in a row . . . chances are that was done automatically."

"Like on a credit card," Tippin added. "Not sure what company delivered them, but I can do some digging around. Hit up all the usual online retailers and then check with any shops around Allison's office."

"Looks like you boys know what you're doing next." A smile came to Parks's face as his cell phone in his pocket began to play the chorus to Poison's Unskinny Bop. "What the hell is that?"

Fairmont and Tippin both held back laughter as they turned back to the folders and papers spread out in front of them.

"What the flip did you two do to my phone?" Parks barked sharply, though not very serious, as he retrieved his phone. "One of you, I don't care who, but one of you better fix this shit," Parks ordered as he waived his phone in their direction before looking at the screen to see the number was blocked. He answered it anyway. "Hello?"

There was only silence from the other end of the line. Parks sighed. He didn't know who had been calling him but this was the third time this week. Someone called. Never spoke. Sounding like no one was there until suddenly a child's laughter came from the other end. Parks never heard more than that, never got an answer when he asked who was calling or what they wanted. He wanted to tell whoever was calling to piss off but he had a feeling that it would be the one time he would be recorded and then there'd be hell to pay. Though he wasn't sure why? He was the one being pranked. He wasn't in the mood and was about to say something when he simply hung up. He was more likely to change his number if this continued. He had done it before.

Moore eyed him with a questioning look.

"Wrong number," Parks said by way of an explanation.

"You getting a lot of those lately?"

"There's worse things going on around us than me getting prank calls."

"Still, you might want to have IT put a trace on your calls. Or at the very least tell Tippin. I'm sure he knows of some way to find out who's calling you. We have too much going on around us right now for you to start losing your cool over prank calls. As it is, it doesn't look like you've been sleeping enough. And I don't care what you've told Hardwick, or what she's willing to believe for the good of the department, I know better."

Moore finished and stared at him, her eyes grilling into him.

"Fine," Parks said, giving in. "I'll have Tippin look at my phone." Moore raised her eyebrows in doubt. "I promise. Now can we please get back to the case in hand?"

"You're the boss."

10

"Parks? Parks?"

Parks continued fiddling with the crossword puzzle as he sat at his desk, feet up on the corner, while he tried to clear his mind of anything case-related. That apparently included hearing his name as Wilkes stood in his doorway and called out to him. He'd finished a Sudoku and several brain teasers on his phone earlier that morning as he waited for the rest of his team to show up. After staring at the files for three hours his brain needed a break. He figured the crossword was as good a way to give his brain a break as anything else.

"Parks?"

Parks looked up from the puzzle on his desk, confusion on his face. "What?"

"Tanaka needs us over at the morgue."

"Us? Together? What for?"

"The Harris case."

"Both of us? You sure?"

"That's what she said. You want to question her?"

"When?"

Wilkes held out his arms and made a face as if to say, what do you think I'm standing here for? Parks noticed Moore bury her face deeper into the binder in her hands as she held back a smile that was fighting to turn into laughter.

"All right. Let's go."

The two detectives drove in silence to the LA County Medical Examiner's Office, which was less than ten minutes from the LAPD's downtown station, though to Parks it felt like an eternity. He had tried several times to start a conversation before giving up and embracing the silence. Wilkes parked illegally in a handicap space near the front entrance, and Parks let it go. If they got a ticket it would be on Wilkes anyway. They made it to the front desk when Tanaka walked out through a side door before they could even address the receptionist.

"Men," Tanaka said, smiling. "Follow me."

"This better be important," Wilkes snapped. "I don't know why he needs to be here. This is still my case."

Parks remained quiet, hoping not to start anything with the other detective. Wilkes was shorter than Parks by a good six inches but was just as fit and had a decidedly shorter temper. And if there was a tumble to be had and Wilkes couldn't defend himself, it was known he had no problem getting on the phone and calling the proper people who could.

Tanaka led the investigators to the morgue, where she had Ian Harris's body out on a table, still opened up from the autopsy that was only halfway completed.

"I just started less than an hour ago, but I sent a vial of his blood in to be examined Monday night. Figured that might be helpful on how and why he bled like he did. So I put a rush on it. Just for you, Wilkes."

"And? What did you find?" Wilkes spat out, proving once again that no matter the situation he was never one to be pleased.

"Methanol," Tanaka answered, putting on two blue latex gloves. "As well as a high level of neurotoxin which I was able to determine came from an acanthophis."

"A what?" Wilkes asked.

"It's a highly venomous snake," Tanaka explained, holding up Harris's hand and showing the two men the snakebite. "More commonly known as a death adder."

"That's it?" Wilkes laughed. "So we're looking for a snake? Shit. I thought we had a killer on the loose. So the man stuck his hand where it didn't belong and got bit. People and their dogs get bit up on Runyon all the time."

Tanaka looked like she was ready to jump up and murder Wilkes herself.

"What is it, Amy?" Parks asked.

"There aren't any death adders up around Runyon Canon. Rattlesnakes? Yes. Death adders? No. And I don't think this was an accident."

"What do you mean?"

"I think that the vic here was poisoned." Tanaka turned from Wilkes and focused on Parks. "On purpose."

Parks took in what she was saying. She thought this case was related to his.

"Wai—what? How do you know that?" Wilkes asked. "It's a snake for crying out loud. You can't order a snake to go and sic someone down and kill them. And you got the bite marks right there. Stupid son of a bitch reached for or grabbed a snake and got bit. It happens."

"No, you can't order a snake after someone," Tanaka agreed. "But that's not what got me thinking it was intentional."

"What did?"

"The methanol."

"How so?" Parks asked.

"Methanol comes in several different forms. It's a sort of distilled alcohol. Like moonshine. It's also in perfumes, antifreeze, shellac, varnish, windshield wiper fluid. But at room temperature it's a liquid that can be swallowed. Tastes a lot like alcohol. Strong alcohol."

"Aren't there housewives who've killed their spouses with that stuff?" Wilkes asked, looking from Tanaka to Parks, who nodded in agreement.

Tanaka turned to Wilkes. "You said you found a half-empty bottle of vodka next to the body?"

"Uh-huh."

"I hope you're testing the bottle for what was in it. I have a feeling that it was mixed in with that. But this was a strong dosage. It didn't come that way. Someone had to have fixed the bottle. As little as ten milliliters can cause permanent blindness. But generally around a hundred milliliters is a fatal dose."

"That sounds like a lot," Wilkes said. "No way he drank that much."

"That's about four fluid ounces," Tanaka corrected. "The average water bottle holds approximately sixteen fluid ounces. If the vodka bottle next to him was mixed fifty-fifty and he drank half of that . . . you get where I'm going with this?"

"Asshole drank a lot," Wilkes muttered.

"And that's what killed him?" Parks asked, skeptically.

"No. Although it is toxic, if discovered in time it's treatable. Plus the symptoms usually show up between eight and thirty hours after consumption. Though at the rate and amount that our vic here consumed, I have a feeling the reaction time was bumped up."

"And what are the reactions?"

"It creates an imbalance of acid in the stomach. Like acidosis. The victim will feel inebriated. There will be haziness in the eyes. Possible blindness. And if it goes on long enough, seizures, possibly coma, and eventually death."

"So someone started poisoning the vic, and when it took too long they sent a snake in to finish the job?" Wilkes didn't believe what he was hearing.

"I don't think so," Tanaka said. "I think the snake was the original, intended poison for our victim. But while a bite from an adder is deadly, it's also treatable. If gotten to in time. And that's if you didn't run away from the snake in the first place."

"So the methanol . . . was a sort of precursor to the snake. To slow him down. Distort his senses." Parks thought aloud. "But why? Why did our victim need to die by snakebite? What's so special about the adder bite? Symptoms-wise?"

Tanaka shook her head. "Chills. Fever. Swelling. Skin discoloration. Heavy perspiration. Vomiting of blood. Bleeding from nose and eyes. Loss of vision. Loss of consciousness. The body was covered in sweat when I examined him. And while there was blood in the mouth area, he didn't appear to vomit any. Most of the blood just came from the eyes."

"That seems like a lot of blood to come from the eyes," Parks said, focusing on the crime scene photos Wilkes had passed to him. "That usually how much they bleed?"

"Not sure. Haven't seen this before. I'd have to check, but I'd say off the top of my head, no. Also, methanol affects the eyes, so maybe the two poisons together worked in overdrive to attack the area."

"He wanted to blind our victim? But why?"

"Something he saw?"

"Or something he was going to see? Or had been watching?" Wilkes added.

"Yes," Parks agreed. "Says in your report that he was found next to a window, correct?"

"That's right."

"Along with a pair of binoculars and an empty camera?"

"Yep."

"He saw something he shouldn't have. And possibly even took pictures of it. We need the film from that camera."

"The cameras were all empty. No film. No memory cards. No nothing. I can send my men back and have them check every angle of viewable space from his seat by that window. Check out what he could have possibly been watching. But that's our only option at this point."

"Is that all?" Parks asked, turning back to Tanaka.

"Nope," she said. "There's one more thing. Come look. Up at the screen. I have it hooked up to my microscope. I never would have seen this had I not already been looking at the eyes due to the blood. But this . . ."

Parks and Wilkes both looked up at the screen and saw the victim's two bloody eyes staring up at them. Tanaka took a dropper filled with a clear solution and squeezed some drops into each eye to clear away the blood, revealing two more plus sign-shaped symbols carved onto each of the corneas.

"Son of a bitch," Parks said as he sucked in his breath and tried to hold back on his instinct to throw up at the sight of the gore. His mind immediately went to paper cuts on the eyes and other such unpleasant images, and he had to squeeze his own eyes tight as if to protect them.

"What the hell is that?" Wilkes spat in disgust as he too turned away from the image and exhaled deeply.

"Killer's calling card," Parks answered. "That also means he came in after our victim was dead. No way had our killer done that while the guy was still alive."

"Nope," Tanaka agreed. "These are precise. Exact. There were no slip ups."

"There was no film in the camera?" Parks turned to Wilkes.

"None," Wilkes said, shaking his head.

"And none of your men found a snake?"

Wilkes remained silent.

"So he came in afterwards and cleaned up," Parks said, looking to Tanaka. "Looks like our guy's struck again after all."

11

"You know my team already went over this entire crime scene," Wilkes muttered to Parks as his team went about inspecting Ian Harris's loft. Each person had taken a different angle, comparing the original crime scene photos to the living space.

"And I appreciate it," Parks replied. "But having a fresh pair of eyes never hurts. Besides, your team was not aware of what they should have been looking for. My team has been working on this case for a week now. It's just a different pair of eyes."

"Hey look, no skin off my teeth," Wilkes shot back as he glared at the back of Parks's head. "You want it. Take it. My guys and I have plenty to do if you want to retrace everything."

Parks pulled Wilkes aside so that the rest of their teams wouldn't hear him.

"Look. I know you guys have to testify next week on the Cosway killings and that all of America will be watching. If you need to work on that then go ahead. Just check it with Hardwick. You know protocol. I'll tell her you have my support, whatever you decide. You'll get no argument out of me about it. As it is, thanks to that trial—and

117

Peter Kozlov—we already have the entire department under scrutiny."

Parks was like most people in the city of Los Angeles. Everyone was captivated by the two brothers who had beaten their parents to death one night in hopes of obtaining their inheritance ahead of schedule. Evan and Wesley Cosway were the latest in a string of spoiled kids who felt they were entitled to more from their parents and had followed the lead of Lyle and Erik Menendez two decades before. They weren't the first. And as most knew, they wouldn't be the last.

Wilkes and his team had been the first ones on the scene while TMZ and Channel 10 news crowded the driveway of the Cosways' fifteen-million-dollar Bel Air mansion. One of 10's cameramen managed to get inside the house and both damage evidence and shoot the crime scene itself, giving America an eyeful of the viciousness of the murders and proving Charles Wyler's willingness to do anything for a story. Charles Wyler and the LAPD had once again become front and center of another scandal. Americans were outraged and the first people to take the blame were the LAPD. Luckily, Wilkes and his team managed to identify the Cosways' killers as two of their three sons who happened to be living at their parents' house at the time, and immediate arrests were made, bringing a little bit of shine back to the department. It wasn't that shocking an accusation considering the two young men had been in trouble with the law multiple times throughout their lives, most notably when they had been accused of sexual assault and distribution of drugs on the PSU campus the year before, leading to both their expulsion from the university and a six-month jail sentence. So little was their price to pay with their father's checkbook constantly waving in the background.

A checkbook that only went on to entice then feed the two young men's greed.

Now, seven months after their parents' murder, a high-profile and ratings-breaking trial was getting underway, with most of America keeping a watchful and attentive eye. There could be no other mistakes made by the LAPD while a trial of this magnitude was underway.

Wilkes glanced around the loft at the two teams.

"We're already here," Wilkes said gruffly. "And you're right. We are under a watchful eye. Let's not mess anything else up. I'll make sure your team is brought up to speed by mine. Once we're finished here, we'll hand everything over to you guys."

"Thanks." Parks said as the two men split up. "Everyone, pay attention," Parks called out, ordering both teams gathered around the room. "We know some of you have already gone over this scene, and we are not in any way commenting on your job on the field. We have in our possession new information regarding this case and have to look at everything from a different perspective. My team has been familiarizing themselves with this killer for about a week now. This is his second murder, that we know of, and if we're lucky, his last. But if the first murder scene was any indication, then that's doubtful. This guy is good. Clean. Careful. Patient. Don't anyone be fooled by him or his methods of killing. Everyone needs to be on their utmost levels of alertness. This is not a game. I don't need any territorial bullshit. There are lives at stake here, and we have a job to do."

Everyone remained silent, most staring on, waiting for the word to get to work.

"Okay. Fairmont, Tippin, and . . ."

"Ramirez," Wilkes announced.

"Ramirez," Parks continued. "You three work on the views from the window and try and figure out what our victim was watching or may have witnessed from this spot. Okay?"

The three men nodded in agreement, and Parks waved them away.

"Rachel," Parks continued. "I want you to sweep the room where the victim was found. Focus on where the body was. And . . ." Parks looked to Wilkes.

"Hayward," Wilkes offered.

"And Detective Hayward will help you out."

"Sure thing," Hayward agreed.

"And us?" Wilkes asked.

"You and I are going to dig through the rest of the loft to try and figure out why this guy was chosen."

"Yeah, right," Wilkes said as he set about to dig through Ian Harris's life once again.

*　　　　　*　　　　　*

"Rach?" Parks said as he walked up behind her. She had just wrapped up checking the room for prints.

"I have nothing," Moore admitted. "I mean, there are prints all over this room, but we haven't come up with anything. They already ran them through IAFIS and got no hits other than Harris."

"Yeah, I get you," Parks said. "And the snake?"

"From what I can tell, the snake was in the box that was delivered. Hayward concurs. It was delivered to our vic, but by whom we're not sure as the prints on the box came up unidentifiable. The snake bit him and he dropped the box and fell into his seat here." Moore moved about the room showing Parks what happened where and how she thought according to the evidence they had recovered.

"The snake slithered out of the box and went over to that hutch there and stayed underneath it. There's no evidence that it left from that area, so I've a feeling that when our killer came here to clean up and leave his mark on both the table and the body, he gathered up the snake."

"How can you tell?"

"When the vic fell, he knocked over his bottle of vodka. The snake slithered through it and left a trail. You can't see it, but it's dried to the floor. Apparently it was citrus flavored, so that's a plus for us. Sugar in the liquid leaves behind a sticky substance."

"Shoe prints?"

"That's one piece of luck we've gotten so far. From what we can tell, they're size elevens. Mens. I scanned them and will have a print made up. Maybe the shoes will have significant aspects to them that will help us."

"That's good, but we need something more," Parks said, still staring at the camera aimed out the window. "This guy cleaned us out. We have next to nothing to work on."

Ian Harris's telephone began to ring, and everyone in the apartment froze as if a bomb was going to go off and no one wanted to be the one to trigger it.

"Where's the phone?" Parks asked as he left the room and worked his way to the kitchen, where he saw Lewis Hayward reaching for a phone on the wall.

"Don't touch it," Parks ordered before picking it up himself.

"Hel—" Parks stopped and remained quiet as he listened. Twenty seconds later he hung up and smiled.

"What is it?" Hayward asked.

"We may have just gotten a break," Parks said as he walked back to the other room and stuck his head out the window, looking down below at his men working in the courtyard of the complex.

Parks whistled. "Tippin."

Tippin looked up, and Parks motioned for him to join them in the apartment.

"What is it?" Moore asked as she walked over to Parks.

"Not sure." Parks shrugged. "Maybe something. Maybe nothing. Won't know until we check it out. Hopefully we'll luck out and it will be something the killer overlooked and couldn't have predicted when he cleaned out this apartment."

"What is it, boss?" Tippin asked as he entered the loft out of breath.

"You know where Samy's Camera is?"

"Over on Fairfax? Yeah."

"Good. Seems our vic has some prints that are developed and waiting to be picked up. Why don't you go see what's on them?"

"I'm on it," Tippin said with the same enthusiasm and spunk he had shown throughout the entire case. Then he disappeared out the door.

Parks turned to everyone else in the room. "Looks like we may have just gotten our first break."

*   *   *

"Milo. What is it?" Parks answered his cell, glad that Tippin had decided to call him from Samy's Camera rather than waiting to get back to him as it had taken him nearly forty-five minutes to get across town.

"I'm not sure, but I think it's the neighbors," Tippin said, excitedly. "The neighbors across the street from him. Yellow building. Three stories up from the look of these pictures. It's a couple. Guy and a girl. Mid-thirties. They're both blond. That's who he took pictures of. It looks like he was spying on them."

"Perfect. Thanks, Milo."

"There is one other thing, sir."

"Yes? What is it?"

"There're other pictures in with this roll of film."

"Oh?" Parks waited, hoping the kid would continue on his own. "What of?"

"You, sir."

"Come again?"

"Well, in particular from the Allison Tisdale crime scene. I think he was one of the paparazzi or newspaper men in the crowd of reporters. There are several pictures of you arriving at the crime scene."

Parks paused for a moment and tried to take in what this meant. Maybe something. Maybe nothing. Maybe just a coincidence. If he believed in coincidences. Either way, he could only tackle one problem at a time.

"We'll deal with that later. Just get back here."

"Yes, sir. I'm on my way right now."

Parks hung up and turned to the team. "Looks like he took pictures of the couple across the street. Wilkes, let's go have a talk with them."

As they made their way out of the building and across the street, Parks surveyed the area around the buildings to see if anything stuck him as being out of the ordinary. The two apartment complexes should have been on the opposite sides of the city, not just separated by a semi-busy street. Ian Harris's building was artier, with open-spaced lofts that had more of the internal structure of the building showing inside the living spaces. There were alleyways on three sides of the building, and numerous homeless people wandering around the area. The neighboring building was twice as high as Harris's and was painted over with a dull, mustard color with a complementary white trim. It felt as if it had been more recently established, one of several new buildings put up in an attempt to rebuild the area. They were nearing what was known by the locals as Koreatown, where on one street a citizen could walk the sidewalks and enjoy the nightlife and on the next one over get mugged and left for dead. Such was the area. Luckily, most who lived nearby were unaware of just how close to danger they were.

Parks and Wilkes entered the building and found a stairwell near the back corner of the lobby area. They quickly made their way up to the third floor and started down the hallway in the direction of the apartment they thought belonged to Ian Harris's unknowing Peeping Tom victims. Parks tried his best to estimate which apartment he was looking for based on the windows in between the apartments that looked out onto the street below.

Parks took out his cell and called Rachel. "Do you see me?"

"I got you. Over two more I think," Moore suggested. "To the right. Try that one. Dave, I haven't seen any movement from within the apartment. I don't think anyone's home."

"Thanks," said Parks as he hung up and turned to Wilkes. "Sounds like they may not be home." He knocked, more forceful than he had intended. "LAPD. Anyone there?"

The two men stood patiently, waiting for a response.

"You smell that?" Pars asked, leaning in closer to the door.

Wilkes also leaned in, took a sniff, and looked up at Parks with alarm. Both men were more than familiar with the scent of a decaying corpse.

"Go find a manager," Parks said. "We need a key."

Wilkes eyed Parks with disdain but knew better than to argue. Parks got on the phone and called Rachel to have her gather the rest of the team and head over to the apartment. He also wanted her to have one of Wilkes's people get a warrant to make sure they kept everything in order.

"That's the Bollingers," a rotund man said as he rounded the corner with Wilkes a few steps behind him. "Husband should be home. Jason Bollinger. Wife is Deborah. But she's out of town visiting family. Been gone since Monday afternoon. The husband should be home, though. He don't have a job right now. Legal problems. Here's the key."

Parks took the key and unlocked the door, opening it all the way.

"Sir?" Parks addressed the manager while holding his hand up at the man's chest. "Please wait outside. Thanks." Parks nodded to Wilkes to be ready to enter. "LAPD. Mr. Bollinger? Anyone here?"

"Doubtful," Wilkes commented.

"Check back there." Parks motioned toward a back room he figured was a bedroom.

Wilkes withdrew his gun and headed toward the rear of the apartment. Parks made his way in through the front room, finding it vacant.

"Find an—" Parks stopped walking when he reached the kitchen and saw what he assumed was Mr. Bollinger sitting in a chair next to the table. The shades were drawn in the kitchen, blocking any view from outside the apartment.

"Mr. Bollinger?" Parks worked his way around the table until he was in front of the man. "Wilkes! In the kitchen."

Wilkes walked into the kitchen and stopped as he took in the sight.

"Dave?" Moore called out as she stepped into the apartment with Fairmont and one of Wilkes's two men behind her. "You find the people who live–Oh, God!"

"Stop," Parks ordered. "Someone call Amy Tanaka and Jackie Isley. They need to see this one."

12

"What the fuck is going on around here?" Wilkes may have not been the most subtle person on the force, but he was pretty good at saying out loud what most everyone else was thinking. Everyone else being both investigation teams standing in the Bollingers' kitchen staring down at Jason Bollinger's lifeless corpse with a peculiar-looking fish in his limp hands. The fish was equally as lifeless as its holder. It was exotic, with spines coming out of the sides and top and stripes going vertically along the body, switching between a vibrant white to a coppery-brown color. Parks thought it might be a zebra fish but had a feeling he was wrong.

"Jake?" Parks called out. "I want photos before anyone else steps in here."

"Got it," Fairmont called back.

By the time the two teams made their way across the courtyard and up the three flights to the other apartment, Tippin was just arriving from Samy's Camera, traffic being lighter heading east than it had been heading west.

"I want to know what the hell he's holding," Parks said.

Tippin grabbed his computer and began researching.

"If you need us, we're at your disposal," Wilkes said, looking to Parks. "But personally, this shit is too fucking weird for me. And what's with all the bread?"

Parks shook his head as he put on a pair of blue latex gloves. On the table next to the body was an open loaf of bread with another two dozen pieces scattered about the table. There were also a few pieces on the ground near the table, as if someone had simply thrown them around the room. Upon closer inspection, he could tell the stale pieces had been sitting out for a few days.

"Not sure," Parks admitted. "But it looks intentional. It has to mean something."

"There's more in the kitchen," Moore pointed out.

Parks walked over to the kitchen and saw that indeed there were several more loaves of bread scattered about the counters and floor. The kitchen sink was filled with water and pieces of soggy bread, most of which had soaked in the water and dissipated into pieces that either floated to the top or had sunk to the bottom, giving the water a filmy, clouded appearance.

"What the—?" Wilkes bit his tongue, appearing to be taking the crime scene personally. As much as Parks wanted tell him to keep it under control, he couldn't disagree with his feelings.

"How about I have my team process the apartment and you have your team work the building," Parks suggested. "Neighbors. Door-men. Manager. Video surveillance. Anything."

Wilkes rounded up his team and left the apartment.

"All right, everybody, you know the drill," Parks began. "Don't touch anything on the body. Fairmont, get pictures. The bread around the body, and in the kitchen. There's something up with that. Not sure what. We'll have it all tested."

"What about the fish?" Fairmont asked.

"I said don't touch a damn thing," Parks repeated. "That includes that . . . whatever the hell it is. Don't touch it. We don't know what it is or what it means. You just photograph."

"It's a lionfish," Tippin answered, looking up from his electronic tablet. "Don't touch it. They're poisonous."

"Of course they are."

"They're one of the most venomous fish in the ocean," Tippin said, skimming whatever website he was reading. "But they're not deadly to us. Just stings. And painful as hell."

"What about after the fish is dead?"

"Not sure," Tippin said, continuing to scan. "Doesn't say. I'd avoid it though."

"So they're venomous but not lethal?" Moore asked. "Then what—?"

"Just wait until Tanaka and Isley get here," Parks ordered. "Probably another compound poison like Ian Harris with the methanol and snakebite. Everyone make sure to keep your gloves and masks on. Just work around the body. Whatever you do, don't touch it."

*　　　*　　　*

"Whoever the flip this guy is, no one can accuse him of being boring or unoriginal," Tanaka said as she set down her kit and knelt in front of Jason Bollinger's body, staring intently at the decaying man. He showed signs of having been one of those guys whose glory days had come and gone, having most likely peaked during his high school days, though that didn't necessarily mean he was lacking. He was still fit and, regardless of his current complexion, was someone who enjoyed life with a beer or two in his hands. Tanaka looked from the man's placid face to the fish he held rather protectively in his hands on his lap. "Scorpionfish?"

"Lionfish," Tippin corrected from behind her.

"This is what killed him?" she asked, looking to Jackie.

"I don't think so," Jackie answered, sliding on a pair of latex gloves. "They're venomous, but human deaths are rare from them. Mostly just result in nausea, stinging pain, and difficulty breathing. Few places carry any specific antidote, but then again some people are more susceptible to them than others. There is a possibility the victim here was one of those people and the fish did kill him. But I'll have to run a full tox screen to check if he was exposed to something else."

"I'll put a rush on it," Tanaka said as she moved the body, releasing both an intense odor and a clear liquid that leaked from the body to the floor. "There's a crusty substance along the lower lip and chin. Looks like saliva. I'll test it too. I don't see any physical signs of restraint or defense wounds of any sort. But, just so you know, this chair stinks."

"Soaked with sweat before he died," Jackie said.

"You think our vic stayed put while he was dying?" Parks asked.

"Paralyzed."

"What's that?"

"He was paralyzed," she repeated louder. "The killer injected the victim with a toxin that paralyzes but kept him alert. Our guy was alive during his death. He knew he was going to die."

"What can cause that?"

"Some animal bites. Rattlesnake. Cobras. Shellfish. The puffer fish. Several plants and fungi. Fool's parsley. Hemlock. Larkspur. Monkshood. Mountain laurel. Passionflower. And several nerve agents. Soman. Tabun. VX." Parks's eyes widened as his heartbeat picked up a beat. "But I don't think it's any of those. They would have dissipated by now anyway, and I'm not seeing any other concurring signs that it's one of those."

"You said he showed no signs of a struggle or defensive wounds. What about his hands?"

"Those punctures were made postmortem," Tanaka answered. "I think our killer placed the fish in his hands after he died. See? There's no blood. Just the punctures. His heart had stopped pumping already."

"So our killer stayed around to stage the scene," Parks surmised. "Just like the last two."

"He's done it three times now?" Jackie asked.

Parks nodded. "You've missed out. With Allison Tisdale he stayed to draw the circle around her with her blood. Ian Harris, he stayed to collect the snake and leave his marks. Speaking of which—"

"I don't see anything visible at first glance," Tanaka said, looking closer at the body for the killer's calling card. "But on the first two vics they were more hidden from sight than out in the open. I have a feeling I won't find it until I get the body back for autopsy. But you're right."

"What's that?" Parks asked.

"If we do find the mark then this makes three. This guy's a serial."

"You could be right about the ten thing. The symbol I mean. Guess ten is going to be our lucky number," Fairmont commented.

"These deaths are painful. No one should have to go like this." Tanaka said as she stood up, having finished her initial observation.

"Hey," Jackie said from Tanaka's side as she maneuvered around her to lean in and get a closer look at the body. "What's that? On the neck."

"What?" Tanaka asked as she too leaned in.

Jackie moved to the side to avoid getting in the ME's way, not noticing the thin layer of liquid that had accumulated under the corpse, placing one of her Cole Haan short wedge boots into the bodily fluids and immediately slipping. Tanaka noticed her friend going down and grabbed at her, managing to keep her up on one foot while her other swung around and brought her to her knees, causing her to land in Jason Bollinger's lap.

"You okay, honey?" Tanaka asked, helping Jackie to her feet.

"Ow. I'll . . . oww . . ." Jackie started to stand but froze when she saw the lionfish move with her, several of its spines sticking into her forearm.

"Oh, shit," Fairmont yelled from behind Parks as his eyes grew wide. "Oh, shit."

Jackie stared down at the fish that dangled from her arm, and tried to maneuver around the protruding spines to remove it.

"Hold on," Tanaka ordered as she worked her way around to Jackie's other side.

Tanaka removed a pair of metal tongs from her kit and reached up and, looking at Jackie who nodded back, grabbed hold of the fish and pulled it free from her arm. Jackie let out a painful groan as she instinctively pulled her arm in close to her body as if to protect it. Parks let out a breath himself, not realizing he had been holding it.

"We need to get her to a hospital," Tanaka said, looking to Parks.

"No. I'm sure I have something—"

"You're going to a hospital and that's final. I'll take her," Parks insisted. "You guys can finish up here and make out your reports just fine?"

"We got it, boss." Fairmont nodded. "Go. Go. Go."

"No problem," Moore added. "Go take care of her."

*　　　　　*　　　　　*

"I'm okay," Jackie said for the tenth or so time. "Really. Doctor's fixed me up. Gave me enough shots and antivenin to cure me from Death himself, and I have some really good painkillers to boot. I'll be fine."

"But you can't drive," Parks replied, tearing away at the wrapper of a Milky Way bar he had retrieved from one of the vending machines in the waiting room. He had felt a surge of adrenaline when Jackie was poisoned and could feel himself coming down from that high.

"No, I can't," Jackie said with concern in her eyes. "But I already called Ricky. He'll be here any minute to rescue me. It's okay."

"I could have taken you home."

"It's okay. Besides, you have a case to get back to."

Parks looked at his watch and finished off the candy bar.

"What's with the chocolate bar? You hungry?"

"It's the caffeine. Or the sugar. Or something. Just a—I just need a fix is all. Bet you're regretting I called you earlier, now aren't you?"

"What? About the case? Not at all. Been waiting for your call."

"You've been waiting for someone else to be poisoned?"

"No," Jackie blushed. "I said I was waiting for you to call. Which I realize you were probably never going to do. But I'll take another dead body as an excuse for you to do so."

"What?" Parks looked confused.

"Nothing. Men. Go on. You have a case to work on. Go," she said as she pulled Parks in and gave him a hug. She felt warm, and he wondered if it was from the drugs she was on or just the way she was. He felt the softness of her skin as she held him, and he started to close his eyes as he took in her natural body odor, which was surprisingly potent for someone just scrubbed down with cleaning alcohol. She started to back away from him, and for a second he could feel her lips about to grace his cheek when she let him go. "Go. I'll be fine. But thanks for worrying."

"I better not see you at the office again today," he joked.

"Don't worry." She smiled. "I have a good excuse for my baby to stay at home and pamper me, so I'm going to milk every second of it I can. But I'll be in early and ready to go tomorrow. No arguments there. You need my help."

"Sounds good to me," he said as he started to step back. "You're sure you—"

"Go," she ordered again. "I'm an adult. I'll do just fine. Thanks for your concern. Go take care of business. We still have a killer to catch, remember?"

"Okay," Parks said as he finally turned and headed for the elevator.

He pressed the button and noticed Jackie staring at him as he waited. The rest of the hospital seemed to disappear as he stared back into her deep, Irish-green eyes, and he felt his heart tug at him for leaving her exposed. He knew she was fine, there was nothing to worry about, but still, he wanted to stay, to make sure she was okay and protected. He wasn't sure why he felt this strong about her, as he hadn't felt this way about a woman in quite some time, let alone this quickly after having just met. He knew his track record with women, most of them never sticking around longer than a week or two. He liked the companionship but wondered if his need to be with another person had more to do with his addiction than an actual desire for a relationship. The elevator chimed, breaking the spell, and the doors opened and Parks stepped aside to make room for a young man who was frantic to get off. The kid's square jaw was clenched and his brown eyes were large and filled with a combination of worry and fear as he pushed past Parks without a word.

Parks pressed the button for the garage. Just as the doors closed he saw the young man rush to Jackie's side, and he realized that he must have been her son. He felt a slight lift on his conscience as he accepted that she would be properly watched over now. The elevator descended, and when the doors opened on the ground level, he stepped out and headed for the garage, mentally preparing himself to get back to work.

13

"All right, everyone, let's see what we have," Parks said as he entered the conference room to find his team sitting around the table and chatting with one another. There were cups of coffee, most of them empty, sitting in front of everyone, letting him know not that they were tired but rather how long they had waited for him. "Sorry for my tardiness."

He had decided to go to the gym after leaving the hospital, getting in a quick workout to help burn off the stress the case had been building in him. By the time he was finished, covered in sweat and his muscles aching, he felt physically exhausted even though his mind still raced. He showered and changed at the gym, then made his way back to the station.

He then spent the next hour alone in his office going over the case so far. He liked looking over the paperwork on his own, in silence, just his own scrambled mind to talk over the facts of the case.

He looked over to Amy Tanaka and recalled the conversation they'd had in the hallway minutes before the meeting and figured it might be best if she said what she was there to explain so she could get back to her lab. "Amy. Why don't you start by telling us what

138 | TYLER COMPTON

you found?"

"All right," Tanaka said, standing up and looking at the open file in front of her. "It's official. Jason Bollinger was poisoned. But he was poisoned by a different poison than either of the other two."

"The lionfish?" Fairmont asked, reading his own notes.

"No," Tanaka said, shaking her head. "The lionfish did release a poison into the victim's body, but it was post mortem. What actually killed him was a lethal dose of a poison called Tetradontoxin. Tetradontoxin affects the nervous system and in particular the nerve impulses. Symptoms can include involuntary muscle spasms, weakness, dizziness, and loss of speech. Again, I'm not a hundred percent sure about this stuff, but I called Jackie and this is the CliffsNotes version of what she told me. She said she'd work up a full profile and make sure we have it by tomorrow. There was also excessive saliva and sweating, which would account for the smell and condition of the body and the seat around it. The secondary set of symptoms includes increased paralysis. Followed by cardiac arrhythmia. There have been reports of people being completely aware of what's happening to them during the entire event of being poisoned."

"What's the reaction time once someone is affected with this?" Moore asked from her end of the table while scribbling notes into her pad.

"Ten minutes."

"And where is this Tetra-whatever . . . where can it be obtained?"

"Not sure about that. Jackie's working on it. But most cases have it coming from what is commonly known as a puffer fish."

"Isn't that that fish they eat over in Japan?" Parks asked.

Tanaka nodded. "The poison is found in the fish's ovaries and liver. But the fish is usually harmless if the poison sacs are removed before cooking. It's considered to be ten thousand times more lethal than cyanide."

"Shit," Fairmont said

"That's not all," Parks added. "Now, these may be pointless but I thought they were worth noting. The toxin is often used in zombie-making rituals in Haiti and West Africa. Because the toxin affects the nervous system—what it does is it inhibits the ability of the nerves to send messages to other parts of the body—well, because of this, it puts people in a zombie-like state."

"I highly doubt our killer is looking to bring his victims back from the dead," Fairmont threw out. "But that would be awesome."

"Now this one is a little more relevant. Possibly. There's a company in Canada that is attempting to develop the poison into a drug."

"What for?" Moore asked.

"There're two reasons. One is to help cancer patients suppress pain."

"And the other?"

"Help heroin addicts wean off their habit by relieving the symptoms of withdrawal."

"What?"

"It's called TTX, or Tectin, and apparently it's two thousand times more potent than morphine but without the side effects, and it's not addictive, which makes it better for longer-term use. It's still in the clinical development phase with protocols being filed with the Food and Drug Administration. But back to the pain-suppressing use, currently opioids are the number one standard for severe pain treatment, representing a more than seven-billion-dollar intake each year. Worldwide. TTX, or Tectin, could seriously challenge and change that figure."

"Damn," Fairmont said.

"You've got to be kidding, right?" Moore asked. "I mean we don't really think this killer is killing people in some twisted attempt to stop a new drug that might possibly challenge a seven-billion-dollar industry. A drug that might or might not even get FDA approval. Or am I the only one who thinks this is way too out of left field? I mean, why not go after the manufacturing company directly? Or else why not kill each victim with this Tetra-whatever?"

"I agree," Fairmont seconded.

"Me too," Parks added. "But we should still look into it. How did this stuff get into him?"

"I found a small needle mark near the C3 and C4 cervical vertebrae," Tanaka said, holding up an x-ray and showing on the picture where the needle mark was. She then held up another picture that was a blown-up view of the needle mark. "I'm not sure how much was injected, but I'm assuming it was at least half to a full vial. We're talking anywhere between ten to twenty-five milliliters."

"And the fish in his hands?" Fairmont asked.

"So far as I can tell it has nothing to do with the murder." Tanaka said. "It was an afterthought. A decoration. A—"

"I'm not so sure," Parks interjected.

"What are you thinking?" Moore asked.

"I don't think it's his calling card," Parks said. "He has one of those already, correct?"

Parks looked to Moore, who nodded.

"We found these." Moore held up three more photos, close-ups of the symbol. "It was painted on the underside of the seat that Bollinger was found siting in. We're having the substance tested, but due to the color and appearance of the substance . . . we believe it's

Allison Tisdale's blood."

"It's a connection," Fairmont said.

"We'll make a note of it," Parks said. "He has his marking, so then this fish left in Jason Bollinger's hands isn't it. Then what is it? What are the possibilities? What if all of these victims are connected? Somehow. Someway. We can connect victim two to victim three. Ian Harris spied on the Bollingers. That's their connection. But what connects Allison Tisdale with Ian Harris? Or with Bollinger?"

"Assuming they are connected," Moore commented.

"I think they are," Parks said. "It might be a long shot, but I think each of our victims is connected to another in some way or another. Like sections of a train. One after the other."

"So what does that have to do with the fish?" Fairmont asked.

"What if the fish is Jason Bollinger's connection to potential victim number four?"

"How's that?"

"I don't know," Parks admitted. "It's just a theory. But what if? So far we haven't been able to find a believable reason why that fish is there. It doesn't serve any purpose that we can find. So what if?" He looked around the table at his team. Their shoulders sagged and their faces were long with glazed-over eyes staring out into nothingness. "Anyway, it's just a theory. Tippin, I want you to look up all you can on the fish and see where they're available around here."

"Will do," Tippin said.

"We met with Bollinger's wife earlier today," Moore added. "She's shaken up and wasn't in any condition to be questioned. She's staying at a friend's house. She agreed we could question her tomorrow and take her by their place to see if there is anything out of the ordinary about it or anything that the killer may have moved or changed. I think you should come with me. You're . . . good with people. She's going to need a delicate touch to her interviewing process."

"Sure thing," Parks said. "And there was nothing else at the Bollinger residence?"

"No signs of breaking and entering," Moore said, going over her notes. "No fingerprints. No strange fibers or biologicals. What about the husband?"

"Bollinger?"

"No. The first one. Tisdale. Our original prime suspect. The chemistry professor?"

"Douglas Tisdale's a bust as of right now. I had a car on him since earlier this week. According to them he hasn't left his house except to plan for his wife's funeral. He was there for a few hours, and they didn't have eyes on him the whole time. But unless he snuck out the back to do this . . . for now we'll keep an eye on him, but I think it's doubtful. Other than that, he's been home all week. So I don't see how he could have planned these let alone carry them out." Parks took a moment to soak everything in. "Did we go over what Wilkes and his men originally pulled from the Ian Harris crime scene?"

"Yes," Moore said, standing up and walking to the murder board, with pictures of the crime scene taped up. "Along with the emptied digital camera, we have a pair of binoculars, a tube of women's lipstick, a bottle of vodka and an empty glass that was on the table next to the body. Each item has been dusted for prints and checked for saliva and DNA. Everything belonged to Ian Harris with the exception of the women's lipstick, which is a MAC brand color Hot Gossip, available at Macy's and various other women's boutiques for a simple $14.50 plus tax. Nothing special as far as anyone can tell.

Hundreds of tubes of the product have been manufactured and can be purchased most everywhere."

"Great. Then what about the message left with the lipstick?"

"Three-one-three," Moore continued. "So far nothing significant regarding either the murder or the victim has been discovered behind the numbers. Before we took over, Detective Hayward, from Wilkes's team, had discovered that three-one-three was the area code for Detroit, Michigan.

"Okay. Anything else?"

"The birth date of Donald Duck. March 13."

"Okay."

"And the frame of the Zapruder film where President Kennedy's head explodes."

"I see," Parks said, not sure what to make of the facts.

"Then there's the empty package that had been delivered to Ian Harris. The package had fingerprints besides Ian's on it, but IAFIS hasn't come up with a positive identification. Detective Ramirez discovered that the prints on the package also matched a print found on the tube of lipstick. There were no identifiable marks on the package showing who had shipped it to Ian Harris, how it was paid for, or how it had even gotten to him."

"Okay. For the rest of the night I want us to keep going over all of the evidence that we already have in our hands. Go over the crime scenes. The bodies. Everything. What we need to do, people, is figure out what our killer is trying to say. Why is he doing this? What's the purpose? Why these people? This isn't all just a coincidence. There's reasoning behind all of this. It may not make sense to us but it does to our killer, and we need to find out why. We need to dissect these people's lives. There's something connecting them. At least in the killer's eyes. Something that should lead us to the next victim before our killer gets to him or her."

Everyone began to stand and stretch as Parks's cell phone rang. He read the number on the screen, not recognizing it.

"Detective Parks," he answered as he flipped open the phone.

"Dave?" a female voice said.

Parks paused for a second, trying to identify the voice.

"Dave?"

"Who is this?"

"It's Jackie."

"Oh, hey, Jackie," Parks said with a smile. "What's up? Is something wrong?"

"No, no. Everything's fine with me. I was calling because . . . you're not around a TV, are you?"

"No," he said, a question in his voice.

"You have one nearby?"

"There's one in the break room. What's up?"

"Turn it on. Channel ten."

14

"Son of a bitch," Parks cursed under his breath as he stood in front of the small television set that sat off to the side in the break room. Unfortunately, Parks's language wasn't enough to get Hardwick to turn from the television. Her eyes, like everyone else's in the room, were glued to what Channel 10 crime reporter Charles Wyler was commenting on.

"While police refuse to officially comment on the murders, sources close to the investigation have confirmed that the two murders in neighboring apartment complexes are related. Our inside source has also confirmed that at this time the police have no solid leads."

"Son of a bitch," Parks hissed again as he turned from the TV and stormed out of the room.

"Parks," Hardwick called out as she followed him into the conference room. "Parks."

"It was Wilkes," Parks said accusingly.

"You don't know that. But if it was, and I find out, I'll nail his ass to the wall and make sure it stays there."

"No leads. Of course there are no leads. We just got the case a few hours ago. Who do they think we are? Magicians? I know it was him. Anything to make a buck on the side and screw me in the process."

"Forget about Wilkes. You have a case to work. It doesn't matter what the reporters say or who told them about it. The fact remains that we have a killer on the loose and it's your job to find him. That going to be a problem now?"

Parks remained quiet.

"Good," Hardwick said, taking his silence to be an affirmative answer. "Now grab your coat and let's get out of here."

"Ma'am?"

"You need a drink. And so do I. Your team is good enough to handle the next hour or two without you. And we should talk. Let's go."

"Ma'am?" Parks hesitated, not sure if he should move or not.

"That's an order, Parks. Move your ass."

*   *   *

Hardwick drove a little over a mile away to Grand Street and parked in an underground garage before leading Parks up to Casey's Irish Pub. The famous downtown pub was located below street level and they walked down two flights of stairs to a brick and wrought-iron patio area where two couples played pool off in a corner. A doorman flirted with a hostess who sat on a stool next to the front door. He turned, ready to ask the two for ID, when he recognized Hardwick. He gave her a hug and a smile as he kissed her on each cheek and motioned them inside, while also keeping an eye on Parks. On the left was a massive mahogany bar while wooden booths lined the opposite wall. Above the booths was a giant chalkboard with various specialties and Irish quotes and historical facts scribbled with sporadic organization.

The bar was empty except for two girls and a guy sitting at the far end, staring up at one of the several flat-screen televisions mounted above the bar showing various sporting events. Hardwick stopped at the bar and knocked twice to get the attention of a female bartender cleaning glasses at the other end. The young woman smiled and walked over as she dried off her hands.

"What can I getcha?" the bartender said with an Irish brogue that was so muddled Parks couldn't determine if it was real and faded after years in America or an act put on by all the establishment's employees. She was cute, in an almost tomboyish sort of way, with short-cropped blonde hair and a powdered-white, pointed nose.

"Two Jameson pickle backs," Hardwick answered.

Parks looked to Hardwick with doubt on his face. Casey's brewed their own pickle juice, which they offered as a chaser for a shot of Jameson. Parks could not recall the last time he had ever had a shot of Jameson, and he wasn't sure he wanted to start with Hardwick.

"Just drink it," Hardwick ordered as the bartender arrived with their shots. "It'll put hair on your chest."

She laughed at the comment and winked at the bartender. She downed her shot then followed it with the shot of pickle juice.

Parks sighed to himself as he downed the shot and followed it with the pickle juice, expecting to begin coughing and look like a fool. Instead, both the liquor and the chaser went down smoothly, and he found himself enjoying it and wanting another. Hardwick smiled at Parks and looked at the bartender, held up two fingers, and circled them around to signal for another round of shots, which were quickly set up.

"Keep 'em comin'." Hardwick picked up her shot then downed

half of it, followed by half her pickle juice.

"Do you know what two of the most commonly asked questions of cops are?" Hardwick asked, staring up at Parks.

Parks sat silently, not sure where the conversation was going.

"Why did you become a cop?" Hardwick said, answering her own question. "And why are you a cop?"

"Really? I would have thought it would be, have you ever killed anyone?" Parks said somewhat mockingly as he took another sip of his drink.

"Been a while since I killed someone. You trying to fix that for me tonight?" Hardwick glared and Parks remained quiet. "Anyway. So I throw that question onto you now. Why?"

"Which question?"

Hardwick stared back. "I've read your files and I've worked with you for almost a decade now. I know the answer to them both. I'm just wondering if you're aware of it. Why did you become a cop?"

"I dunno. Because I was looking . . . for . . ."

"Bullshit," Hardwick said, finishing her drink. "Bullshit. Bullshit. Bullshit. I was lost and looking for a way. Blah, blah, blah. I say most cops were born to be cops. The good ones at least. Put on the path one way or another before they knew it. You say you became a cop because you were lost after your divorce? I say you got a divorce to become lost to give you a reason to become a cop without knowing it."

"Yes, Zen godmother. Is this one of those chicken-egg riddles?"

"I swear, Parks, if you make me take my gun out in here and use it," Hardwick said, shaking her head and motioning for more shots. "Seriously. You think you simply became a cop because you were bored and needed purpose? Bullshit. Sure that happens. A lot of cops are like that. But the good ones. The really good ones—like you, Parks—I feel are born to be cops. And I don't mean it's in your blood, passed down from generation to generation. Your father wasn't a cop and his father before wasn't one either. But you don't think your father's suicide helped put you on a path to become a cop? Not to mention your mother's abandonment not much longer after that?"

"Despite my parents, I didn't have a traumatic upbringing."

"Didn't say you did. I don't think all good cops need to be flawed like that. The classic, haunted past or whatever. But you can't tell me that what happened to you as a child has had no effect on the rest of your life. You've been withdrawn most of your life. A loner. But that makes you stronger. You've learned not to depend on anyone else and you work great on your own. Your failed marriage? You can't tell me the thought of your father and mother's abandonment had nothing to do with the destruction of your marriage. You and Jennifer were going strong until you got married. She was your first. First love and first heartbreak. Don't tell me that Doc Black hasn't had a field day with you on the subconscious parallels between what happened with your parents and your own failed marriage. Even I can tell you about those."

"There was more to it than feeling pressure from ghosts," Parks said steadily.

"I know," Hardwick said, realizing she was close to stepping over a line, which wasn't her goal in this conversation. "What about why you are a cop? Why are you a cop?"

"To make the world a safer place, I guess," he answered. "Just like most other cops, I would imagine."

"See, but unlike every other cop, who are you making this world a safer place for? You don't have a family. No wife. No children. No siblings. A mother you don't talk to and a father who's dead. An aunt and uncle who raised you, yet you rarely ever see. So I ask you again, who are you making the world a safer place for?"

Parks glanced away from the table as if to say for everyone else out in the world that needed it to be a safer place to live.

"I'm not the only single officer on the force."

"Yeah, yeah," Hardwick said, brushing off Parks's comment. "Only problem is, that's such a global answer for such a small effect. Most cops want to make the world a safer place. But as an individual there's not much difference one can make other than for their own little spot in the world."

"What are you getting at?"

"We have some of the smartest men and women I've ever met working with us day and night. Yet you're one of the few people I know I can have an intelligent, human conversation with. You're well educated. Always reading, enlightening yourself to learn and know more. You push yourself. You're attentive. Observant. Gentle when needed but tough as well." Hardwick chuckled at this observation and took another swallow of her drink. "Unfortunately, I think your biggest assets are also your biggest flaws."

"And what are those?"

"For starters? Your need to be needed. Most likely due to being so alone."

"Come again?"

"For some reason you can't help yourself. It's what helps drive you. Your need to be needed. To help people. To be in control. To do everything for everyone at once. To be piled upon until it's almost too much. You know how to delegate, yet you still manage to let it all stack up around you. You take care of your own. Even sometimes when they don't want you to. You feel it's up to you to fix everyone's problems. You want everyone on your squad to get along like a family and succeed. To be the best they can be. And that's not bad. But you take it so personally. As if their failures were your own."

"What are you getting at?" Parks repeated as he downed his shot and chaser.

"How are you doing?"

Parks looked at Hardwick, one eyebrow raised. "What do you mean?"

"Kozlov. Levinson. You and I haven't exactly talked about it. I mean outside the official reports and meetings with the department heads. I know you're seeing Doc Black several times a week and he's yet to report to me that I need to take you off duty, so I'm assuming all is good there. But you and I haven't spoken about it. I can tell you're not sleeping well. At least not since the start of this case. I know you've got PTSD, and don't tell me you don't. I've been there."

"I keep seeing children, standing in the dark. They open their mouths and blood comes pouring out. I also see Kozlov and his razor blades every time I close my eyes. I know the bastard's locked up. I know it's silly. But I keep seeing him everywhere. Little flashes in crowds out in public. I don't know why either. That's what really bugs me about it. I've been attacked by perps before."

"He almost killed you, that's why. Sure the ambulance got there to save you in time but you were pretty cut up. Lost a lot of blood. I can't recall a time you were ever that badly hurt."

"I was fine," Parks said, brushing off her comment.

"You weren't. Maybe that's your problem. You haven't admitted how bad it really was. It was bad, Dave. You had slices made into your body. You needed stitching through your skin just to hold you together after the attack. It was pretty fucking bad. Then there was your partner."

Hardwick finished the rest of her shot and signaled to the bartender for another round, hoping that Parks would take over the conversation.

"He was my partner for five years. It would be weird to not feel anything. There was the funeral. His wife. Dammit, they have one kid already and another on the way. And to hear what everyone's saying about him now? I don't blame her for wanting to move back with her folks. I mean, I play a million scenarios in my head. Why he was there? What if he wasn't? What if it had been me? Why . . . I don't know. I want to be angry at someone. Anyone. But what difference would it make? It won't bring him back. So what can I do about it? I should have been there. He was my partner. I should have known and I should have done something about it."

"But did you know? You proclaim you didn't and I honestly believe you. Part of the reason I spoke so passionately on your behalf. The higher-ups believe me. You've met most of them. They know you. You're not responsible for Aaron Levinson. That's something you need to comprehend. And accept. You're not him. You are your own man. And a good one at that. We're lucky to have you. As it is, you barely got out of it alive. It's not like you weren't unmarked by all of that."

Parks focused on his scarred hands, the multiple cuts that were still healing a month later. He remembered those scars, because he saw them every day. It was the cuts on his face he often forgot about. They weren't anything life changing, just little nicks here and there.

"It could get worse for you, you know," Hardwick said.

"It can always get worse. That's life. Only cure for that is to stop living. And I don't see that as an option."

Hardwick stared out into the relatively empty bar and shook the blankness off. Four college-aged kids had entered and sat at the other end of the bar, laughing and being loud as they began to drink away the night. Two men in business suits sat at a booth near the front of the bar, each one staring up at an opposing sporting event.

"I don't blame you, you know? For what happened. You're his partner? Hell, I'm his boss. I should have known. I'm going over all of his past cases myself. Forget the inquisition board. I want to know. *How* did this happen? I'm not saying it doesn't. There are corrupt cops just like there are corrupt people in any other profession. But when did it start? Was this the first time? Or had he been doing this for half his career? Why? These are things I want to know. But I don't blame you. Not now. Not ever. Not for him. I want you to know that. Forget everyone else. The department will survive. The rest of the squad will survive. They'll come around. You're too good a cop for any of them to doubt you for too long."

"I appreciate that," Parks said, downing another shot. "But I think what's pissing me off, even more than Levinson's betrayal, is the fact that Kozlov might go free. And that, because I wasn't aware of my partner's actions, *will* be on me."

Hardwick didn't respond to his comment. "How's Tippin doing?"

Parks tilted his head at the change of conversation and took a swallow of another shot as he digested the question.

"You know, it used to be you needed experience to be a good detective. Years working cases, being on the street, familiarizing yourself with the human condition. But nowadays it's all so different. Now, people like me—with all the experience in the world—are becoming extinct, and people like Tippin, with no experience on the street whatsoever, are becoming the direction of the force. We didn't use to have computers, and trace evidence, and all this technology. We just had good old-fashioned police work. Digging into a victim's life and putting it all together like pieces of a puzzle. Now we scan for fingerprints and fibers and DNA. You just need to press a button and, voila, out pops a killer. The bad guys out there have gotten more sophisticated and so must we. It's just the way the world works now. Times change."

"Being able to work a computer will never make up for years of experience."

"No. But it sure helps level the playing field." Parks finished off his drink. "Don't get me wrong. Tippin is a good kid. A hard worker. And I don't mean anything against him personally. He's doing well. You were right." Hardwick raised an eyebrow in triumph. "His instincts aren't all there yet, but he's new to it all. Over time he'll become a great asset to the team. He's smart as hell and ready to learn and prove himself. It's all just . . . interesting to me."

Hardwick downed one more shot.

"Son of a bitch." Parks bit his tongue and finished off his drink.

Hardwick noticed him peering up at the television over the bar. The seven o'clock news was on, with captioning below the faces to let them know the current events. Charles Wyler was going on about the inefficiency of the department and how there was no forward movement on the case concerning the two slain victims that had been discovered.

"Ignore him," Hardwick ordered. "Nothing you can do about what they say. I'll have Public Relations contact the station and deal with them. Nothing for you to worry about. Your only job is the case. You understand me?"

"It's just that sometimes—"

"I know. I know. Free speech and all that rubbish. It still doesn't change anything. Forget about Charles Wyler. He has nothing to do with this case. What you need to do is focus on who your possible victim number four could be . . . and then get to him before our killer does."

15

"Anything at all. Anything out of place. Something that wasn't here before. Something that's been moved. Anything at all." Parks stood off in one of the corners of the Bollinger's living room while Rachel guided Mrs. Bollinger throughout her apartment, hoping she might see something that would lead them in the direction of the killer's identity. Parks was losing patience with the "grieving" widow and was about to wring her neck and throw her out a window himself.

"We don't have much," Mrs. Bollinger snapped. "As you can see."

The longer Rachel guided Mrs. Bollinger around the apartment, the more he noticed how sparse and empty it really was. As the two women walked around he heard the hollow-sounding echo their shoes made, as if they were inside of a museum. There were no pieces of art on the walls, only a few sporadic pictures of the couple. A simple couch resided in front of a twenty-two-inch TV that Parks thought was older than he was. There were no DVDs or walls of CDs, let alone a stereo to play music on. The kitchen was equally vacant, with only a kitchen table and a single chair left, as the other one that Jason Bollinger had been found dead in had been removed and tagged as evidence. The small kitchen had a microwave, refrigerator, and oven/stove. He couldn't remember the last time he had seen such a dreary-looking apartment.

"Why is that?" Rachel Moore asked breaking the silence.

"What?"

"Why don't you have much? I mean, it almost looks like you two didn't actually live here. I thought you were a fitness instructor and your husband was . . . ?"

"Unemployed," Mrs. Bollinger admitted, her posture becoming more erect. "We've only been here a year. Jason used to be an investment consultant." She paused. "He always said he got paid to play with other people's money."

"And—?"

"Twelve months ago we got served," Mrs. Bollinger continued, biting her lip. "Jason was being investigated by the IRS and FBI for money laundering or extortion or something. Some Ponzi-type scheme. He never actually showed me the papers. I only know what little I was able to get from phone calls through walls or papers that were delivered when he wasn't here. He was accused of stealing money from several companies and hiding it in offshore accounts. He denied it of course. And I believed him. I stood by his side. Even as everything we owned was taken away and we were reduced to this. I stood by his side."

Mrs. Bollinger finished looking around the kitchen and fell into the single chair at the kitchen table. Parks wondered if maybe Mrs. Bollinger wasn't hiding something from them. Or perhaps her husband had been hiding more from her. The apartment, sparse in its decorations, was by no means a cheap place to live. Something wasn't adding up. It was like the Bollingers had put on the face of being poor without being so.

"Why did you go home to visit your family this past week?" Parks interjected.

"I . . . I just missed them. That's all. It was a holiday this weekend. Had a longer weekend from work. So I chose to go visit them."

Parks didn't buy it. He had seen his share of liars over the years, and Mrs. Bollinger showed plenty of signs. She wouldn't make eye contact with either one of them. She couldn't stop fidgeting either, and it was starting to get to him.

"But the three-day weekend was Saturday through Monday. Most people get back to work on Tuesday."

"Yeah? And? So what?"

"So you didn't leave to see your family Friday after work or even Saturday morning. You didn't leave to see them until Monday morning, the last day of your vacation. And you were still gone Tuesday and Wednesday. So again, why did you go home to see your family?"

Mrs. Bollinger wiped away several tears, her mascara running, not that it mattered to anyone in the room. The woman wasn't a screaming Hollywood beauty, but she would have made most men turn their heads. Despite her only reaching five foot four in height, her body was fit, as was in accordance with her job.

Parks wondered if she had been aware of the fact that her neighbor, Ian Harris, had been spying on her. Taking photos of her. Desiring her. That's when it hit him.

"You were leaving him," Parks said. "Weren't you?"

Mrs. Bollinger nodded her head and cried some more.

"Why?"

"I . . ." Mrs. Bollinger sighed and inhaled deeply. "He *lied* to me. All these months. He lied to me. His wife. He did do it. What they accused him of. Stealing. He did it. Worse than that, he lied to me about it. I mean, I was his wife. I would have stood by him. Supported him. But everything . . . it was too much. All he did was shut me out of everything. Out of his job. His legal troubles. His life. It was supposed to be our life. Ours. But he chose himself instead of us. So yes. I was leaving him. I went home to talk about it with my parents. To get their help and support. I didn't know what to do. Then you called." Mrs. Bollinger reached for her purse on the table and dug through it for something. "There's nothing here that isn't the way it was before." Mrs. Bollinger retrieved the compact mirror and began fixing her makeup. "Nothing new. At least that I'm aware of. Nothing moved. Nothing changed. Nothing missing. It's all here. And it can all burn as far as I'm concerned."

"Okay," Parks said, motioning to Moore. "We thank you for your time."

"Thanks," Mrs. Bollinger huffed, staring out the window.

"Oh, one other thing," Parks said, turning back around. He motioned for Moore to hand him something from the briefcase in her hands. She retrieved a photo of the lionfish and handed it to the grieving widow. "Does this have any meaning to you?"

Mrs. Bollinger took in the photo, staring through it as if it wasn't in front of her at all. Finally, she shook her head.

"We've never had any fish. It means nothing to me," she said, sighing.

"Thanks for all of your help."

Parks wasn't sure what else to say and backed out of the apartment, leaving the woman alone to grieve in her own way.

*   *   *

"All right, ladies and gentlemen," Parks said, getting his team's attention. It was noon and he knew they would want a break soon, and he hoped after their midmorning recap that he would be able to let them go for an hour. "There's a connection here. We're just not seeing it. This lionfish—whatever it means—it means something. What have we found on it?"

Tippin was looking down at his laptop opposite of Moore and Fairmont, both of whom were frustrated and out of answers. Long days and late nights with no results had left everyone burnt out.

"Sorry I'm late," Jackie said, rushing into the room like a breath of fresh air, waking everyone up. "Morning from hell. But I have paperwork."

And that she did. Jackie set the pile that she had been carrying with two hands onto the conference table, and for a second Parks thought the table might collapse underneath the weight.

"What's all that?"

"Information dealing with poisons," Jackie said, pulling a strand of hair out of her face and tucking it behind her ear. "Particularly dealing with Los Angeles. Not sure what will be helpful, so I grabbed it all."

"And?"

"And what? I just got here," Jackie shot back, smirking. "But never fear. I know there's something in here. Somehow. Somewhere. Who supplies whom with what and how much and why. Everything. And wherever it is, I'll find it."

Jackie plopped into her chair with a smile plastered on her face. She brought with her an air of optimism that most in the room were not used to. Then again, this wasn't her job, and once this case was over she would be able to escape the reality they lived through day after day. It was almost as if the near-death experience the day before had changed her somehow. Given her a different perspective.

"Uh, boss," Tippin said quietly, raising his hand like a student waiting to be picked on.

"What is it, Milo?" Parks asked.

"I think you need to see this, sir," Tippin said swiveling his laptop around so everyone else could see it.

"What are you watching?" Parks asked, somewhat upset by being sidetracked.

"It's live," Tippin said as Parks stared at the screen in front of him. "It's a special report. Charles Wyler."

"What's that guy talking about now?" Fairmont asked.

"It's not important," Parks snapped. "I want us to focus on our case. Not what this jerk thinks he has that we don't."

"Did you know they're calling him the Palisades Poisoner?" Fairmont laughed at this bit of information.

"The Palisades Poisoner?" Parks said with a roll of his eyes. "What the hell is that? He hasn't killed anyone in the Palisades."

"Yeah, yeah," Fairmont agreed. "But you know they need the moniker to sound catchy, and a repeated letter helps. Remember when you took down the Silver Lake Strangler two years ago? Or like, let's see . . . the Pasadena Pedophile? Or was it pervert? Or puncher?"

"Jake," Moore snapped.

"Anyway, there's also the Compton Killers or Bel Air Burglars. Get it? Or us, Hollywood Homicide."

"That's the stupidest thing I've ever heard," Parks said, shaking his head.

"Hey, it's not us," Fairmont said defensively. "It's the damn news people. They need something catchy to get people's attention. Palisades Poisoner sounds catchy. It sells."

"It's misinformation and will get the wrong people thinking the wrong things," Parks replied, now even more upset by how Charles Wyler's inaccurate reports were affecting their investigation. "It doesn't matter. Forget him and focus back on what we're doing here. Milo, put that away."

"But, sir," Tippin said. "Look where he's at."

"Where?" Parks asked. "Looks like downtown. Union Station."

"Yeah. At the end of the metro line. But don't you see it?"

"What?" Parks asked as he leaned in closer to the laptop screen along with the rest of his team. "What am I looking at? So he's doing a report from downtown. So what?"

"Behind him," Tippin huffed, getting fed up with no one seeing what he had caught so quickly.

"So he's in front of a fish tank. It's always been there. It's at the entran—" Parks stopped talking as he saw what it was that Tippin had been trying to point out since he first turned his laptop around. Swimming in the giant aquarium at the Union Station were several lionfish. "Are we sure there's a connection?"

"What do you think?"

"I think we need to get down there. Can you keep watching?"

"I got a live stream."

"—who has been terrorizing the streets of Los Angeles since Labor Day weekend," Charles Wyler said over the screen. "The Palisades Poisoner has already claimed the lives of two innocents. That we know of. This leaves the top questions on the public's mind: Will he strike again? And where? And who?"

"Son of a bitch," Parks cursed. "Let's go. Everyone grab your stuff. Come on."

"Something's wrong," Tippin said stopping everyone from moving. Parks maneuvered himself over to Tippin's side and stared down at the screen. Airing live, the cameraman was focused on Wyler, who appeared to be stalling when someone off screen yelled his name. Both Wyler and the cameraman turned at the sound.

A homeless person threw a Styrofoam cup filled with a reddish liquid into Wyler's face. Wyler held up his hands to block the liquid but missed most of it as it flew into his face, getting into his eyes, mouth, and every other crevice it could seep into.

"Oh my God," Moore exclaimed, throwing a hand to her mouth.

"Let's move people," Parks ordered. "Now!"

Wyler immediately began screaming.

The cameraman was still filming everything, broadcasting live across every television in the Los Angeles area.

"Cut that shit," a professional-looking woman ordered the cameraman, almost pushing him over as she rushed to Wyler's side to see if there was anything she could do for him.

"Help me," Wyler cried, the tears pouring from his bugged-out eyes mixing with the red substance all over his face, making him look as if he was reenacting the prom scene from Carrie. "Help me!"

16

Dave Parks and his team arrived at Union Station less than ten minutes after they saw the attack on Charles Wyler play out live on television. Sirens wailed as blue and red lights flashed off buildings and vehicles to help build a passable lane, but the traffic was already congested that late Saturday morning as people tried to leave town to enjoy the rest of the weekend. As the team walked toward the entrance to Union Station, Parks could hear the sounds of ambulances echoing off the downtown structures in the distance. It was only fifteen past noon, but it was already gearing up to be another hot day. He wondered what the records for the month of September in Los Angeles were and whether they might break any that year with the oncoming heat. As it was, if it kept up, he was going to have to buy a whole new wardrobe just to counterbalance his already sweat-stained clothes, which were still waiting for a wash back home.

Moore and Fairmont flanked behind him on his right while Tippin and Jackie carried up the left side like a flock of birds traveling in the well-known V, though the only kind of birds he could see them being compared to at the moment were carrion-sniffing buzzards, circling around until they dove in for the kill.

"Are you the medical team?" a short, slightly overweight Spanish woman spat as she spun out from behind the back of the news van. She wore a pin-striped brown suit with a black undershirt. She was frantic and disoriented; as if she had woken up in some foreign place other than her own bed. She had the look of one who had at one time been considered a great beauty, but unfortunately a stressful life of ruthless business meetings and liquid lunches had caught up to her, aging her somewhat beyond her years. Makeup plastered her face in hopes of bringing out her faded beauty, though it failed to hide the bags under her eyes.

"Dammit," Parks cursed. "No. LAPD. They're not here yet? Where's Wyler?"

"Come," the woman said as she led them to the back of the van, where Wyler sat in a chair, clutching his arms and panting heavily.

"Rachel? I want you and Jake to see if you can locate the man who attacked Wyler and keep everyone who witnessed what happened secured and controlled," Parks ordered.

"Got it, boss," Fairmont said as he and Moore broke formation.

Parks and Jackie rounded to the back of the news van and stopped immediately in their steps.

"My God," Parks exclaimed, keeping his distance from the man, who was clearly in pain.

Charles Wyler rocked in his chair, breathing heavily and making deep, husky sounds from his throat. His clothes were drenched with sweat, his face flushed with heat. His arms and face were covered in a red rash that the man couldn't stop scratching, his fingernails leaving marks.

"I've been poisoned!" Wyler screamed in agony at the group of men and women standing before him.

"Okay," Jackie said, setting her medical bag down and removing a pair of latex gloves and a mask. "Everyone, gloves and masks. I don't know what we have here yet." She moved to Wyler and stared at the man, assessing his condition. "What was thrown at him? Does anyone know?"

The Spanish woman shook her head and stammered a barely audible no.

"Poison. Dammit," Wyler quipped.

"That doesn't help me," Jackie replied, digging through her bag.

"Then get me someone who that does help."

"Listen," Jackie shot back in a forceful tone that got the attention of everyone around her.

"Don't you 'listen' me—"

Jackie smacked Wyler across the face, grabbed his cheeks with her right hand, and held him steady.

"Now you listen to me, you scumbag piece of shit. You brought this on yourself by playing with fire. I ought to let you rot. Right now I'm the best bet you have at surviving whatever was thrown at you. If I can't help you, then no one can. I don't have time for bullshit, and neither do you. You've been infected with whatever it was you were poisoned with, so you had better calm yourself down and pay attention. I need your cooperation, or this will prove pointless and you'll be dead. Then I'll simply fill out a report, grab a beer, and go home to my son. Do you understand me? Nod if you do."

Wyler remained quiet. His cheeks puffed up as if he was about to throw up, but he held it back at the last second.

"Now I need a sample of what he was infected with," Jackie said to no one in particular. "I don't care if you scrape it off a rat's ass in

168 | TYLER COMPTON

the bottom of the sewers or tackle the mayor himself to get it off his shoes. I need a sample. Someone get on it. Now." Several footsteps move frantically about behind Jackie while she continued her study of Wyler. "I need whoever has been around him since the symptoms began. I need answers."

"I can help," the woman said from behind Parks as she dug her way toward Jackie through the team of people who had begun circling around the panic-stricken man.

"And you are?"

"Diane Gandara," she answered as she flexed her hands, trying to figure what to do with them. "I'm the producer."

"Diane, good," Jackie replied. "I'm Jackie Isley. I'm going to ask you a few questions, and I need honest answers. If you don't know, that's all right—but say so. Don't make stuff up. This man's life may depend on it. Understand?"

"Y-yes, ma'am." Diane's hands shook even worse than Wyler's, and Jackie wondered how much help she would get out of the woman. She didn't even know what she was dealing with yet and therefore didn't know the timeline she had to work with.

"Okay," Jackie said with a smile and calming whisper. "A substance was thrown in his face. Did you see it?"

"Yes."

"Liquid? Powder?"

"L-liquid. R-red colored."

"How much?"

"J-just a cupful. Only on Ch-charles."

"Just the same, I'm going to need everyone who was standing around him at the time. Other people may be infected, and they'll need to be tested." Jackie looked up at Parks. "Make sure everyone's wearing gloves and masks. We don't know if this is an airborne contagion or not. Most likely not. But even a drop of this stuff on someone's skin could affect them, so until we know what it is, I need everyone rounded up."

"Got it," Parks said through his own mask.

"Okay. You're doing good," Jackie said while she took Wyler's temperature. "A red liquid. A cupful. Good. This was about twenty minutes ago. Then what happened? Did he feel any immediate sensations? Burning? Itching? Hot? Cold? Anything?"

"No . . . I don't . . . no. I don't think so," Diane stammered. She began to lose it again as she turned from Jackie to Wyler, whose color grew paler as he continued to shake and cough.

"Hey," Jackie snapped as she grabbed the woman by her shoulders and pulled her around the side of the van so she couldn't see Wyler. "Focus on me. Okay? Forget about him. No immediate symptoms?"

"No. I got some water for him, and he cleaned off his face and flushed out his eyes with it."

"Good," Jackie said, resuming her physical consultation of Charles Wyler. "Pupils dilated. Now his skin feels cold but his temperature's rising. Labored breathing."

"Can I have some water?" Wyler asked. "I'm awful thirsty."

"I'm sorry, Mr. Wyler, but I can't allow that at this time," Jackie said, swabbing off his arm. "I need to draw some blood to do some tests. Okay? Is that okay, Mr. Wyler?"

Wyler nodded.

"Now it's important, Mr. Wyler, that I find out if you are on any medication. Anything I need to know of?" Wyler shook his head in the negative. "Anything at all? Antidepressants? Viagra? Anything illegal? Marijuana? Cocaine? Even alcohol? Any alcohol in your system? Any anything? I need to know, Mr. Wyler. Your life depends on it.

"N-nuthing," Wyler stammered as he continued to shake his head in the negative to each item that Jackie reeled off.

"Mr. Wyler?"

"I had a shot of whiskey and a bump to take the edge off. That's all. Nothing else."

Jackie breathed her disapproval.

"I want s-s-some w-water," Wyler repeated.

"I understand," Jackie said calmly as she could under the circumstances. Parks was impressed with the woman's bedside manner and wondered how much practice at this she had. "But I can't allow that at this time. I don't know what it is you were infected with, and there are numerous toxins out there that can be triggered by being mixed with something as simple as water. Do you understand me?"

"I already gave him some water," Diane said, starting to get frantic again.

"It's okay," Parks said as he grabbed Diane and sat her down.

"How much?" Jackie asked.

"He took a few swallows from a bottle, cleaned off his face, then finished off another bottle."

"To get rid of the t-t-taste in my mouth," Wyler explained. "That st-st-stuff tasted like sh-sh-shit."

"What did it taste like specifically, Mr. Wyler?" Jackie asked.

"Like bitter sh-shit."

"What water?" Parks asked, trying to keep Diane occupied.

The woman turned her head, but Parks stopped her from looking around the corner into the news van. "He has a personal supply flown in."

"Tell me," Parks said gently.

"In the van. There's a case of it. We have it ordered. For Mr. Wyler only. He's very picky about what he drinks."

"Stay here," Parks said, making his way around Jackie and into the van. He found a small refrigerator in the back corner and inside were a dozen purple-labeled bottles of Kobra water.

"Never heard of this," Parks muttered.

"It's f-f-foreign," Wyler said. "I have it imported. The best st-stuff in the world."

Parks reached into the fridge and picked up a bottle. He stared down at the neon-blue lettering with the outline of a hooded cobra above the name and thought to himself about what some people were willing to pay for in life.

"What is it?" Jackie asked, looking up past Wyler, whose face she kept pointed out the back of the van.

"Not sure," Parks said, squeezing the bottle. He expected a stream of water to burst out and when none did he let out a deep breath. "I was expecting—" Parks stopped when he felt something cool touch his gloved hand. He looked back down and saw water leaking out from underneath the plastic wrapper around the bottle. Parks ripped the label off and squeezed the bottle again; this time a stream of the liquid shot out through his fingers.

"Shit."

Parks dropped the bottle, reached for another, and squeezed it. When nothing happened he ripped the label off and felt another stream of water come spraying out.

"We have a problem. A very serious problem."

"What is it?" Jackie asked.

"These bottles have all been tampered with. I think you were right. Only we're too late and you have it backward."

"What?" Jackie said, checking Wyler's heartbeat and pressure.

"You said water might trigger the chemical that was thrown on Wyler's face. What if he's already been taking in the toxin through his water and the chemical that was thrown at him was the trigger."

"Okay, Mr. Wyler, we're going to have to induce vomiting," Jackie shouted. "I have something for you to swallow. It's important you take this or I'll have to induce gastric lavage."

Jackie was reaching back into her medical kit when she first started hearing the sounds from Charles Wyler that let her know her pill would not be necessary. She turned around when suddenly he opened his mouth and began throwing up all over himself and Jackie like a scene out of *The Exorcist*. She let out a startled scream as she jumped back, already sprayed with the reddish liquid the man had just vomited. Charles Wyler clutched his stomach as he moaned in pain. Parks imagined that if wailing banshees truly did exist, this was what they would sound like.

Wyler began vomiting again. The vomit was red, not from the chemical thrown at Wyler, but from the blood mixed in with it. Charles Wyler jerked himself up and threw up another small amount and slammed his mouth shut, his teeth closing down on his tongue, the tip of which hung by a thread through his clenched teeth. Wyler lurched forward and opened his mouth and threw up once more. When he was finished, the tip of his tongue was no longer attached, having come free in the chemical waste.

"M-m-my thwoat," Wyler groaned through the spasms that continued to attack his body. "M-my thwoat is b-buwning."

Parks looked at the dying man but then noticed that Jackie hadn't even paid attention to what Wyler had said. Instead, she was trying her best to clean herself off, having been a side victim of the killer's poison yet again. Parks tried to get around Wyler and slipped in the blood, almost falling to the ground before catching himself on the side of the van. Wyler threw up more blood, making the back of the news van look like something out of a Wes Craven horror movie, blood flying everywhere. Parks finally got out of the van, his shoes and pants covered in blood, and reached Jackie and grabbed her.

"Jackie," said Parks. Jackie looked up, tears in her eyes, as she frantically tried to clean herself off. She didn't have to say it. He knew what she was thinking in that moment even though he himself had never been a father. She was worried about not being there for her son. Sure he was full grown, a man now, but she was still, first and always, a mother.

Two ambulances raced up to Union Station and four EMTs jumped out and hustled over to the back of the news van.

"Keep your distance," Parks shouted at the approaching men and women. "Check her." Parks handed Jackie off. "But stay away from this van. Don't get any of the red substance on you. Understand? Fairmont? Moore?"

"Boss," Fairmont and Tippin both called out through muffled masks. Both men stopped suddenly, backing off a few steps at the sight of their boss covered in blood.

"Rope this entire area off," Parks ordered as he jumped back from Wyler. Wyler began making painful, retching noises as he continued throwing up blood. The wheezing noises coming out of the man made it sound as if his insides were being squeezed together as his organs fought over one another to get oxygen. "Get those people over there who were with Wyler during the attack to the EMTs to be checked out, and keep everyone else away. We'll all need to be checked and tested."

"What about Wyler?" Fairmont asked.

Parks turned back to the news van, already knowing the answer. Wyler laid face-up, covered in the vomit he had choked to death on because of his body's uncontrollable reaction to a poison that had been introduced to him by a sadistic madman.

17

"It's not your fault," Parks said quietly from a chair facing Jackie while she sat on a hospital bed in the Cedars Sinai emergency room. They were alone, sealed off from the rest of the room by a cloth curtain, giving them some privacy, which Parks felt they were entitled to after the day they just had. Both were dressed in blue nurses scrubs as their clothes had been taken for testing and ultimately burning.

Every member of his team had been cleared, at least as far as they were able to determine at this early stage. They had been at the hospital all day, each getting poked and prodded. More blood had been drawn from each of them for testing than Parks thought they could physically reproduce to keep living. Each had been given numerous immunization shots and would be required to return for further testing. But for now, all had been cleared to go home.

"But I left Wyler alone. I just freaked. I should have never stopped administering—"

"You're human," Parks said, trying to console the woman, who was doing her best to hold back the tears. He could see it on her face. She was distraught. And not just about the fact that she could have died by some unknown, foreign substance, thereby leaving her son an orphan. She was also genuinely disturbed by her conduct on the job. Performance was everything to the people Parks worked with; he saw that day after day. He felt the same way. They all took pride in what they did. "You panicked. It happens. We don't know what we're dealing with. It's scary. Damn-right freaky. Anyone of us could have died today. It's not your fault about Wyler. Blame that sick son of a bitch out there running around poisoning people."

Jackie threw on a fake smile that let him know she wasn't buying it. Parks stared at the woman before him, her hands trembling as she tried to get a grip on herself.

"You talk to your son yet?" Parks asked.

"Ricky? No." Jackie shook her head. "He's not home today. Or tonight. Staying on campus. Some frat party. I think he's pledging. Not sure. Only know he's out of contact for the weekend."

Parks stared intently at her. "How are you getting home?"

She shrugged and smiled. She had no idea. Why would she? She wasn't worried about how she was going to get home. Only about trying to survive the day.

"I'll give you a lift," Parks said.

"Are you good to drive?" Jackie asked. "Because I'm sure as hell not. How can you be?"

"Believe it or not, but I've been through worse things than today." Parks smiled and held his scarred up hands in front of her. "I've learned to control my adrenaline flow. I know how to manipulate it. Use it to my benefit. It's what helps keep me cool under pressure. I'll pass out tonight and sleep like a log. That's when it hits me."

Jackie and Parks stared at each other, enjoying the moment of silence.

"Yes," Jackie said, breaking the silence.

"Yes?"

"Yes, I'd like a ride. If the offer still stands?"

"Sorry. That was a ten-second offer. I have to leave you here for the night now." Parks smiled again and even uttered a little laugh as she playfully punched him on the shoulder. "Come on. Let's get out of here."

"Actually," Jackie said standing, pausing to grab her purse. "You know what I could really use right now?"

"What's that?"

"A drink. You game?"

"Dressed like this?"

"What? So they'll think we're doctors or something. What do you care what other people think?"

"I think that after today, we've earned a drink. Let's go."

                    *   *   *

"How do you do this? Every day?" Jackie almost finished her beer then set it down on the bar top and stared at Parks, genuinely wanting an answer.

"Well, honestly, it isn't like this every day," Parks said. "I mean sure there are days from hell. Days when we wished we'd never gotten out of bed. But the good days far outnumber the bad ones. And day's like today . . . well luckily those are once in lifetime. If you're lucky."

Parks stirred the ice in his glass and remained quiet. There was no consoling her. No words that would make it better. She simply had to purge the experience from her being. He had been there. Numerous times throughout the years.

They had found a small hole-in-the-wall bar near Jackie's place in Venice so that she wouldn't have far to go after the several drinks she planned on downing. Parks was accommodating. He liked the beach area and the sound of the waves in the background was having a calming effect on them.

"I panicked," Jackie said, shame on her face.

"You're human," Parks said, correcting her. "That's all it is. Nothing more. Nothing less. You were no worse at your job today than you were yesterday. You can't foresee these things. They simply happen. Shit as it is. It's true. But you're not a bad person. Simply flawed. That makes you human. Trust me, that's a good thing. Okay?"

"Thanks," Jackie said, a smile lighting up her face before she finished off the beer.

"For?"

"Trying. That's more than most people would do. It's not working. I know you know it. I can see it on your face. But you're still trying. Thanks."

"Then how about this. Forget that you're a human being. Remember that you're a mother." Jackie tensed up and Parks paused, letting her take his words in. "That's why. It's understandable. No, I cannot comprehend. I'm not a parent. So I'm not even going to begin to try and convince you that I know what you were feeling. But I do know that that's why. You're a mother. You have a child to think of. True, he's grown now. But that doesn't mean you stop becoming a mother. You'll always think of him. That's just the way it is. It's nothing to be ashamed of or to beat yourself up over. So give yourself a break. It was scary, yes. You hesitated, yes. But it's over and you're alive and all is okay. So just take a drink and breathe. You'll be fine. Tomorrow you'll wake up and feel like a fool for having overreacted so much. Trust me. I've done it myself."

Jackie smiled, appearing to actually accept Parks's words of comfort. When it came to her child anything was game and all was excusable.

"You know you still amaze me," Parks continued. "The way you handle your job. I'd be scared shitless being around those toxins and poisons and whatnot. But you're in control. Fearless. You take charge. The way you handled Wyler when we first got there was amazing. You took no shit. You had a job that needed to be done, and in order to save lives you did what had to be done. And the other crime scenes. Around the bodies. Most people wouldn't be so calm and collected. That's a gift. Don't sell yourself short."

"Fine," Jackie said. "I'll agree with you and relax if you buy the next round."

"Sure thing," Parks said with a smile.

*   *   *

"You want to come in?" Jackie asked while Parks kept his car in idle on the street near her house. She lived in one of the remodeled two-story houses that lined the historic canals in Venice. There was a small, gate-enclosed yard in the front of the house, along with a covered patio that gave a homey feeling of relaxing evenings watching the sunset. "I . . ." Jackie bit her lip, cutting off her thought. "For a drink or . . . something?"

Parks remained quiet as Jackie stood, balancing herself against the car door.

"I shouldn't. I know we're all ordered to rest up and stay away from the office, but I'll probably go back and keep looking things over." She stared at him in disbelief. "Sorry. It's just what I do. I don't stop until the case is wrapped up."

"Then what about the next one? Or the one after that? Does it ever end?"

"No. I guess not. That's just the life I lead."

"The case will still be there tomorrow. And the day after. If you want, I'll even go in with you and look it over, just the two of us. In peace and quiet. The detective and his poison expert."

"That sounded like . . ."

"It's exactly what it sounds like. Look Dave, I don't want to be alone right now. I don't feel like it. Ricky's away for the night. I'm going to go in and fix myself some food. Knock back a few Tylenol PMs and hope I can sleep through the night and late into tomorrow. That's all I'm offering. Nothing else. Good conversation if you want. But maybe we're too frazzled for that. That's fine too. If you want to go back to the office, then after you've eaten and after I've passed out, you can go. I won't think anything of it. Okay?" Parks contemplated the offer and what else went with it that wasn't being said aloud. He stared at her. In the darkness her eyes shined brightly, calling to him, coercing him to obey her. He couldn't explain it, but when he looked at her, listened to the words coming out of her mouth, he felt compelled to give in.

Jackie stood outside the car with her door open until he finally turned off the car. She smiled with satisfaction and walked toward the house. Parks shook his head at his stupidity but didn't care as he exited the car and followed Jackie over a bridge, through a white-painted gate, and into her home. Jackie set her keys down in a bowl on a table near the front door then turned around and kissed him. Parks let her kiss him as he stood there, waiting for her to finish.

"I'm sorry," she whispered. "I don't know if it's the adrenaline or the fear of death that was around us today, but I . . . I don't know, I just . . ."

But she didn't need to explain, because, just like the adrenaline, this was a feeling that he was accustomed to. He knew what she was saying even without her saying it; he just wanted something more than another one-night stand that he wouldn't even remember come the next morning. Not that he was looking for more from life; he just felt a stronger connection to this woman. He reached down and grabbed her, pulling her in and kissing her back. He could feel her maneuver herself in closer to his body. She removed her jacket as Parks did his own then she began to unbutton his shirt. He finished with the rest of the shirt and yanked off his tie while she unzipped her skirt, dropping it to the floor as she reached up and removed her blouse. She stood there in front of him in her underwear, her heart beating wildly, her breasts rising and falling with each breath.

Parks reached for her, picked her up, and began to kiss her as he found his way to the nearest bedroom. Once they reached it they spent the rest of the night wrapped in each other's bodies, falling asleep after they finished having sex, only to wake a few hours later and go at it once more. It was four in the morning when they finally passed out and stayed asleep for the rest of the night.

They were both wrapped in a slumber so deep and fulfilling that neither one heard the person who entered Jackie Isley's house and made his way down the hallway to the entrance to her bedroom, and stared at the couple as they slept in each other's arms.

PART THREE

18

"Good morning." Jackie smiled as she opened her eyes and saw Parks staring at her from his side of the bed.

"Morning," he replied, holding back a yawn.

"That was, um . . ." Jackie blushed. She looked around her trashed room, their tossed clothes lying sporadically across the floor and items knocked off her desk, evidence of their escapades of the night before.

"Agreed."

"Please tell me we caught the killer and we're waking up on some exotic island right now."

"Sorry to ruin the delusion," Parks said, chuckling.

They remained quiet for a minute, the sounds of the nearby ocean soothing them both into yearnings for the placidity that wasn't yet meant to be. Gulls cried out in the distance and broke the hypnotizing stare Parks had been giving Jackie.

"I'm gonna go shower," Jackie said, sitting up, holding the sheet around her body even though Parks had explored nearly every inch of it hours earlier. "You can either wait here for me—"

"Have any coffee?"

186 | TYLER COMPTON

"You read my mind. There's a pot in the kitchen."

"Sure thing," Parks said as he leaned in to kiss her. Jackie pulled back, the embarrassment of having just woken up and not yet brushed her teeth hitting her.

"I'm going to go clean up. I'll see you in a few," Jackie said. She stood up and walked into the neighboring bathroom and turned the shower on.

Parks fell back into the bed and lay there for a few more minutes listening to Jackie humming while she cleaned herself off in the shower, hypnotizing him.

His phone began to vibrate, obviously Fairmont or Tippin and fixed the ringtone on his phone and he picked it up and looked at the screen. The caller was blocked. He didn't even bother answering it. He was in too good a place to let someone spoil his morning.

"Gotta get up," Parks said to himself as he forced himself out of bed and searched around for his clothes. He found his underwear and threw on his shirt, buttoning two of the buttons and forgetting about the rest.

He rubbed the sleep out of his eyes and made his way down the hallway to the kitchen. He was opening and closing cupboards, looking for the coffee supplies, when he smelled something and turned around. There on the counter was a freshly brewed pot of coffee, and he wondered why both Jackie and he had not noticed that from the bedroom. His cop instincts kicked in, and he became alert and on edge.

"Good morning," came a voice behind him, forcing Parks to spin around and come face-to-face with the young man he had bumped into getting off the elevator at the hospital. The kid sat at the dining table reading the morning paper. "Figured after that performance you both gave last night you guys might need some of that."

Parks stared at the kid—Jackie's kid—who lowered his eyes back to the newspaper.

"You must be Ricky," Parks said by way of introduction as he became self-conscious about the way he was dressed.

"And you must be Parks," Ricky replied.

"Your mother thought you were staying at some frat house last night," Parks commented, buttoning the rest of his shirt.

"That was Friday night," Ricky said without looking up. "Last night was just a date. I'm usually home on the weekends. Mom knows that. She prefers that." Ricky smiled. "Mugs are in that cupboard up over your left shoulder."

"I'm sorry we had to meet like this," Parks said as he found a mug and poured himself a cup.

"Why? We're all adults. It happens," Ricky said, taking another sip of his coffee. "I mean, you don't think you're the first person my mother's ever brought home, do you?"

Parks stood silent, not sure of what to say or how to respond, and sipped his coffee.

"You're not," Ricky continued. "It happens. Then they leave. They all leave. Then it's just me and her. You'll leave. Which is fine. I'm okay with that. So long as you do leave. I don't need to see my mother getting hurt again."

"I'm not out to hurt your mother."

"That's what they all say. But that doesn't change the facts, now does it? You all still manage to do it just fine anyways."

"I don't know who 'they all' is, but I'm not—"

"You have a job to do. Because of that you met my mother. But don't go thinking you're in love already. Because you're not. You have your fun then you leave. Understand? They all do that. Nothing more. It's not allowed. If that means you need to bolt out the front door right now before my mother gets out of the shower, then you damn well better do that. Do. You. Understand. Me?"

Parks stared at the young man whose words cut through the air and stung him like a million bug bites. He had heard words like those before, with the meaning and tension behind them that was meant for him, he just wasn't expecting it from someone Jackie had brought into the world. Someone attached to her.

"Just watch yourself," Ricky continued as he stood up from the table. "My mother's all I have. And I'm all she has. We won't let anything happen to each other we don't think isn't good for the other person. You understand me?"

Parks stared at the kid as if they were in a pissing contest in a bar when he heard Jackie walking down the hallway.

"Mmm, smells good," Jackie called out. She walked in, wrapped in a terry cloth robe and drying her hair with a towel. "Guess you figured out—oh, look who showed up after all. What are you doing here?"

Jackie walked over to Ricky and gave him a hug and a kiss on the top of his head.

"Oh, just taking a break from college life. What are you up to?"

"Well I was about to make breakfast. What if we all take a walk down to the beach and hit up some brunch place nearby?"

"Actually," Parks interrupted. "I should probably get going."

"What? No. Why?" Jackie asked.

"Well you've got Ricky here. You should spend some time with him. Just mother and son. Besides, I have a case I need to work on."

"I thought you were ordered to take today off?"

"I was. But I'm not really expected to do so. Just to stay out of the office. I'm going to drive around and visit the crime scenes. Take some new notes. Stuff like that."

"Well why don't we have breakfast and then I can join you?"

"It's okay," Parks said with a smile. "I appreciate that. I really do. But this is something I should do on my own. Besides, you have your son here today. I know you miss him. You talk about him all the time." Parks looked past Jackie and eyed Ricky. "Spend the day with him. I'll see you tomorrow. Promise."

Jackie moved to Parks and pulled him out of the kitchen and toward the bedroom. "This a little too much Normal Rockwell for you, isn't it?"

"It's nice. I'm fine. I promise. I enjoyed last night and I would like to see you again. But you really should spend the day with your son and I really should work. The sooner we crack this case . . ."

"Oh, is that a date you're scheduling?"

"That's a promise," Parks said as he leaned down and gave her a kiss. "Something for me to look forward too. I work so much better with inspiration."

"Well then . . ." Jackie said, pulling Parks back down for another kiss. "How about one more for the road. Just to make sure you don't forget what's motivating you."

"Like I could."

*　　　　　　*　　　　　　*

Parks spent the rest of the day doing just as he said. He stopped for coffee then went home and played with a new puzzle for an hour before he decided it was time to work and dug through the notes he had on hand. He mapped out the four crime scenes so far and then spent the afternoon driving from location to location. He checked the times it took to get to each place. The surroundings. Buildings. Businesses and residential. People. Landmarks and any other distinguishing objects of merit. Nothing new stood out to him but he felt he had a stronger hold on the events as they had played out. Locations were irrelevant making the subjects more noteworthy. There was a reason each person had been chosen. Somehow, someway, they had to be linked.

On his way back home he stopped by the Tisdale residence stakeout and checked with the officers. There had been no movements anywhere. Tisdale had become a recluse. Parks felt the man was a weak suspect, but he was still their lead prime suspect. Even though there had been no connection made between him and any of the victims (with the exception of his wife), he was the one person they knew had knowledge of chemicals and toxins. Parks wished the officers luck, knew that he'd most likely have to pull them the following morning.

Parks was heading home when his phone began to ring. A number popped up that looked familiar but he couldn't place.

"Detective Parks," Parks said, answering his phone.

"You shouldn't have involved her. It was not wise," said a voice on the other end. The person calling didn't need to identify themselves. The man's Russian accent was thick.

"Kozlov?" Parks said as the line went dead. What the hell was Kozlov doing calling him? How? Why? The man had to know Parks wasn't the lead investigator on his case anymore. And what did he mean by—

Parks pulled over to the side of the road and dialed Hardwick who answered on the first ring. It was almost as if she had been expecting him to call. Or was about to call him.

"What happened?" Parks asked before she could say anything.

"Look, Dave. We don't—"

"Don't bullshit me. What happened? Where are you?"

"Parks—"

"Where, dammit!"

*   *   *

Parks arrived at the Kozlov residence just south of the West Holly-wood area, between Fairfax and Houser, to find the entire property tapped off with caution tape. The house was on the corner of a residential intersection, a white house with dark brown trim and a lawn in front with numerous flowers around the front walkway. Three black-and-whites were parked out front, police officers standing around; making sure no one entered the premises. Crime scene technicians were entering and exiting the house, their booties covered in blood.

"Hardwick!" Parks shouted from the front door when he was stopped by an officer.

Hardwick arrived from a back room and signaled to the guard to allow Parks entrance. He rushed in, almost out of breath and quickly put on booties and gloves of his own. Plastic tarp was laid out all over the front room and leading down the hallway to the back bedroom, which was a good thing, because despite booties, blood was being tracked everywhere.

"Where?" Parks asked.

Hardwick started down the hallway. "I need you to brace yourself, Parks. It's a mess in there."

"What happened?"

"We still don't know," Hardwick admitted. "Or rather we don't know who did this to her."

Parks followed her down the hallway and to a back bedroom where Natalie Kozlov was found lying in her bed, her head up against the headboard, blood everywhere in the room. It looked like a slaughterhouse massacre had occurred in the room. Up above Natalie's head, written in what was most likely her blood, were the words:

ШАХ И МАТ

"What the hell?" Parks said, almost in a whisper, barely audible, while he took the whole scene in.

Parks noticed that Hardwick wasn't looking at the body, rather she was faced away, side by side with Parks in case he needed anything. It was the woman's body. Parks took a step closer, leaning in and taking all of the damage that had been done to the woman.

"Everything that was done to her was done with a razor," Tanaka's voice sad from behind Parks. He turned and saw her, covered in blood, having done the initial observation. "We'll move the body now if everything's been photographed and catalogued."

Hardwick looked across the room, probably to the detective in charge, though Parks couldn't focus on them. They didn't matter. Natalie Kozlov was what mattered.

"Tell me," Parks said.

"Dave—"

"Tell me," Parks repeated, more forcefully this time.

Tanaka looked to Hardwick who nodded that it was okay. He would find out one way or another anyway.

"Each of her fingernails has been removed, sliced off from under the skin. Whoever did this dug in and literally severed each nail from the root. She's got numerous cuts along her body, legs, arms. Defensive wounds on her hands. He sliced open her face. First her mouth. Her attacker almost cut her jaw off. Then he removed her eyelids. Both below and above the eyeball. Her nose was removed. As well as both ears. He really disfigured her."

"This was anger," Parks said. "For her testifying against her husband."

"Her breasts were cut off. Body parts and skin were found all over this room," Tanaka said, almost as if she couldn't stop once she had started.

"I get it," Parks said, by way of letting her know she could stop. He needed to know but he could see the damage. He didn't need to make anyone else relive it. Especially not Tanaka. "Where is he?"

"Kozlov?" Hardwick said. "Still locked up. I've had him checked on three times since I got this call. It wasn't him."

"But he was behind it," Parks said, getting pissed off. "We know that much."

"And?"

"And what now? What does this mean for Kozlov? What does this mean for anyone else who might testify against him? And more importantly, who did this? Who's helping Kozlov?"

19

At quarter past eight, Monday morning, Dave Parks was fiddling with the LA Times's daily Sudoku while his entire team, plus Jackie Isley and Amy Tanaka, sat on one side of the conference table, awaiting their instructions for the day. He was in a foul mood and knew he needed to get out of his funk. Everyone had heard about Natalie Kozlov by now and were keeping their distance, knowing full well that condolences weren't what Parks needed right then. Hardwick stood near the entrance to the room as if waiting for someone to deliver some pressing news. Parks wasn't sure why she had called the meeting for first thing that morning or why she had ordered his entire team on one side of the table, but he hoped the bad feeling he had about it was wrong. Something told him that after the public attack made on Charles Wyler on the Channel 10 news the mayor would be implementing a task force of some sort in the LAPD to help take care of the Palisades Poisoner. Los Angeles had local FBI headquarters within the city limits, but the LAPD was rarely ever "taken over" by the FBI, due to the already sizeable amount of manpower they had at their disposal. Mysterious men and women in trench coats, showing up out of nowhere, taking over investigations and blocking the LAPD out, were more the stuff of fiction than real life. Personally, Parks had rarely ever worked with the FBI, and on the few occasions he had it wasn't anywhere near as territorial or intense as was often portrayed. An FBI-led task force was not one of his biggest concerns at the moment.

Someone behind Hardwick cleared his throat, and Parks looked up to see Detective Wilkes standing in the doorway.

"Your whole team here?" Hardwick asked without turning around and acknowledging the man's presence.

Wilkes grunted, and Hardwick motioned to the empty side of the table. Wilkes made his way into the room followed by Detectives Ramirez and Hayward, each taking a seat at the table.

"Good. Right," Hardwick said with a huff, walking to the front of the room, commanding the attention of everyone in it. "Now I want everyone to listen to me and listen good. We have one sick fuck out there killing innocent people with some seriously scary—and dangerous—substances. Our expert on the topic, Dr. Isley, has already been infected once, and we got off lucky on Saturday. It could have been a hell of a lot worse. It's a fucking mess. And all on TV."

Hardwick glared at everyone, driving the point home.

"I can't afford to lose anyone in this room and yes, I'm saying this both professionally and personally. Now, with that out of the way, I've been on the phones and in meetings all weekend with both the mayor and the commissioner and every other person who outranks me in this damn town. Things are not looking good. We have four deaths already. And considering how he's killing he's being given a high priority. I've assured the proper higher-ups that we have the situation in hand and in return we have been given full cooperation by everyone you guys may need it from. FBI. CDC. Whoever. But this is also why I'm bringing in Wilkes and his team to help assist."

There was an uneasy silence to the room as everyone looked around while keeping focused on Hardwick.

"You're all familiar with Detectives Wilkes, Ramirez, and Hayward." Each man nodded with the mention of his name. "They begin their testimony on the Cosway murders this week, so I can't have them in rotation to accept new investigations until they're finished. So until that time comes when their entire team is ready to work again, they will be at your disposal to help with whatever you may need. I also have members of Parks's team being pulled and interviewed by the DA about the Kozlov case. So, if you haven't noticed, we've all got quite a bit on our plates. This arrangement is nonnegotiable for anyone in this room. If you have a problem with this arrangement, then I will accept your resignation effective immediately. Lives are at stake here, ladies and gentlemen, make no mistake about that. This is not the time for petty office bullshit and hurt feelings. Understand? You all work as one team on this until it's finished. Parks takes lead with Wilkes as his second-in-command. Dr. Isley is still our lead expert on the matter. Tanaka, I understand you work out of a different division and have your own set of protocols, and I'm not asking you to break them. You have been more than helpful with this case from what I've been informed of so far. I thank you for that and for being here, though this is more so you know what's going on in this office in case you need to relay any further information about this case to anyone."

"Yes, ma'am," Tanaka replied.

"Good," Hardwick continued. "Copies of the murder book were made for each member of Wilkes's team. I expect everyone in this room to know every aspect of this ongoing case, inside and out.

Now, I want us to go over victim number four: Charles Wyler. What do we have from the attack on Saturday?"

Parks looked to Jackie and Tanaka and nodded. The two women stood up and began going through their notes.

"As we suspected from what's happened on several of the other murders the death of Charles Wyler was a compound poisoning," Jackie began.

"Meaning?" Wilkes asked.

"Meaning that Wyler was poisoned by not one, but two poisons that worked together. Like Ian Harris, who was poisoned with methanol, which slowed down his reaction reflexes for when he was attacked by the death adder."

"And Wyler?"

"We figure the substance thrown in Wyler's face was the second agent, which only had an effect on him thanks to the water he had been drinking for who knows how long."

"Water?" Wilkes asked.

"Yes," Parks piped in. He paused for a moment. He had to put Kozlov on the back burner. For now. He had another serious, more imminent threat to deal with. "Yes, Wyler has his own special brand of water, Kobra Water, flown in especially for him. Nothing special about the water other than the amount of filtration it goes through. Its origin is somewhere in the mountains of India. But again, nothing overtly special about the water. We're checking the shipping history on his last few cases just to be safe."

"Except in this case the bottles of Wyler's latest shipment had been tampered with," Jackie continued. "Each bottle had a high-quantity injection of both diphenylhydantoin and barbital."

"In English please," Hardwick snapped.

"Dilantin and phenobarbital."

"And those are the two poisons that killed him?"

"No. Wyler had already been drinking the contaminated bottles, though for how long we don't know."

"What do those two poisons do?" Wilkes asked.

"They're quite similar actually," Jackie explained. "Usually, both are given to control epileptic seizures. Sometimes as a sleeping aid. There are no outrageous effects or symptoms of phenobarbital other than chills and lowered blood pressure."

"What's its reaction time?" Parks asked.

"Immediate."

"And the Dilantin?"

"This one's a little nastier. Its symptoms can include fever, liver and kidney damage, anemia, slurred speech, confusion, and swelling of the gums."

"So that's what caused the scene you witnessed in the back of the van," Hardwick said, more as a statement than a question.

"No," Jackie said. "I think these two drugs served a different purpose."

"Such as?"

"Phenobarbital can react with many drugs to speed up their half-life. Or the amount of time the drug remains active in the body. It also causes them to be eliminated more rapidly."

"So the phenobarbital and Dilantin were mixed together to work off each other more rapidly and then dissipate without being noticed?" Hardwick asked.

"Kind of," Jackie said. "To do that, yes. But not with each other. With the third drug that was introduced into the body."

"What third drug?" Hardwick asked.

"The red chemical substance that was thrown in Wyler's face by the homeless man."

"So it was a poison?"

"Yes, quite. Sanguinaria canadensis. Or more commonly known as bloodroot."

"And what does that do?"

"That does what we witnessed in the back of the van. Skin rashes. The poison reduces the heart's action. Basically, death occurs after intense vomiting and cardiac paralysis. Generally, it takes one to two hours to take effect, but because of the phenobarbital, the reaction time was sped up."

"So why was the Dilantin used as well?" Wilkes asked, confused.

"We're not a hundred percent sure on that, but I believe it was used for the same reason that the bloodroot was used. They do many similar things, but where they really overlap as far as symptoms go is in the effect they have on the throat and mouth."

A low murmur went through the room at this.

"Keep in mind that it's just a theory at this point," Jackie said. "But I think I'm right. He basically bled from his mouth and then choked to death on his vomit."

Tanaka agreed with this explanation.

"He was being silenced," Parks muttered.

"More like shut up," Wilkes replied. "The killer didn't want him talking. But what did Wyler know? I think if Wyler had known anything pertinent he would have said something on air about it."

"Maybe it wasn't to shut him up for the reasons we're thinking," Parks surmised. "Maybe there's another meaning as to why this was done to him. What about the other murders. Did any of those poisonings have any specific targeted effects on the human body?"

Jackie peered back down at her notes to look over the names of the victims.

"Allison Tisdale, no. Nothing specific with cyanide. Ian Harris, n—actually, yes. He bled from the eyes. There are multiple symptoms to the two toxins that were introduced to his body, but where they overlap is in the effect they have on the eyes. With Bollinger, I'm not sure that I can tell. The poisons used on him are paralyzing agents, but neither are specific to any particular portion of the body like Harris's and Wyler's were."

"All right," Parks said. "But that's something. Maybe Harris saw something and Wyler was going to say something. Maybe not. But it's an angle to check into."

"What about the homeless man?" Hardwick asked.

"No sign of him since the attack," Parks said. "We searched all of the area, issued a BOLO for him. Used pictures of the man from the live video feed. Nothing so far. Witnesses at the attack saw the man but no one saw where he disappeared off too. No one was watching him. Just the show Wyler was putting on. We've got some patrol officers in the downtown area who say he's a local on the homeless scene but they haven't been able to locate him so far. We're still searching. My guess is that he's dead somewhere. Not that we'll ever find a body. But we're still looking."

"All right," Hardwick said with a sigh. "Keep on it."

"What about all of these poisons that have been used so far?" Wilkes asked. "This bloodroot and phenobarbital? Are they traceable? How's this guy getting all this stuff?"

"Not sure, but we're working on it," Jackie said. "Bloodroot is found in and around North America, in the southeastern states and Canada. But it's not in season right now, so whoever this guy is, he's either been storing it all this time or manipulating the plant. Either way, it takes precision and caution."

"Keep looking into it. See what you can find," Parks said.

"What else are we working on?" Hardwick asked.

"I'm working with Fairmont on processing the crime scenes to see if there's anything we overlooked," Moore began.

"Actually, I walked through each one again yesterday. I didn't spot anything new so I'd like Wilkes and his men to go over them since they have to review them as it is, and to get a fresh pair of eyes on them," Parks said.

"Yes, sir," Moore replied.

"You two work with me on the timelines of each of the victims, and we'll try to determine a connection between them," Parks said.

"I have something," Tippin said raising his hand.

"Yes?"

"Well it might be nothing. I mean it probably is nothing. But if we're checking every little thing—"

"What is it, Milo?"

"You remember Ian Harris's pictures that you had me pick up?"

"Yeah?" Parks wondered where Tippin was heading with this.

"I was looking through them again. And besides the pictures of the Bollingers there are also the few of you."

"Yes," Parks said, nodding. "We actually haven't explored what that means. We know Harris doesn't do freelance work like that anymore. Following people around and the such. So why does he have those pictures? If it wasn't for personal reasons then obviously it was for a job."

"Someone hired him," Milo said, agreeing.

"You mean to follow you around?" Hardwick asked, looking to

Parks.

"It's a possibility," Parks said.

"Why?"

"Couldn't tell you. No idea."

"Could it be related to this case?"

"It's a possibility. Not sure why. But we should consider every possibility."

"But then that means—"

"There's a possibility that whoever hired Harris to follow me around is our killer. Like he knew I would be on this case. In which case the timing of these murders is more than intentional. As was Harris' murder. To keep him silent. Again, there's no proof of this. But it is a theory. I've thought of this." Parks turned to Tippin. "Was that what you wanted to bring up?"

"Sort of," Tippin said. "But there's more. Most of the pictures on this roll of film were of the Bollingers. A few were of you. Then there's these three of some mysterious guy. Can't tell who as they're slightly out of focus."

Everyone leaned in and looked at the three photos. They appeared to be of a young man, in his twenties or thirties, leaving an apartment. Parks would have guessed the area to be West Hollywood or around the UCLA campus. But there were no distinguishing landmarks in the picture to eliminate any of the possibilities.

"But we don't know who this is or where this was taken," Parks said.

"It's Kyle Oni," Tippin said.

"The baseball player?" Wilkes asked, leaning in closer to the photos. "Yeah, I guess it could be. It kinda looks like him."

"Have you guys heard?" Tippin asked, looking around. "In the news this morning. About Kyle Oni?"

"We've kind of been focused on this," Parks said, motioning to the murder board. "What happened?"

"Look," Tippin said, punching away on his computer screen. Immediately the screen lit up with several online news blogs about Kyle Oni. Each one was accusing him of being caught with a gay lover.

"No, shit. He's queer?" Wilkes asked.

"Hey," Hardwick snapped. "What the hell does this have to do with anything? We don't have time for gossip rags."

"They're accusing him of having stayed the night at a friend's house several times over the past few weeks," Tippin began explaining. "They have pictures—"

"What's this have to do with us?" Parks said, interrupting him.

"Look," Tippin said, pointing to the screen. He scrolled down and there were the pictures that were accusing baseball phenom Kyle Oni of having a gay lover. The same exact pictures that had been taken by Ian Harris. "You said this could all be about timing? What are the chances that the photos that were used to out Kyle Oni, and of a Palisades Poisoner victim, and of the lead investigator of the Palisades Poisoner case, all found together, taken by a victim of the Palisades Poisoner, is simply a coincidence?"

"Someone get a hold of Kyle Oni's people," Parks said. "We need to see him now. He either knows something, or he's in danger."

20

"Uh, sir," Fairmont said, hovering near the hallway leading to the interview rooms. He had the look of both awe and trepidation upon his face. "They're here."

"Who?" Parks asked, looking up.

"Kyle Oni. And his manager and coach."

"Where are they?"

"Interview room two."

"Thanks," Parks said, standing up and gathering his notes. He worked his way down the hallway, pausing at the door to interview room two then entered.

"I hope you've found the son of a bitch who's done this to my team," shouted John Duran, coach of the Los Angeles Dodgers, as he walked right up and into Parks's face. "Because if you haven't and I do, then I swear to you—"

"Sir, let's try and keep this as calm and civilized as possible, okay?" Parks said looking from Duran to the other two men in the room.

"Kyle Oni is one of the hottest and most-sought-after players in the league," began the other man who could only have been Oni's manager. "He didn't come cheap, but so far he's paying off tenfold. Despite all of the off-field, behind-the-scenes, soap-opera drama occurring around the team for the past few seasons, attendance at Dodger stadium had risen nine percent in Oni's first year and another seven this past season. The owners are pleased with the numbers. As they should be. This is someone's idea of a smear tactic, simply trying to ruin—"

Parks looked at the kid while his manager continued to ramble. The fact that Kyle Oni was only twenty-four, with model looks and a hard-toned physique that he didn't mind showing off at the beaches for the paparazzi to snap photos of also didn't hurt the press the team got. Nor did the frequent sightings of him at some of LA's hippest new clubs and on the arms of Hollywood's most-desired, up-and-coming actresses at their movie premieres. Oni had the makings of a superstar that was rarely seen in baseball players in this day and age.

"Again, I truly am sorry for what you're going through right now," Parks said, cutting the manager off. "Your life is your life. And it's nobody else's business. I wish I could do something about that for you but that's not why I've called you in here."

"What can we help you with?" Oni said, finally speaking. He had an innocent way about him. He was from a small town in northern Michigan and wasn't yet used to all of the glitz and glamour of the big-city life, despite having lived here for two years already.

"There's an ongoing investigation I'd like your help with. If you can. I have some photos I'd like you to take a look at," Parks said, setting several photos down in front of Oni. On each one was a different photo of a victim of the Palisades Poisoner. "Just let me know if you can identify any of these people."

"I know this man," Oni said pointing to the picture of Charles Wyler.

"You mean professionally?"

"Yes. I've never had personal contact with him, if that's what you're asking. Never had any professional contact with him either. Guy seemed like a snake."

"No comment there. Thank you. Anyone else?"

"I'm sorry," Oni said, shaking his head, seriously studying the photos. The kid was still of a small town mind where the law was final and one did their civic when asked upon to do so. "None of them look remotely familiar. I'm sorry."

"What's this about?" Duran said, interrupting. "This should be about the man who's ruined this young kid's life. What are you going to do about that, huh? What's all this bullshit matter? You should be out there trying to locate the man who—"

"While I personally find the events surrounding your client to be . . . disgusting, that's not a legal matter I can deal with. I work homicide. But the man who took the photos we believe were used to out Mr. Oni is in fact dead," Parks said, bluntly, nodding toward the photo of Ian Harris.

Parks stared at the kid, into his deep, lime-colored, cat-like eyes as he swiped a lock of midnight-black hair out of his face. The kid had clean, clear skin the likes of which even Photoshop couldn't improve upon for a magazine cover. Parks felt bad for him, but knew he had nothing to do with the Palisades Poisoner.

"What . . . what happ—" Oni said, barely audible.

"It's still an ongoing investigation. I can't go into details right now. I just needed to know if you knew any of these people. Had any association with any of them. The man's name is Ian Harris. He at all remotely familiar to you?"

"If I've seen or met him before I have no honest recollection of it," Oni said. "I'm sorry."

"No need, son."

Oni continued to stare at the pictures, moving them about, studying them, putting the pieces together.

"You don't suspect Kyle in that man's murder do you?" Oni's manager interrupted.

"No," Parks admitted. "I should. He would be our prime suspect. But no I don't believe he had anything to do with this man's murder. Of course I can't simply dismiss him because of my gut feeling. But he's a pretty public figure. I've got my people searching into his whereabouts over the last few weeks. I'm sure they'll have an alibi built for him by the end of the day. If not sooner."

"How dare you!" shouted Oni's manager as he jumped to his feet. "You have no right ambushing my client like that. This is a violation of privacy. We're out of here."

"We'll sue if we have to," Duran threatened. "This is on you guys. You think you can ambush us like this? Is that how the LAPD gets things done?"

"That is not what this is about," Parks said, getting defensive.

"Are all of these people dead?" Oni asked, looking at the rest of the pictures displayed out in front of him.

"They are." Parks said. "This is a serious situation, Mr. Oni. I don't believe you had anything to do with these people's deaths. But if you're not a suspect, then I am afraid it's possible you might be a target."

Oni's eyes widened in fear and he quickly looked to his manager and coach.

"This is outrageous," Duran shouted. "How dare you? First you scare us with false allegations, then you threaten us? We will sue. We'll take this whole damn department down, do you hear me? Come on, Kyle." Duran got Oni to his feet and started for the door. "Do you hear me? You stay the hell away from our client."

"We don't know what the hell is going on around here," Oni's manager hissed, stopping Parks by the doorway. "But don't think you've heard the last from us. You can expect to hear from our lawyers later today."

"We can offer protection," Parks offered.

"Stay the hell away from us," Duran shouted over his shoulder, mumbling and cursing the entire way out of the station.

"Well that didn't go so well," Moore said, sneaking up behind Parks. "You want us to keep an eye on him?"

"There's no real reason to," Parks admitted.

"Other than your gut?"

"Yeah," Parks said with a sigh. "Other than that."

"And when has your gut ever led you astray?"

"They refused police protection," Parks said. "There's nothing we can do about Oni for now. Let's just hope Oni isn't next and catch this guy before he gets to anyone else."

*   *   *

"Guess who has a brother?" Hardwick said, rather excitedly and almost sing-songy as she entered Parks's office.

"What is this? A new game?" Parks put down his phone, which he had been playing a game of some sort involving popping rows of bubbles and looked up at Hardwick. "Who?"

"Kozlov," Hardwick said matter-of-factly. "Our favorite razor-wielding psychopath."

"And?"

"And guess who was snuck into the country, illegally?" Parks stared at her, holding back a smile. "One Victor Kozlov."

"Do we know where he is?"

"Let's just say that Peter was the one with the brains. Victor's been using his brother's credit card to live on. Apparently he's never heard of this thing called cash." Parks stood abruptly. "Whoa there, cowboy. Remember, you are to have nothing to do with any of the Kozlovs. Peter. Victor. Natalie. Any of them. Alive or dead. We need this to go through."

Parks stared at her, knowing she was right, and slowly, and against his wishes, sat back down.

"So what's the plan?"

"The plan? The plan is to pick up Dumb Ass Number Two and hope he really is as stupid as he appears. We can then hope to either use him to convict his brother. Or if need be play brother against brother. Offer deals, see who wants to spend less time in prison, yadda, yadda."

"You'd really offer up a deal to Peter Kozlov?"

"Hell no," Hardwick said, scrunching up her face in disgust. "But for starters it's not my choice. The DA's the man in charge of this one. And hell no, he has no desire in letting either of those two walk. Especially the child killer. How would that look to the voters? But neither Dumb Ass Number One or Dumb Ass Number Two need to know about that, now do they?"

"I suppose not," Parks said, genuinely happy about the situation. They were finally closing in. He just wanted to be done with this whole mess.

"Besides, from what little we can tell, it seems Older Kozlov is somewhat protective of Younger Kozlov. Part of the reason he got him shipped over here to the good ol' U.S. of A. was to both keep an eye on him and keep him away from the less desirables in Russia."

"There are less desirables than Kozlov?"

Hardwick shrugged. "The world's filled with all types. So, anyways, we'll see what he has to say when we threaten to charge his brother as a co-conspirator in the death of children. Something tells me he won't go for that. Might just break down and confess to everything. And if not, we can always threaten to deport his brother. If he wanted him over here bad enough we can hope he doesn't want him over there even more. One can hope, right?"

"One can hope." Parks doubted that would happen, but he had seen people in the same situation do stupider things for lesser reasons. You never did know. "You'll keep me in the loop? As to what's going on?"

"Like they could stop me if they tried," Hardwick said with a wink as she left the room.

Parks could have sworn he saw a bounce in the woman's step. Hell. He knew how she felt. And he couldn't blame her.

21

It was the morning of the fifteenth, the third Thursday of September, and Parks and his team were no closer to finding their so-called poisoner than they'd been on the first day after Allison Tisdale's murder. Parks stood in front of the murder board, writing down information that he was sure led to nowhere and didn't help them one little bit. They had added a second board, and at the rate they were going, he would soon need to add another one and move the whole case out onto the main floor. The problem right now was that he didn't know what else to write. He tried to focus on what was important. His mind was sharp and clear, most likely thanks to the seven miles he had run that morning before arriving at the station. He had also managed to get in three cups of coffee and thirty minutes on the Babel puzzle that he was close to finishing. His mind felt clear and ready to absorb anything.

"What about the symbol?" Wilkes asked from his position on the edge of a desk.

"What about it?" Parks asked, somewhat frustrated.

"Do we know anything else about it? Was it found on Charles Wyler's body? I mean, how could it be? He died in our custody. It isn't like the killer could have snuck in there and carved it on him."

"Best as we can tell, it's still just the number ten. We think it's our best explanation—though we don't know why. And no, it wasn't carved into his body, but when we went through his personal effects, inside his wallet we found . . ." Parks pulled a plastic baggie with a business card in it off the murder board. Printed on the card was the symbol that had been found on each of the other bodies. "No prints on it. Professionally printed. The card itself and the ink are both being analyzed to see if we can track the job or purchaser, but so far nothing."

"What about the location of the mark on the bodies? Does that have any significant meaning?"

"It might. Probably does since it's been found in a different place on each victim. But as to what? So far we've got nothing. Still working on that."

Jackie walked into the room with Tippin at her side, the two having just finished another checklist run through universities and businesses that may have missing quantities of poisons reported.

"Find anything?" Parks asked.

"Nothing," Jackie said. "No schools up and down the west coast or any businesses that may be housing any of the poisons used so far are reporting anything missing or stolen. But with the toxins being used to kill people, no one's willing to admit they're actually missing anything. Go figure."

"Great," Parks sighed.

"But we got Milo here doing a little under-the-radar sneaking through online corporate files." Jackie winked. "Maybe he'll come up with something."

Parks shook his head and held back a smile as Lewis Hayward

and Cal Ramirez arrived to take over the next shift of mindless paper chasing from Rachel Moore and Jake Fairmont. All four sat at the table, each one surrounded by stacks of various papers.

"What the hell are they doing?" Wilkes asked, staring at his two men settling in.

"Going through phone calls we've been getting ever since Wyler's death on Saturday," Parks explained. "People are claiming to have seen the killer. To know the killer. To be the killer. People who claim they know something about the murders and whatnot. Mostly just rubbish."

"Exactly. Sometimes it's just people claiming to be the killer, even though they don't know who the victims are or how many people have been killed," Moore explained. "Luckily, for as much as the public is aware of what's going on, they really don't know anything. It's making it that much easier to determine who's full of it."

"Right," Fairmont added. "And sometimes it really is just rubbish. One guy called in, we think, to confess to killing another person then halfway through the recording just started spouting gibberish that made no sense about taking shits in May and whatnot."

"Shits in May?" Wilkes practically groaned.

"May poop," Fairmont said with a smile, looking back to his papers, trying to hold back a laugh. "Or maybe it's fly turds. Isn't that a type of fly? The mayfly?"

"You're an ass," Moore said with a roll of her eyes.

"Wait," Jackie shouted, causing most around her to jump. "What did he say exactly? May poop or maypop?

Fairmont made a face at Jackie as if she had lost her sanity then began digging through his papers for the phone call.

"Oh, uh . . . maypop, I guess."

"Anything else besides maypop? What exactly did he say?"

"He said . . . hold on, 'I've gone and done it again.' 'Excuse me, sir?' 'I poisoned him.' 'Where are you calling from, sir?' 'Maracujo.' 'Excuse me?' 'Maypop.' 'I'm sorry, sir, but this is a police line. This is not the place for prank calls.' 'I've gone and done it again.' 'Done what, sir?' And that's it."

"That's it?" Parks asked.

"That's it," Fairmont confirmed.

"For starters, you said it wrong. It's Maracuja. That's our guy," Jackie said. "When did that call come in?"

"About an hour or so ago," Fairmont, said looking to Parks, confused.

"Why is that our guy?" Parks asked.

"Maypop. Maracuja."

"What about them?"

"There's also passion vine and apricot vine."

"What are those?"

"They're all names for the passionflower."

"What's that?"

"A very deadly plant. I'm telling you, that's our guy."

"Where did that call originate from?"

Fairmont flipped the paper over and looked again.

"Hollywood. The Roosevelt Hotel."

*   *   *

"We don't even know who we're looking for," Fairmont said.

Parks ignored Fairmont and pulled off Hollywood Boulevard, south of the Hollywood and Highland shopping center, and up to the valet area of the Roosevelt Hotel.

"Checking out a 911 call," Parks said to the valet, flashing his badge. He was immediately waved on to an area where he could temporarily leave his vehicle.

The Roosevelt Hotel was a twelve-story, Spanish-style hotel in the heart of Hollywood, built in the 1920s and named for the president. Famous for hosting the first Academy Awards, it also housed several Hollywood stars, including Marilyn Monroe back when her career was just taking off. Though often just seen as an historic building, since its renovations in 2005 it had become more of a hot spot for the younger crowd.

"There's a callboard for the hotel," Parks said to Fairmont as they exited the car. Wilkes and his two men pulled up and parked behind them. "Every call that's placed from the hotel has to go through a switchboard. They can dial straight out, but the hotel keeps track. I have Tippin trying to find out who placed a call at 9:33 a.m., the time our call was received."

"Got it," Tippin called out, trying to keep up with the rest of the team with his face down in his portable computer. Jackie kept pace with him, one hand on his shoulder, guiding him where to go so he wouldn't have to stop researching. "Call came from Room 928."

"Who's it registered to?"

"A . . . uh . . . shit. It's register to a Roy Hobbs."

"Who's that?" Fairmont asked.

"That means nothing to me," Parks said. "Let's get going."

The group B-lined it for the front desk and Parks retrieved his identification and addressed the man behind the front counter.

"Can I help you, sir?" the man asked with a rather peppy smile. His nametag read Justin. He was in his early thirties, thin with sharp, angular features and a recently shaved head of reddish-brown hair that did nothing for his complexion. In a town so focused on looks and appearances, Parks wondered how the kid had gotten a job that required him to be the face of a major hotel.

"Yes," Parks began. "I'm Detective Dave Parks. We have it under good authority that someone staying in this hotel may be in danger or possibly worse. We need to be taken to his room immediately."

"Are you sure, sir? Nothing's been reported."

"Would you mind calling the room?"

"Not at all, sir. What room?"

"Nine twenty-eight."

The desk clerk paused for a moment then picked up the phone and dialed the room number. Parks wondered about the man's reaction to the room number. Who was Roy Hobbs? The name was familiar.

"There's no answer," the desk clerk replied hanging up the phone. "Would you like me to take you up there?"

"No," Parks said. "Just the key. Thanks."

The man was miffed but searched for a room key and handed it over.

"You don't want me in that room," Parks said, stopping the desk clerk. "Who is Roy Hobbs?"

The man paused, wondering how much he should say.

"Some of our clientele like to remain anonymous," the desk clerk answered. "They use aliases."

"So Roy Hobbs isn't a real name? Who's really staying in that room?"

"You have to realize we're under the strictest of confidentiality—"

"Uh, Parks," Tippin interrupted.

"—and that forbids us from simply giving out names—"

"What is it, Milo?" Parks asked.

"Roy Hobbs."

"What about it?"

"It's Robert Redford's character's name from *The Natural*. He's a baseball player."

"Shit, you were right," Wilkes hissed.

Parks spun on the desk clerk. "Is Kyle Oni in that room?"

"We'd lose business if we told people every person who stays here," the desk clerk said, trying to stand his ground.

"On second thought," Parks added, "I don't need you calling anyone about this. Come with us. Show us where this room is." As they started for the elevators, Parks stopped Wilkes. "Two of you stay here in the lobby and keep an eye out. If for some reason this guy is still here, we need to make sure we have every angle covered."

"I'll stay with Ramirez. Take Hayward," Wilkes agreed. "We know what to do."

"Perfect. Thanks."

The desk clerk led the group to the elevators, where a bell hop was waiting with the doors open to one of the cars. The entire team piled in, each appearing nervous and agitated.

"When did he check in?" Parks asked.

"Monday afternoon," the clerk replied. "Said he couldn't go home. What with what all happened to him in the news. Are you aware of what they're saying?"

"So he checked in Monday afternoon?" Parks wasn't interested in answering any questions or letting any information the department may have had out into the world.

"Just after two in the afternoon actually."

"Any complaints or visitors to his room since then?"

"No complaints. Just ordered room service. Other than that, only his agent and lawyer have been here to see him. No one else. There's no one in any of the neighboring rooms either. He was specific about wanting privacy, and since we're not overbooked . . ."

"All right," Parks said as the doors chimed and opened up. "Where is it?"

"Down the hall," the clerk pointed. "Near the end. On the right."

"Okay. Hayward, stay here with him." Parks nodded toward the desk clerk. "Keep him back. Make sure if anyone else pops out of their rooms to keep them inside. We don't know what we're dealing with. Guy may still be there, may be gone. We're not sure what kind of poison we're dealing with here either."

"Yes, we are," Jackie corrected him. "If he did use the passion-flower, then we'll all be fine. Just so long as we don't touch it."

"All right." Parks said. "You hear that, everyone? Don't touch anything. Everyone make sure you're wearing gloves no matter what."

Parks checked each member of his team to make sure they were all wearing their latex gloves, as he wanted no one to take any chances with this case.

"It might not even be our guy," Moore whispered next to Parks.

"We had him in our interview room on Monday," Parks said, referring to Oni as if that said it all.

"Trust me," Jackie said, shaking her head. "It's him."

"Let's just check it out." Parks reached for the door and knocked on it three times. "Kyle Oni? LAPD. Please open up." After thirty seconds without a reply and hearing no movement, Parks knocked again, even louder, and stated his identity once more.

"All right," Parks said, looking back at his team. "We're going in. Everyone be ready. Hayward, notify me if you see anything suspicious."

"Will do," Hayward replied, wiping the sweat off his brow.

"You stay out here until we stabilize the room, understand?" Parks said, looking to Jackie. She was disappointed but understood. "Milo? You ready?"

Tippin nodded, somewhat shaken up but with his gun drawn at the ready. To Parks he was like a kid with a water pistol. He wondered if it was the wisest choice to let him follow but knew this was what the kid was trained for.

"Okay, then," Parks said. "Let's do this."

Parks took the dark-gray keycard with gold lettering on the front that the desk clerk had given him and slid it through the slot until the red light turned green and the door unlocked. He pulled down on the handle and pushed the door open. Parks paused as the smell of alcohol hit him, as if the room had been soaking in wine for the past few days.

"Kyle Oni. LAPD. Identify yourself if you can hear me." Parks stepped into the room, checking every direction in the hallway while Moore covered his back. They inched their way down the hallway to the first door on the left, which led to the bathroom. Moore moved into the bathroom while Fairmont moved up to cover Parks's back. Tippin stayed behind Fairmont, his gun pointed to the ground. Inside the bathroom were six bottles of wine, each one emptied, with the bathroom sink clogged and filled with another two bottles.

"Moore?" Parks asked.

"Kenwood. Beringer. Francis Coppola. Pinots. Cabernets. Sauvignons. We have everything from Two-Buck Chuck to hundred-dollar bottles in here."

"Okay. Let's keep going. Kyle Oni?" Parks called out again, working his way down the hallway. In the next room, on mute on a TV played a movie with Dennis Quaid and Meg Ryan. On the dresser next to the TV were another dozen bottles of wines. Most stood upright while several lay on their sides, having drained out as wine was spilled all over the white carpet. Parks worked his way further into the almost blindingly white room with black furniture, quickly swinging his gun around and aiming it at a body that lay in a bed. He was able to tell immediately that it was too late to save him.

The Palisades Poisoner had claimed his fifth victim.

Kyle Oni lay on the unmade king-size bed with several dozen of the passionflowers laid across his nude body. Also on the bed, in between the various flowers, were several bunches of grapes, most still on the vine, and another six emptied bottles of wine.

"Oh my God," Fairmont said, taking a step back from the bedroom.

"We're clear," Moore said, putting her gun away. "Damn. Looks like Dionysus had a party in here."

"Isley," Parks called out. "Isley, get in here. Jackie! *Fairmont*. I need pictures. *Now*."

The sound of Jackie's pumps could be heard across the floor as she made her way into the room and gasped at the sight of Kyle Oni's body.

"Is that the passionflower?" Parks asked Jackie.

"Yes." Jackie answered. "Those are them."

"Dave," Moore whispered as she composed herself and moved in closer. "Look."

"What?" Parks whispered back.

"The flowers," Moore said. "The petals on each one."

"What about them?"

"There are ten of them on each flower."

Parks didn't comment but took it in and pondered what this meant, if anything, to the killer and what his ultimate aim might be.

"Excuse me," Fairmont said, beginning to take pictures of the body.

Parks turned to Moore. "I want this entire floor sealed off. Get anyone staying in any other room on this floor relocated. And I want everyone on this floor interviewed too."

"I'm on it," Moore said.

"Hey, boss," Fairmont said from behind Parks, trying to get his attention.

"What is it?" Parks asked, turning around.

"What's that?" Fairmont said, nodding toward the body. "In his hands. What is it?"

Parks leaned in and saw in each of Oni's hands, partially hidden by flowers, were two halves of a small four-by-six photograph that had been ripped down the middle.

"You get pictures?" Parks asked.

"You're good to go."

Parks used tweezers to pluck the halves from Oni's hands and held the two pieces together. In the photo were two teen-aged girls, one Caucasian, the other of Spanish descent, staring at the camera, with large smiles on their faces. Both of the girls were attractive, full of life, and Parks felt a chill run up his spine.

Who were these two girls?

And what did they have to do with the trail of corpses that were being left by a sadistic madman?

22

After Fairmont finished taking pictures of the crime scene and Moore scanned the room for prints and fibers, they collected a total of twenty flowers, ten white and ten purple, a number that Parks took to have significant meaning for the killer. The entire room was dusted, gone over with every piece of machinery the LAPD had to offer in the form of forensic science. Exactly 234 bottles of wine were photographed, dusted, bagged, and tagged before being shipped back to the station.

Was all the wine from one order? But if so, from where? And who placed the order? And how did it get into the room without anyone seeing anything?

Parks already had Tippin trying to research it.

Two hours later, Kyle Oni's body was zipped up in a body bag and escorted downstairs to the vehicle that would take him to Amy Tanaka's lab to be autopsied.

Parks had hoped they had gotten there in time. They had never been this close to a murder, with the exception of Charles Wyler's, which hadn't even been directly committed by their killer. This time Parks hoped they would be able to find something that would help

225

them.

Seven hours later, Parks felt like kicking the wall or punching something hard. He knew this wasn't the example he was supposed to set for his team, but he was sick and tired of this. The stress was getting to him, and he knew it. He needed to control himself. Have another cup of coffee or something. Anything. He saw the Rubik's Cube on the corner of his desk, picked it up, and began to fiddle with it, letting his mind wandered. This was all it seemed they did any more. There were no clues. No evidence. At least none that helped further their investigation. Nothing turned up. There were no connections between any of the victims.

How was that even possible? There had to be some reason each victim was chosen.

"Boss? Boss?" Moore tried to get Parks's attention and failed. "Dave?"

"Wha . . . huh? What?" Parks said, turning from the Rubik's Cube which he had the entire red side completed.

"What's going on?" Moore walked up to Parks to keep their conversation from the rest of the room as she handed him a Hershey's bar. "You look like you're spacing."

"I'm, uh, um, sorry," Parks apologized, setting down the Rubik's Cube (green side completed) and taking the candy bar. "Something has to change."

"What do you mean?"

"This case. It's not working for us. We're not getting anywhere. We're making no progress. We simply stand by and wait for the next victim to show up." Parks stared at his group, along with Wilkes and his two men, not sure what to say.

"It isn't like that. You know it's not."

"So what do we have on Kyle Oni?" Parks said, ignoring the comment as he ripped open the chocolate bar and looked to Fairmont.

"According to the gossip mags—"

Parks cut him off. "I want facts, not gossip."

"Boss, no disrespect, but Oni was a celebrity. Gossip may be as close to the facts as we get with this guy. And in this town, that may be a lot. I mean, who pays more attention to the rich and famous than the paparazzi? Who knows who was watching him and when and where? Maybe something was even caught on tape."

"You're right. Sorry. Check it all out. See if anyone was particularly focused on Oni. See if they have anything. Take Tippin with you to check it all out. Maybe we'll get lucky. But what were you going to say?"

"Rumor has it he was with Caroline Maddox for the past six months."

"The actress?" Parks asked.

Everyone knew who Caroline Maddox was. One of the hottest women on the planet, Caroline Maddox had been on the cover of Maxim twice in the last two years and was a Vanity Fair and Rolling Stone favorite. She sold copies. Besides that, the three movies she had made in the last two years, though sordid thrillers that were more commonly referred to as "trash," had raked in big money, especially considering the cheap price tag it took to make them. She currently had a film in theaters, a European noir where she played a femme fatale, a role that was gaining her Oscar talk, her first in five years since playing the abused witness of a violent gangster in a Scorsese drama.

"Yup," Fairmont said.

"They're together?"

"According to the online blogs."

"But what about the whole . . ." Wilkes looked around the room, not sure who he might offend, making sure to carefully choose his words. "Gay thing."

"Like Oni was the first closeted gay celebrity with a 'girlfriend,'" Parks said sarcastically, finishing his candy bar and picking back up the Rubik's Cube. "But if she was his 'girlfriend,' then find her and bring her in. We need to question her. Also, if he was seeing some guy . . . bring him in as well. We need everyone involved here. Agents. Managers. Coaches. Those two aren't going to be a piece of cake after this, I can tell you. Oh, and teammates as well."

"We already got a list going," Fairmont said, writing something down in his notepad before digging into his pocket for another piece of Nicorette.

"So what about these passionflowers that were found all over Oni? What do we know about that?" Parks turned to Jackie and sat down, hoping she'd take over that part of the discussion.

"Based on the 911 call, we're assuming Kyle Oni was murdered today, right?" Jackie asked from her position at the table.

"Right," Parks confirmed.

"And when did he come out? I thought I heard someone say he came out publicly, is that correct?"

"It broke sometime late Sunday night early Monday morning," Parks said.

"All right," Jackie said, disappointed. "It doesn't matter. I mean, you probably already know to figure out his timeline, but it doesn't matter for what I was thinking."

"What's that?" Parks asked.

"I hate to say this, but I kinda wished he'd been killed on Sunday. Or Saturday. That would have helped us a lot."

"How so?"

"In narrowing down the list of suspects," Jackie explained. "See, the flower has meaning. The killer chose it on purpose. But if Oni hadn't outed himself to the entire world, then the list of suspects could possibly have been limited to those who knew he was gay."

"You're saying those flowers we found all over his body have some sort of gay connection?" Wilkes asked.

"Let me explain," Jackie said. "I'm getting ahead of myself. The passionflower is an interesting flower. Yes, it has what you call a 'gay connection,' but it also has a strong religious connection. Particularly where the passionflower got its name from. The Passion of Christ. If you look at the flower . . ." Jackie turned in her seat to point to the five different enlarged photos of the flower that were up on the murder board. "The stigma here, in the center of the bloom. Many believe these to symbolize the three nails used in the crucifixion. Next we have the stamens. I'll try to spare you all the technical details of the flower, so just go with what I'm saying. The stamens are located behind the stigma and in front of the petals. They're usually representative of Christ's five wounds. The most recognizable feature of the passionflower, though, is the corona."

"It comes with its own beer?" Fairmont joked.

"No," Jackie replied, not letting the joke get to her. "The corona is this part." She pointed on the diagram to the area she was talking about. "Anyone want to guess what this symbolizes?"

"The crown of thorns worn by Christ," Parks answered, barely audible.

"Correct. Next are the petals. It may appear that the flower has ten petals, but actually there are only five. The remaining five are sepals. But together, the ten of them are said to represent the ten faithful apostles."

"Ten," Parks muttered, but everyone heard him.

"So what? You're telling me that this nut is killing people because he thinks he's Christ and he has in mind ten dead victims as his apostles?" Wilkes asked gruffly.

"It's a possibility," Parks said. "Look. We don't have to agree with why this guy is killing, but it will help us stop him if we can figure out why he's doing what he's doing. No matter how crazy it is. But that definitely sounds like a possibility."

"Christ wouldn't want his apostles dead, would he?" asked Moore. "I mean, they're his apostles."

"So then maybe this guy is working for the other side?" Wilkes suggested. "Getting revenge for what's-his-name?"

"Wait? Weren't there twelve Apostles?" Fairmont asked.

"Traditionally, they are Peter, Andrew, James the Greater, James the Lesser, John, Philip, Bartholomew, Matthew, Thomas, Thaddeus, Simon and Judas Iscariot," Parks answered to the best of his recollection. "Judas is generally considered one of the Twelve but when he betrayed Jesus, he killed himself. Then I think Judas was replaced by someone else. But if you look in some of the other books, like Mark or John, they give different names of the apostles. So I have no idea. Someone look it up to be sure."

Jackie and Moore both stared at Parks with awe.

"What? I went to Sunday school," Parks smirked, looking back down at the Rubik's Cube and finishing off another side. "Anyway, that's something we should look into fur—"

"Wait. Wait. Wait," Tippin said, cutting Parks off, as he looked up from his tablet. "Apparently, the ten petals represent the ten apostles, minus Peter, who denied Jesus, and Judas, who betrayed him."

"So then maybe this guy thinks he's Peter or Judas getting revenge by poisoning these ten people?" Wilkes suggested.

"But why these ten people?" Moore asked. "They're not apostles. They're just average, everyday people. Why them?"

"That's what we need to find out," Parks said. "But at least it's an angle. Which is more than we had a few minutes ago. Maybe it's a stretch. But it's something to work with."

"What about the gay angle?" Wilkes asked.

"What?"

"Doc here said the flower had both religious and gay connections. What's the gay connection?"

Parks turned to Jackie.

"Most of the Passion references originated through the Catholic religion. But over in Japan there isn't a whole lot of Catholic symbolism. The passionflowers there are generally referred to as Clock Face flowers, but in some of the larger, more urban areas, the flower is a symbol of homosexual youths. There are several reasons for this, and I won't bore you all with the details now, but I'll make a report and attach it to the murder book."

"So chances are that our killer killed Kyle Oni because he was gay?" Parks asked. "That would make this a hate crime."

"It would," Jackie began, "if that was why he was killed. I believe he was chosen because he was gay, I don't think he was killed because he was gay."

"Excuse me?" Wilkes said.

"Our killer is complicated. He's thought this out. In great detail.

He's not randomly choosing blonde or obese women or dirty hookers off the street who remind him of his mother or the schoolyard bully. He's killed both male and female. Young and old. Of various races. None of that matters. He's doing this for a reason. There's a purpose to all of this as far as he's concerned. He's sending a message of some sort. Might not make sense to us, but he is. I think in accordance with whatever message he's trying to spread, he's sought out the people who best help spread that message. I think somewhere in there was the need for a gay man. But though he's part of the message, I don't think it was a personal attack because Kyle Oni was gay. If that makes sense."

"Yeah, tell that to the LGBT and whoever else handles this sort of thing," Wilkes snapped.

"Don't worry about them," Hardwick said, storming into the room. "I've got Media Relations handling them. Just make sure you get me everything there is to know about his death so they can properly do that."

"So you're saying he wasn't attacked because he was gay?" Wilkes said. "He just came out a few days ago. And very publicly. Every gay rights group will be all over this."

"And I said I'll handle them. You all stay focused on the case. What's next?"

"They're going to play it off as an unrelated suicide, aren't they?" Parks muttered.

"That's not for you to worry about," Hardwick said. "This case is your only priority. Not what the public believes."

"I don't mean to be racist or anything, but what's the possibility we're looking for a Japanese killer?" Fairmont interjected.

"How so?" Parks asked.

"Well, if the gay themes came from Japan—"

"Actually," Jackie interrupted, "though the gay references regarding the flower are more pronounced in Japanese culture, it is thought that the connection may have started in America and simply worked its way over to Japan. Difference is, over there they're slightly less conservative in regards to these matters, so it's simply more vocalized than what we're used to over here."

"And this is in regards to all gays?" Parks asked.

"If you're asking about men versus women, the flower is more associated with young gay men as opposed to women," Jackie said. "Wakashu, they're called."

"It's an angle," Hardwick said, getting everyone's attention focused once more.

"Agreed," Parks said, standing up. "And so far one of the best ones we've gotten. We may be reading more into this particular type of poison, but it's a start. See if there's any connection between the flower and each of the poisons that's been used so far." Parks looked to Jackie when he said this. "Then see if there's any reason behind these particular poisons being used, period. Maybe someone famous used them in a speech. Maybe some report out there done sometime in the past named all of these poisons for some reason. Check it all."

Jackie nodded, as did most of the others sitting at the table.

"He's punishing these people," Parks said out of nowhere, staring at the murder board.

"What's that?"

"These deaths. These murders. They're painful. There's definitely a reason they're being chosen and killed with the poisons they're being affected with. They're being punished."

"What makes you say that?"

"Take Kyle Oni. When was his death?"

"Tanaka hasn't given us an official time yet, but she thinks early this morning," Jackie said. "Between five and nine am."

"I think it's closer to nine."

"Why's that?"

"Think about it," Parks said. "How did we even find out about Kyle Oni?"

"Because of the phone call," Fairmont shot out.

"And when did that come in?"

Several people began looking through the files in front of them.

"Seven after nine," Parks answered without needing to look. "The killer called saying he'd killed again. The call came from the room where Kyle Oni was staying. He was still there at nine. I don't think he would have called if Oni was still alive for fear of the chance that we could possibly save him. Or get any information from him. So Oni was one hundred percent dead when the killer placed that call. And I don't think he would have stayed around too long after he died. Chances are he died close to nine."

"Why not?" Moore asked.

"What?"

"Why wouldn't the killer have stayed around the death scene a while after the time of death? Some killers like to stay around and be with their victims after they're dead."

"Agreed. But not this guy. He's not in it for the thrill like a strangler or rapist going for the power. He's sending a message. He's doing what he feels he has to do and nothing more. Besides that, like I said, with the passionflower it could take anywhere between fifteen minutes to an hour before the symptoms began to show. Then there's still the time between that and the actual death. Our killer already spent plenty enough time with our victim. It's the process they go through that turns him on, not the end result. Death is simply a side effect. What gets him off is watching them suffer. Pay for their sins, so to speak."

"So you're sticking with that theory?" Hardwick asked.

"We don't know for sure. And any direction is possible. But personally, I would say yes. This is painful, what he's doing. Tortuous. He wants his victims to suffer. And they are. I feel he's delivering a message. I don't know what that is just yet, but I'd say that's exactly what he's doing. He's punishing these people. There is a connection somewhere."

"What do any of the items he's leaving around the crime scenes have to do with that so-called message?" Hardwick asked. "The honey, the bread, the wine and grapes. The three-one-three written in the lipstick? The photograph?"

"Tippin? You find something for me yet?" Parks asked.

"I think I may have," Tippin said, looking up from his computer.

"Go on," Hardwick ordered.

"You're right. Honey. Bread. Three-one-three. The grapes and wine. Individually, they mean nothing. Together, they mean nothing. But then Parks suggested I look at each of the items individually, and in association with poison."

"And?" Parks asked. "What did you find?"

"Quotes. Like famous quotes. I think that's all they are."

"Explain," Hardwick said.

"Let's go in order. Take the honey at the Tisdale scene. 'Deadly poisons are concealed under sweet honey.'"

"That's a famous quote?" Parks asked.

"By a guy named Publius Ovidius Naso Ovid. Yes."

"What was it again?"

"'Deadly poisons are concealed under sweet honey.'"

"I want a copy of that printed and put up on the board next to Allison's information. All right. Next? Three-one-three?"

"Three-one-three, I think, is actually in reference to a Bible verse."

"Son of a bitch," Wilkes cursed.

"Which one?" Parks asked.

"Romans. Chapter three, verse thirteen. 'Their throats are open graves; their tongues practice deceit. The poison of vipers is on their lips.'"

"He was killed by a poisonous snake," Fairmont offered.

Parks nodded at Tippin for him to continue.

"Okay. Bollinger. The bread. Particularly the bread in the sink," Tippin began. "'People who treat other people as less than human must not be surprised when the bread they have cast on the waters comes floating back to them, poisoned.' That was by James Baldwin."

"Print it up too," Parks said nodding toward the murder board. "And last? The wine?"

"'Bacchus, that first from out the purple grape crush'd the sweet poison of misused wine.'"

"Milton," Parks said.

"Yes," Tippin confirmed. "So that's it. At least that's what I think."

"Strong possibility," Parks said. "Something more than nothing. Thanks. Good work, Tippin. What does it mean, though? Something . . . or nothing? We should look into the meaning of the chosen quotes. Maybe there is a reason each one was picked. I mean, the first and last one have no special meanings besides describing the way in which the victims were killed. But the second one focuses on lies and deceit and the third one on being mean to others. Maybe our killer felt those two were liars and abusive, respectively. Something to check. But again, why? Just another way the killer leaves his mark on the scene? Possibly. Though I'm not sure why yet. Maybe he's a former teacher or professor of literature or something. Another angle to check. There's got to be a reason why he's doing this. Fairmont?"

"On it," Fairmont said.

"What about the photograph?" Wilkes asked.

"We don't know who these two girls in the picture are or what their connection to these murders is. Not sure how old this photo is either, but we'll have CSA look over it," Parks said.

"We don't have anything on it?" Wilkes asked. "You just spent the last six months in and out of schools, looking for Kozlov. Anything about these girls correlate anything you can remember from any of the schools? One of them is in a cheerleading uniform. We can't see a name or mascot, but look at the colors on the top of her uniform. Red, gold, and black. Familiar at all?"

Tippin raised his hand to speak, but Parks cut him off.

"I spent the last six months looking for a man attacking elementary school-aged kids," Parks explained. "These two girls are at least in high school. I'm not familiar with which one they come from."

"Fairfax High on Melrose," Tippin interjected, not even bothering with raising his hand this time.

"Say again?" Wilkes barked back.

"Those colors? They're Fairfax High's colors. Crimson, gold, and black."

Wilkes opened his mouth to challenge the kid, but considering

Tippin looked as if he had come from high school only a few months before, chances were he knew what he was talking about.

"Then Fairfax it is." Wilkes smiled slyly. "Have your kid and Hayward work on it. Hayward's my best man when it comes to computers. Bet they can get online and look through past yearbook photos or something."

Parks looked to Tippin, who rolled his eyes but nodded, then looked to Hayward, who appeared amenable to the task.

"Good. As for Oni, we do the usual," Parks said. "Interview the next of kin. Family. Friends. Find the girlfriend and boyfriend, if he had both. Get them all in here. See if they noticed anything out of the ordinary recently. Maybe someone somewhere saw something. Same goes for the paparazzi. We question them as well. They'll be more difficult, as they're basically considered right there next to cockroaches in this town, but we have to just the same. Get what we can out of them. Any way we can. I don't want to find out the identity of our killer because some sleazy paparazzi sold his photos to the highest bidder. Everyone with me?" There were murmurs and nodding but nothing more. "Actually, Wilkes, I know we just talked about your men going over this case from the beginning, but if you could have your team work on the paparazzi, that would be helpful."

"We'll take care of it," Wilkes grunted.

Parks could tell by the man's sagging shoulders and deep breathing how he felt about the extra workload they had just been given, but with Hardwick in the room there wasn't anything he could say about it. Most likely Wilkes would retaliate at some time later, when Hardwick wasn't around. Parks didn't exactly like that idea, but as it was, his team was spread thin and everyone was worn out. He'd just have to see where the chips fell and deal with what was what from there. What he failed to realize was that Wilkes was actually charged for the first time since being assigned this case. He felt they had a solid lead to work on and he liked progress. Especially if it made him look good.

"All right, everybody. Let's get to work," Parks said, dismissing the table.

"Parks," Hardwick called out.

"Yes?"

"I hope you don't mind, but in light of keeping outside resources out of this mess as long as possible, I've asked for Dr. Black to take a look at the murder book and give us some insight as to who we should be looking at. Profile-wise, I mean."

Parks was surprised it had taken this long for Hardwick to involve the department shrink, considering he was the closest thing they had to a forensic profiler to help out with cases. As it was, Dr. Black was mostly around to make sure everyone in the department was stable enough to handle a gun, but perhaps he could contribute something useful.

"I'll make sure he gets a copy of the murder book," Parks said, smiling in agreement.

"He already has one," Hardwick said, turning from her lead detective. "He'll be down in an hour to go over his notes with you."

23

"He's showing off," Dr. Black said as he stood in front of the murder board, staring up at the physical evidence that was taped and tacked all over the white board. Dr. Lucas Black had been with the department for over a decade now, though physically he looked to be no older than his late thirties or early forties. He had wild, shaggy hair that gave him an earthy, inviting touch while also having the feel of professionalism. The glasses he was prescribed only added to his attractiveness, enlarging his already round, owl-like, hazel eyes.

"He's saying, 'Look how good I am. You want to catch me? Then you better be better than me. Otherwise, you don't deserve to catch me.' He's making a statement. Making himself feel better about what he's doing so that if he's ever caught he can say, 'Look how good I was. It took a lot to catch me. I'm that good.'" Black had a gravely if not soothing quality to his voice that could either calm a person or drive them crazy, depending on whether they were a friend, co-worker or patient.

"This guy's sick," was all Parks could think to say.

"He's made these murders into something of an art show for

241

himself."

"How so?"

"Look," Black said, pointing to the various photos of the five murder scenes plastered up on the murder boards. "Take the first one. Allison Tisdale."

"Yes."

"All alone. In a solid-white room. The only other color in here is the purple flowers and the circle of the victim's blood. That's serious. This is a work of art. I bet you anything, both her blood and the flowers mean something."

"Why's that?"

"Everything else in the room blends together. Blur your vision and look at this photo. The only thing you see is the bouquet of flowers in the center of a circle. That's not by accident. This guy did that on purpose. Those flowers mean something. Everything he leaves behind, everything he takes with him, what he touches, what he does in this room, everything has one thing in common: our killer and the crime he committed. They all lead back to him. Why? To the killer himself, everything about this room serves a purpose. Why he chose this place. This room in the house. This victim. The dress she was found in. Why she was dressed as opposed to found nude. The flowers. Her hair. The scent of her. The poison he used to kill her. The chair she's in. The pills found in her pockets. Everything. It's all part of the reason he killed this victim the way he did and it all leads back to him."

Parks made a note of this on his notepad. "And victim two?"

"This guy's different," Black continued, referring to Ian Harris. "He's not posed. This crime scene is different. It's messy. Chaotic. Painful. Bloody. Look at all that blood. I take it whatever he was poisoned with focused on the eyes mostly?"

"Yes."

"That was done on purpose too. Maybe the victim saw something he shouldn't have."

"We've considered that. He spied on the neighbors across the courtyard. The wife mostly. But the wife's husband was victim number three. Killed earlier the same day."

"I would almost say Ian Harris was an accident," Black said. "He witnessed the third murder, which was actually the second murder chronologically, and therefore he was taken out."

"Couldn't be," Parks argued. "He had to be planned too. The way he was poisoned took time and premeditation. He was mailed a bottle of vodka that was mixed with methanol and then someone hand-delivered a package that contained a poisonous snake. This killing wasn't some last-minute break-in or jealous rage of passion. No one suddenly decided to stab him with a needle full of poison." Parks thought about this. "Maybe the killer knew Harris spied on the wife, and so he knew there was a chance he might be seen killing the husband?"

"So then why such a mess?" Black asked mostly to himself. "Why not staged and posed like Allison Tisdale and Jason Bollinger? Unless the chaos of the crime scene is the way the killer wanted him posed. Look at Bollinger. He's sitting alone in his kitchen, holding this fish. Is the fish what killed him?"

"Nope. More of a tease, beforehand, to the next murder. Like a link."

"See, but Jason Bollinger is posed again like Allison Tisdale. Holding that fish in his hands. He's showing off. Why did he change for Ian Harris? Why not move the body like the others? Why not have him sitting up for all to see when they first entered his loft? Why leave him slumped over, face down, in a puddle of his own blood? Was he not as worthy as the other victims? What's the difference between him and the others?"

"Maybe the killer was interrupted? Or ran out of time?"

"I'd check with everyone in his building."

"We have."

"Do it again. Someone knows something they're not saying. There's a reason the killer didn't mess with Ian Harris's body. Then again, you found him before Jason Bollinger, even though they were killed in reverse order. Was the order in which they were killed and the order in which they were discovered switched on purpose? I'd say most likely. Our guy knows what he's doing. I wouldn't take anything for granted. Everything he's done so far has been according to plan. Make no mistake about that."

"Maybe there was a more personal reason for Harris?"

"Possibly, but you and I both know that the killer's not touching or moving Harris's body actually makes his murder seem less personal," Dr. Black said. "Then victim four. Charles Wyler. Everyone watching TV saw that attack. That was public."

"But Wyler's murder wasn't staged."

"Not like one and three, with the bodies posed in death, but still staged. Theatrical. The killer lured Wyler to that location on purpose."

"Giving purpose to the fish. If we would have seen the fish earlier we could have saved him. Wyler was on the air for over ten minutes before the attack. If we would have seen it right away we could have saved him. Maybe."

"He gave you the opportunity to do that. But with the poison that was used on Wyler, was there really any chance of saving him?"

Parks thought about this. "Most likely not. He was already being poisoned for a few days through his water supply."

"And the killer knew that. He wasn't calling you there to see if you were good enough to save him. He called you there to throw it in your face. He's saying, 'It doesn't matter how close you get to me, there's nothing you can do to save these people. I've already chosen them all, and there's nothing you can do to stop me. I'm on a mission, and I'll finish when I choose to. Be in awe.'"

"Dammit."

"And five?"

"Kyle Oni."

Dr. Black focused on Kyle Oni's crime scene photos on the murder board.

"This goes right back to Tisdale and Bollinger. Oni's posed. And look at the flowers. It's like victim one. And the vines coming off from the body are circular like the circle of blood from victim one. Were any of these people killed in their homes?"

"Just two and three. Harris and Bollinger."

"Anyone else live with those two victims?"

"Just Bollinger. The one whose wife was spied on."

"Has she seen these photos?"

"No. We've taken her back to the crime scene and she said nothing was out of place."

"Show her these," Dr. Black insisted. "It's harsh but necessary. Something's been moved. Posed. Just like the victim. Most likely it was moved between the time the body was discovered, when these photos were taken, the time when the room was cleaned up for the wife's return. I'm telling you, I know it will be hard, but show her these. There has to be something there. The first and fifth crime scenes are too well cleaned up and posed. They're perfect. He had to have done the same for this one as well. Only two and four were chaotic, messy. But possibly that was done on purpose. Perhaps he didn't like victims two or four. He had no respect for them. It was as if they had to be killed instead of him wanting to kill them." Dr. Black paused and perused his notes some more. "There's a reason he's killing all of these people. He's trying to fulfill a fantasy that one victim hasn't satisfied. As I suggested, he's probably sending a message. If so, then us not knowing what it is based off the first few victims, will only fuel him to keep killing. And he'll keep doing so until you figure out what he's trying to say. There's a purpose to all of this." Dr. Black paused again, this time lost in thought. "Of course, it could be that it's not about a message at all. Maybe he's trying to exercise a demon of his own, and by taking the first life he had hoped to take care of that problem. It didn't work."

"How can you tell?"

"Because he's still killing. If the first victim had solved his problem, then you wouldn't have more victims beyond her."

Dr. Black stood silent and composed, staring at the board. He turned back to the murder book and flipped through several pages before looking back to the board.

"What's the date of the first murder?"

"August thirty-first. It was a Wednesday."

"And the second?"

"Victims two and three were killed on Labor Day. September fifth. Monday. Then Charles was on Saturday the tenth. And Kyle Oni just today. There was a clump of them and then he took a break before getting to Oni."

"Two and three were on the same day. Only you didn't find Jason Bollinger's body until two days later on the seventh of September. So that changes things. If we take that into account, then there could be a pattern the killer uses to claim his victims. Maybe not. Maybe it's all just a coincidence. But I think it means something."

"What? What is it?" Parks asked as he noticed Wilkes walking into the room, drinking Coke from a can. He was one of the people in the department who never got along with the shrink, and he kept quiet, standing off in the corner.

"He's killing people five days apart from each other. On the thirty-first you have Allison Tisdale. Five days later, on the fifth, you get Jason Bollinger and Ian Harris. Five days later, on the tenth, you have Charles Wyler. Five days later, Kyle Oni."

"So then the next murder . . ."

"Tuesday," Dr. Black said, finishing his thought. "You have until Tuesday to stop this guy from killing again."

"We make any progress?" Fairmont called out, walking into the conference room, unwrapping a piece of Nicorette.

"And what if he does kill on Tuesday and we don't stop him?" Wilkes asked.

"Then your next deadline is the following Sunday, and then the Friday after that, which is the thirtieth," Dr. Black answered bluntly.

Though it was late and the team had had a full day, everyone was more charged by the new developments than from all the caffeine they had been drinking. They had something. They could do it if they focused. This could be all over come Tuesday night.

"Thanks, Doctor. You've been a help," Parks said.

"No problem," Dr. Black said, picking up the copy of the murder book. "This was just a quick assessment. If you want, I can keep reading and give you a more detailed analysis."

"Anything you can do to help." Parks said as Dr. Black left the room. "Anything at all."

"I'll type out my findings and have them to you by the end of the day."

24

"We got him," Hardwick said standing in front of Parks and his and Wilkes's entire team, as well as numerous other members of the LAPD. "We not only found and arrested Victor Kozlov but in the process of interrogation and, maybe a little strong-armed cohesion, have sealed a deal with the two Kozlov brothers that will see them being locked up, in a maximum state facility no less, for the rest of their natural lives."

"Without a trial?" Fairmont asked.

"No trial. No more publicity. No chance of parole. Lock. Stock. And fucking barrel." Hardwick was grinning from ear to ear as everyone else cheered. Parks could feel a release from within his entire body, as if he had been holding his breath ever since he had first heard the name Kozlov. He almost felt himself physically collapse as he leaned back in his chair. People were patting Parks on his back and shaking is hand as they congratulated him.

"That's right," Hardwick said, walking up to him and offering a hand. "Ladies and gentlemen, it's been a long and bumpy road, but we have succeeded. Let it be known the LAPD never gives up. And we have this man to thank for getting that piece of scum shit off the streets of LA. You all better be buying him drinks when you see him out and about. This is good work. Honest work. Parks, you, and everyone else in the department, should be damn proud."

As the rest of the department continued to celebrate, Hardwick pulled Parks aside.

"I don't care what you do. Go out and get blind drunk. Call up a friend. Go to a movie. Get laid. Go to sleep for the next twenty-four hours. Anything. Just make sure it's fun. You've earned it. We've had a lot of shit lately. This is a win. We accept and celebrate our wins for they are few. Tomorrow's another day and we still have the Palisades Poisoner out there. But for today, tonight, whatever, you celebrate. You go out and wash your mind, body and spirit of Kozlov. I know he's been eating away at you and now it can stop. Time to hit the rest button and start afresh. Tomorrow, you show up, you're going to look at the Poisoner case with whole new eyes. I can feel it. Now get out of here. Go celebrate. And Parks . . . be happy."

*   *   *

"Someone's gonna be late . . ." Jackie said, teasing her son who was rushing throughout the house looking for scattered items that he refused to tell his mother about. Parks thought it was only because he was there and the kid didn't want to look dependent in front of him. Parks stared at Jackie with a face that could have said anything from leave the kid alone to what's he looking for? "I think he's going out on a date tonight and he's having trouble finding the con—"

"Mom!" Ricky shouted from the neighboring room.

"You do realize you're probably not doing our new-found relationship any favors by embarrassing him in front of me, right?" Parks was trying to hold back laughter.

"Oh, he's my son and I'm his mother," Jackie said, waving Parks's comment away. "It's my job to occasionally embarrass him. He wouldn't remember who I was in the scheme of things if I didn't."

Parks was wondering what they were waiting for, simply sitting at the kitchen table, staring at one another. After having heard about Kozlov he realized there was no where he would rather be. No one he would rather celebrate this victory with. "Are we waiting for him to leave before we start doing something in particular?"

"Well, I'm waiting to rip your clothes off," Jackie said, not the least bit embarrassed. "But I figure I should at least wait until Ricky leaves for that. Figure my son can only handle so much shame from his mother."

"Mo-om!"

"Would you like a drink?" Jackie offered.

"I think I'm going to have to insist," Parks said, the eagerness to change the subject displayed across his face.

Jackie got up and began retrieving items from the refrigerator as she cut limes and salted the rims of two glasses.

"Rocks? Salt?" Jackie asked, holding up a glass. Parks nodded. "I figure while we have this glorious day that we'd head out to the yard, sit back, enjoy some margaritas, and soak in the sun. Relax. Nice conversation. Just . . . take it easy. Even if only for an hour."

"Sounds good to me," Parks said, agreeing.

"I mean I don't get why my son gets to be the only one having sex, but whatever," Jackie said, smiling.

"Mo-*om!* Stop it!"

Parks could hear footsteps stomping across the floor above him.

"You just couldn't help yourself, could you?" Parks asked, shaking his head.

"What? I'm his mother," Jackie said, pouring the two drinks into their respective glasses. "Ready?"

"Yes. Please. Thank you," Parks said standing up and taking his drink from Jackie.

Ricky came into the kitchen, a gym bag over his shoulder, finally prepared for whatever adventures he had planned for that evening.

"And where are we off to?" Jackie asked.

"School," Ricky replied, not wanting to elaborate in front of Parks.

"See that?" Jackie said turning to Parks. "You raise them to love you and when they're older they turn on you."

"It's Village of the Damned unleashed," Parks said, smiling.

"I'm going out with some friends from school," Ricky replied, practically rolling his eyes. "How is that turning on you? Besides, I'm a grown man, mom." Jackie simply stared at her son, the look of pride and enjoying torturing him apparent on her face. "You're just messing with me, aren't you?"

"Go have fun," Jackie said, answering him. "You're young. Go get wild. Not too wild. Have fun. But not too much fun. And remember, you can call me anytime from any place. I'll be there, right?"

"Right," Ricky said giving his mother a hug and a kiss. Ricky caught Parks's eye line on his way out. "Sure you're up for this?"

"Whoa, whoa, whoa," Jackie said, being purposely melodramatic. "Did my son and the man I plan on spending some time with just gang up on me? What's going on here? My own flesh and blood turning on me. I think it's time you left. And before I kick you out permanently."

"Oh, mom," Ricky called back.

"Don't you 'oh, mom' me. Oh, make sure you have on clean underwear, honey," Jackie said, harassing her son, calling after him as he walked for the front door.

"Mo-*om!*"

"See? They turn on you." The front door opened and closed. Jackie turned back to Parks. "Trust me, if you ever have any of your own, you have to do that to them. Was it just me or did my son kinda just have a semi-bonding, not totally hostile moment with you?"

"I, uh—" Before Parks could spoil her moment Jackie threw her arms around his neck and kissed him.

"Let's take this outside," Jackie said.

"But what would your neighbors say?" Parks asked.

"Screw em," Jackie said, laughing. "I don't care. I meant your drink, silly."

Jackie playfully punched Parks on the shoulder then grabbed her drink and headed out back to the patio area. There was a little patch of grass beyond the cement deck before the waters of the surrounding canals began. Each of them took a white, plastic lounge chair and relaxed.

"If you need to talk about it—about him—now's your chance. I'll let you. But I want you to get it all out. Now. Kozlov is captured and going away. That's a good thing. But I don't want him haunting every minute we have together. So speak now or . . . you know the rest."

Parks stared at her, took everything about her in, before turning and staring out across at the canals. There was nothing more he needed to say. She was right. He would not let that man haunt him any longer.

"I love it out here," Jackie said, soaking in the ambiance.

"How'd you end up here?" Parks said, taking a sip of his drink.

"Well my mother's from Mexico City," Jackie began. "Father was Italian-Irish. Gee, I wonder which heritage prevailed in me?" Jackie twirled her hair through her fingers. "Her family migrated up here. He was already living here. Had left home back in Chicago when he was eighteen. They met, fell in love. And a year later out popped me."

"Happily ever after?"

"Not quite," Jackie admitted. "I mean my parents divorced. Like most everyone else's. They remained civil. All things considering. Mother stayed here and father moved back east. Got remarried."

"Ohhh, there's an evil step-monster?"

"No. not really. Honestly I think I love my step-mother more than my father. But I never said that out loud." Jackie smiled. "I think my father remarrying was one of the best things he could have ever done. He's not the most . . . humane person. Or the most personable person. I think she's helped bring that part of him out. He's still distant but at least he tries to make an effort every now and again. We're fine. Mostly cards. Phone calls once or twice a year. It's my mother I was always close to growing up."

"She helped you with raising Ricky?"

"She did," Jackie said, taking another swallow of her own drink. "She was my rock. Couldn't have done it without her."

"Surprised she doesn't live here with you still . . . ?" Parks was fishing and she could tell.

"Oh, she's still alive and kicking. Lives back down south near Baja or even more south I think. She keeps on migrating south. Lives on the coast. Gorgeous views. She loves it there. Closer to her family. All that. I get down there to visit a few times a year. Bring Ricky with me. We love it down there. She gets up here to see me all the time as well. We're still close. Trust me, you don't want to see our phone bills. She's probably my best friend. I didn't have a lot of those growing up but my mother was defiantly one of them."

"Even during your rebellion phase?" Jackie eyed Parks, wondering what he was talking about. "I thought Ricky was the result of . . ."

"Oh, that. Yeah," Jackie said, chuckling. "Not much of a rebellion phase. That was mostly against my father. My mother I still went too. Even during all of that. My father never accepted Ricky. That's part of what put a rift between us. Ricky's my son. My father didn't care."

"And Ricky's father?"

"Just some guy," Jackie admitted. "I mean he was more than that. I knew the guy. He wasn't some one night stand. We were together almost a year. Surprisingly, as much as I started dating him as a way to piss my father off he was actually a descent guy."

"Until Ricky came along?"

"No. No. I mean he would have done the 'right' thing. Whatever that would have been He would have married me. Or supported me financially. He did actually. For a while. He was there when I needed him to be. But being a father wasn't one of his strongest suits. See, he never had a good relationship with his own father. Actually his father was a bastard. And he was always scared of turning out the same way with his own children. So he swore he would never have any. I don't think he would have been a bad father. He would have stumbled, that's for sure. But not a bad father. But I understand his fear. That is a lot of responsibility to take on. And his father was a bad man. I can understand being scared of passing that on to another generation. And while it might not always be valid, I think it takes a lot to admit you might not be what's best for a child's future. Takes a lot to give up your parental rights for the greater good of the child."

"Sure that's what he did?"

"He didn't bail," Jackie said, firmly. "I mean that. Ricky's father was around when I needed him. But as far as Ricky's concerned it's just him and me. And I was good with that. Ricky's had his ups and downs about it but I feel he's made peace with it. He understands. Might not always agree with it, or like it, but he understands. I think part of the reason I was okay with Ricky's father not sticking around had something to do with my issues with my own father. " Jackie paused, as if deciding to admit something or not. "Truth is I say I'm fine with the way things were, and considering how they turned out, how can I not be? But there isn't a day that doesn't go by that I don't think I screwed up my son somehow. I've been told that's the same of all parents, regardless of the conditions. I'd like to think things turned out all right. Ricky's in college. Going to have a bright future ahead of him. But somehow I just keep waiting for the ball to drop and reality to hit me that I screwed him up somehow and every-thing's going to turn to shit."

"You can't be the only parent to have those concerns."

"I'm sure I'm not. Sorry to get maudlin on you."

"Well then, what about you?"

"Me? Oh, me, me. Oh, you know me. I'm a bucket of laughs. Truth is I don't always connect with people. I think that's why I got into the field I'm in. Keeps me segregated from everyone else. I get to work alone a lot. I like it like that to be honest. I work best by myself. Growing up I was such a bookworm. A total nerd. Then I had Ricky, got into college, and I blossomed. Decided to get out and see what the world had to offer. "

"Yeah, I understand that," Parks said, agreeing.

"You know, you're not as damaged as everyone would like to make you out to be," Jackie said, eyeing him.

"Oh? And who says I'm damaged? And why would they?"

"Oh, I hear the talk around the station. Everyone's got their own opinions. You're a man of mystery in some ways. They're a little concerned about you after Kozlov. And with losing your partner. But you seem to be holding it all together to me. Then there's your broken childhood. A mother who's not around? And a dead father? I think they're all waiting around for you to have a breakdown or something."

"That's what I don't get," Parks admitted, almost laughing about it. "I didn't have a traumatic childhood. At least not as far as I can remember. Maybe that's why I'm so mellow about it. My father died when I was like four. But I barely recall any of the circumstances revolving around it. Why he did it? Was he depressed? Running from something? Exhausted? What? My mother was no help after my father committed suicide. She was never around after that. Has almost never been around my whole life. But I was raised by her sister and brother-in-law in Newport Beach. I mean, it wasn't exactly a lacking childhood. They had money. Clout. Treated me like their own. Never made me feel like an outsider. I went from being an only child to having a brother. I was never lacking growing up. Sure I was a bit of a loner, probably spawning from my immediate family's circumstances, but I wasn't some off the wall wild-child. Did baseball in high school. Was semi-popular, if I do say so myself. Especially considering I wasn't really outgoing. Dated. Was nominated for Prom King. Lost both Junior and Senior years. Had a memorable time those four years though. Got married. That didn't last. That was probably the most traumatic experience in my whole life. I was bitter after that. Real bitter. But I was never self-destructive or anything like that. I joined the force, found focus and direction. And . . . just been living my life for the last fifteen years. I date here and there. I've had a few serious girlfriends, but nothing worth proposing my undying and eternal love for. I'm a bachelor, probably for life, and that suits me just fine. I like where I'm at in life and see no reason for any major changes. Not that I'm not open to them if something right was to come along, but I see no reason for it. I'm good. There are far more people a lot worse off than me."

"Right? Amen to that."

"So I've got some tics and whatnot. Who doesn't? I'm not out committing crimes or hurting myself or anyone else. I feel I'm pretty well grounded. Why do I need to be flawed and damaged goods?"

"Hey, don't look at me," Jackie said finishing off her drink and setting it aside. "I think you're good just the way you are."

"Do you now?"

Jackie got up and moved over and sat down in Parks's lap. She leaned in and began to kiss him.

"I do. And just so you don't question me, let me prove it to you."

Jackie slid into the chair and Parks's arm, the two of them laying there, kissing as they relaxed and took in all that was around them. This, to the two of them, at that moment, was paradise.

And both of them wondered how long it would really last.

25

"Parks. Parks!"

"What is it?" Parks shouted, looking up from the iPad he was playing brain teaser games on. He was testing his memory skills, his logic skills, and just plain playing games and forgetting the rest of the world for a few minutes. He had been in a much better mood since the Kozlov ordeal was finalized. He could move on. Was determined to. He had even slept good, through the entire night.

"The pack—what are you . . .?" Parks made a face that encouraged Fairmont to continue with what he was there to discuss.

"Um, yeah. That package . . . that was . . . that was delivered to Ian Harris," Fairmont said, almost out of breath. "The one . . . that held . . . the death adder? With . . . the prints on it? Remember?"

Good thing he's trying to quit smoking, thought Parks. "You mean the prints that we didn't get a hit on? What about it?"

"I have a match."

Fairmont smiled from ear to ear.

"How?" Parks was genuinely shocked by this information. "We ran them through IAFIS. We didn't get anything."

"I know," Fairmont said. "But I had a hunch, and I had them run against everyone else connected with this case. Maybe someone who didn't have prints on record with IAFIS."

"And? Who did they match?"

"Deborah Bollinger."

"The third victim's wife?" Parks wasn't expecting this.

"The one and only." Fairmont was excited. "So now what?"

"Now?" Parks said. "Now we go have a chat with the widow Bollinger."

*   *   *

"Deborah Bollinger," Parks shouted through the closed door. "LAPD."

Parks knocked forcefully on the door to the Bollinger's apartment and waited with Moore and Fairmont at his side. He went to knock again when the door opened. Mrs. Bollinger appeared as if she was still accepting the fact that her husband was never coming home again. She wore sweats, and her greasy, matted hair was down, giving the appearance of having been untouched for the past few days. She was without makeup and looked like she'd been doing her fair share of crying, her eyes all puffy and red, aging her a decade. The look on her face was anything but welcoming to the detectives.

"Detectives," Mrs. Bollinger said, recognizing Moore and Fairmont. "What is it?"

"I'm Detective Dave Parks," Parks explained. "We have a few questions for you."

She hesitated for a moment, huffed mostly for show, took a swallow of whatever alcoholic beverage was in the short glass she held, and let them in. She didn't walk to the couch so much as moped her way to it before plopping down, staring at the coffee table in front of her as if remembering a moment from her life before her husband had been murdered. She uttered a short laugh then made a face as if deciding whether she should cry or not.

"I'm supposed to be planning a funeral. Though with what money, I don't know."

"We wondered if you were familiar with this person," Parks said, holding up a picture of Ian Harris. Mrs. Bollinger stared at the picture, puzzled, as if she knew the face but couldn't place how or why, before taking another swallow of her drink.

"Who is he?"

"Have you seen this man before?"

"No. No, I don't think so."

Parks stalled as he thought of the best way to advance the interrogation now that he had caught the woman in a lie.

"But he . . . he does look familiar. But I can't tell why."

"His name is Ian Harris," Parks said, pausing to see if the name struck a bell with her.

Mrs. Bollinger shook her head. She couldn't place him.

"He lived across the courtyard," Parks said, nodding toward the windows behind her. "He—"

"Lived? You mean he's dead? Was he another victim of the same person who killed my husband?"

"We're not at liberty to discuss an ongoing investigation. We—"

"Oh!" Mrs. Bollinger threw up her hands. "Oh. Oh. Across the courtyard. That's where. Yes. I-I-I do know him. I mean, I don't know him, but I met him. Just once. The day my husband died."

"Yes?" Parks sat up on the edge of his seat while Fairmont and Moore who had been pacing behind him, stopped and leaned in to hear what she had to say.

"When I was going to leave, to go see my family, I noticed a package on our doorstep. But it didn't have mine or my husband's name or address on it. It had that other man's on it."

"Ian Harris."

"Yeah. I saw the address was just next door, so I decided to drop it off on my way out of town."

"So you took it to Mr. Harris?"

"Yes."

"And what time would that have been?"

"Early afternoonish. Around twelve thirty. Maybe one. But I think earlier than that."

"Did you speak to Mr. Harris?"

"Yes," Mrs. Bollinger admitted. "When I handed him the package."

"Did you notice anything out of the ordinary about Mr. Harris?"

"How would I know what was out of the ordinary for him? That was the first time I had met him. But he was drunk."

"Drunk?"

"Yes. Really drunk. He slurred his words and could hardly stand. He tried to cover it up, but it was obvious. Place reeked of booze."

"The methanol," Moore muttered to Parks.

"There was something else actually," Mrs. Bollinger continued. "He seemed . . . oh, um, I don't know. Ashamed."

Parks thought about this.

"Spying," Fairmont mouthed to Moore, who nodded back.

"Ashamed?" Parks asked.

"Sorta. Like I had caught him doing something he shouldn't have been doing. But I'd never met him before. So how would I know what he should or shouldn't be doing? Anyways, that's how he acted. Caught. Didn't say much of anything. Just took the package and that was it."

"And this package . . . you don't know where it came from?"

"No idea."

"You looked at it?"

"At it, yes. Not in it. No idea who it was from. It didn't say on the box. Just the delivery address. So I took it over there."

"Thank you for your time. There is one other thing, if I may. I need you to look at some photos."

"Photos?"

"Yes. They're of your husband's death scene. I've had the portions of his body blocked out, but I need you to focus on the rest of the scene. Around him. See if you notice something out of place."

"Dave," Moore muttered. "What are you doing?"

Parks ignored his associates. "If you're not up to it, I understand Mrs. Bollinger. But it would really help us."

"Help you catch the man who did this to my husband?"

"It could."

Deborah Bollinger turned and stared out a nearby window and didn't say a word. She appeared lost, confused, more frail than Parks figured the woman usually was. He was about to stand up and leave when she turned back to him.

"Okay," Mrs. Bollinger replied, finishing off her drink, the ice clinking against the side of the glass. "Show them to me."

Parks retrieved the pictures and handed them over and let the grieving woman look through them. The area where her husband's body was supposed to be in each photo was blacked out so that she wouldn't have to look at him. As much as it was there to help, it didn't, and Mrs. Bollinger began crying at the sights displayed before her, as she knew her husband was still in them, sitting there, lifeless.

"There's . . . nothing," Mrs. Bollinger finally said. "Nothing. I don't see anything."

She held the photos in front of her and stared at them without even looking at them while they rested limply in her hands, the last connection she had with her deceased husband. Parks knew when he was defeated, and this exercise, though a good intention, proved fruitless.

"I'm sorry to have taken your time," Parks said as he stood up and reached to take the photos.

As he grabbed the pictures, Mrs. Bollinger's grip on them tightened and she pulled them in closer, focusing on them for the first time. She looked to the kitchen then back at the photo. "Did your people remove anything from the apartment?"

"I'm sure some things were removed that the body touched or when we dusted for fingerprints," Parks explained. "We have a log list." Parks motioned to Fairmont. "What in particular have you noticed?"

"A baseball," Mrs. Bollinger said, pointing to a five-shelved stand next to the kitchen table. On the shelves in the stand were various knickknacks and mementos. Glass figurines of animals were spread throughout each shelf, while photo frames were filled with the generic pictures that had originally come with the frames.

"A baseball?"

"It was special. To my husband. It was a signed baseball that he had up on the . . . the . . . over there. It's not there. It was always right there. I know it was there the day I left."

Fairmont shook his head from side to side as he glanced through the log list.

"Nothing here about a baseball," Fairmont said. "Plus, we didn't take anything on those shelves, so there's no reason we would have taken just the baseball."

"Now this baseball, you said it was special?" Parks asked.

"Yeah, I guess so," Mrs. Bollinger said. "At least to my husband it was. It was signed."

"Signed? By whom?"

"A baseball player." Mrs. Bollinger shrugged.

"Yes." Parks smiled, trying to keep his patience. "Do you know who? Was it from—"

"Yes," Mrs. Bollinger interrupted. "It was the Dodgers. I remember that. Jason loved the Dodgers. Only team he would watch on TV. We have—well, used to have, season tickets."

"Do you remember who? Or when?"

"It was late spring or early summer. Just this year," Mrs. Bollinger recalled immediately. "I remember that because we saw him out with his girlfriend, and I remember her because she's that actress that everyone loves. I don't remember the guy's name. But he was cute. That much I know. It was a short name. And foreign. Not his first name. His last name. But then again, most of the players these days are foreign."

"Does the name Kyle Oni sound familiar?"

"I'm sorry. All those names sound the same to me."

Parks turned to Fairmont. "Tell me we have a picture of Oni on us?"

Fairmont dug through a folder and shook his head.

"Mrs. Bollinger," Parks broke in. "Do you perchance receive the LA Times?"

"Um . . . yes," Mrs. Bollinger answered. "Why?"

"Do you happen to have a few copies lying around?"

"There's a recycling bin in the kitchen."

Moore left for the kitchen and, after some rummaging, came back with the Sports section from a few days before, when Kyle Oni's face was plastered all over for his coming-out story.

"Is this the guy?" Moore asked, holding up the paper.

"Looks like him." Mrs. Bollinger said, not entirely sure.

"He's dating Caroline Maddox."

"Yes," Mrs. Bollinger finally said emphatically. "That's her. That's the girl. I remember. People say I look like her. Like I could be her sister or something. Even though she's a redhead and I'm blonde."

"Thank you," Parks said, hoping his skepticism didn't show. "Thank you so much. That helps us a lot. Thanks."

Parks stood and turned when Moore pulled in closer to him.

"How exactly does that help us?"

"Not sure," Parks admitted. "But at least we're finding some kind of a connection."

26

"So what do we have, ladies and gentlemen?" Parks asked as he rubbed the several days' growth that he could have sworn he had shaved off just that morning. "It's Tuesday morning. This is it. If he's working according to schedule, then today's the day. Anything?"

Parks looked around the conference room and saw nothing but blank faces staring back at him. With sunken eyes, disheveled clothes, and unkempt hair, the entire team looked as they had slept at the station over the past weekend. Tempers flared and nerves were short. Detectives Wilkes and Ramirez were in court testifying that morning, leaving only Detective Hayward to help.

"Well, Oni kept his sexuality hidden from most everyone pretty well," Moore spoke up. "According to his manager, agent, coach, lawyers—all of whom we spent all weekend tracking down and interviewing—no one had any idea that he was gay. Not even his family. Before he came out publicly, that is."

"What about the girlfriend?" Fairmont asked.

"She's been in Florida filming a movie for the past few months," Parks explained. "She just flew in last night. We've got an appointment with her this morning. See if maybe she can't help us. What about a boyfriend?"

"He's some lawyer who's been out of the country since before Oni's coming-out announcement," Moore said, coming alive. "We've talked with him on the phone, and he's agreed to come in for a formal interview once he gets back into town. But he's clueless as far as we can tell."

"Stick with it," Parks ordered. "Okay, look. I know we're all tired here, but this is it. The last," Parks looked at his watch, "fifteen hours if he's going to do this today. Okay? You can all have tomorrow off to do as you please, if we just do our jobs today. Jackie?"

"What's up?"

"Poisons."

"Yes?"

"Have anything for us? Anything special about what he's using? The order he's using them in? Why them?"

"I have a new report on the passionflower but nothing substantial. There's no rhyme or reason to why he's picking what he's picking. At least as far as I can see. You'd think we'd have enough based on this many victims but really, no idea. Nothing. These murders are so sporadic the only pattern is that there is no pattern to them at all."

"None that we can see, but there's always a pattern," Parks said. "Okay, I know I'm swamping Milo with work, so see if you can use Hayward a little."

"Will do," Jackie said.

"Anything on the girls in the picture?"

"We're scanning through yearbook photos," Tippin said. "But we've got years to go through and we don't really have a starting point based on that photo. That photo could be from this year or a decade or two ago. So . . . still working on it."

"Good. Thanks. Keep on it," Parks said. "Oh, anything on the homeless man who attacked Wyler?"

"Still no sign of him," Fairmont admitted. "Maybe he wasn't a homeless person. Maybe he was our killer in disguise?"

"Well, keep checking out the video footage of the attack," Parks suggested. "See if we can't get something from it."

"We're on it."

"Okay, Rachel, let's go. Time to visit this girlfriend of Kyle's and see what all she knows."

*   *   *

Parks pulled up to the valet area of the Chateau Marmont just off Sunset Boulevard and handed over his keys. Parks and Moore made their way to the front desk area and, after a few minutes of explaining who they were and that they were legitimately there on official police business, were finally given the room number for Caroline Maddox's two-bedroom penthouse suite.

Parks knocked and waited patiently, knowing his patience was more than going to be tested with this visit. He had done several interviews with celebrities, and while most were more than accommodating, there were the few who thought they walked on water. Based on the few articles and YouTube videos that Tippin had pulled for him, Parks figured he had his work cut out for him.

The door was finally answered and Caroline Maddox stood there with a smile on her face, though for just the briefest of moments Parks could have sworn he saw disdain. She was one of the few actresses who were just as beautiful in real life as they were up on the big screen with makeup and computer effects in full overload.

"Caroline Maddox?" Parks asked.

"Yes," Caroline answered.

"I'm Detective Dave Parks and this is Detective Rachel Moore of the LAPD," Parks announced, both of them flashing their badges. "We have a few questions for you regarding Kyle Oni."

"My people said you were coming. Come in." Caroline smiled and stepped back to allow room for the two detectives to enter. "Uh, in there." She pointed down the hallway to the living room and closed the door, only to have someone knock on it not a second later. "Are there more of you?"

"No," Parks replied, instinctively going for his gun.

"I, um . . ." Caroline opened the door and beamed. "Oh, I'm so stupid. I forgot I ordered this. That was like two hours ago." Caroline stood back and a man pushing a cart with her lunch on it stepped into the hallway and made his way down into the dining room. "Oh, not in there. In the living room, please. Thanks. I have some stuff to go over with my guests. Thank you. Oh, um . . ." She looked up at the two detectives then around the room, trying to figure out what to do with her lunch.

"You go ahead," Parks said. "We don't mind. We just have a few questions for you anyway. We shouldn't be long."

"Thanks," Caroline replied as she turned to the doorman. "Just over there."

She pointed to a coffee table and then tipped the man before he left the room. She closed the door behind him, locked it, and walked back into the living room and sat down at the table.

"Would you like some?" Caroline asked as she took the lid off the plate to reveal a radish and butter lettuce salad with Chianti vinegar dressing on the side. "There's plenty."

"Thanks," Parks said. "But we're fine. Do you mind?"

"No, no. Go ahead. I know my lawyer said he wanted to be here for this, and he's on his way, I believe, but I don't see why we can't begin? I mean this is just routine questions about Kyle, right?" Caroline focused on the salad and began preparing it, removing a few unwanted items and tossing in the dressing.

"Right. More or less. You're not a suspect or anything like that."

"God, I hope not," Caroline said with laughter. "What do you want to know?"

"Particularly if you knew or know anything about Kyle Oni's . . . other life," Parks said, hoping he wouldn't offend the woman.

"You mean about his gay lovers?" Caroline shot back.

Parks cleared his throat and tried not to blush. "Yeah."

"No. Sorry," Caroline said, taking a bite of the salad. "I honestly had no idea the guy was a fag. Though I guess it does explain a few things about him now."

"Okay," Parks said. "That's fine. You know of any friends he has that might be associated with that part of his life? Anyone you weren't particularly close to?"

"Particularly close to? Please," Caroline retorted, finishing off a bite and preparing another. Parks was almost willing to offer to come back and let the woman eat in peace as she devoured the salad at a rather rapid pace. "I didn't know diddly-squat about Kyle's life. I mean, yeah, sure we were boyfriend and girlfriend. So what? It was all publicity anyway. He mostly hung out with the guys. Go figure, right?"

"You mean the other players?"

"Yeah, them," Caroline said with a look on her face as if to ask, Who else would I be talking about? "He mostly hung out with them and practiced all the time. Hell, they're probably all fags. He never drank or . . . did anything else. He was such a goodie-goodie. We'd only been going out a few months and he was in the middle of the season, so no, we really didn't do a whole lot together. Other than pose for pictures occasionally."

"So," Parks huffed, trying hard to keep from rolling his eyes at the woman, "how exactly did you two meet?"

"What's that noise?" Moore asked, practically jumping up and looking down the hallway.

"What? Oh . . . oh, that's nothing," Caroline said, waving the question off. "We met at some after party event. We had mutual friends who introduced us."

"Miss Maddox, what is that noise?" Parks asked, also looking down the hallway.

"It's just my assistant," Caroline said, somewhat offended. "She's sick. So she's back in my room sleeping it off. I think she has a hangover. Whatever. Bitch can't handle her liquor and I warned her."

Parks's cell phone began to ring.

"Excuse me," Parks said, standing up and taking a step away from the two women. "Detective Parks."

"Dave," Fairmont said. "I know you're in the middle of an interview—"

"Yes, I am actually."

"I know. Sorry. But I have Deborah Bollinger on the line and she swears it's an emergency and she says she'll only talk to you. Says the killer took something else from her apartment."

Parks looked to the two women, who were both waiting patiently, when there was another groan from the back room.

"Rach," Parks said as he got her attention and gestured toward the back room.

"Dave," Fairmont said through the phone.

"Yeah, sorry. I'm here. Yeah, okay. Go ahead. Put her on."

"Okay, wait a minute," Fairmont said. "Patching her through."

Parks waited while Moore started down the hallway. Caroline rose to follow her when Parks stopped her. "If you don't mind, could you just wait here? On the couch. Please. Thank you."

Caroline sat back down then rubbed her throat before grabbing her glass of water and proceeding to drink all of it. Parks stared at her, the paranoia of Charles Wyler's tainted water digging into his mind, when Moore called out his name and drew him back to reality.

"Stay here," Parks ordered.

Parks left her and made his way down the hallway to the bedroom on the right, opposite the kitchen, where he found Moore checking the pulse of a young woman lying in an oversized bed. She was young, in her early twenties, and of Spanish descent though with her pale complexion it was hard to tell.

"Detective Parks?" Mrs. Bollinger's voice suddenly came through from the other end of the phone, taking him off guard, and almost startling him.

"Yes, Mrs. Bollinger," Parks replied. "What's up?"

"You told me to call you if anything else was missing."

"And? What's missing?"

"I only thought of it because of the missing baseball."

"We know about the baseball, Mrs. Bollinger." Parks covered the mouthpiece of the phone and addressed Moore. "What's wrong with her?"

"Not sure," Moore answered. "Fever. Heart's beating rapidly. Some kind of a skin rash. Vomit. Urine everywhere. Loss of bodily functions."

"Possible poisoning?" Parks asked. "Yes, I'm here, Mrs. Bollinger."

". . . only reason I remembered the baseball player was because of his girlfriend."

"Caroline Maddox. What about her?" Parks looked back down the hallway, realizing he couldn't see the other woman and hoping she hadn't heard him call out her name.

"The reason I remembered them both was because they were together when Jason got the baseball signed," Mrs. Bollinger explained. "And since he got the baseball player's signature and I liked her so much, I got her signature. Just on a napkin."

"So what?" Parks asked.

"So after I thought about the baseball, I remembered the napkin she signed and went to check. Detective Parks, he took that paper too. It's not where I left it."

"You're sure you didn't misplace it somewhere?"

"No," Mrs. Bollinger said, dragging the word out. "I know exactly where it was, just like Jason knew where his baseball was. We never touched each other's stuff. Whoever killed my husband took that napkin. Though I'll never know how he knew where it was. I had all but forgotten about it."

"Dave," Moore said, stepping back from Nina's body and bumping into her boss. "Something's wrong with—Dave, I think that's one of the girls from the photo."

Parks took another look at the sick girl and immediately recognized her from the photo as well. The girl let out a loud retching sound and coughed up some blood. "Call an ambulance. Now!" he shouted and ran out of the bedroom.

Parks reached the front room and saw Caroline Maddox lying half in her chair and half on the floor. The actress was sweating profusely, her hair plastered to the side of her face, while the front of her was covered in vomit. She moaned in pain, though her face showed no signs of suffering. Parks moved in front of her and could tell she was trying to focus on him, though to no avail.

"Call an ambulance!" Parks shouted again when Caroline's body began to convulse.

Parks hung up his phone and dialed Jackie's number when the woman beneath him stopped moving. Parks noticed three-fourths of the salad had been eaten and that her glass of water was empty. It could have been anything. Could have been something else from before they arrived.

"Come on, dammit, pick up," Parks hissed into the phone.

He brought his focus back to Caroline and noticed her breathing had slowed down as if she was having trouble getting air into her lungs. She continued to lie in the chair, her face a mask of nothingness—no pain or fear showed upon it. It was as if she had been paralyzed from displaying any emotion, something her career had always depended upon.

"Jackie!" Parks shouted when the line was answered. It took him a few seconds before he realized he was listening to a recording. "Dammit, Jackie, where are you? I'm with the next two victims. They're dying before me. I don't know what to do. We called for an ambulance already but I don't know if they'll be able to help us. Call me back. Immediately."

Parks hung up when he saw Moore stumble toward him, a look of defeat across her face.

"Is she—" Parks stopped when he noticed the first tears streaking down Rachel's face as she shook her head from side to side. The girl from the photo, whom they had yet to properly identify, had died before her very eyes while she could do nothing but stand back and watch the woman succumb to death.

Parks felt bad for his partner and realized he was most surely about to find out exactly how she felt. Caroline suddenly let out a gut-wrenching yell as her body jerked up, and her face contorted in pain, as if her fingernails were being torn off. Parks went to grab the woman when she stopped and fell back, her breathing becoming even more labored.

"Did you call an ambulance?" Parks asked.

Rachel nodded frantically, unable to say anything, scared that whatever toxin was attacking the women may possibly be airborne.

Parks turned back to Caroline's body and noticed the look of fear in the woman's eyes as she lay there, her breathing picking up its pace, though her face had become more porcelain-like, as if she were a living doll. Caroline breathed quicker and quicker, her eyes revealing the pain and terror she was experiencing while her body refused to move.

"What's wrong with her?" Moore asked from behind Parks.

"I have no idea," Parks said when his phone began to ring.

He answered his phone without looking at the ID. "Jackie?"

"Dave? What is it? I didn't hear your message. I just saw that you—"

"Stop. Stop. Stop. We've have another victim here," Parks spat into the phone. "She's still alive, but it looks bad. Been screaming in pain. Convulsing. Having trouble breath—" He stopped when Caroline's body jolted as if she had been electrocuted and her breathing suddenly stopped, her body stiffening then relaxing.

Parks grabbed the woman's wrist and felt for a pulse. He stared at the living idol while her pulse, as well as her breathing, both stopped functioning right before his eyes.

PART
FOUR

27

Parks stood off in a corner of his bedroom, staring out through the window at the Hollywood sign resting atop the hill north of the city. The sun was beginning to disappear over the horizon, taking with it all evidence of the smog that had attacked the city during the day. Everything was covered in an orange glow, as if a giant fire was blazing in the distance, just waiting to consume the world.

It was Friday night, three days since Caroline Maddox and her assistant, Nina Mendola, had succumbed to horrific and painful deaths right before his eyes. The depression had hit him. Mostly it had manifested itself in him physically, as he slugged around, his head and shoulders hanging heavy—while he did practically nothing. His eyes had become large and glassy, sinking into his face, bags forming under his eyes. When he wasn't with Jackie, he was in his office—both at the station and at his home—the door closed, with the lights on and papers rustling about. She knew he was working the case, without anyone's help—his own personal, macabre murder puzzle.

He wasn't alone though. The knowledge that the killer was stick-

282 | TYLER COMPTON

ing to the time table embedded itself in everyone's mind as the countdown to Sunday's inevitable death loomed closer. They were no closer to figuring out who was committing the murders than they were to figuring out who was going to be killed next.

In the days that followed Caroline Maddox's and Nina Mendola's, deaths most everyone at the station was lethargic, only speaking when spoken to, and only when necessary. It was as if everyone was afraid to talk, the only words to come out of their mouths the admittance of defeat and failure. It wasn't rare that a murder went unsolved. It happened. More often than one cared to admit. But this was different. The team effort seemed so hopeless. They had tried so hard. Had put so much into the investigation. This killer was different. They had to stop him.

But how?

"Monkshood and haloperidol," Jackie had said at the meeting the day after the deaths of Caroline and Nina. "Or more commonly known as haldol. That's what those two women were poisoned with."

"What are those?" Fairmont had asked.

"Haldol is a major tranquilizer and is often used for people in highly psychotic states. It's a depressant that attacks the central nervous system. From what we could determine, the killer injected a box of chocolates with the substance, and Nina Mendola, Caroline Maddox's assistant, had been eating them over the past two weeks. This would account for her sickly complexion. Her drowsiness, blurred vision, headaches, confusion, and skin rash. Her difficulty breathing. There was no hope for her once she finished off the box of chocolates. I'm sorry, Dave, but there was nothing you could have done to save her."

"And Caroline Maddox?" Parks asked to keep the conversation going, though he hadn't lifted his head.

"Caroline Maddox was poisoned with monkshood," Jackie continued. "The entire plant is deadly, especially the leaves and roots. You saw the signs almost immediately. It works fast. After the initial symptoms and pain, you get paralysis of the facial muscles and rapid breathing followed by paralysis of the heart. She ate enough so that her death occurred within ten minutes of finishing the salad."

"The salad?" Moore asked.

"Yes. Monkshood is often mistaken for radish. The leaves were put into her salad. She never even noticed it with the dressing on. You never would. If either of you two had eaten any of it yourselves . . . she ate her death. There're no known antidotes for monkshood either. There was nothing you could do about it. Our killer knew this. He knew all you could do was watch."

The knowledge of this did little to ease anyone's conscience.

On the plus side, the death of Nina Mendola had led to identifying one of the girls in the photo found at the Kyle Oni crime scene and therefore had limited the timeframe Tippin and Hayward were looking at to identify the blonde girl in the photo with her. Unfortunately, the blonde girl hadn't been shown in the class photos the same year as Nina Mendola, leaving Hayward with a list of thirteen girls who hadn't been photographed. He had tried to track them all down through the DMV, but of the thirteen girls, eight of them were not the blonde-haired girl, and the five others did not have driver's licenses. It was as if this one girl had been chosen simply because the Poisoner knew it would be next to impossible to locate and identify her. Or had he erased her trail himself?

Parks had spent his days in the station tearing through files and reports, while nothing filled him with any sort of satisfaction as he tried to stop a killer he did not know, to save a victim he could not yet identify. At night he went with Jackie to her place, neither one wanting to be alone, though neither finding the energy to do much more than fall asleep next to each other, rarely touching one another throughout the night.

Earlier that day, Parks had called it quits for the team and sent everyone home to recharge before returning for the last forty-eight hours before the next inevitable attack. Jackie had followed him back to his place, where they made love for the first time since the first night at Jackie's place. Now, an hour later, Parks stood at the window while Jackie stared at him. The usual sounds of the city could be heard behind the pane of glass that separated him from the outside: cars running, sirens wailing, people wheeling and dealing. No matter what happened, no matter how traumatic or euphoric, the city would always remain a hustle-and-bustle metropolis that would continue to move on. No matter what pain any single person felt, Hollywood was more than that. The city was a survivor and knew how to keep on thriving.

"Is there something you want me to do?" Jackie asked. "Something you need me to do?"

He didn't answer. She sat up in the bed, the sheets falling to the side, and held up her arms.

"Come here," she cooed. "Come on."

He worked his way across the room and fell in the bed on top of Jackie. He wrapped his arms around her and lay naked on top of her and the sheets. The warm summer air had worked its way into the room through the open window, mixing with the sweat that had built up on their bodies from the hour of lovemaking they had just finished.

"I know I'm not in the same department as you," Jackie said, playing with his hair, outlining patterns on his head. It was still short, yet long enough to show the scars on the top of his scalp. "Not officially. Nor the same . . . job, really. I may think I know what it's like for you, but no one really knows anyone else's pressure. I'm sorry. I wish I could help. I wish there was something I could do to relax you and help you focus. Concentrate. Spark some immediate . . . something or other that would help you solve this case. But I can't. And I'm not sure what you want me to do, because you won't talk to me." Jackie held his face and positioned it so that he stared into her eyes. "You have to talk to me. No matter what. I don't know what it is exactly that we have here. Maybe something. Maybe nothing. Maybe as soon as this case is over I'll never see you again." Jackie paused when she felt his body tense. But she had been here before, and they were both adults. She knew the rules of life just as he did. "I can handle it. All of it. The falling for a co-worker. Being impressed not only by his gorgeous, physical being but also by the way he conducts himself in life. The way he interacts with others. The way he thinks. But along with all that can come heartbreak. And it's all right. I've been there before, and I expect to be there again. But that's not what you need to worry about right now. Right now we have the case. That's your focus. My focus is on you. And what I can do to help you with this case."

Jackie stopped. She wasn't sure if this was what she had meant to tell him but had lost track of what she was saying and wasn't sure where to go next.

"You know I don't look at you like that," Parks said calmly. "As an accessory. To this case, I mean. You're valuable here. Very. We couldn't have done as much as we have without your help."

"But what have we really done?"

"You've helped a lot. Identifying the poisons. Helping us with the symptoms. Helping us avoid getting killed ourselves. We couldn't have done this without you, Jackie. I mean it. You're valuable to us all."

"It hasn't shown," Jackie replied. "Not you personally. I mean on the case."

"By the end, it will all pay off. Somehow. Some way. It will all be worth it. I'm not sure what it is just yet, but it will be. You'll see."

"We'll all see," Jackie corrected.

He kissed her and then lay back down.

"You know I'm not sure what comes next," he added. "After all this, I mean. I do like you. I'd like to see where this goes. But you also have a son."

"A wonderful son," Jackie corrected him again with a smile.

"A wonderful son, who doesn't much care for me."

"He's just protective of his mother. That's all," Jackie said. "Realistically, he wants what's best for me. But it's not up to him to like or dislike you. He won't be home in a few years, if not sooner, and then what? I'm all alone? Why shouldn't I have someone? I wish I had found someone earlier. A father figure for him. He deserved that much at least. If there was any area where I failed as a mother, that would be it. Not that he needed it. At least if you ask him. He did just fine on his own. Puberty. Girls. High school. Sports. All of it. He appears to have gotten through it just fine without a father. So who knows? Maybe he and I alone are enough."

They were both silent for a while, again letting the time pass though neither was aware of just how much had come and gone.

Parks lay face down in Jackie's lap, and she calmly drew her finger along his shoulders, subconsciously outlining the patterns of ink permanently etched into his body. She had stared at the tattoos for hours now and had only begun to put the pieces of the literal puzzle together. Starting in the center of each shoulder was the outline of a three-inch puzzle piece. From the one piece on each shoulder there were connecting pieces, forming a sleeve of ink on each arm, each piece outlined in a different color. Where the two sides differed were in the detailed and colorful pictures in the center of each puzzle piece. Each piece held a lone, symbolic picture, a part of Parks's history. Jackie had put together that the pieces on his left side told the story of his personal life while the pieces on his right told the story of his professional endeavors. In the center piece on his left shoulder was the sign for Pisces, which Jackie took to be Parks's astrological sign. Next to that was a picture of an A+, which she took to be his blood type (something she knew men who served in war often did in case they were injured on the field of battle, though she couldn't recall Parks ever having served), followed by one of a baseball, most likely a link to his high school days. The names Peter & Kelly were written in a bright red font on a third piece, though she wasn't sure who the two people were or what their connection to Parks was (possibly his aunt and uncle?). On the professional side there was a picture of a razor blade half hidden in a piece of candy, symbolizing his recent tangle with Peter Kozlov, the tattoo no doubt obtained during his three week vacation from work. Next to that were the letters SLS in bright blue, though again, Jackie had no knowledge what the initials referred to. The main difference between the left and right sides was that on the right side, the center piece on his shoulder, from which all the other pieces stemmed out, was still blank. Jackie wondered what that piece was being saved for.

"We still on for dinner after this?" Parks asked, startling Jackie.

"Why not now?"

"You feel like going out?"

"Not really." Jackie smiled. "But I'm sure you have something here we can eat so we don't have to leave."

Jackie left the room. Parks heard her poking around in his kitchen, and the next thing he knew he was jerking awake. He had fallen asleep, though he couldn't remember closing his eyes. He had to be more tired than he thought. He knew his sleep over the past few nights had been sporadic and unfulfilling, filled with tossing and turning—the thought of another victim weighing on his conscious. And it wasn't just attacking his sleep. He could feel his insides becoming wracked with a physical guilt that was just as exhausting as the mental kind.

"All I could find was breakfast foods," Jackie said. "So we have cereal, grapefruit, toast, orange Juice. And coffee's percolating. What's with that anyway?"

"With what?"

"With just breakfast food?" Jackie said. "I've noticed that. You mostly only eat breakfast foods. I've actually never seen you eat anything but breakfast foods, now that I think of it. No matter what time of the day. Only breakfast. What gives?"

Parks smiled to himself. "I don't know. I've only recently noticed it. But I am aware of it. Don't know why I do that. But for some reason that's all I eat. I don't know for how long I've done that. Long as I can remember, I guess. Everything else just makes me physically sick for some reason."

"Might want to have Doc Black take a look at your brain while you're in the station one of these days," Jackie joked.

"Been seeing Doc Black on a weekly basis for weeks now," he admitted. Jackie looked confused and he explained. "I'm not quite as perfect as you paint me to be." Jackie stayed quiet.

"Sure about that?" The look on her face wasn't one of an accusation, rather of genuine concern.

"Let's just say I've had a full year when it comes to traumatic events," Parks admitted.

"Year's not over yet," Jackie said. "Maybe it will pick up. You never know." Jackie bit into a piece of toast. "You're not Aaron Levinson. You need to realize that."

"I know that. I do. Aaron was well-liked. A good detective. A good man."

"Like you."

"But not an honest man." Parks stared off into a corner of the room, and Jackie ate quietly while she gave him space. "How do you tell people that a fifteen-year decorated veteran of the department who died while trying to save the life of a repeatedly-abused victim was also dishonest? I mean, I didn't know. Never did. And I was his partner for five years. But I never had a clue."

"How bad was it?"

"It's never how bad is it but rather how bad can it get. I figure once you start down that path it can only lead to darkness. If you're willing to plant evidence, how long until you're willing to take the life of a man you deem guilty that you know won't be prosecuted by the law?"

"Is that your decision to make?" Jackie asked, making Parks look sharply at her. "I'm not judging you; I'm asking if this is something you should let weigh on you. Other people's ethics? I know it's enough to struggle with one's own values when working in this line of work. Is it worth your sanity to worry about others? How bad was it?"

"Kozlov was harming children. Levinson was expecting a child. It was too much for him. The chances of Kozlov getting off were too much for him." Parks contemplated this. "That's why we always worked so well together. We never gave up. Always worked a case until the bitter end. But where I'm detail oriented, Levinson was sloppy. Careless even, you could say. That was why they really partnered us up."

"What did he do?"

"Kozlov was guilty. We had the evidence. But Levinson was in a rush. Always rushing through things. He forgets to do things in order from time to time. Warrants and the such. So the evidence we had, was worthless. So what did it matter if the new evidence was manufactured? As long as he was guilty. I don't know. Kozlov was a bad man. We just wanted him off the street. But the way we went about it—"

"The way *he* went about it," Jackie interrupted. "Right?"

"Right. We were suspended. That case was a mess in our hands. But it was a mess case to start with. Harming children. Everyone's common sense just goes right out the window. Can't help it. We're a protective species by nature. But Levinson didn't care. Once the suspension came down he decided to take care of Kozlov on his own. He called me. His partner. He knew I was the only one who could talk some common sense into him. That was my job. As his partner. To be there for him. And I failed. Even Hardwick's called me on it. My need to be needed. My loyalty. But I blew it. I couldn't save him in the end. Maybe it was karma."

"You mean Levinson losing his life at Kozlov's hands due to him planting evidence? You really think that?"

Parks smiled and shook his head. "If only it worked that way. No, I don't. But what do I do? What does it matter now? Levinson's dead. Kozlov is locked up. Along with his brother. For life. Case is closed. Is this just something I live with?"

"Is it something you can live with?"

Parks didn't answer, and a minute later Jackie leaned in and gave him a kiss.

"Well . . . if you ever need to talk about this or anything," she said, going back to her food. "I'm here for you. I mean it. Off the record or whatever. I'm here. No judging. Only listening. It goes no further than these walls. I can promise you that if nothing else in life."

"Thank you. But I think I've done enough talking lately."

"Even though, apparently, breakfast foods were never brought up."

"Considering the other things that I've been through, if only eating breakfast foods is a problem, then I'm not doing too badly."

Both were quiet for a second.

"Sorry," Jackie finally said as she burst out laughing uncontrollably.

Parks burst out with laughter as well and they both felt the tension in the room break.

"You forgot to add coffee and chocolate freak to your list of my weird traits."

"You're right," Jackie said, still laughing. "And I'm sorry, but what's with all of those massive puzzles you have everywhere? There has to be at least fifty or so of them around this place. They're huge."

"It's a tic I have," Parks admitted. "They calm me. Make me forget about other things I'd rather be doing or. . . whatever. Once I start one, I can't not finish it."

"I'm sorry," Jackie said again, trying to control her laughter. "I don't mean to laugh at it."

"No, it's no problem." Parks laughed himself.

"I didn't mean to start something. Or dredge up something uncomfortable for you. I was just wondering about it was all. Sorry."

"No need to be. Never learn anything new if we don't ask. I just don't have any answers for you. Perhaps some buried childhood trauma I've yet to face."

"You know, actually, all things considering I think you're one of the most grounded people I know. Considering your upbringing, your past traumas, most men would be raging alcoholics or bordering on the edge of sanity or whatever it is men who experience similar things like that do. But you're actually pretty normal. You're not weird. Closed off a little maybe, but that's not all that bad. I can understand that. Just as long as you don't close yourself off from me, okay?"

Parks smiled and kissed Jackie. A few minutes later they made love for the second time that night. Afterwards, they were lying there enjoying the silence when Parks's cell phone began to ring. He noticed that the sun had set while they were preoccupied, as the entire room was dark. He picked up his phone and saw that it said 5:43. It must have been Saturday morning.

"Parks," he answered into his phone. "What? Yes . . . what? What? Are you sure? Right away. Be there within the hour. At the latest. Call everyone else. Now."

He hung up and jumped out of bed and stormed into the bathroom where he turned on the shower.

"Dave?" Jackie called out.

He popped back into the room, a look of excitement on his face.

"Let's shower and get dressed," Parks said.

"What is it?" asked Jackie when her phone began to vibrate.

"I'm trying not to get my hopes too high, but Milo thinks he may have just figured out why our killer's doing what he's doing."

28

Milo Tippin stared down at the red-colored Converse he was wearing, squeezing his sweaty hands together, trying hard to control the nerves that swam through his body while the team assembled itself before him in the squad room. The conference room that Parks had started out using had become too small for the amount of murder board space needed to accommodate all of the victims and for all of the detectives he now had working on the case.

Parks looked around, satisfied that everyone was present and ready.

"You can begin, Milo."

"Yes, um . . . well, I'm sorry if I appear a bit on edge. I haven't gone home since yesterday." Tippin chuckled, but when no one else replied, he continued. "I think I may have discovered a few different things, and all of them may lead into what our killer's doing and why. I'll explain. I was looking around on the Internet at the different meanings behind ten, like Parks suggested, and found a few things. I also did a cross reference search into crime and punishment and—"

"Just tell us what you found, Milo," Parks interrupted.

Tippin stopped as Amy Tanaka joined them, looking relaxed and fresh compared to everyone else.

"Sorry," Tanaka said, grabbing a chair next to Hardwick, who looked questioningly at her. "Sorry, but I've been a part of this one since the beginning. I want to hear this." Tanaka smiled at Tippin as if to say, Thanks for remembering me.

Hardwick turned back to Tippin. "Continue."

"During the sixteenth century, the use of poison as a form of murder had become a sort of, uh . . . a profession, I guess you could say. There were actual schools teaching people how to use it. As a way to kill."

"You mean like a college course?" Fairmont asked.

"Not exactly. More like . . . Jason Bourne style."

"You mean assassins?" Parks asked. "Government trained?"

"Sort of. Yeah. Like that. Anyway, before this, there was a group of alchemists formed known as the Council of Ten."

"Council of Ten?" Parks repeated.

"Yeah. Um . . . think like the Freemasons. Or Illuminati. But not. They were originally formed to help preserve the government from corruption as well as help intelligence services and military affairs. But they were also a group of assassins who carried out contracts for people who paid them enough money to do so. The way they killed was with poison."

"Where was all this?" Hardwick asked.

"Venice. Mostly. Between the thirteen hundreds to the late seventeen hundreds. The Council was generally composed of ten members, who each served a one-year term. No member could serve for more than one successive term, and two people from the same family could not be a part of the group either. The leadership went to three members of the Council, known as Capi, who were elected from the ten members. They were only in position for one month though. During the month they served they weren't allowed to leave their, like, um, headquarters, or whatever it was."

"So you're saying what, exactly? That this guy is a . . . he thinks he's a member of this Council? Or that he's formed a modern-day version of this Council of Ten?"

"That is a possibility." Tippin shrugged. "Could be a good reason none of our victims have a connection. Because each one could be chosen by a different . . . assassin, we'll say. But I don't think he's formed a modern-day version of the Council. I think this is one person we're dealing with here. It's why he's doing what he's doing that we're interested in. I think he's using a bastardized version of the Council and what they did as an excuse for what he's doing. No, that's not right. Not as an excuse. As an inspiration for how he's carrying out his murders. And why?"

"And what's that?" Wilkes chimed in.

"Punishing," Tippin answered. "Like Parks suggested. He was right about that. We thought he was punishing the people he's killing, and he is. He thinks he's in the right. So then I got to thinking, who deserves to be punished?"

"According to him?" Fairmont asked.

"In general? We're the police. The law. Who do we think needs to be punished?"

Everyone looked around the room, somewhat lost.

"The bad guys," Parks said, smirking. "People who commit crimes."

"Exactly. And what constitutes what is a crime or not?"

"The law," Parks answered. "Criminal law."

"Yes. But what laws? Who makes them? Which ones are severe or not? Think back. What are the oldest laws we know? As man."

"Milo, I'm sure a history lesson is greatly appreciated, but right now?" Hardwick said, getting irritated.

"There has been law since before Christ walked the earth," Parks said, going along. "Thousands of years before. There's evidence of it. Maybe not the same as what we have today, but they had it. In one form or another."

"Yes," Tippin agreed. "But think back only as far as the Council of Ten. Think back to that time. Or, yeah, even before to when Christ walked the earth. What laws did they follow then? That might pertain to what we're doing here. Think ten . . ."

"The Ten Commandments," Moore blurted out.

"Yes," Tippin said. "Parks actually came up with that idea, but I've no idea where."

Several people turned to Parks.

"I was doing a crossword puzzle that asked about a gun-toting Moses. Or something along those lines. Then I got to thinking about the number ten . . ."

"You're saying this guy kills based on the Ten Commandments?" Hardwick asked, turning back to Tippin.

"He is." Tippin beamed for a moment, taking in his glory. "He's picking and punishing people based on what commandment they have broken," Tippin said, flipping the white board over to reveal the Ten Commandments written on the backside in black erasable marker.

Thou shalt have no other gods before me

Thou shalt not make for yourself an idol

Thou shalt not take the name of
the LORD thy God in vain

Remember the Sabbath day to keep it holy

Honor thy father and thy mother

Thou shalt not kill

Thou shalt not commit adultery

Thou shalt not steal

Thou shalt not bear false witness
against thy neighbor

Thou shalt not covet your
neighbor's house, wife, etc.

"Now these are just in my words, and there are several different versions of what the Ten Commandments are, according to which religion you refer to. But I think these are as close to what our guy is going by."

"This is nuts," Wilkes muttered.

"Hold on a sec," Moore said, waving Wilkes quiet. "He just might be onto something."

"Let's take this one at a time," Tippin continued. "So, starting with not coveting your neighbor's wife or anything else that belongs to him, we've got Ian Harris. He spied on Mrs. Bollinger. We know that. Found the roll of film with her picture. He coveted her. Or he coveted the husband's life by wanting to be with his wife? It's basically the same difference, either way you look at it."

Parks nodded in agreement, as did everyone else.

"Two. Thou shalt not steal. Jason Bollinger was accused of stealing from his clients and was under federal investigation."

"Continue," Hardwick said, looking up from her notepad.

"Do not take the name of the Lord in vain. I rewatched Charles Wyler's last broadcast from the night before he died. He used the name of God a lot to say how what the killer was doing was wrong and that he would be punished. He spoke for God. I looked back at his broadcasts over the past few years and found he did this quite a bit. Condemning the guilty on behalf of God. So I think Charles Wyler broke this commandment."

"And Kyle Oni?" Hayward asked.

"Kyle Oni played baseball. Lots of games on Sundays." Tippin grabbed the marker and wrote Oni's name next to one of the commandments. "Remember the Sabbath and keep it holy."

"It's fu—reaking baseball for crying out loud," Wilkes bitched, catching Hardwick's stony glare.

"Doesn't matter. These aren't my rules. They're his. They're why he's doing what he's doing. And this fits."

"I thought he was killed because he was gay?" Wilkes asked.

"No," Tippin replied. "It's like Jackie said: the poison he was killed with was chosen because he was gay, but he wasn't killed because he was gay. He was killed because he didn't honor the Sabbath."

Everyone around the table took in what Tippin had just said.

"Keep going," Parks urged.

"Caroline Maddox. You shall not make for yourself an idol. I'm not sure if this was taken in the same spirit it was originally written, but I think it fits. She was worshiped. By millions. People idolized her every day. Everywhere she went paparazzi followed her around, invading her life. Everyone loved her. Including her assistant, Nina Mendola . . . you shall have no other gods before me. You've talked to a few of Caroline Maddox's previous assistants and her managers and agents, and they all confirm. None of them were as dedicated to Caroline as Nina was. She worshiped Caroline Maddox. Unconditionally. And it cost her her life. Now we know the chocolates were addressed to Caroline, but I think we can safely assume that our guy had something planned for both women. I mean, they were both killed, and I don't think there's any doubt that if he wanted both of them dead that either one would still be alive."

"What about Allison Tisdale?" Moore asked.

"She's the only one I can't one hundred percent place."

"See," Wilkes said. "This is bullshit."

"I didn't say she doesn't belong," Tippin said cutting him off. "Just that I couldn't concretely connect her to a particular sin. All we have to go off of so far is . . . Parks's feelings of an affair. But we've no real evidence."

"We didn't find proof of an affair, but we did find a connection between Allison Tisdale and another person on the list," Fairmont offered.

"Who?" Parks asked.

"We looked through Allison's portfolio of houses she's sold in the past. She doesn't use him anymore, but when she first started, guess who took the pictures of the houses she used to put up online when selling them?"

"Ian Harris," Parks said, nodding as if he should have known all along.

"Si, señor," Fairmont said, pleased with himself.

"That's not all," Tippin said as the group began to get riled up.

"What else?" asked Parks.

"I think I know who his next victim is. Or rather victims."

"How? Who?" Hardwick said, all but jumping out of her chair.

"He's getting splashier. More daring. Making a bigger show of this. First Charles Wyler on live TV, then Kyle Oni, a national figure in the sports world. This was followed by Oni's girlfriend, a multi-million-dollar actress. So far we've managed to keep a lid on most of these murders. Or at least the link between them. Where technology usually spoils things and alerts people to what's going on in the world, this time it's actually working to our benefit, and too much information leaked. No one knows what's what. As far as most people are concerned, each of these events are just random events. They aren't making the connection. Each person is such a superstar, people think they're each their own . . . event. Which is good for us. But maybe bad for our killer. Maybe he's feeling neglected. Like he's not getting the publicity he desires. In which case, how does he go about changing that?"

"How?" Parks asked.

Tippin pointed to "Honor your father and mother" on the board.

"How's that lead us to the next victim?" Parks asked.

"We're looking for someone who's dishonored their father and mother," Tippin replied.

"So what?" Wilkes said. "That's just about every damn teenager in this flippin' state."

"Think closer to home," Tippin said.

"Is this someone off some reality show?" Parks asked.

"No," Tippin said with a roll of his eyes. "Come on, guys. No one can think of this? None of you?" Tippin looked to Wilkes's team when he made this last accusation. "Nothing?"

"What?" Confused, Wilkes turned to Ramirez and Hayward.

"What have you guys been working on for the past few weeks when you're not working on this case?"

The realization of what Tippin was talking about came to Wilkes.

"Cosway," Ramirez muttered.

"Those two little shits who offed their parents?" Wilkes spat.

"You know of anyone locally more famous right now who's known for not honoring their mother or father?" Tippin asked.

"Where are they?" Hardwick asked, picking up a phone and dialing a number.

"Parker Center," Wilkes answered.

"Here?"

"At the Metropolitan Detention Center. It's where they're locked up in-between days in court."

"Wait," Hayward said. "How do we know they're next? Couldn't one of the other crimes be before the honoring parents one?"

"Don't think so," Tippin said. "Monday is final summations from both sides. After that the jury goes away to make their decision. No idea how long that could take. But if it's a short deliberation—which, who doesn't think they're guilty—then there's no time left. This guy wants this to be public."

"Call whoever you need to, but get those two boys up here today," Parks said, turning to Hardwick. "We need to put them under twenty-four-hour guard. We'll do it ourselves if we have to. No deliveries of any kind without everything being checked. Isley, I need you to be there too. You'll know what to search for. We need everyone on this."

"So if this guy kills both of the Cosway brothers, does that count as one or two murders?" Fairmont asked. "I mean there are two of them. Plus, not only did they disrespect their parents, but they also killed them. Shall not kill, isn't that one?"

"Honestly, who knows? Could go any number of ways," Tippin said. "Remember. He's killing based on the Ten Commandments. I don't think he cares how many people who committed the sin are murdered so much as at least one person is held accountable. Think of the Cosway brothers as a sort of two-for-one type of a deal."

"Great," Fairmont said with a roll of his eyes.

"We have a problem," Hardwick said, slamming down the phone.

"What's up?" Parks asked.

"They're not here."

"Where are they?"

"USC's downtown medical center."

"What happened? We're supposed to have a whole other day before his next attack."

"Looks like this one started early. They complained about aches and blood in their urine. They're being checked out. Apparently there have been sores and rashes spotted all over their bodies and severe peeling on the hands and feet."

"Why there? I mean at that particular medical center?"

"They specialize in urology. I think peeing blood falls under that."

"Right." Parks turned to Jackie, who frantically typed away on her laptop. "Jackie?"

"I'm already working on it," Jackie said. "How long until we can be there?"

"Ten, fifteen minutes, depending on traffic," Parks said, getting everyone's attention. "All right, ladies and gentlemen. This is it. We may finally have the upper hand in this game. Everyone be alert. And be careful. We have no idea what's next."

29

P arks drove down Hope Street, through downtown Los Angeles, passing by the University of Southern California, until he came to the Doctors of USC-Downtown building and parked in front, his lights still flashing while he left the car on the side of the street. Jackie hopped out of the front passenger seat with Detectives Moore and Fairmont getting out of the back. Parking haphazardly next to Parks was Detectives Wilkes, Ramirez, and Hayward in a second vehicle. Hardwick had kept Tippin behind to continue researching other possible future victims.

Parks burst through the sliding-glass doors with his badge in hand, looking for the closest person he could talk to. A rather robust woman sitting behind a front reception desk rose at the sight of the approaching detectives. She was dressed in a maroon and yellow uniform with a nametag that revealed her name to be Rita.

"The Cosway brothers," Parks said. "Where are they?"

"Upstairs, on the sixth floor, being checked by Doctor Lynch," replied Rita.

"How do we get there?" Parks asked.

The receptionist pointed down the hallway while leaning halfway over the counter.

"Take the elevators on the right and go up to the sixth floor."

"Any staircases that lead up there?"

"Two. One next to the elevators and one over there." She pointed in the opposite direction of the elevators to the other side of the main lobby. "They already have police up there with them though," she continued as the team walked away.

"All right . . . I need Fairmont and Hayward to handle the stairs. One on each set and head up. Don't argue with me—you're both the youngest and most fit here. Okay? Take them from the ground up and check for anyone suspicious. Probably nothing to see, but I want to cover all bases."

Fairmont went up the staircase next to the elevators while Hayward started across the lobby for the other staircase. The elevator doors opened to unload a group of people including a doctor, two nurses, and a man in a wheelchair. Parks and everyone else made it onto the elevator and worked their way up to the sixth floor. The doors chimed open and Parks walked off and looked around for the closest reception desk or person in charge. He spotted two officers standing outside a door down the hallway.

"You guys guarding the Cosway brothers?" Parks asked the two officers. There was a foot-and-a-half difference in height between the two men and about a decade and a half in age. The younger, shorter one had a nametag that read Hunter, while his taller, older partner's read Conrad.

"More like watching than guarding." Officer Conrad shrugged. "Who're you?"

"Detective Parks. This is Moore and Wilkes," Parks said, flashing his badge. "We're taking over from here. They're in our custody for now. But don't go anywhere. We may need you guys."

Jackie walked into the room containing the two criminals with Parks at her heels.

"Doctor Lynch?" Jackie asked the aging man reading off a clipboard, the two Cosway brothers sitting before him, each one handcuffed to a chair.

The two men in their early twenties looked up at Parks and Jackie when they entered the room, each brother showing only marginal interest in them, each paying attention to a different person. Wesley Cosway, the older of the two brothers, was the one most watching the trial felt was the leader. He had a more natural, outgoing charm about him, with his long, darkened hair and piercing brown eyes. He had an engaging Spanish flair about himself and a rather soothing voice. His younger, more introverted brother, Evan, usually shied away from the cameras during the trial, appearing more meek and mild-mannered, especially compared to his brother, who was known for his short temper. Evan had been born with lighter, blond-colored hair and fairer looks, the yang to Wesley's yin. Evan had often been considered the "brains," while his brother had the "brawn." This might have mattered at one time to the brothers, but they had since grown up and moved on past such childish labels, each choosing his own path in life, even if both of those paths had kept the two brothers at home during their college years. Though with their father covering their bills while they were at home, no one was all that surprised by their decision. A decision that had apparently led down the path to murder.

Everyone in Los Angeles, and across the United States, had heard of the two young men who had murdered their rich Bel Air parents in hopes of gaining access to their inheritances just a little quicker than was intended. Both had shouted their innocence, claiming a mysterious pair of persons had been in the house the night their parents had been sliced open with the kitchen butcher knife, but no one believed the story. The trial had been a long and engaging one, with live broadcasts across the country every day for the last two months, making it the most watched trial since OJ Simpson's. Their lawyer attempted to show their movie producer father's love-less, and at times, abusive relationship toward them, or how their mother spent most of her days in a pill-and-vodka-induced coma. The DA felt that this trial would produce one of the quickest verdicts in his entire career.

If the brothers lived to hear a verdict.

"Yes?" Dr. Lynch replied, looking at Jackie through his thin, rim-less reading glasses. He was in his early sixties, with a round body and an equally round, bald head, save for a snow-white goatee.

"I'm Detective Dave Parks, LAPD, and this is Doctor Jacqueline Isley," Parks said by way of introductions.

"What's this about?"

"We believe that a threat has been made on their lives," Parks said nodding toward the Cosways, "and we're here to check it out."

"What kind of a threat?" the doctor asked, looking concerned. Both young men also perked up at this information and looked to one another. Parks noticed Evan Cosway scratching at the palms of his hands, which were swollen, red, and peeling.

"What the hell you mean, a threat?" Wesley Cosway barked.

"Doctor," Jackie said, interjecting herself into the conversation. "I'm a forensic toxicologist." She paused a moment and let the infor-mation sink in. He looked at the two young men, then back at Jackie, the blood draining from his face. "Now if you don't mind, I'm going to help, if not take over. But if you could tell me what you've done so far, I'll see what I think should come next."

"Yo! What kind of a threat? Are we in danger?" Wesley Cosway asked again.

"Sit down," Parks barked in a tone that got everyone's attention. Wesley even held back any further comments, swaying from foot to foot, deciding what to do or say next.

Jackie motioned to Parks that she had control of the situation for now and that she'd let him know what she came up with as soon as she had something.

Parks glared down at the two young men handcuffed to their chairs. Wesley stayed puffed up, trying to prove he was still the big man in the room, while Evan scratched at his throat. Parks left the room without another word.

"So what's up?" Wilkes asked when Parks was back in the hallway.

"Not sure yet. Isley's going over the medical reports with the doctor to see what's wrong with them."

"They look like they've been affected with something already?"

"For sure. They have rashes, just like we were told."

"Shit." Wilkes spat. "So we're too late?"

"No idea," Parks admitted. "Could be something that was already done to them, or something that's still waiting for a second poison to be added to complete the deal. Not sure. But they're still alive, so we're standing guard until we know something definite."

Jackie walked away from Dr. Lynch over to the group. "So they ran some preliminary blood tests on the guys, and it's been determined they've been poisoned already."

"They going to die?" Wilkes asked.

"Not from what they've been given," Jackie explained, "though they are in danger."

"What were they given?" Parks asked.

"It's an exotic cocktail like I've never seen," Jackie said. "Doctor Lynch either. Not sure how it got into their systems, but it's there just the same. It appears to be a mixture of brown recluse venom—"

"You mean the spider?" Wilkes asked.

"Yes."

"So it's possible they weren't poisoned and they were just bitten by some spider?"

"No," Jackie retorted. "They've been poisoned. The levels of toxin are too high for a spider bite. But it's not just spider venom in their bloodstream."

"What else?" Parks asked.

"Warfarin and acrylamide. Now we've determined the acrylamide is why their hands and feet are peeling like they are. We're not sure how they were given it, because it can be absorbed through the skin, inhaled, or swallowed. But we're thinking ingestion because that's usually the reason for the redness and skin peeling. But we don't think it's too high a level of the toxin because they haven't been experiencing any hallucinations or disorientation or seizures. At least from what's been brought to our attention."

"How long?" Parks asked.

"What?"

"How long ago were they given this acryl stuff?"

"Few days. They're being given vitamin B6 to counteract the effects."

"Okay," Parks said, thinking this through. "And what's the reasoning behind the spider venom? Your opinion."

"Other than to kill them?" Jackie shrugged. "Painful. Very. But they weren't given a high enough dose to be fully effective since it was discovered in time. It's like he just wanted to torture them."

"And what about the third poison?"

"Coumadin. Or warfarin," Jackie reminded him.

"Yeah, that. What's that do?"

"Basically, it's a blood thinner."

"Blood thinner?"

Jackie nodded and stayed quiet while Parks rolled over the facts.

"Toxic?"

"Can be, but not necessarily deadly. It's not but a five or six on the toxicity scale. It's painful and bad for the body. You can bleed to death, but that's not dying by poison. Per se."

"This is complicated," Parks said, looking to the rest of the team. "He's doing this one in stages."

"What do you mean?" Wilkes asked.

"The spider venom and the amly—"

"Acrylamide," Jackie finished.

"Yes, the acrylamide and the spider venom aren't put in them to kill them. It's like Milo said, he's torturing them. But it also serves a second function."

"Which is?"

"To get them to the hospital," Parks said, looking around. "But why? I don't get it. They're guarded twenty-four seven. Even here. So they're not more accessible. But if there was no way for him to get to them before, then how did he poison them enough to get them here? And if he could do that then, why not just poison them enough to kill them while he had the chance?"

"I've told you before. It's poison. And as precise as it is, it's not an exact science. Things go wrong. Things you can't count on. Not everything's controllable. These poisons are attacking people and the human body is as different person to person as fingerprints. Everyone reacts differently and for different reasons."

"You're saying he might have messed up?"

"I'm saying, I don't know. It's complicated and complex. Why? You'd have to ask our killer. I'm not sure what he intended."

"Is this the only place where they would be brought to?"

"Considering the toxins have them peeing blood . . . yeah, this is the closest place they would have been brought to, no matter what," Jackie said, thinking about it. "Closest place to where they were held."

"It's a trap. Even if it wasn't the plan, it is now. He's adapting. I think this guy's going to strike. Today. We need to relocate them."

"Not tomorrow?" Wilkes asked. "I thought tomorrow was the date of his . . . thing he follows or—"

"No," Parks said. "This is one of those out-of-his-hands things. He had probably hoped to hold off until tomorrow but risked the chance it wouldn't happen. He's messing with poisons, here and he's not God. He makes mistakes. But I think there's a good chance he knows what's going on with the people he's trying to kill. He has an eye on them somehow. I think he already knows they're here. We need to be alert. Wilkes, call Fairmont and Hayward and see where they are. Everyone buddy up. I want everyone to stay in radio contact with each other at all times. Five minute call-ins. Wilkes, you find Hayward and check this floor, room by room. I'll get Fairmont and start on the floor above. We're checking for anyone suspicious or anything out of place. Everyone else stays on this floor and stands guard over the Cosways. We don't know who we're dealing with here and what he has planned. Go."

Wilkes took off and headed for the staircase by the elevator as he pulled out his walkie-talkie and tried to reach Fairmont on it.

"Detective Fairmont, what's your ten-twenty?" Wilkes said into the walkie-talkie.

"Working my way up the fifth-floor staircase," Fairmont replied. "Almost to you."

"Okay. Once you get up here check in with Parks. Something's up."

"Will do," said Fairmont.

Wilkes left the stairwell and started across the floor toward the opposite end where the door to the other staircase was.

"Detective Hayward, what's your ten-twenty?" Wilkes said into his walkie-talkie.

Wilkes opened the door and stepped into the stairwell and found it abandoned.

"Detective Hayward, what's your ten-twenty?" Wilkes stood there getting more impatient by the second. "Detective Hayward, do you copy?"

As Wilkes clicked off, he heard feedback from another walkie-talkie a few flights below.

"Hayward?" Wilkes called down into the stairwell, his voice echoing throughout the metal surroundings. The walls, steps, even the window treatments in the stairwell were all painted white, giving a sanitarium feel to the whole place. "Hayward?"

Wilkes retrieved his gun and started taking the steps down. He'd made it halfway between the sixth and fifth floors when he turned the corner and saw a body lying on the stairs, facedown, with a slash of blood along the wall leading to his head, beneath which a puddle had formed on the lower steps.

"Hayward?" Wilkes said.

Wilkes was about to leave the landing for the stairs when he heard a noise from behind him. As he turned, a lead pipe slammed into his head and knocked him down the flight of stairs to the floor below. He moaned for a second before passing out in the stairwell.

30

"So what's he planning next?" Parks asked Jackie. "What poison? How? Where? The warfarin is what made them pee blood?"

"Mixed with the spider venom? Yes," Jackie said. "But it's mostly a blood thinner. I think that's the key. He plans to bleed them out somehow."

"Are there poisons that can cut through the skin?"

"Yes," Jackie said, nodding. "There are acids and whatnot that can eat through the skin, but those take time. They're messy and unstable. I'm not sure what he's planning. But if they're cut, they will bleed. Badly."

"I have some more tests I need to check on," Dr. Lynch interrupted. "Do you want me to inform you of the results?"

"Can I go with you?" Jackie asked before turning to Parks. "I'll call you on your cell and let you know if there's anything immediate that needs to be relayed."

"Sounds good," Parks said. "Okay, Ramirez. I want you to stay with the brothers." Ramirez nodded. "You two," Parks said pointing to Officers Conrad and Hunter. "You're going to stay with me.

317

318 | TYLER COMPTON

We're going to check this place out floor by floor."

"I hate to say it, sir, but we've been instructed that at least one of us has to stay within eyesight of the two prisoners at all times," Officer Conrad said. "And no one's called us to tell us otherwise."

Fairmont made it back onto the floor, catching Parks's line of vision. "Oh, good, Fairmont. You're joining me." Parks turned back to the two officers. "One of you stay here then. You two decide who."

"What about me?" Moore asked.

"You're going to stay here and keep guard. Go through the paperwork at the front desk over there. All admissions. All patients. See if anything sticks out as odd or wrong. But give Hardwick a call first and give her an update on what's going on here."

"Will do." Moore agreed.

"Dave," Fairmont began when Moore gave him a look. "Detective Parks. Look, doesn't this seem a bit . . . wasteful? I mean, how do we even know this guy is going to attack today?"

As if on cue, the fire alarm in the building went off, lights flashing as sirens began to wail throughout every room on the floor. The tension raised as everyone on the floor began to panic and move about quickly as if fleeing the Titanic.

"When was the last time you had a coincidence that was just that?" Parks asked.

"Got it," Fairmont agreed, retrieving his gun.

"Let's go. Coming with me is . . . ?"

"Conrad," answered the older officer.

"All right," Parks said looking to Fairmont and Conrad. "You two, let's go. Starting with the floor above us."

Parks led the way to the staircase and up to the seventh floor.

✳   ✳   ✳

"Think we should leave the door open like that?" yelled Officer Hunter.

Ramirez mentally rolled his eyes at the kid almost half his age.

"What's it matter?" Ramirez yelled back over the siren.

"Isn't someone trying to kill these two?" Hunter asked.

Evan and Wesley were still handcuffed to their chairs, looks of concern growing on their faces.

"Yeah, but he's not going to shoot them," Ramirez replied. "He wants to poison them. It's all right. We have a guard outside as well. No one's getting into this room."

"I gotta go," Moore said, sticking her head through the door.

"What's up?" Ramirez asked.

"There's a fight breaking out because everyone's panicking. Nurses need help. I'll be right back."

Ramirez looked past her and waved her on. "Go."

Hunter's breathing deepened and his eyes bulged to the point that the fear in the air was becoming infectious.

"Fine," Ramirez said, nodding toward the door. "Go ahead, if it makes you feel better."

"Just until she gets back," Hunter said, closing the door.

The thick steel door latched shut, and Hunter stared out through the wired-glass window in the center of the door then turned and went back to his post in the other corner, keeping an eye on the two brothers. Evan continued scratching the top of his scalp as if digging for something he could not locate.

"Man, this is fucked up," Wesley said. "We can't die in here. You can't keep us in here if we're going to die. That's, like, unconstitutional or something. We need to get out of here. Like, now."

"Shut up," Ramirez yelled back. "You'll be fine if you just shut up and don't do anything stupid."

"Yeah, whateve—" Wesley stopped talking and eyed the air around him, sniffing at it, as if he suddenly noticed something out of place. "Does anyone smell that?"

"Shut up," Ramirez said again.

"No, seriously, man," Wesley continued.

"Shut! Up!"

"Don't you smell that? That can't just be me."

"I don't smell nothing. Now shut the fu—"

"No, wait," Hunter said. The young officer turned his head around to face the air duct above everyone's head. "What is that?"

Ramirez sniffed the air when suddenly his eyes began to water and he coughed deeply. Though chained to the chair, Wesley tried to stand, looking around wildly at the air above him. Then his brother began coughing.

"Shit," Hunter said.

"Something's coming in through the air duct," Ramirez said. "We gotta get out of here. Get their handcuffs."

Ramirez went for the door only to find it wouldn't open. He banged against it, yelling as loud as he could, not realizing he went unheard thanks to the one-and-a-half-inch-thick metal door and wailing fire alarm. He continued to pound away at the door when Moore showed up, looking confused as she jiggled the handle.

"What's wrong?" Moore shouted at the window in the door.

"Locked," Ramirez mouthed inaudibly, also motioning toward the air vents to try and signal what was happening within the room.

Moore tried the handle while Ramirez continued pounding against the door, his eyes tearing up as his lips swelled and his nose began to run.

"Hold on," Moore said. "We'll get you out of there. How's every-one doing?"

Ramirez turned around to see for himself and to allow her a view, something she wished she could take back. Officer Hunter was doing the same as Ramirez, his eyes turning pink and tearing up while the rest of his face swelled up and became flushed. The two convicts, still handcuffed to their chairs, screamed in pain as the poison being released into the air affected them more. Their mouths bled as they coughed up blood, while their noses became leaky fau-cets that couldn't be stopped. Their faces were red and swollen, as if their entire bodies were on fire. The handcuffs around their wrists dug into their skin as they jerked against them. The undersides of Wesley Cosway's wrists bled freely, and he began to cut through the skin with his teeth in an attempt to free himself from his restraints.

"Dammit," Moore cursed as she retrieved her cell and dialed Parks.

"What is it?" Parks shouted over the sirens wailing throughout the hospital.

"The attack. It's going on. Now. Ramirez and the other officer are trapped in the room with the Cosways. The door is locked, and we can't open it. And the room is filling up with some sort of gas. Not sure what, but everyone's reacting badly to it."

"I'm coming right down," Parks shouted back. "Call Jackie. Get her up there with the doctor right away."

"Okay," Moore replied. She hung up and dialed Jackie's number while looking back into the room. Inside the locked room, Evan Cosway choked on some of his blood as he screamed in pain while also gnawing away at his wrists, trying to free himself. He stopped and jerked his hands back violently from the handcuffs, trying to apply enough force to break them. Ramirez heard a snap and looked over at Evan as he freed his right hand from the still unbroken cuffs.

"Dammit, Cosway, stop it," Ramirez choked.

Evan Cosway ignored Ramirez's orders and with his free hand immediately went about wildly scratching at his neck, his fingernails digging deep to get at the root of his pain. He let out a sigh of relief when he broke through the skin on the back of his neck, drawing blood as he continued to scratch.

Moore looked on in horror, realizing there was nothing she could do to stop what was happening, when Jackie broke her concentration.

"What's up?" Jackie asked through the phone line.

"Get up here with the doctor, right away. Something's happening. The room with the Cosway brothers is filling up with some sort of gas, and Ramirez is trapped in there with another officer. We can't open the door."

"On my way," Jackie said and hung up.

"Get this door open," Ramirez shouted, still not realizing he was going unheard.

Moore ran off to find something to help pry the door open, running back a few seconds later with a fire extinguisher in her hands. She motioned for Ramirez to back up then began to bang the extinguisher against the glass window in the door. She was able to crack it but not break it enough to allow for fresh air. She then began to slam the extinguisher against the handle in the doorway. Moore peered in through the shattered glass and saw that everyone looked worse than before, the two brothers now bleeding through their eyes and ears as well as their noses, mouths, and ears. As she looked to Ramirez, she saw his nose began to bleed.

"Hold on," Moore shouted when she started banging against the door handle again. "Almost there."

"Rachel!" shouted Fairmont from down the hallway as he and Parks swung through the door at the stairwell and ran toward her. "Stop!"

Over the commotion of nurses and patients evacuating the hospital, and the fire alarm that had yet to stop, there was no way for Moore or anyone else at the other end of the floor to hear Fairmount's shouts.

"I got it," Moore gasped as she slammed against the door once more and broke through the lock.

The door swung open at the same time the extinguisher slipped from Moore's hands. Both the door hitting the metal wall and the extinguisher hitting the floor caused not one but two sparks, and immediately the room erupted in a ball of flames. The fireball was big and quick, consuming the entire inside of the room. The two brothers shouted in pain while their bodies burned up, both of them still handcuffed to their chairs, Evan Cosway's one free hand waving wildly, neither one able to run away or do anything about the flames.

Detective Ramirez and Officer Hunter had also both been engulfed in the flames and flailed about as they tried to get out of the room. Hunter ran into a wall, slipped on the floor, and banged his head against the corner of the counter as he fell. Ramirez made it out of the room, but had no clear direction to go as he couldn't see with his face on fire, and he fell over a nearby couch, crashing through a glass coffee table. He writhed about on the floor, his body still in flames, his neck sliced open by the glass shards, his life rapidly bleeding out. As his blood soaked into the hospital carpet, it began to cook from the flames, emitting a foul smell into the air. Parks and Officer Conrad ran to his aid and began patting the fire out.

The ball of fire that had swept through the room quickly dispersed, but not before sending a wall of fire out the door and engulfing part of Moore. Fairmont tackled her and beat at her sides as he tried to put out the fire consuming her clothes. A few seconds later, Jackie was at his side with a blanket to help smother the flames.

"Doctor!" Parks shouted to no one in particular. "I need a doctor."

Dr. Lynch was at Parks's side, checking on Ramirez and shouting at several of the fleeing nurses, all of whom ignored him. Parks backed away from the doctor to allow him room to conduct his business on the detective. He turned toward the room Ramirez had escaped from, everything inside black from the fire. Parks walked past Fairmont, who cradled Moore in his arms as tears made clean tracks down her soot-covered face. Parks approached the doorway to the room and saw the two Cosway brothers, both dead, looks of horror forever burnt into their faces, while their charred bodies remained chained to their chairs. In the corner of the room the young officer lay face down, his body burned almost beyond recognition. The smell of burnt flesh filled the hallways of the sixth floor, making everyone left breathing ready to gag as their eyes watered.

This was an absolute nightmare. In all his years on the force, he couldn't recall a more horrifying sight.

They had tried. He wasn't sure what went wrong, but they had still lost. And just like Tippin had warned, there were casualties. The people who had tried to stop the Palisades Poisoner had paid a price. And as Parks looked over his beaten team, he wondered who else would pay with their life as they tried to stop this madman from killing again.

31

"So?" Jackie stared across the table at Parks as he hung up the phone. The lights from the neighboring downtown buildings were lighting up the sky with the sun disappearing behind the horizon. Parks, Jackie and Tippin were sitting around a conference table in the center of the squad floor, each covered in soot, their clothes smelling of sweat and ash, each waiting to finish with their interviews with their superiors about the day's events. The smell of burning flesh was still imprinted on Parks's brain and the taste of blood on his tongue.

"That was Amy," Parks said to no one in particular. "Evan and Wesley Cosway are dead. Fourth-degree burns on the majority of their bodies. But we knew that."

"We don't give a shit about them," Jackie said. She blushed when Tippin turned to her. "Sorry. Sorry I said that. They were still people."

"No, you're right," Parks agreed. "Cal Ramirez died an hour ago. He had second- and third-degree burns but he actually died from blood loss. The . . ." Parks was gesturing to his throat and the injury that Ramirez had sustained from his fall on the table. "You know he's got two ex-wives and four children. His son is in the academy right now. He graduates in the winter. I can't . . ."

"What about Rachel?" Jackie asked.

"Oh, she's a fighter, I'll tell you that," Parks said, smiling. "She's one of the toughest women I've ever known. She's got some first- and second-degree burns as well. But she'll be fine. Still at the hospital. They'll keep her overnight, maybe even two. Then she'll go home. Take a few weeks off. Then she'll be back to us good as new."

"Where's Detective Fairmont?" Tippin asked innocently.

"I had him stay at the hospital to keep me updated on everyone there."

"What about Wilkes and Hayward?"

"They're all right as well. Just a little banged up. Hayward said someone jumped him in the stairwell and when Wilkes went to check on him someone got him as well. They'll take some stitches and bandages but they'll be back tomorrow."

"Or today," Jackie said.

Parks turned to her and she looked to Hardwick's office where Wilkes had just disappeared. Wilkes's heightened voice bellowed from behind the closed door.

"Well this can't be good," Jackie said, shaking her head.

"What do you suppose that's all about?" Tippin asked, lowering his head to the desk. Everyone was tired and just wanted to wash the day's events away. Go home, have a strong drink, and sleep the nightmare away.

"I'm not sure," Parks said, still eyeing the office.

"Oh, you know what it's about," Jackie said. "Get ready for some blame to come your way. The great Detective Wilkes—not to mention his men—were injured on the job today. On your case." Jackie eyed Parks, giving him pity he was too tired to accept.

"You don't know—Oh, here we go," Parks said, standing up. Chief Hardwick was motioning for him to come to her office. "How do I look?" Parks winked.

"Like a million bucks. Although it's kinda obvious you didn't spend it on that suit. Or cleaning supplies." Jackie winked. "Good luck."

"All right . . ." Parks said, walking into Hardwick's office. "I know this looks bad, but this can be seen as a good thing."

"How's that?" Wilkes shot back. "What about all the dead bodies we accumulated today? How do you figure that's a good thing?"

Parks tried to keep his cool in check as he avoided locking eyes with the other detective. Wilkes had a right to vent after what had happened that day. Wilkes was bandaged from the blow to his head and taking whatever drugs had been prescribed for him. Both men's eyes were swollen and bloodshot. Parks's lungs were still cleaning themselves out, and he'd been coughing since leaving the hospital. Parks felt like he had been given an injection of adrenaline as he couldn't stop his hands from shaking.

"Look, we all suffered a great loss today. I know that. But we need to focus on the positive right now."

"Positive?" Wilkes snapped, jumping out of his chair, knocking it back against the wall.

"Wilkes," Hardwick said, staying put behind her desk.

"What the fuck is positive about anything that happened today? Ramirez is dead. Along with another officer I didn't even know. Hell, even Hayward and myself didn't get out of that unscathed."

"And we still have an active case to wrap up," Parks said, not backing down. "A very serious case that could put a lot more lives in jeopardy if we don't stop this guy. We've never been this close to this guy before. Hell, we were there before the attack. We're catching up to this guy. We're putting all of the pieces together. We're going to get him. Now are you going to help with that? Or not?"

"What? Are you saying I haven't been?" Wilkes asked. "Well, fuck you."

"Of course not—"

"Fuck you!"

"No one's saying that," Hardwick interrupted. "No one's saying anyone associated with this case hasn't put in a hundred and ten percent. But the truth of the matter is this guy's still out there. And yes, we suffered a loss today. A big, fucking loss. So the question is, what are we going to do about it? As it is, I have the press hounding me, as well as the mayor and the commissioner. What happened today isn't likely to be forgotten any time soon. Luckily, most everyone was evacuated out of the hospital before the attack, so there aren't many eyewitnesses to deal with. It's being reported as a bomb scare, and for now we're getting away with that. It's believed we can keep this under wraps for the most part."

"What about the Cosway brothers?" Parks asked.

"That's not your problem to concern yourself with," Hardwick said. "Honestly, I don't know yet. We're still dealing with that. Who knows what they're going to say about them."

"Fuck that," Wilkes said, pacing the room, building up tension like a tea kettle waiting to explode.

"It was a very public attack," Parks said. "The chances of this guy doing what he did and not being seen by anyone, someone, somewhere, a security camera, something, is unlikely. I had our guys pull forensics off you and Hayward and anyone else who was attacked to try and figure out what you were attacked with."

"I'll tell you what I was attacked with," Wilkes said, still pacing. "A psychopath you can't seem to stop."

"Now listen here," Parks replied, standing up and getting in Wilkes's face. "This wasn't my fault. Shit happened. No one's blaming anyone."

"Well, I'm blaming you," Wilkes shot back.

"Wilkes," Hardwick said sternly from her desk. "Cool it and sit down."

"You know what? I am blaming you," Wilkes continued as he poked his finger into Parks's chest. "This is all your fault. I lost damn near my entire team today. And that is your fault. You are in charge. This is your investigation."

"Get the hell out of my face, Wilkes," Parks said, swatting Wilkes's finger out of his face.

The gesture immediately ignited Wilkes, who shoved Parks back against the wall with his whole body and then pinned him up against the wall.

"Wilkes," Hardwick shouted. "Knock this off. I will not tolerate this."

"I lost them all today because of you. If you had just spent some more time planning instead of listening to that little faggot spout conspiracy theories," Wilkes spat into Parks's face as he held him up against the wall.

"We didn't have time! And watch—"

"Fuck that!" Wilkes's face was red and his pulse raced, the veins in his neck and forehead throbbing. Several officers ran into the room and pried Wilkes off Parks, which only infuriated Wilkes more, forcing the officers to hold him back as he kept trying to get back at Parks.

"Fuck you!" Wilkes continued. "This is your fault!"

"Wilkes!" Hardwick shouted. "Get the hell out of my office. Get out of here. Go home. You're suspended. Now!"

Parks massaged his neck while the other officers pulled Wilkes out of the office. He continued to scream and struggle to get at Parks the whole time. Jackie and Tippin were standing at the conference table, concern and fear on their faces, as they watched Wilkes be dragged away.

"God dammit," Hardwick cursed, throwing her pen down on her desk and having it bounce up and almost hit Parks. "Sorry."

"It's not your fault. And it's not his either. It is my fault. He's just short-tempered. Always has been. It's just who he is."

"That's no excuse. He'll be suspended, and that's all I need is for another detective to be out of service right now. He's right. We already lost one good man today. Dammit."

"I won't press the matter," Parks said, trying to control his shaking hands.

"Doesn't matter. He has a short temper and it needs to be dealt with. And it all happened in front of me. And other witnesses. What am I supposed to do? Pretend it never happened?"

"I'll go along with whatever you decide." Parks breathed deeply. "Our department is thinned out enough as it is. We need more people. I understand the difficulty of suspending him. Maybe restricted duty for a few weeks."

"It's my decision either way," Hardwick said, ending the subject. "Where's your report on today's events?"

"Not finished yet."

"Then that's your priority right now," Hardwick said matter-of-factly. "It's Saturday. Finish your reports. Then you and your whole team go home for the night."

Parks nodded.

"Maybe we'll get lucky and this asshole will poison himself planning for his next attack," Hardwick muttered to herself.

Parks realized he had no proper reply for his boss's comment as he left her office.

32

"You're never going to believe what we found," Fairmont said with a smile across his face.

"What's that?" Parks asked, not sure he would believe much of anything right now. It had been a little less than forty-eight hours since the catastrophe at the hospital, and while everyone was physically better, no one's moods had repaired quite so quickly.

"The connection between Allison Tisdale and Ian Harris," Fairmont replied.

"I thought you already said he took pictures of houses for her?"

"I did. He does—did. But there's more."

"More?" Parks got up out of his chair and sat on the end of the table, picking up his nearby Rubik's Cube and playing with it as he listened to Fairmont and Tippin.

"Well, it was my idea, but Tippin here helped me figure out how to find the information," Fairmont said, beaming.

"I got it, I got it," Parks said, rolling his hands, signaling for Fairmont to continue. "You're brilliant. How would we ever survive without you. What do you have?"

"We followed the flower trail."

"What flower trail?"

"Remember the flowers that Allison was receiving? How we thought they were from whoever she was having an affair with. We found out who was sending them."

"Ian Harris."

"Ian Harris," Fairmont confirmed.

"So what does that give us?" Hayward, who had been listening quietly, asked as he set down the file he had been scanning from the far corner of the room.

No one had had much incentive to do any intensive investigation work ever since the fire. They all needed something to pep them up and get them going again, and this might have been what they needed. Parks had been left with only Fairmont and Tippin of his original team, since Rachel Moore was at home recovering. Wilkes's entire team had been dismantled, as Ramirez had been killed in action and Wilkes had been ordered to deskwork as part of his probation for his attack on Parks. That left the only working member of Wilkes's team, Detective Hayward, loaned out to Parks's team for the remainder of the case in light of Rachel's absence.

Jackie had been out at Newport Beach all day, investigating a body found near the beach that had, according to the officer who had called it in, a "bizarre" skin rash. She had checked in earlier that evening and informed Parks that the rash, though still unconfirmed, was unrelated to the Palisades Poisoner. She promised to stop by and help with the case when she could afford it, but the coroner's office had requested that she return to her regular duties and work on her own active case load. In other words, she wasn't sure when she would be back.

Parks turned to the murder board and thought.

"Parks?" Hayward said, standing up.

Fairmont turned to Hayward then back to Parks. "Dave?"

"We're not looking for a typical serial killer. We're looking for a pattern," Parks said to no one in particular as he sipped his coffee, which reinvigorated him some.

"What do you mean?" Fairmont asked. "This guy has killed at least eleven people that we know of. I think that counts as a serial killer in my books."

"A serial killer is generally defined as a person who kills three or more people," Parks explained. "They have cooling-off periods between each murder, though that time can shrink as the killer's need for satisfaction escalates. Their motives for the murders are sexual, anger, seeking a thrill . . . and typically their victims all have something in common, such as race, gender, appearance, age group . . . like black women or prostitutes or college girls. Ted Bundy, Green River Killer and so on . . . there's a reason behind what they're doing, even if it only makes sense to them. Then there are serials who attempt to rid the world of a certain type of people. Prostitutes. Women in general. Homosexuals. Someone of an opposing religion. They see themselves as ridding the world of something . . . wrong. Something that needs fixing."

"So, what are you saying?"

"This guy's sort of a mixture. He's all over the place. I mean, why? Why is he doing this? Is he ridding the world of people who have sinned? Broken one of the Ten Commandments? That only rids the world of ten people. Then what? Once that's done, does he start over again? Back at square one looking for another set of ten people who have broken the commandments? Or is he finished? Or is he hoping we'll stop him before he gets to the end? Does he need to keep killing, or will he be satisfied with this group of ten? And if so, then why this group of ten? What makes them so special?"

"What do you think?" Fairmont asked, looking to Tippin, who simply shrugged.

"I think it's easier in the movies because the cops always stop the killer before he gets to the end and they never have to ask these questions," Parks said with a sigh. "But really? What is his ultimate goal? It's obvious he's enjoying this so I don't see him stopping. But then what? If you look at these murders, they've gotten more and more elaborate. At first this was a mission. The murders had a purpose. But he's come to like them. He's thriving off the thrill of the murder and the game of cat and mouse with us. I don't know if he'll finish after these ten like he might have originally planned. This has become so much more to him. It's become . . . it's become an addiction for him. But that doesn't take away from the fact that these ten are different. There's a connection between them all. There's a reason he originally picked these ten."

"We know that most of them are connected one to the next," Fairmont said. "Like a chain letter."

"No," Parks said, still staring at the board. "There's more to it. There's one central connection between all of these people and the killer. He knows them all."

"Of course, he's killing them all." Fairmont wasn't sure what more to say.

"What set him off?" Parks wondered. "Why did he start this series of killings? Something set him off. A catalyst. What was it?" Parks turned around and faced the rest of the room. "The beginning. What was the beginning? What started this all?"

"That's what we don't know." Fairmont shrugged.

"Allison Tisdale," Hayward answered as he leaned back in his chair and repeatedly clicked a pen in his left hand. "She was the first murder, right?"

"And her connection?" Parks asked. "We already tried her."

"And if her murder is what started all of this. How?" Hayward continued. "Her sin, according to the kid's chart, is what? An affair? I don't know about you but when it comes to murders, good, old-fashioned jealousy is more often than not a very simple motive. One of the oldest in the Bible."

"An affair?" Fairmont rebuked. "That's what we're saying now? That's what started all of this?"

"What if we're looking at this all wrong?" Hayward asked. "What if this was a simple homicide? To begin with. A simple motive. Jealousy. Then a fit of rage. What if this was all a more personal murder? Tisdale discovers his wife's infidelity and kills her. Then, in an attempt to cover his tracks and throw us off, he elaborated. Took what tools he had available to him and used them to take the heat off him and direct it onto other possibly unrelated victims. And on the journey, he went overboard in trying to cover his tracks."

"You're saying Douglas Tisdale?" Parks asked, looking back at the murder board. "But we've already checked him, and he was cleared. We had a squad car parked outside his house, and they said he never left during the second and third murders."

"And he had an alibi," Fairmont said. "For his wife's murder."

"No, he didn't," Hayward rebutted. "Not according to the murder book. He was at home. Unaccounted for. When the other murders began, you simply wrote him off. Did you check his alibis for any of the other murders? They say they never saw him leave his house, but did they actually see him in it the whole time? Windows open, putting on a show to make sure the world knew he had an alibi? Or was he simply last seen walking through his front door and they don't know for sure?"

Parks looked to Fairmont, who shook his head, and turned to Hayward, who shrugged. They turned to Tippin, who was off in his own world, not focused on anyone else in the room while he took in what Hayward had just said.

"Milo?" Parks called out.

"No," Tippin said, coming back to focus. "We never went back to him. We just wrote him off, like you said. Plus . . ."

"Plus what?"

"Don't forget the reason he was our original prime suspect. What he teaches." Tippin let everyone think for a second. "Biochemistry and molecular biology. He has the know how to pull this all off."

"Dammit. All right. It's enough to at least find him and pick him up. Just to question him. We don't know anything for certain, yet. If it is him, then chances are he's not around anymore."

Fairmont and Hayward started out of the office, but Parks held Tippin back a second while the room cleared out.

"I was wondering if you could stay here and do something for me," Parks said.

"Uh, sure," Tippin said, looking around and realizing they were alone.

"You're good with the computers. And you spent all summer working on uploading our past case files. So what I need is a search."

"Okay. What?"

"Poisonings in LA County going back the last two years. Maybe even as far back as five."

"Sure thing," Tippin said. "I can do that, no problem. Homicides from poisonings. I'll have something for you when you get back from Tisdale's."

"No," Parks said, stopping Tippin. "Not homicides."

"Not homicides? But our guy is killing people by poisoning them, right?"

"True. But that's not what I'm looking for. I need you to search for all poison-related deaths ruled accidental, suicide or undetermined."

"Uh, okay . . ."

"That's what I need," Parks said firmly.

"Then consider it done," Tippin said with a nod and left the room.

33

"What do we have?" Parks asked, sneaking up behind Fairmont and Hayward, who were watching Doug Tisdale's place from across the street. Four black-and-whites awaited command a block away so as to not be seen. Parks intended to only question the man, but when Hardwick had been informed of their latest theory, she decided to take no chances. If Douglas Tisdale was the Palisades Poisoner and he felt the police were finally onto him, chances were he wouldn't go down without a fight. She could spare the men at the moment and would rather they weren't needed as opposed to allowing him to escape once again. Three cars were waiting north of the residence and another four were parked south, each waiting for a command of what to do.

"You do realize that there is a chance this guy isn't our killer?" Fairmont asked, not taking his eyes off the target.

"Yes, I'm aware," Parks replied. "Which is why we need to do this right. Hopefully we can just bring him in and question him. But something tells me we might not be so lucky. Is he there or not?"

"From what we can determine, he's there. There's movement

from behind the curtains. But nothing specific."

"He's there," Hayward replied. "I say we take this son of a bitch and do it now."

Parks agreed. "All right. Fairmont you come with me. Hayward, you take two men and go around the back to make sure he doesn't run. Everyone stay on your radios with open communication. Maybe this guy won't put up a fight. Okay?"

They all checked their guns then started across the street.

Parks knocked on the door to Doug and Allison Tisdale's house on North Crescent Drive and waited for any sign of acknowledgement from within. He glanced around at the yard and noticed that it didn't appear as if the gardeners had been by in a few weeks. Most likely not since Allison's death. He wondered about this and knocked on the door again.

"Hayward? You guys in position?" Parks asked into the mic attached to his vest. "Hayward?"

"I saw movement," Fairmont said, stepping over from Parks's side and making his way toward the front window.

"Hayward, come in," Parks said into the mic. "See anything? Hayward, you there?" Parks turned to Fairmont as he switched over to one of the officers in the back of the house. "Why isn't he answering? Hayward—"

The lights in the house went out, and everyone froze.

Fairmont tried looking through the front window to see if he could determine anything when two bullets shattered the glass, just missing his face by inches.

"Are you all right?" Parks asked.

"Parks, what was that?" Hayward asked through his walkie-talkie.

"Jake?" Parks shouted.

"I'm all right. Get him. Get him," Fairmont shouted back.

"Shots fired. Shots fired," Parks said into his mic. "I repeat, shots fired. We've got a four-seventeen with shots fired. Officers in need of backup." Fairmont worked his way back over to Parks, gun drawn, as blood trickled down the side of his face from the wound on the top of his forehead. "Ready?"

Fairmont nodded and Parks kicked at the door. It didn't budge, and he kicked again until it finally opened. Parks entered the house, gun drawn, with Fairmont ready at his side. They worked their way into the interior, which was completely dark.

"Be alert," Parks said.

There was a noise from above them and both men immediately turned toward the stairs before they noticed the two patrol men working their way from the back of the house.

"Where's Hayward?" Parks asked.

"He ran in ahead of us," one of the officers answered.

"Dammit. Spread—" Parks stopped as he saw Tisdale standing on the ledge, holding Hayward hostage with a syringe inserted into his neck. Whatever the contents of the needle were, they had yet to be injected into the detective. "Just take it easy." Parks took his gun off of Tisdale and aimed it toward the ceiling.

"I . . . uh . . . uh, back off," Tisdale spat at the police as he looked wildly from one officer to the next, searching for a way out with his highly dilated pupils. He was sweating profusely and breathing rapidly, as if he was on something, and continued to lick his lips, his mouth dried out. "Back the . . . back . . . back off. *Now!*"

"All right." Parks said. "All right. We can work our way through this. Nobody has to get hurt here."

"I didn't do it," Tisdale continued while he eyed the front door.

"You're not—You hear me? Now back off! I'm getting out of here and nobody's stopping me." Tisdale hugged Hayward tighter, his pulse picking up speed, as he looked around like a trapped animal. He worked his way down the stairs, one step at a time. Sweat rolled down Hayward's face, and Parks could only imagine the fear pumping through the man's body.

"Whatever you want," Parks said as the officers began to back up.

"Into the kitchen," Tisdale ordered, continuing down the stairs, nodding toward the back of the house. "Go on. All of you. Get into the kitchen. And none of you come out until I'm good and gone. You hear me? Or this one gets whatever's in here. Go on. Back off! Now!" Tisdale's words were slurred and barely made it out of his mouth, as if he couldn't find the words to go with the thoughts in his brain. He kept smacking his mouth, in need a drink of water.

"Okay. Okay. Okay," Parks said, making sure everyone behind him continued on into the kitchen. He was almost out of sight of Tisdale and wasn't sure he wanted that. The man was a killer. He had taken so many lives—what would stop him from taking one more on his way out?

"Back!" Tisdale shouted once more, forcing Parks to take another step into the kitchen. He bumped into Fairmont, as none of the men had moved deeper into the already darkened room. Parks kept inching backward until he was far enough around the corner to be out of sight of Tisdale and Hayward.

They stood for what felt like an eternity when Parks heard a car engine rev up. He ran out of the kitchen and saw Hayward lying on the ground, rubbing his head, having been hit over the head to stop him from chasing after Tisdale.

"Go," Hayward yelled, waving Parks on.

A car flew out of the Tisdale's garage, not bothering to wait for the door to open, as Doug Tisdale drove out in his wife's BMW. He missed hitting the patrol car across the street by inches as he spun his car around in the middle of the street and gunned it north for Sunset.

"Suspect on the run," Parks announced into his mic as he and Fairmont ran for their car.

Parks jumped in the car and started it up just as Fairmont made it into the passenger seat. He turned on his cherry light and sirens as he sped up the street, barely catching sight of Hayward getting into his own vehicle in the rearview mirror.

Tisdale sped through the intersection at Sunset, not stopping for the red light, causing several cars to swerve and collide with neighboring cars. Parks sailed through the intersection, skirting the wreckage and both cars sped north on North Beverly Drive.

"Call it in," Parks ordered Fairmont.

Fairmont picked up the mic and said, "Officers in pursuit of suspect heading north on North Beverly Drive toward Coldwater Canyon and Mulholland. Send backup," Fairmont gripped the dashboard as Parks swerved around a car and sped up once again. "Careful. These streets are about to get dangerous. It's windy up here."

"I know," Parks shot back, swerving again.

"Where the hell's this guy going?"

Parks remained quiet, focusing on his objective, honking the car's horn as he swerved in between two vehicles, finally catching up with Doug Tisdale's BMW as it turned onto Mulholland Drive. Lights flashed and sirens wailed as Parks tried his best to keep up with Tisdale's car, which began to swerve in the lane.

"What's he doing?" Fairmont asked.

"I'm not sure," Parks said.

Doug Tisdale's car pulled to the right and ran up against the guardrail, sending a spray of sparks out over the edge of Mulholland. As the two cars sped along the road, all of Los Angeles could be seen far below the mountaintop, the lights of the city stretching away into darkness. Doug Tisdale pulled his car off of the guardrail but overcompensated and drove into the opposing lane. A car came right at the BMW, and Tisdale pulled the vehicle back into the right lane at the last second, swerving several more times.

"Coming up on a sharp bend," Fairmont announced, keeping an eye on the road.

"I see it."

"If he doesn't slow down he's going to go right over the edge."

"Dammit."

Suddenly Doug Tisdale's car jerked into the opposite lane, just missing one car and passing another before going off the road and running straight into a telephone pole. The whole front of the car wrapped around the wooden post as Doug Tisdale flew through the front window, his face and hands getting ripped to shreds as he flew up and back down onto what was left of the hood of the car.

Parks pulled his car over to the side of the road. Fairmont jumped out and stopped the passing traffic as Parks made his way across the road. Smoke rose from the totaled vehicle as he approached and found Doug Tisdale dying on top of the hood of his car.

"Call it in," Parks said.

Fairmont called in their location when Hayward and two other black-and-whites pulled up and cut off traffic. The two officers began redirecting traffic while Hayward made his way to Parks's side and looked down at Tisdale's body. Blood covered the shattered windshield, and glass stuck haphazardly out of the man's face, neck, and hands. His left eye had been completely detached, a shard of glass now resting instead in the man's vacant socket. The top of Tisdale's scalp had been taken clean off, along with a portion of the man's skull, to reveal his throbbing brain as it slowed down in function. Tisdale's gaze reached up to Parks and Hayward and he tried to mutter something but only emitted a stream of blood as the entire insides of his mouth had been cut open.

Parks remained quiet, pissed off at the situation.

Even though he could hear the sirens of an ambulance in the distance, he knew there was no saving Doug Tisdale, and in losing Tisdale, they'd lose any hope of finding out why he had committed the murders. They figured his wife's infidelity had triggered the man's rage and murderous rampage, but Parks still felt there was more to it and wished he could ask the dying man about it.

"Do you smell that?" Fairmont asked as he lowered his head in close to the driver's window, which had been shattered.

"Some kind of gas," Hayward said from behind the detective. "His car smells like it's filled with it."

"Then why was he driving it? And why was it filled with it?"

"That's probably why he began to swerve."

"But why? Why do it? Why get into the car if it was filled with poisonous gas?"

"Suicide?" Hayward shrugged. "Figured he'd go the way he was killing others? If he was punishing according to the Ten Commandments maybe he was saving himself for last? Thou shalt not kill."

"That could have been his endgame all along," Fairmont said, agreeing. "Brings everything around full circle. Makes sense. Maybe this was a suicide mission from the start."

Parks remained silent. He didn't know what to think or say right then.

Tisdale's last breath finally escaped from between missing teeth and sliced lips. Those were questions they would most likely never have answers to.

34

"Fill out your reports tonight before leaving," Hardwick said. "All of you. What you have. Everything. There's a full-on press release going out in the morning and Media Relations needs to know everything possible about this entire case."

"Everything" wasn't as much as Parks would have liked at the moment, but they were still working on wrapping things up five hours after Doug Tisdale's unfortunate demise up on Mulholland. CI and detective teams tore through Tisdale's UCLA office and Beverly Hills house, causing more than enough commotion for the gossipy neighborhood despite the growing hour. Every aspect of Tisdale's life was being dissected and gone through with a fine-tooth comb. Though connections to the suspects were being made, irrefutable and damning evidence had yet to be produced. Word throughout the department was that he had to have a "place" where he conducted his business outside of the home and office, though they'd found nothing so far that had been able to lead them to a concrete location.

"We just need the proof that Tisdale's our guy," Hardwick went on. "This entire case doesn't have to be wrapped up tonight. You guys can take as long as you need with what all you have to go through. We just need to assure the public that the Palisades Poisoner is done and finished with and that they are all safe once again. Luckily, it's after nine, so we've missed the early evening news, but there's still late night and we only want them to get trickles until tomorrow morning. Okay? Fill them in. Then go home. Parks. Fairmont. Hayward. All three of you. Good job. We got the son of a bitch."

Hardwick stared at Parks, who was avoiding eye contact.

"We did get him, right?"

"We'll have all of our reports for you by the end of the evening," Parks said. "Mine included."

Hardwick breathed deeply, both mentally and physically exhausted. She wasn't satisfied with his answer, but was not in the mood to argue at this time of night. Parks felt the same way.

"We'll make the connection," Parks assured her.

Hardwick went to leave the conference room and stopped by Tippin, who was at the end of the table with a dozen files spread out before him while he typed away on his computer.

"You too, Tippin," Hardwick added. "No idea what the hell you're doing now, but we couldn't have done this without you. Get some rest."

"Just finishing up some paperwork for Parks," Tippin said with a smile.

Hardwick nodded and left the room.

"Milo," Parks called out. When Tippin didn't reply, he tried again. "Milo? You find me something?"

Tippin scrunched up his face, unsure how to answer.

"Hayward?" Tippin asked, trying to be sensitive. "You worked on the Cosway case, right?"

"What about it?" Hayward asked.

"I mean from the beginning. You did the initial investigation into the two brothers."

"What do they have to do with anything? That case is closed. The suspects are dead, and as sick as this Palisades Poisoner guy was, he saved the city a lot of money by offing those two whack-jobs. What are you doing?"

"I just have a few questions I'm trying to answer is all," Tippin said.

Hayward tapped his pencil rapidly on the table and looked to Parks.

"I've asked him to look into a few things," Parks said.

"Fine," Hayward huffed, getting up and leaving the room. He reentered the room and dropped the Cosway murder book onto the table next to Tippin. "Here you go. Everything you want to know but were afraid to ask about the Cosway brothers. Help yourself."

"Thanks," Tippin said, beginning to dig through the navy-blue binder.

Though he couldn't hear for sure, Parks thought he caught Hayward mutter something to express his irritation.

*   *   *

"That's it for me," Hayward said, looking up two hours later.

Fairmont had finished twenty minutes before and, after thanking everyone in the room, left quietly and quickly. Parks had the sneaking suspicion that Fairmont was off to check on Rachel Moore again. He wasn't sure what was blossoming between the two detectives (if at all), or had possibly been blossoming, but figured either way it was an issue for another day. They were each allowed their lives outside of the job. Who was he to interfere?

"Feel like a drink once you're done?" Hayward asked Parks.

"I'm going to be at least another hour," Parks said, tapping his report. "Probably two. And I still have to go over the entire case with Hardwick. And honestly, I'm exhausted. I need to do nothing but sleep for the next twenty-four hours and not be disturbed. I plan on taking the battery out of my cell and unplugging my home phone. I hope no one needs to get a hold of me at all. But I'm game for tomorrow night if anyone's around."

"Sounds good to me," Hayward said, standing and gathering his report. "Thanks for everything. It's been good working on this case with you. Even if the circumstances have been less than desirable."

"You too," Parks said, shaking Hayward's hand. "And thanks for your help on this case. We couldn't have done it without you. I mean that. It's been noted and will be acknowledged."

"Thanks," Hayward said. He turned to leave and noticed Tippin still digging through the murder book. "Night, kiddo."

Tippin looked up and smiled before digging back into the casebook. Hayward disappeared out the door without another word.

"You've been done with your report for the last thirty-seven minutes," Tippin said without looking up.

"Is that so?" Parks wasn't at all surprised by the comment. "What have you found?"

"You really want to know?"

"I do."

"Even if it might upset you?"

Parks sighed, telling Tippin to continue but tread lightly.

"It might take your entire case and shake it apart," Tippin said, his voice barely audible.

"I've been waiting for you to say something like that. Luckily for you, I'm not buying this Tisdale as our killer angle anyways. Tell me what you have," Parks said as he searched for another cup of coffee, realizing he had already drank too much if he was planning on going to sleep within the next decade.

"You're still wondering why he's poisoning people, aren't you?" Tippin asked. "That's why you had me dig through the old files, isn't it?"

"Well if we go with Tisdale as our killer it's because he knows poisons and has access to them," Parks said. "But poisons weren't really his forte. I mean, that would be a good reason. But why do it? Poisoning someone is complicated. There has to be a reason behind it. A meaning. And I don't think it's access. As we've stated several times, it's a hell of a lot easier to get a knife than cyanide or methanol. These poisonings have meanings behind them. Like the Ten Commandments and the Council of the Ten. But Tisdale doesn't fit the bill for either of those two things. He wasn't a religious man, and he didn't care two hoots about history from what I've been able to tell by his home and office studies. So why the Ten Commandments and the Council? There's no connection."

"And you're hoping the answer was in what I was digging through?" Tippin asked, getting a nod from Parks. "Okay. So the archives. Starting with this year going back to find what I was looking for."

"The original murder that set this whole thing off," Parks said, calmly.

"Let's go back to the original theory of the Ten Commandments being the link between the ten murders."

"Yes."

"What are the two commandments we don't have a victim for?" Tippin asked. "If we assume Allison Tisdale broke the commandment about committing adultery."

Parks turned to the murder board.

"We have thou shall not bear false witness against your neighbor and thou shall not kill," Parks said.

"Yes. Okay," Tippin said, standing up and getting energized. "So, searching through the files, I think I found what you were looking for. I found one which I think not only counts as a death by poisoning but also links up with the commandments up there."

"Who?"

"Female student from PSU. Two, two and a half years ago now," Tippin explained. "Twenty-two-year-old named Julie Hammond."

"Is this the other girl in that photo?

"It is."

"There's connection number one. What about her?"

"Seems she had an affair with one of her professors." Parks was tempted to say something to stop Tippin but knew the kid was on a roll. "Anyway, she used him to get a better grade in class or something like that. Whatever. Doesn't matter why they were sleeping together—just that they were. They were secretive, but apparently some of her classmates found out about the affair and threatened to go to the dean with what they knew. But she beat them to it. She filed complaints against the students and had them expelled from the university. An investigation was launched by the university, on behalf of the students who were expelled, and they found out that Julie Hammond had made up the charges against her classmates."

"Shalt not bear false witness against thy neighbor," Parks muttered, putting it all together and wondering what that meant for his case.

"Possibly. So the school launched an investigation into Julie Hammond's life and uncovered a whole slew of accusations. Sleeping with a professor. Cheating on exams. Drugs. Blackmail against other students and teachers. Lots of things. Rumors began to fly."

"True?"

"Who knows? But people talked. People like to gossip. Especially on a campus. I've been doing research online about it. No two stories are the same."

"So the false rumors she spread came back to bite her in the ass."

"Big-time karma. Part of the problem was that she was also bipolar. Apparently suffered from depression and had been on medication since she was sixteen or so. She blamed the other students, saying they'd messed with her medication, as part of the reason she behaved the way she did. But then she accused the psychologist who was evaluating her of blackmailing her into sleeping with him in exchange for a clean bill of health. No one believed her though. Kind of the boy-who-cried-wolf syndrome."

"This psychologist that she was seeing . . ."

"He was assigned to her by the university to help testify for their side of the lawsuit. You know—she has her own people check her out then they have theirs. Sort of a he said-she said sort of deal. This was all for the legal process that they were going through."

"This psychologist," Parks said. "You know his name?"

"Um . . . I know he's a part-time professor at the university," Tippin said, digging through some notes. "He did the psychology thing on the side. Here it is—Professor Fredrick Knott. Anyway, no one believed Julie Hammond's allegations against him. She spiraled after that. Couldn't handle that no one believed her story."

"And don't tell me . . . she killed herself?"

"Was found in her dorm room. She choked to death on her own vomit."

"Pills?"

"They found two empty bottles next to her," Tippin said, nodding. "Bottle of codeine and one of Percodan."

"Same two pills we found on Allison Tisdale's body at the first crime scene. So there's connection number two." Parks whistled. "So in effect, she was poisoned."

"Yep. Or at least whoever took her death personally saw it that way."

"Who was she survived by?"

"Not just yet." Tippin smiled. "First, you want to know how the other nine people poisoned connect with her?"

"You can connect all nine poisonings to her?"

"Pay attention. And prepare to be dazzled." Tippin walked over to the murder board, uncapped a dry erase pen, and began making marks from each person on the board to the next. "First, because of the legal case against Julie Hammond, her family had to hire lawyers to handle the accusations brought up against her by the families of the other students expelled, as well as the school's accusations. The family lost a lot of money. And in the shuffle they had to sell their house. Guesses on who sold it once they lost it?"

"Allison Tisdale."

"Bingo. Sure, she had acquired the house after it was seized, but she still sold it. I did some more digging. Apparently Julie confronted Allison about selling their house. Made a scene at the job. Police were called and a complaint was filed. But it did no good. And two years ago, who was taking pictures of the houses that Allison Tisdale was selling?"

"Ian Harris."

"Yup. He was also listed as a witness on the complaint filed against Julie."

"Okay. Next? Jason Bollinger? How does he fit in?"

"What did Jason Bollinger do?"

"An investment advisor or something."

"Actually, two years ago he was an insurance broker. Until he lost his license and became a private investment advisor. Works on your finances and makes sure you get the best insurance possible. Medical. Life. Home. Everything. And guess who one of his clients were?"

"The Hammonds?"

"Yep. He was hired to help with the financial strain they felt due to legal and medical bills. The mother had cancer and spent most of the time this was happening in and out of hospitals. Now, I don't believe that Bollinger was quite to the corrupt stage of stealing from his clients, but he was mishandling their affairs. And they were already in a tight spot. It wasn't the straw that broke the camel's back, but it was another stone on the pile. Next?"

"Charles Wyler?"

"Wyler was the reporter on Julie Hammond's story. The controversy of what happened at the university was what helped make his career; moved him from second-rate stories to the channel's lead crime investigator. And guess who misrepresented Julie Hammond to the public in exchange for a large payout from the school? Of course, he would deny it if he were still alive, but I dug into his financial history."

"You're kidding me."

"Nope. I mean, there's no direct connection, but it appears Wyler has been receiving payoffs from various groups or people for years, probably in exchange for manipulating his reports. And he did receive a rather large payoff of close to fifty thousand around the time of Julie Hammond's accusations. I've gone back and pulled his reports on the whole affair. She was slammed in the news. Unfairly so. It looks like a witch hunt. Next, Kyle Oni . . . oh, did I mention the name of the professor Julie Hammond first slept with that started all of this? Lee Oni. Guess how a simple, underpaid college professor was able to afford a big-time lawyer to get him off of any wrongful allegations?"

"His brother the baseball player?"

"Ding. Ding. Ding."

"But this was two years ago. Kyle Oni wasn't signed on with the Dodgers and making big bucks yet."

"No, but he was being scouted. This meant good publicity for the university he was attending. And the university he was being scouted from?"

"The same school his brother taught at."

"Correct. So the school, wanting to keep the profitable and future alumni Oni brother happy, paid for the other Oni's defense and made his allegations disappear."

"Then what about Lee Oni or the school? Why didn't our killer go after them?"

"Six months after this all settled down, Lee Oni died in a head-on collision with a drunk driver," Tippin explained. "Kinda hard to punish him anymore. And the university . . . who are you going to punish for that? That's an entire establishment. This is personal. The killer wants to make it more personal. But, I do think our killer found a way to make the university pay for their part in all of this. I'll come back to that though."

"All right. And Caroline Maddox and Nina Mendola?"

"Nina Mendola and Julie Hammond, our victim, had been best friends since grade school," Tippin continued, picking up the picture of the two girls. "But halfway through this entire mess, Nina up and left her best friend for a career as a personal assistant to Caroline Maddox. When she needed the support of a friend, possibly someone who could vouch for her credibility, most in her life, Julie felt abandoned. Nina left Julie for Caroline. Or at least that's how it played out in Julie's mind. Thus helping lead to her suicide."

"And the Cosway brothers?"

"I have two different things to comment on about them. First, in addition to being parasites that fed off their father's wealth, they had dabbled in various jobs and lines of education. Part of their father's requirements to be allowed to keep living at home was to continue their education. They'd already been banned from UCLA, Santa Monica, and Pepperdine. So the next closest school to daddy?"

"Pacific Southwest University."

"Right. And they were at the school the same time as Julie Hammond. Guess who two of the people were that she had kicked out under the so-called 'false' accusations?"

"The Cosway brothers."

"Yep. Make you wonder how false those accusations really were?"

"Yes, it does. I'm beginning to wonder if maybe anything she said was actually a lie."

"Who knows? She was sick. Unbalanced. She was prey. And in a world filled with predators. But with the Cosways' parents' money, they fought back legally in a way that the Hammonds could never have competed with."

"And what was the second thing?"

"Huh?"

"You said there were two things about the Cosways you needed to comment on?"

"Oh yeah. Second, the Cosways could take one or two of the places on that list of commandments broken. They broke two of them. Disrespecting their parents and killing someone. So there is a possibility that while each brother committed both sins, one could have been killed for one sin and the other brother for the other sin. Or both brothers for both sins. Either way," Tippin said looking up at the board, "that takes us to ten commandments broken and ten victims."

Thou shalt have no
other gods before me — Nina Mendola

Thou shalt not make for yourself an idol
— Caroline Maddox

Thou shalt not take the name of the LORD thy
God in vain — Charles Wyler

Remember the Sabbath day to keep it holy
— Kyle Oni

Honor thy father and thy mother
— Cosway Bros?

Thou shalt not kill — Cosway Bros?

Thou shalt not commit adultery
— Allison Tisdale

Thou shalt not steal — Jason Bollinger

Thou shalt not bear false witness against thy
neighbor — Julie Hammond?

Thou shalt not covet your neighbor's house, wife,
etc. — Ian Harris

"All right," Parks said. "This is seriously messed up."

"Tell me about it."

"So then tell me, who was Julie Hammond survived by? Mother? Father? A father could be doing this."

"Could be. If any of them were still alive to avenge her death."

"You've got to be kidding me."

"Mother battled breast cancer all throughout the events at the school. After her daughter's suicide, she simply gave up and succumbed to it. Here. I found some old Facebook pictures from Julie's old page. It hasn't been updated, obviously, but look."

Tippin moved some pages around on his laptop and showed Parks the girl's social media page. He motioned through several pages of photos until he stopped on one of Julie and her mother and enlarged it. There was a picture of the two women having just received tattoos at a local parlor. Signs of tears were prominent, but pride overcoming the mother daughter bonding experience. On top of the mother's right foot, matching the tattoo in the center of her daughter's left shoulder was the Japanese symbol for ten.

"You've gotta be shitting me."

"According to the date they probably got them about the time the mother found out about her cancer and six months before the daughter started getting into trouble at school."

"That's connection . . . whatever it is. It doesn't matter. It's a link. Did they ever express why they got them or what they mean?"

"Not here on the page they didn't. It might be somewhere else on here. I can search. But there was nothing immediate."

"They're not alone," Parks said, nodding to the photo. Tippin knew what he was referring to. While Julie and her mother were the main focus of the picture, there was another person, from the looks of it a man, on the other side of Julie, though only his arm wrapped around Julie's shoulder was visible as the rest of him had been cut off by the frame.

"We'll come back to that," Tippin said.

"Who is that?"

"We'll come back to that. Let's keep going."

"You're pissing me off. You better make it quick. What about the father? Is it the father in that picture with them? That would fit."

"It isn't the father. He couldn't handle what had happened to his family, so he took his own life as well. Double barrel in the mouth. Top of the head was completely gone. Terrible. I saw the crime scene photos. Took his teeth and fingerprints to ID him. And according to the coroner's report he did not have the symbol tattoo anywhere on him. I checked."

"And?"

"No siblings. No cousins. Both parents only children. No other relatives left alive."

"So who's that leave us with, Milo?" Parks demanded. He knew the kid had a theory and wondered why he wasn't divulging it. Tippin avoided Parks's eyes. "Milo, what is it? What aren't you telling me?"

"Now, none of this is for sure. I mean, this could all just be a co-incidence. Douglas Tisdale could be the real Palisades Poisoner."

"Bullshit," Parks shot back. "You know that's bullshit. Doug Tis-dale was a patsy. And if this whole Julie Hammond connection is simply a coincidence, then that's the biggest fucking coincidence of the century. And you and I both know it. What is it? Spill."

"There's only one other person I can think of who's associated with this entire thing," Tippin said, finally breaking.

"Who is it?"

"Julie's boyfriend."

"She had a boyfriend? I can buy a boyfriend doing this."

"There's more," Tippin said, hoping to build the suspense even more before the revelation.

"Go on."

"Apparently, they had been high-school sweethearts. Together for like six years or something. He's two years younger than her though, so he didn't show up for most of the events at the college. But he was adamant about the lies being presented against Julie Hammond during everything that was going on. Argued with Wyler on TV and everything. Took offense at the way the school handled the whole event. Like they brushed it under the rug and forgot about it. Plus, now he's old enough to go to college and is currently en-rolled in the same school where Julie went. I think that's where he's getting some of the poisons to carry out what he's doing. Sort of his way of getting back at the school. I did some checking earlier . . . several of them are kept at the school. If someone knew what they were doing, they could have easily manipulated the numbers of what was in stock to cover what was missing. If word gets out that the Palisades Poisoner got his poisons from the university, it would be some seriously bad publicity for them. And that's going back to how I think the Poisoner plans to hurt the university."

"Okay. But who is it, Milo?" Parks asked. His mind raced. He knew he wasn't going to like the answer.

"Also, he's been around toxic chemicals most of his life, so he's familiar with them. He knows all about them and how to handle them. That's why I think he chose poisons as the way to kill people. Plus, he loved Julie Hammond. And poisoning is seen as a more intimate way of killing someone. He's showing his love for her by doing this the way he is."

"Who is it, Milo? Who was Julie Hammond's boyfriend?"

Tippin looked to the ground then finally up at his boss again, the hurt etched in his eyes. He hated to say it but knew the time had come. There was nothing left to say. Tippin clicked the arrow button on the computer and the next photo in the series popped up on the screen. In it was a picture of Julie with her boyfriend. He too had gotten a Japanese symbol for ten tattooed upon his body. Square in the center of his right shoulder. He had his sleeve pulled back and he was flexing alongside Julie, tatted shoulder to tatted shoulder, making the evidence irrefutable.

"Rick Isley," Tippin said, his voice barely a whisper. "Julie Hammond's boyfriend was Jackie's son."

35

Fifty minutes later, after making it out of the downtown area to Venice Beach, Parks managed to navigate his way through the canals to Jackie's front door. The sun had set, but the neighborhood was brightly lit with street lamps and porch lights reflecting off the water in the canals.

He rang and knocked and waited to be let in. He hadn't called in advance, hadn't told her he would be by. He wasn't sure if Ricky would be there either, or what he would say if he was. He felt the anticipation build in his body as adrenaline pumped throughout his system, and he tried to shake the nerves out while he waited for a reply.

He reached for the doorbell again and noticed his hands shaking. He stuck them in his pockets, hoping that he would calm down before Jackie answered the door. He felt like a teenager waiting for his first date. Or worse, a traitor. He wasn't sure what to say—what he would say to the woman he felt himself falling for.

Just as he was about to wonder if maybe no one was home the door swung open. Jackie stood there in a pair of form-fitting jeans and a green Fighting Irish t-shirt that brought out the reddish highlights of her hair. She smiled at him without saying a word, her face lighting up and taking off a decade of tiredness at the sight of him. They had seen less of each other since the fire at the hospital, as she had been called to other investigations throughout the Southern California area, though none were of the murderous tone set by the Palisades Poisoner.

"I hear you caught him tonight," Jackie said, breaking the silence with a wide smile. "Here to celebrate?"

"Actually," Parks said, looking down at the doormat before looking back up at her, "here to talk, if we can?"

Jackie studied his face then took a step back. "I'm in the middle of making dinner. You can help. Come on in."

Parks stepped into the house and Jackie gave him a kiss, holding him tight, both of them taking in each other's scents, their warmth, before she let him go. She turned away and headed toward the kitchen in the back of the house.

"Leave your coat and gun on the rack and come help me," Jackie called back to him. "I need some garlic pressed and tomatoes chopped."

Parks stood there, looking around at the Norman Rockwell-esque home with sounds of the ocean in the background while food cooked in the kitchen. Pictures of Jackie and her son were scattered about the home, hanging on the hallway walls and spread out on various tables, showing a life they had built for each other, with soccer games, Cub Scout camping trips, academic trophies—all in the absence of any true male figure in either of their lives. They had done the best with what they had, which was better than most. Love held them together and sustained them through what most others might have seen as a bad situation. Both were stronger than might have been given credit. Jackie had nothing to feel guilty about. She had done good.

Then again, how could he say that knowing what he knew about her son. This would destroy her. Her every worst fear come true. She would blame herself until her last breath. All the deaths brought about by her own flesh and blood. She would never forgive herself. She would never forgive him.

Parks removed his jacket and gun and hung them up on the rack.

"You know, I think we should talk," Parks said, walking down the hallway toward the kitchen.

"So then talk," Jackie said, laughing as she stirred something on the stove.

"It's not about us," Parks said as he walked into the kitchen and stopped at the sight of Ricky sitting at the bar divider between the dining area and the kitchen. The teenager watched his mother cook and glared at Parks upon his entrance. He had a look of finally accepting Parks's place in his mother's life on his face.

"Then what's it about?" Jackie asked, still moving about the kitchen like a master. Stirring one pot, moving another from one burner to the next, chopping food. "Dave?"

Jackie looked up to Parks and noticed him staring at her son.

"All right, you two." Jackie stopped and flipped on the faucet to clean off her hands. "We need to get this out of the way once and for all. I'm not dealing with this any longer. Ricky . . . Ricky? You hear me. If you have something you need to say, then I want you two to deal with it. Here. Now. With me around to witness it all. No tough guy, bullshit. You hear me?"

Parks and Ricky continued to stare intently at each other, each one wondering what the other was thinking.

"Does she know?" Parks finally asked.

"Who?" Jackie asked, grabbing some wine glasses and a bottle of merlot off the counter. "Me? What? What do I know?"

"Does she?"

A brief look of confusion flashed across Ricky's face.

"We figured it all out," Parks said. "Everything. All of the pieces of the puzzle. We put them all together."

"What are you talking about?" Jackie asked as she looked from Parks to Ricky. "Ricky? What's he talking about?"

Parks paused for a moment. Was he wrong? He could have been. This could have been one last mistake in a long line of them. Only he wouldn't have minded this one.

"Julie Hammond," Parks said, drawing the attention of both mother and son.

Ricky glanced at his mother, a look of having been caught with his hand in the cookie jar across his face.

"Julie? What does she have to do with anything?" Jackie placed the wine glass down. "She hasn't been . . . she hasn't been a part of our lives for two years now. What are you talking about, Dave? What does she have to do with anything right now?"

"Why don't you ask your son?" Parks said. "He should be able to tell you about her."

"Look," Jackie said, getting frustrated. "I know all about Julie Hammond. And if you don't mind, this isn't something I care to talk about right now. The past is the past. Look, Dave, I was there through it all. It was a bad time for all of us. But especially Ricky. It's all in the past. We've moved on. That's not a part of our life anymore. Why are you bringing her up?"

"Because of her connection to the Palisades Poisoner," Parks replied.

"What?" Jackie asked, confused.

Ricky looked to Parks with shock on his face.

"Didn't think we'd put it all together, did you?" Parks asked. "But we know. The poisons the Palisades Poisoner has been using came from the university where Julie went to school. The same university Ricky currently attends. I know you know all about them, how to use them. Handle them safely." Parks turned from mother to son. "I know all about the victims who have been poisoned."

"What about them?" Jackie asked, her eyes wide in disbelief at what she was hearing.

"I know about their connection to Julie Hammond. And why they were chosen."

"What?" Jackie asked, startled. "What are you talking about?"

"It was all about revenge. Wasn't it, Ricky?"

"What?" Jackie stood up in Parks's face. Her entire body shook with the rush of adrenaline. "You think my son is the Palisades Poisoner? You think that? How dare you! How dare you!"

"It all fits." Parks grabbed Jackie by the shoulders. "I hate to be the one to tell you this, but we know all about it. Everyone's connection. Your son's connection to Julie Hammond. He's the only one left to do it."

"To do what?" Jackie spat.

"To seek revenge," Parks replied calmly.

"That's bullshit," Ricky said, his face full of rage as he tried to compute what Parks was accusing him of, shock taking over his body and petrifying him in a state of immobility.

The front doorbell rang, none of them registering it.

"I know this hurts, but it's the truth," Parks said.

"Fuck you!" Ricky shouted.

"Ricky, stop!" Jackie ordered, standing between Parks and her son, the mother lioness moving in to protect her young. "That's not helping."

"There's nowhere to go," Parks said turning to Ricky who tried holding back the tears of a past pain. "Everyone at the station knows about this. I'm asking you, for your mother's sake, both of you, come in calmly. Let me take you in. We can work this out. It doesn't have to end in any more deaths. He has the symbol. On him."

"What? What symbol?"

"The Japanese symbol. The one that's been carved into the bodies of the victims. Ricky, Julie and her mother each got the symbol tattooed on themselves a few months before Julie's death. I've seen the photos. Online."

"What?" Jackie almost gasped as she turned to her son, the news that he had a tattoo—no less the same symbol matching the victims of the Palisades Poisoner—obviously shocking her. "No. But I've seen it before. It's not . . . it can't be. I would have . . . it is—how did I not know?"

"You're his mother," Parks consoled. "You couldn't have seen it as associated with this. Your subconscious wouldn't allow you to ever condemn your own child. I understand that. But it's true."

The doorbell rang again and Jackie jerked her head toward the hallway.

"Is that them? The police? Are they here to arrest my son?" she asked with tears coming down her face as she moved right up to Parks. "I'm telling you, Dave. If you ever trusted me. If you feel anything for me at all, I'm telling you my son did not do what you are accusing him of."

"I'm sorry, Jackie." Parks placed his hands on her shoulders once more. "I wish it could be another way. I wish it wasn't so. But it is. Convince him to come peacefully with me, and I promise you, I'll look out for him the best I can." The doorbell rang again and Parks turned toward the front door then back to Jackie. "Talk to him. If he runs, it won't end well for him. I'm . . . I'm so sorry."

Parks left Jackie's side, tears streaming down her face, her mascara leaving black streaks as she smeared her eyes with her hands. She turned to her son, who stood silent, stunned by the accusation. He walked to the front door as the doorbell sounded one more time.

His hand froze on the doorknob. He knew they were waiting, just on the other side of the door. They would come in, arrest her son, and tear apart her house, her world. She would be finished as well. They would no doubt blame her. She would never be allowed to practice her profession again.

Could he do it? Could he ruin two lives? But what about the lives of the victims? The dead? Did he really have a choice? He could tell them that he was alone there. He hadn't found anyone at home. How would they ever know? Sure it was wrong, but it happened all the time, right? Look at his partner. Aaron Levinson did stuff like that all the time. His partner had thought he could take the law into his own hands and look where it got him. But he wasn't Aaron Levinson. He knew what he must do. No matter how he felt. It didn't matter what everyone else thought. Let them judge. He was stronger than that. He was his own person. He had to make his own decisions in life and not be affected by the actions of those around him. He knew what he must do. Even if he didn't like the options.

The doorbell rang once more.

*   *   *

"Tippin," called out Hardwick when she entered the conference room. "What are you still doing here? Everyone else has already left for the day."

"I . . . uh . . ." Tippin stammered. "I was just looking up some old files on one of the cases related to the Poisoner. To help Detective Parks, on some back research stuff."

"What back research stuff?" Hardwick asked, knowing she wasn't going to like the answer.

"A new theory."

"What theory?"

"We stumbled upon something. I mean, I did. A different . . . avenue. A different theory about who the Poisoner really is."

"What theory? Where's Parks right now?"

"Out chasing down a lead."

"Son of a . . ." Hardwick retrieved her cell phone and dialed Parks's number. "I don't know where he is or what you two are up to, but I'm getting him back here right now. I have a press release to work on, and if he hasn't wrapped—*sonofabitch*."

Hardwick slammed her phone closed then opened it up and dialed the number again.

"What the hell are you looking at anyway?" Hardwick gestured to the files all over Tippin's desk and began picking up a few of the papers and looking them over.

"Julie Hammond."

"Who the hell is that?"

"She's the girl we think is at the center of this whole conspiracy. She's why this all began in the first place." Tippin reached for the papers Hardwick had picked up and began to reassemble them in a sort of mishmash order that only made sense to him.

"How's that?" Hardwick asked, demanding an answer to all of her problems. "Who is she?"

"All of these poisonings are an act of revenge for a lost loved one," Tippin explained rather dully. "Julie Hammond. It's her boy—" Tippin stopped shuffling the papers and stared at one particular piece.

"Yes? Earth to Milo. Who is she?"

"That . . . doesn't . . . that doesn't add up," Tippin whispered.

"What doesn't add up?"

"Julie Hammond's parents."

"What about them?"

"They got married here in LA. After Mrs. Hammond relocated here."

"Yeah? So? Who are these people?"

"She met Chris Hammond here in LA. After she moved here. But she already had Julie. Before she moved her. You know what that means?"

"No. What? What are you talking about?"

"It means Chris Hammond isn't her birth father. He can't be."

"And that's wrong? What's that mean?"

"It means Julie Hammond was survived by a blood relative after all."

"Who?"

"Her father. Her biological father."

"And who's that?"

"I have no idea," Tippin said as he turned in his seat and began pounding away at his keyboard. "Try and reach Parks again. I think he's about to make a big mistake."

36

"Wha . . . what are you doing here?" Parks asked with confusion at the familiar face that had no business being there that time of night.

"Funny," Detective Lewis Hayward said, smiling. "I was going to say the same thing to you. I thought you were still at the station."

"I was," Parks said as his cell phone began to ring. "I had to speak to Jackie about something."

"Yeah," Hayward said, shaking his head. "That's too bad. I'm sorry about that."

"About what?" Parks asked as he looked down at his cell.

Hayward used the distraction to grab Parks and insert a needle into the side of his neck. Parks tried to fight back and managed to knock the needle out of his neck, but not before half of its contents were pumped into his body. Parks immediately felt the left side of his body heat up even as it stopped moving and he fell into Hayward's arms.

"Sorry you had to be here," Hayward whispered into Parks's ear while he lowered the man to the floor. "Now don't fight it. There's nothing you can do." Hayward set Parks on the ground then stood up and closed the front door. "It really is too bad you were here. I picked you, you know? You don't know how many times I wanted to tell you, you were right. When we were standing around the station, bouncing ideas off one another. You were right about some things. But others . . . you just seemed to miss the point. That was very disappointing. I was counting on you to piece it all together. To understand. I need you to understand. No one else ever could. But you, you're different. You get things. You've suffered. Unfairly so. Just like me. That was why I picked you. We're so alike and you don't even know it."

"Why . . . innocent people . . ." Parks could feel himself slowing down, almost like he was drunk and no longer in control of his body.

"Who? Those people whom I helped?" Hayward was shaking his head in disbelief. "Those people were not innocent. They failed to see the harm they had done to those around them. Sure, some of them began to feel the shame of their actions. So they were ready and I was there to release them. But most of them were guiltless. They needed guidance. Punishment for their actions. You know best about that. For every action there is an opposite and equal reaction? Or something like that. That's what I was there for."

"Dave?" Jackie called out from the kitchen.

Hayward peered down the hall then hid around the corner and reached into his pocket to retrieve another syringe.

"Dave? Who was at the door?" Jackie walked into the front room to find Parks lying on the floor. "Dave? What are you doing down there?"

Jackie flipped on a light and rushed to his side.

"Dave?" She could tell he was paralyzed as he tried to make noise while his eyes fluttered about inside his skull as if he was trying to talk to her through them.

"Sorry," Parks gasped when a gloved hand gripped Jackie from behind. Hayward placed his hand over her mouth and stuck a needle to her neck but didn't yet inject the contents.

"Scream and I'll kill you," Hayward whispered in her ear.

Jackie let loose a muffled yelp and tried her best to control herself. Fresh tears flowed down her face.

"Call for your son," Hayward ordered her. "Real calm like."

Hayward removed his hand from over Jackie's mouth but kept it hovering nearby. The needle he had stuck into the side of her neck drew the faintest drops of blood, and she sucked in a breath as his threat of emptying whatever was inside loomed.

"Ricky?" Jackie wavered as she tried to fight back the tears. "Ricky?"

"Mom?" called out Ricky from the other room.

"Ricky . . . *run!*" Jackie yelled at the last second when she jerked her head to the side, the needle becoming detached from her skin.

"Bitch." Hayward grabbed Jackie by the throat and tossed her to the side. She flew away from him and tumbled over Parks's body, a nearby coffee table breaking her fall as she hit the floor.

"Mom?" Ricky yelled, running into the room. He immediately stopped at the sight of his mother, bloody and cut up on the floor.

"Move and I'll kill her," Hayward said to Ricky as he whipped out his police-issue gun and aimed it at Jackie's prone figure. "So help me God, I will."

"Who the hell're you?" Ricky said.

"Someone who wasn't good enough to be in the picture. Now go be a good boy and put these on," Hayward said, taking his handcuffs from a back pocket. "From behind."

Ricky looked to his mother and glanced at Parks lying immobile on the ground and put the handcuffs on. He stood there, both frightened and angry at what was going on as he glared at Hayward, trying his best to control his breathing, assessing the situation. Hayward walked up to him and checked to make sure the handcuffs were on tight and secure.

"Good." Hayward smiled. "Now sit." He shoved Ricky aside, causing him to trip over his feet and fall onto the couch next to where his mother lay on the floor. Hayward took in his three captives and relaxed, a large smile spread across his face.

"Well, looks like I'm going to be able to wrap this all up nicely after all."

Jackie sat herself up as she tried to stop some of the bleeding from the cuts she'd obtained in her run-in with the coffee table.

"What's going on? Who are you?" Ricky said from his place on the couch. "What do you want with us?"

"Now, now, now," Hayward said, pointing the gun in Ricky's direction. "Let's not take that tone of voice with me. Okay, son? I'm still your elder. You were always so well-mannered from what I had observed. No reason to become uncivilized now. Be the boy you promised to be for my daughter, even though you lied to her."

"What the . . ." Ricky looked from Hayward to his mother, who tried to pull herself toward him, then he glanced over to Parks, who continued to lie on the ground, not moving at all.

Parks took in every sight, every smell, every sound he could, the whole time knowing there wasn't a thing he could do about anything going on around him. If Jackie or her son weren't able to take control of this situation somehow, then all three of them would for sure end up dead. But there wasn't anything he could do. He still couldn't move. Couldn't feel any part of his body as he lay there on the cold tile flooring of the front entry not far from where Hayward stood threatening Jackie and her son. His head was a swirling mess as heat rose from within his body, fighting to get out, spreading from his neck down toward his toes.

"She was my wife. Forever and ever. We were supposed to be a family. We had a plan. But she deviated from it. Then just up and disappeared one day. Out of nowhere. I had thought she'd been kidnapped. But there was no note. No ransom. Nothing. She was just *gone*," Hayward said, shaking his head and addressing no one in particular. "Come to find out she ran away. Why? Why would she do that? Why would she leave me? Our dreams? She changed her name and everything. Did a good job of it too. But she forgot one thing— I'm a cop. Come from a cop family. Got it in our blood. She should have realized that one day I would find her again. And that's when I found out we had a daughter."

Ricky looked from Hayward to his mother, confusion splashed across his face once again. He knew the pieces of everything should have been fitting together for him, but they weren't all connecting just yet. Something was missing.

"We had a daughter. Together. Why my wife chose to hide her from me I'll never know. But Julie knew. Of course. Not originally. Though I feel that deep down somewhere inside of her she always knew. That she had a father out there. Looking for her. And when she got older, when she started dating you, she suspected. That that prick wasn't her father. That she belonged to another. Think that's what contributed to her . . . unbalance. Not me. I'm not to blame. It's that bitch of a wife of mine. She's at fault. But that's okay. Eventually, I confronted her, and she realized everything she thought was true. That's why she cut everyone off when she left for college. And she would have been all mine. Except for you. She didn't cut you off for some reason."

Parks could hear the words echoing throughout his skull but they weren't making sense. If Julie Hammond had cut off her family—her mother—for lying to her then why was she getting tattoos with her just months before her mother died. And why had Julie been around up when her parents had both died. Was he confused? Or was Hayward in his own world?

"You were the one thread that held her to her old life and eventually sucked her back in when she needed help. When those rumors about her began around the college. She should have come to me for help. But instead she held onto you. Little good that did her. You didn't do shit for her. None of you did. My baby still died, and it was all your fault. God had already taken care of Julie's mother by giving her the cancer. But you . . . you promised her the most. You promised her a future. Protection. To love her for better or worse. And you lied. You backed out of your promise to my daughter. When no one else was around to protect her, that was your job."

"No, that was your job," Ricky yelled back. "You were her father. Where the hell were you?"

"Don't you fucking tell me my job!" Hayward spat through gnashing teeth. "I know my job. I did it best I could. I was there for her. Until the end. You're the one who left her. You abandoned her. She had no one left fighting for her and nothing left to fight for."

"Your daughter's suicide was not my fault," Ricky said. Ricky glanced past Hayward and saw Parks blinking at him, slurring and coughing. He wasn't sure what Parks was trying to tell him but knew he had to do something or he and his mother would be killed. "Where the hell were you?"

"I tried to take care of her," Hayward shouted back as he stepped closer to Ricky. "I was her father. I tried to get her back, but you wouldn't let her. She wouldn't leave you. I tried to talk her into leaving you, but she wouldn't. That wasn't my fault. She was scared. And confused. She tried to fight me. Her own father. I only wanted to subdue her. Long enough to get her out of there and away from that world. It wasn't my fault. But she wouldn't calm down. I thought the pills would calm her. Help her. But no matter how many I gave her she wouldn't settle down. Then . . . then she just . . . stopped."

Ricky glanced down at his mother, who kept her face low while she tried to reposition herself next to her son. Through the hair hanging down around her face she made eye contact with Ricky and let him know she was preparing to do something.

"It wasn't . . . your . . . fault," Parks slurred, in between huffs of breath and mouthfuls of saliva. He was having difficulty spitting out the words, he could feel his throat closing in on him, but he got them there. "It wasn't . . . you . . ."

"Yes, that's it." Hayward practically jumped for joy, beaming at Parks. "I knew you would get it. Out of everyone. It wasn't my fault. I wasn't to blame. I did nothing wrong. I only tried to help. You understand. Just like with Kozlov. You were only trying to help. I couldn't control the outcome. It wasn't your fault. Just like with my daughter."

"You . . ." Ricky tried holding back the tears while he processed what Hayward had told him. "Guess you're just a failure as a father. No wonder she wanted to leave you. Run away with me forever. Always said you were a shit father. Guess she was right. You just messed up one thing after another, and look what it got her! It got her killed! And you! You did it!"

"Don't you fucking talk to me about my daughter!" Hayward shouted, focusing all of his rage and anger on Ricky, when suddenly Jackie reached up and slammed a shard of glass from the broken coffee table straight into Hayward's thigh right above his knee.

"Run, Ricky!" Jackie shouted.

Hayward swung out and smacked Jackie in the face, knocking her back, her head hitting the floor, dazing her. At the same time, Ricky fell back onto his hands and pulled his legs up and kicked out at Hayward, sending the man back, where he tripped into Parks's body and flew over him into the front door.

"Mom," Ricky shouted. "Mom!"

"Get out of here," Jackie ordered, regaining her focus.

"Not without you."

"Get out of here!"

Ricky flipped backward over the sofa as Hayward aimed his gun and fired in his direction. Ricky ran out of the room and down the side hallway for the kitchen.

"Get the fuck back here, you little shit!" yelled Hayward, getting to his feet.

Hayward disappeared after Ricky, cursing and yelling as he made his way down the hallway. With Hayward gone, Jackie crawled her way over to Parks and checked his vitals.

"What did he give you?" Jackie whispered.

Parks only muttered slurred words as Jackie found a faint pulse. Her face was placid, and Parks could tell she had put on her "professional" demeanor that was required when dealing with an infected patient. The right side of his body had a little movement but not enough to be controlled.

"Your heart isn't slowing down," Jackie said. "We need to get you to a hospital. Not sure what he gave you. But it might be wearing off. If it was some kind of muscle relaxant it might not last that long depending what kind it is. You need to calm down. Your heart is pumping the poison through your body."

Parks moved his eyes hard to the left then focused back on Jackie. He could feel a tingling sensation in the tips of his fingers once again, but wasn't able to move them about enough to draw Jackie's attention.

"Don't worry," Jackie said. "I'll call 911 right away."

Parks grunted and looked sharply to the left once again.

"What? I don't know what you're trying to tell me," Jackie said. "What's—"

Jackie stopped talking and followed Parks's line of sight as he looked to the left once again. A few feet away from him, near the edge of the shadows, lay one of the syringes that Lewis Hayward had dropped when he tripped over Parks's body.

*   *   *

Ricky couldn't outrun Hayward with his hands cuffed behind his back. He stood in the corner, surrounded by shadows, trying to maneuver his hands under his legs and around back in front of him. Despite his strong build, he was at a disadvantage. The only hope he had was to catch the man off guard.

Hayward made his way into the kitchen area, tossing chairs aside, looking for the boy, when he heard a noise from behind him. He turned and saw Jackie standing there holding one of his syringes aimed right at him.

"You stay the hell away from my son," Jackie ordered.

"Or what?" Hayward smiled. "You couldn't even start to get close enough to me to do anything with that."

He heard the noise first, and Hayward turned just as Ricky collided with him from out of nowhere, sending the two of them through the glass door that led out to the backyard. The glass shattered and fell to the ground as the two men slammed into the concrete deck that was enclosed within the white-picket fence that separated the house from the canals around it. Ricky tried to roll away, covering his back and shoulders with more of the glass as Hayward pushed himself up to his knees and grabbed the young man by his ripped shirt and spun him around. He grabbed Ricky by his throat and began to strangle him, squeezing every ounce of life out of him, when he heard someone behind him. He was turning toward the sound when he felt the syringe plunge into his neck.

"Make one fucking move and I'll do it," Jackie threatened.

"All right," Hayward said, holding up both hands. "You win. All right? You win."

Jackie breathed deeply from behind the man as she fought back tears.

"Ricky, baby? Can you get up?" Jackie asked.

Ricky tried to maneuver out from under Hayward, grunting as he shuffled along the concrete on his back. Jackie loosened her grip on Hayward's neck, and he used that moment to take advantage of the situation. He grabbed her hand and flung her to the side. He pulled the syringe out of his neck and looked at it. The vial was still filled with the light-blue liquid. He reached down for Ricky, grabbing the boy once more as he raised the syringe up over his head, preparing to stab the boy with it, when the gunshot rang out through the night sky, shattering the silence of the neighborhood.

Ricky gasped in horror at the stream of blood that sprayed out across his face from Hayward's shoulder as the man's arm dropped to his side and the syringe fell to the cement below. Hayward blinked at Ricky in confusion as he looked up at Parks, leaning against the doorframe, his gun still aimed at him, the tip smoking.

Hayward stared, lost in disbelief at how far he had come, how near he'd been to realizing his plans finally coming true, only to be stopped this close to the finish line. His eyes scanned around him as his brain tried to think of what to do.

"Hayward, *don't*," Parks barked hoarsely, the muscles in his throat still getting their strength back. Parks could feel the weight of the gun beginning to weigh down his arm but he kept his focus intact and Hayward in his line of sight. The night air was suddenly sliced open with the sound of police sirens growing louder. "Don't even think about it. I will put a bullet through you and end you. So help me God. You're done."

Hayward fell to his knees and Ricky kicked his way out from under the man. Jackie came to his aid and tried to help Ricky to his feet and out of the grasp of the Palisades Poisoner once and for all.

EPILOGUE

Parks stared intently, focused on the task at hand even if he wasn't sure what the task was. He knew he was trying to get signed off on his mental state but, all things considered, wasn't quite sure how to go about doing that. Parks gazed out the office window. The sun shimmered above the horizon, the start of another day. There was a slight chill in the air, signaling the official end of summer and the approaching fall-like weather that many in Southern California had been eagerly waiting for. Children were in school, and before he knew it, signs of Halloween, then Christmas, would be up all over town, bringing with them the end of another year.

"So I guess the rumors of your impending death were somewhat exaggerated?" Dr. Black asked, not taking his eyes off the detective. He had been observing Parks for the better part of an hour, taking in his movements, gestures, reactions to questions. It was his job, after all, to evaluate. To determine whether or not the man was fit to carry a gun and roam the streets of Los Angeles to provide protection to those who required it. The meetings with Dr. Black had been made mandatory by the department, something Parks felt he would have to go through for the rest of his career.

388 | TYLER COMPTON

"Naw. Just a temporary paralyzing agent. Something called Sux-amethonium chloride or something like that. I guess Hayward meant to do me in himself once he finished with Isley and her son. Or may-be he planned to pin it all on me. Who knows. Guess unless he de-cides to start talking, none of us will ever know."

"And what of Lewis Hayward?"

"He'll live. If that's what you're asking. Think he's already work-ing on a plea deal with the DA to try and avoid the death penalty."

"Will he get it?"

"It's a possibility." Parks thought about this. "They're trying their hardest to keep as much of this under the radar as possible. Don't want to cause a panic. Not that I think it would."

"No?"

"Not really. People don't want to be in harm's way. But to find out the danger has already passed and they're safe—but that there's an interesting story behind it? True crime sells. Death sells. People would be fascinated by the Palisades Poisoner for years to come. If word ever gets out."

Dr. Black nodded and kept quiet.

"Does that bother you?"

"My job is only to catch the boogeyman. It's someone else's job to figure out what to do with him once I do. If I worry too much about everything else, then it will all get to me. We each have a job to do, a piece of the puzzle to fill." Dr. Black made a face that didn't reveal how he felt about this comment while he made a note in his pad. "But since we're here—as a citizen of this city, yeah, it would piss me off to know he could get away with everything. Not that I think he will. But then again, what is justice for what he did?"

"What, indeed."

Dr. Black made a few more notes in Parks's file then flipped the page.

"Hayward's good with a computer. I'll give him that. He's actually managed to erase most of his past. This makes me wonder about the few things we have found. His 'history' with the NYPD and Philly PD? Why didn't he erase that stuff as well? Or was that all planted just to get him his position with the LAPD. It's hard to tell what's true and what's bullshit. We're trying to find people he's worked with and even that's proving to be difficult. It's like he's a phantom. No one's claiming to have ever heard of the guy. Is that true? Or do they just not want to be associated with a serial poisoner? And if it is true, then where did he come from? What's his story? Who is Lewis Hayward?"

"They'll search. Get their best on it and try to find out."

"True. FBI's working on it. Tippin's even helping out with that. Even though Hayward managed to make himself a ghost, he wasn't able to do as good a job with his ex-wife. She had filed reports against him. There's over a dozen hospital visits for her that we've been able to dig up so far. Fractured bones. Broken noses. Concussions. He was an intense one. You see the reports?"

"Not my position. I'm here for you guys. Not them."

"No, I guess not. Apparently he never knew about the daughter. When the wife found out she was pregnant she up and left. I don't mean like she went home and figured things out. She went straight from the doctor's visit and disappeared. Did a good job of it too. Managed to stay hidden for fifteen years before he found them. Apparently she's good with computers too. Or was. Maybe that's where he learned? Or maybe they're former CIA spies." Parks smiled. He had said this mostly to see if Black was still paying attention. The

390 | TYLER COMPTON

doctor simply raised an eyebrow in question. "Oh, who knows how much of what they're saying is true and what's made up. Chances are we'll get more out of the press and tabloids than we ever will in court. If there is a trial, that is. If he's smart he'll have one."

Parks didn't feel like talking about Hayward anymore. Too much of his time had been devoted to the man already. He turned back to the window and stared at the city around them. The doc had a good view, all things considering.

"It's incredible the lengths the human mind will go in order to achieve something it sets its sights on. We are a strange animal, that's for sure."

Parks remained quiet for a few minutes, and both men enjoyed the silence. As much as they were usually there to talk, both men had learned to enjoy and appreciate the silence if it ever built up around them.

"Eh." Parks shrugged. "We're still piecing together how exactly he got to each victim. But we're getting there. Most of Milo's theories about the ten being chosen, and why, hold water. But I don't think our 'why' holds up."

"Oh?"

"Hayward still hasn't acknowledged his part in his daughter's death. That *he* killed her by feeding her the pills to keep her quiet. That's a hard truth to face. Killing one's own child. He couldn't face what he had done. That was our connection. His and mine. Or so he said. He felt I was the same way about what happened with Kozlov."

"Were you?"

"What happened with Kozlov wasn't my fault. I know that. I can't control everyone and their actions. I am only responsible for myself. I have to take responsibility for my actions. But nothing more. I need to stop punishing myself. I know that too."

"And the victims?"

"He couldn't process his guilt. For his daughter's death. So I think he projected his shame—his *guilt*—onto those around him. Especially those involved with his daughter's collapse. Allison Tisdale was having an affair. She felt remorse and admitted her actions to her husband and he forgave her. We know this because he was aware of what she had done yet they were still together. Working on it. But Hayward didn't feel she had been punished enough. Bollinger stole money from his clients and lied about it. He felt no guilt. The Cosway brothers who killed their parents. The same. Kyle Oni hid his sexuality from the world. I think Hayward felt Oni was ashamed of who he was—though I doubt it. According to his people he had plans to come out after the season. I can go on for all of them like this. These people whom he killed he did it to punish them for not admitting the truth to themselves, much like him. He couldn't admit the truth.

"We found a throwaway cell with an untraceable number that he used. We found a few phone calls between him and Doug Tisdale, but we still don't understand how he was able to make the man run away from us when we went to arrest him. Blackmail? Maybe. Tanaka's going over his body again. Thinks maybe he was injected with something toxic and told what to do if he wanted the antidote. Who knows? It's as good a theory as anything else."

Parks shrugged.

"This whole series of murders was personal to him. I'm sure there'll be many psychologists and doctors going over the case for years to come. They'll have numerous theories as to why and how. They're already lining up to be the first to write their papers and claim their theories of insanity and emotional disturbance and . . . whatever. I'm sure Hayward's lawyer is having a field day with all of this. The publicity alone is worth the price of admission. It's just crazy."

"And how's the rest of the team?"

"Moore's mending fine. About to come back to work. There's something . . . there's something between her and Fairmont. But I guess you already know about that. From having to see both of them." Dr. Black neither confirmed nor denied this as he crossed his leg and let Parks continue. "I think it's getting serious. But I'm not dealing with that right now. Until there's something to worry about. The new kid, Tippin. Did a good job with this case. Young. Fresh. Still learning but made a hell of an impression with this case. He has a promising future."

"How are things between you and Jackie Isley?"

"Jackie?" Parks went quiet while he thought about her. "She's managing. Little battered up, but she'll live. Her son too."

"I asked how things were between the two of you."

"Haven't spoken to her since that night. Probably won't again either."

"That bad?"

"I accused her son of being the Palisades Poisoner. Even though he wasn't. And even though she worked on the case and has most likely seen the evidence and knows how and why I made that assumption . . . I still made it. One of those things you can't take back. Kind of hard to forget. It's fine. They have each other. They've learned that's all they need in life."

Dr. Black remained quiet and scribbled something in his notebook. "And you're okay with that?"

"I'll live. Been through worse. You know that."

"Yes. But I have the feeling Isley meant more to you than just a one-night stand. I know you have enough of those."

"Does it matter? It is what it is. Life goes on. For some of us. I still have my puzzles. My routines. I keep to them. It works for me. It's what I like. Maybe it's the life I was meant to live."

"But is it enough?"

"What's 'enough'?"

Dr. Black didn't answer. Not because he couldn't, but because it wasn't a question for him to answer. That was a personal question that could only be answered by each individual.

"I'll tell you what's enough," Parks said. "Living. A day at a time. Some days are harder than others. Some days we spend laughing and others we don't smile once. In the end I'd like to think it all balances out. I hope so. I think that's what keeps me going. That hope."

"Everyone has to hold onto something different."

"So what do you say, Doc? Am I fit to get back to work?"

"I see no reason to keep you from doing what helps you get along in life," Dr. Black said, finishing off a few more notes in his pad. "So until I see otherwise, you're fit to continue."

"That's good, Doc." Parks smiled when his cell phone began vibrating and lighting up. He turned on the screen and read the message. "Cuz it looks like I'm needed."

"No rest for the wicked?" Dr. Black asked when Parks stood up and headed for the door.

"Not in this town, Doc," Parks said as he left the room, heading for whatever crime scene he had just been called to. "Not in this town."

ACKNOWLEDGEMENTS

Thanks to the many different people who helped make this book possible, in one way or another—and if I have forgotten anyone here it was unintentional. To Gabe Robinson (editor extraordinaire), Lori, Dani, Derek & Davey who each read the many drafts of *P10* and gave helpful comments and suggestions. They caught many errors yet were never negative, always pushing me to do better and never settling for less. And to the (hopefully) few that are still around I thank my future readers who will kindly ignore them. It amazes me how many times I've read this book and still find the simplest of errors.

To my family for their unconditional support and constant asking of when they could finally get to read something of mine. It means more than you'll ever know. To Kendra who's been one of my strongest supporters since the day we first met back in college. I thank you from the bottom of my heart. To Randy and Yari—this is it girl: The first book. Get ready for many more. You'll have work to do soon enough! To Tyler for his help with the web site and other various online activities—thanks for constantly listening and tolerating my many questions and suggestions. To Eric M. for joining me on adventures throughout LA when I needed to explore and find new settings. The scene in Casey's Irish Pub would not exist without your help. And to Eric S. for allowing me many hours of sitting in the back room of The Coffee House typing away. And with the greatest of debt and gratitude I give thanks to Cindy for her patience and unconditional support in this never-ending journey. I most definitely would not be here right now without her friendship, inspiration, guidance and understanding. And a special added thanks to Rita for finding several red letter errors "after the fact."

And to everyone else who helped simply by asking questions, listening to my rants (or morbidly curious questions), sending me (often bizarre) news stories, or politely pushing me forward when needed—I truly am thankful.

And to the faceless strangers who pick up this book—giving both it and me a chance—I thank you.

I received help from many people regarding police procedures, poisons and their effects and other small tidbits. I received much help from the *Book of Poisons* by Serita Stevens and Anne Bannon. The locations, geography and poisons are as accurate as possible—with the exception of minor changes when the good of the story outweighed the truth. Any errors are strictly the fault of the author.

ABOUT THE AUTHOR

The son of a prison guard, Tyler Compton graduated from CSU, Sacramento in 2002 with a BA in Theatre Arts and a minor in Film Studies. An Eagle Scout, he has worked in the pool industry, as a server, bartender and (for one hilarious evening) as club security. He currently resides in Los Angeles where he has witnessed various forms of crime, including someone breaking into his apartment while he was in it. The second book in the Detective Parks series, *Wicked Games*, is due out in the winter of 2013, while he is currently at work on the third book.

Follow @tscompton on Twitter or visit TylerComptonBooks.com for the latest news and details about future releases.